WHY did top-level Soviet defector Viktor Rahmovich decide to return to his Russian homeland, and then come back to America as a key member of the Russian nuclear disarmament team?

WHY did special agents Ross and Lyle of the ultra-secret U.S. Defense Intelligence Agency find themselves in savage struggle not with the KGB but with the CIA?

WHY did fabulously beautiful and sensually skilled Julie Klein draw Ross ever deeper into a labyrinth of kinky sex-and-snow, while murder after murder turned Washington, D.C., into a capital of death?

WHY did the Russians want so desperately to take America's newest weapon out of the arms race—**and what would happen when the Russians' foolproof plan succeeded?**

SCIMITAR

It gives you all the answers—
even the terrifying one. . . .

*"Vivid, absorbing . . . clever twists
and careful details."* —LIBRARY JOURNAL

"Powerful, tough-minded!"
—CINCINATTI ENQUIRER

INTERNATIONAL INTRIGUE FROM SIGNET

SCIMITAR

PETER NIESEWAND

A SIGNET BOOK

NEW AMERICAN LIBRARY

Copyright © 1983, 1984 by Peter Niesewand

All rights reserved. For information address Stein and Day, Incorporated, Scarborough House, Briarcliff Manor, New York 10510

This is an authorized reprint of a hardcover edition published by Stein and Day, Incorporated

SIGNET TRADEMARK REG. U.S. PAT. OFF. AND FOREIGN COUNTRIES
REGISTERED TRADEMARK—MARCA REGISTRADA
HECHO EN CHICAGO, U.S.A.

SIGNET, SIGNET CLASSIC, MENTOR, PLUME, MERIDIAN AND NAL BOOKS are published by New American Library, 1633 Broadway, New York, New York 10019

First Signet Printing, November, 1985

1 2 3 4 5 6 7 8 9

PRINTED IN THE UNITED STATES OF AMERICA

1

Viktor Rabinovich made his attempt at escape just before the arrival of the lamb chops at lunch on a warm spring day in New York when, pushing back his chair, he muttered, "Comrades, I'm sorry. I must be excused again."

He placed his crumpled napkin on the tablecloth with a hand that was not quite steady and saw Travkin catch the eye of Lappa, then glance questioningly at Nikitin. A waiter came forward to help with the chair. For a second it seemed as if one of the others would go with him, as they had on the previous aborted occasions, but unexpectedly the leader of the team, Fedor Fedorovich Konev, came to the rescue. With a slight gesture of his hand, he kept the others in their places.

"I think our comrade's digestion is not equal to the demands made on it by American cooking," Konev remarked jovially. To Rabinovich he said, "Don't worry, my friend, we'll soon be back in Moscow."

"I think it may be the water," Rabinovich replied with a bleak smile. "Just a slight upset. It will pass."

He moved from the table, feeling the thick carpet beneath his shoes, the thumping of his heart against his ribcage, and the sick anticipation of taking an irrevocable

step. As he walked through an archway, he could hear
Konev saying to the others, "These Armenians aren't as
tough as people give them credit for. My father . . ."

Rabinovich passed out of earshot. He knew the sort of
story that would follow. He hated being referred to as an
Armenian almost as much as being called a Georgian. He
was neither. He was a Jew, a title assiduously avoided by
top echelon Soviets. In polite conversation, he and others
of his race became Armenians, or Georgians, and everyone knew what was meant.

A waiter carrying a tray of plates stood aside for him,
and as he passed Rabinovich looked back to see if one of
his comrades was following him after all, but there was no
sign. The restaurant entrance was in the other direction in
any case, easily observed by Konev himself. But there had
to be a rear door also, giving access to the kitchen.

Rabinovich paused for a moment, gathering courage,
beside a swinging door marked "Private," then he took a
breath and pushed through at a fast pace.

After the opulence of the decor in the public rooms, the
kitchen was so bare and functional, and the contrast so
blatant, it seemed it could not belong to the same establishment. A gauze of steam misted against a wall, and the
smell of cooking was strong. The chef, clad in white, his
front spattered with something dark, called instructions to
two assistants.

Someone was broiling meat, and a waiter in a black
dinner jacket peered preoccupied at an order form, trying
to read the writing.

For a moment no one noticed Rabinovich because he
came in quickly, but then he had to pause to orient himself, and by the time he had located the service door, the
waiter had seen him and was approaching him with a
trained smile to explain that no, this wasn't the way to the

toilet, and the chef was glaring from the other side of the kitchen. Rabinovich brushed aside the waiter and ran.

He was scarcely aware of opening the door and only half heard someone swearing at him. Then he was out, heading toward the street. At the end of the alley, he glanced back, but no one was following and he couldn't even be sure which of the anonymous doors belonged to the restaurant.

Rabinovich turned and walked hurriedly, mingling with the crowds and trying to determine precisely where he was. After a while he stopped a thin, well-dressed woman and asked in halting English, "Please, where is Madison Avenue?"

She stared at him as if he had come from another planet and was about to ask for money. "You're on it, sugar plum," she said and walked on.

Rabinovich looked uncertainly up and down. If he could see the Empire State Building, at least he would . . .

But instead he saw Lappa, and behind him Nikitin, moving fast in his direction. It was clear they had seen him. He was easily spotted: a short, dumpy man in a dark suit, not quite in fashion, who looked obviously lost and now very frightened.

Rabinovich gave a small involuntary cry, and ran. On East 25th Street, he flailed his arms at a passing cab, and almost wept with relief when it pulled over to the curb a short distance away. He jerked open the door and flung himself inside. The interior was plastered with signs banning cigarettes and announcing that the driver was allergic to smoke.

"Please," Rabinovich gasped. "Please, quick!"

The driver, a young black man in a T-shirt advertising beer, turned to look over his shoulder. "Sure," he said. "Just say where to."

"Anywhere!" Rabinovich cried desperately, craning to

look out the back. Lappa and Nikitin had rounded the corner. "Please!" He sank down into the seat in an attempt to make himself inconspicuous. The comrades were less than a hundred yards away. He heard a sound like a sob and realized it was coming from himself, and then to his infinite relief, the driver put the car into gear without another word and they pulled out—but so slowly, because of the traffic, that from his slouched position Rabinovich could see Lappa racing past the cab, the muscles hard and clenched in his jaw and his face wet with sweat. Rabinovich slumped lower, not daring to look.

The cab accelerated, gathered speed and then, just as he was starting to relax, inexplicably it stopped.

"What's wrong?" Rabinovich cried.

He could see the driver's shoulders shrug. "Just a li'l ol' red light," he said. "Thought I'd stop so you can see how purty it is."

Rabinovich found himself grinding his teeth. He sneaked a look through the back window, scanning the crowds on the sidewalk. Because he hadn't been watching, he wasn't sure how far they had driven, but he knew it wasn't far enough. He saw no one familiar. Perhaps Lappa and Nikitin had turned back.

Suddenly there was Nikitin—in the road, not on the sidewalk, getting out of a cab and running toward him, and inside he could see Lappa arguing with the driver. He heard again that low cry he knew was his own, but blessedly the lights changed and they were moving! Nikitin charged back to his cab.

As they accelerated, Rabinovich's driver asked matter-of-factly, "Those guys giving you trouble?"

Rabinovich could see the calm eyes watching him from the narrow rectangle of rearview mirror. "Yes," he said dismally.

"They police?"

"No. Comrades."

"Your friends?"

"My enemies." Rabinovich knew now, beyond any doubt, that they were.

The driver grunted. "Dunno if I can lose them," he said. "The traffic's heavy this time of day. Have you decided where you want to head? You want your Embassy?"

Rabinovich gave an anguished yelp. "Please, no!" He stared out the back, trying to spot the other cab in the traffic. For a moment he thought he saw it, then he wasn't sure. The driver took a left turn. The traffic was lighter now, and they picked up speed.

"I want somewhere where there are many people," Rabinovich announced.

"You've come to the right town," the driver said, catching his eye again in the mirror. "I could let you off here if you want."

"A little farther, please. Let us get some distance."

"Uh-huh. This isn't a good place anyway. Your friends are still back there."

Rabinovich swung around peering at the traffic.

"Two cars behind," the driver said.

The Russian seemed to sag in the seat, on the verge of tears, so when the lights changed as they reached the next intersection, the driver took pity and put his foot flat on the accelerator, jumping the red. "I don't usually do that," he said as he slowed down twenty yards on. "Makes people nervous. Especially me."

"Thank you."

"I could drop you off at Times Square? That sound good to you?"

"Yes, that's good."

Five minutes later the cab drew up beside a shop selling tape recorders, radios, and porno video tapes. "Times Square," the driver said, "and that'll be $8.50."

Rabinovich fumbled in his pocket for the money, remembering that he had been kept short of foreign currency and had only a little more than $20, but he handed the driver a ten and did not wait for change.

He hurried to the doorway of a shop and glanced around. He had lost them. He was free. Rabinovich went into a hamburger joint for a cup of coffee and to work out what to do next. He took a table well inside but facing the window so he could watch the street.

He needed to contact someone highly placed in government—perhaps one of the Americans on the negotiating team at the UN? He would telephone and arrange a meeting.

Twenty minutes later, feeling better, Rabinovich stepped out into Broadway, walking more casually, looking for a telephone.

He might not have noticed the one black limousine pulling up to the curb a little ahead of him, had there not also been another directly behind; but when he half turned, in curiosity more than fear, he saw Lappa and Konev jumping out of the first one, Nikitin and Travkin from the second.

His body went numb. He watched frozen for what seemed like many seconds, aware that his hands were cold and tingling and that his escape had been cut off both to left and right. Suddenly, instinctively seizing the last possibility, Rabinovich bolted headlong for a gap between the Embassy limousines and straight out into the traffic. He hardly saw the shape of a car bearing down on him from the right. The screeching of tires, the angry blare of a horn, seemed to come from far off. Before he realized it, he was onto the opposite sidewalk and running—aware that everyone except Konev was fitter than he, and it could only be a matter of time before he was caught.

He looked over his shoulder and discovered he had a good lead on them. They'd obviously been more careful crossing Broadway. Rabinovich was tiring quickly, and his breath came in painful pants.

On his left loomed a movie theater, and a woman, middle-aged and respectable, sat with her knitting inside the ticket booth. He ducked in, fishing his last $10 bill from his pocket. The woman pushed the change toward him, and the turnstile clicked. He was through, immediately facing a door. There was still no sign of the others, but they could only be seconds behind. Rabinovich pushed on.

The darkness was total, except for the blurry images on the screen. His eyes had not adjusted, and he had no sense of anything other than his blindness in the auditorium itself, but he fumbled on, along where he imagined the aisle to be, his hand brushing the plush sides of seats.

The cinema might as well have been deserted. The sound system crackled noisily at him. Beneath the static, as if coming out of a bucket, was something barely discernible as human groaning. Rabinovich focused on the screen and what he saw caused him to give an appalled gasp. What were they doing? What had he come to?

A small red sign glowed in the corner: Exit. Rabinovich stumbled toward it, spurred by the crackling and popping of the speakers, and the voice repeating dully through the echo: Give it to me give it to me give it to me.

Rabinovich found himself in another alley, blinking in the sunlight. He could wait no longer: he would go to the police. The comrades had nearly caught him twice, and the third time he feared they would succeed.

He was no longer sure he had made the right decision, but it was too late to do anything about that.

He ran toward the traffic.

2

"Rabinovich is the token Jew," General Lyndon Yardley observed. "He hasn't played any part in the arms limitation talks as far as we can tell, but they always make sure he's around when the press are there and photographs are being taken."

"He is a scientist of note, General," Clive Lyle said. "Maybe they consult him privately on technical matters."

Yardley inspected his fingernails and frowned as if he'd seen something that offended him. He picked delicately at the cuticle of an index finger. "That may be, Clive," the Director of the Defense Intelligence Agency replied, "but if it is, it's a breakthrough. No doubt Rabinovich has some muscle in his laboratory when he's designing bombs or whatever it is he does. But in New York, comrade Konev has all the technical know-how they need. No, he's window dressing, I think. You may not have noticed, but recently they've been including a Jew with a Jewish-sounding name and a high position in all their delegations. It helps people get the idea the Soviets do things other than just persecute them."

Yardley glanced at the two agents across the enormous expanse of his mahogany desk in the DIA headquarters in

Washington. Lyle watched him steadily. His eyes, a very light brown, were calm and alert. David Ross gazed at the ceiling, big hands clasped behind his head and his body sprawled uncomfortably over a formal chair, which he had tilted to balance on its back legs.

"I wish you wouldn't do that, David," the Director complained. "First, that chair's not very strong, and second, you'll go over backward and break your head open. I'd rather that didn't happen if you don't mind. We've got a lot of money invested in you."

"Sorry," Ross said. The wooden front legs made contact with the carpet again, and the young agent tried without success to rearrange himself into a more comfortable position. Lyle grinned at him. It wasn't easy fitting a 6 ft. 2 inch frame into such a ridiculous chair although Lyle, who was more conventionally proportioned, had no difficulty.

"So what has Rabinovich got for us?" Lyle asked, turing his attention back to the Director.

"I don't know yet," Yardley replied. "The CIA has him in a safe house, and they're keeping him on ice for the moment. But whatever it is, I've got a feeling there are politicians in this country who won't want to know about it. And I don't like the idea of the CIA being in charge, either."

No one took Yardley up on this remark. It was an article of Defense faith that the CIA was either inept or leaky—and sometimes both.

The DIA, on the other hand, considered itself to be a secure, professional, low-profile operation. It reported directly to the Pentagon and through the Secretary of Defense to the President himself. The DIA was essentially a spy shop for the three services, more powerful than the CIA and spending considerably more money. An indication of its effectiveness could be gauged by the fact that, in the years since its establishment by Robert McNamara in 1961, it had remained virtually unknown to the public and, as Yardley never tired of pointing out, it was hard to keep failure a secret.

More than once, Defense Intelligence had come into direct conflict with the CIA, and it seemed the Rabinovich affair might provide another occasion.

David Ross, who was considered a rising star because of the circumstances of his arrival and the success of his one and only operation so far, was sufficiently new at the Agency to ask, "But surely we can trust the CIA to look after Rabinovich and find out what he wants to tell us?"

Yardley awarded him a fleeting, indulgent smile. "You'd think so, wouldn't you?" he said. "Lesson one on day one. Frankly, I wouldn't give a nickel for the chances that one of the KGB rezidenturas here in Washington or New York doesn't get to hear exactly where they're keeping him and under what security. So it really comes down to the CIA's will to hold Rabinovich as much as their ability. As I say, I think there are people around, not a million miles from the White House, who'll hate the fact of his defection and what it does to their negotiations. And they're not going to like what he's got to say, either, you can bet on that."

"What is he going to say, General?" Ross asked.

Yardley pushed a file across the polished expanse of desk, but the distance it had to travel was too great; so Ross got up to retrieve it.

"As you know, the linchpin of the negotiations is the agreement on banning the neutron bomb," Yardley said. "Now you remember we decided to go ahead with neutron production in '81 because we didn't fall for the line about it being the ultimate capitalist weapon—destroying people by radiation but leaving property intact. For myself, if it comes to war, I'd sooner have nothing left of Moscow that's higher than three feet. I don't want to save Red Square so we can let Americans line up to see Lenin's body. But that's a personal opinion. No, we wanted the neutron bomb because the radiation can penetrate the armor of a tank and kill the crew inside and because, after that, it's relatively clean. No significant fallout. You can walk into the area a few hours later with complete safety. And don't forget, it was important in '81 because the Russians had a hell of a lot more tanks than we did. They still do. In that file, you'll find all we know about Rabinovich. As our side is now having second thoughts about the neutron program, he becomes a particularly interesting man. With his background he ought to be able to help us a lot.''

David Ross turned to his colleague. ''Clive, you want to come take a look?'' Without waiting for a reply, Ross headed over to the side of the large office where leather furniture was arranged around a glass-topped table, and he and Lyle could sit together in comfort. Yardley noticed the flicker of a grin on Lyle's face as Ross unilaterally moved the center of operations from the desk where the Director was indulging himself in the role of big chief to a less formal, more equal situation.

The agents sat together on the sofa, sharing the file, while Yardley stayed where he was, his face expressionless, wondering what the right psychological moment would be to go and join them, or even whether he ought to insist they resume their much less comfortable chairs in front of him. He might be able to bring that off with Lyle and not make himself look ridiculous, but Ross presented a problem. He was not a military product, and he'd had a lot of outside experience—much more than showed on his face.

Ross had a brilliant mind, particularly if it had anything to do with his special subject, computers, and the consensus was that he would more than pay his way on general assignments. But he needed careful handling.

Yardley sighed inaudibly and crossed the room to join his men. Ross had already finished reading and had passed the file to Lyle, whose brain functioned less swiftly and who was still on the last page.

"Rabinovich seems quite a man," Ross said. "It must take a fair amount of courage to be a member of the Academy of Sciences and Jewish and still not join the Communist Party. I'd have thought his religion made him specially vulnerable."

"But you see what I mean about him having a lot to tell us?" Yardley asked.

"Sure. It would be interesting to hear about the Dubna atomic center, even if these arms limitation talks weren't going on. But Rabinovich ought to have details on the actual production of Soviet neutron weapons."

"Maybe our negotiators can learn something useful," Lyle offered.

"Maybe," Yardley said. "Did I tell you the Soviets called off today's session without giving reasons? I guess the lines to Moscow are buzzing about Rabinovich. They've already asked us to hand him back. They claim he'd been indulging in illegal economic activity—I think that was the phrase—and he's got to face criminal charges in the USSR."

"What did we say?" Rosss asked.

Yardley's expression was neutral. "We're reserving our position," he said.

Lyle closed the file and dropped it on the table. "It'll look bad on the front pages."

"Nothing's been made public about his defection, so in theory we could hand him back without anyone getting egg on his face."

"Except Rabinovich," Ross said.

Yardley ventured a thin smile. "It'll be something more

solid than egg," he said. "The problem is the Pentagon's very worried about these talks, but the politicians won't listen. I suppose that shouldn't surprise us too much. There's been such a massive international campaign against neutron weapons. As if," he added bitterly, "it's crueler to kill a tank crew with radiation than by giving them third degree burns with a conventional shell so they die screaming two weeks later, or cut them half to pieces with shrapnel. Still, that's the great Western public for you. So now the White House wants to sign a ban on neutron weapons in exchange for arms limitation in other areas. And if you've seen the latest polls, you'll know most Americans agree with them."

"What do you want us to do?" Lyle asked.

Yardley chose his words carefully. "I want to make sure that Rabinovich gets a fair hearing. I want him in a good, calm condition so we can listen to, and evaluate, his evidence. I want to make sure the CIA doesn't mess up."

"Does that mean we're taking him over?" Ross asked.

"Unfortunately not. The CIA got in first, and they're claiming he's theirs. The best I've been able to negotiate— and believe me, it was a fight—was that we could help babysit and make sure he's in prime shape for the interrogation. Oh, and we'll be in on that as well."

"So we move into the CIA safe house, under CIA security?" Lyle wanted to know. "No additional Defense protection?"

"No, but it should be okay with the two of you there. from what they tell me, they've got the place sewn up like Fort Knox."

Lyle looked disbelieving.

"It's a question of morale, Clive," Yardley explained. "The CIA says, and I can see their point, that if they can't be trusted to look after a simple defector, they might as well pack up and go home. But they did agree the two of

you could come in, on the firm understanding that it's a
CIA show.''

"Does that mean we're under their orders?''

"No," Yardley said. "You're under my orders. And
they're these: don't go in there as if you own the place.
Don't make jokes about pickle factories. If you want
something, ask for it, don't just take. Don't give them a
hard time. Be polite and diplomatic. Of course," he added,
"in an emergency all that goes by the board. You're there
to see that Rabinovich is kept safe, and if you have to
knock some heads to do it, I'll be here to fight the political
battle for you.''

Lyle glanced at him with affection. That was the sort of
thing Yardley did pretty well. He could be relied on to
stand by his agents when something went wrong, as it
occasionally did, even in the DIA.

The red scrambler phone on Yardley's mahogany desk
began buzzing in a low, insistent way, and the Director
walked swiftly across to answer it. Calls on this line came
either direct from the Oval Office or from a select few in
the Pentagon. Ross and Lyle watched him take the call,
and then, after a few seconds, begin scratching the top of
his gray, crew-cut head with a finger: a bad sign, as Lyle
knew from past experience.

Yardley spoke forcefully into the phone. "No, Mr.
Secretary," he said. "With respect, that is unacceptable to
me . . . Of course I realize the problem. But the President
must know . . . well, it just isn't good enough. I'm aware
of the stakes. God knows I'm aware. And I know you are
too, sir . . . Sorry to sound off like this. But we've got to
stall them. At least can't we do that? . . . Let's say until
tomorrow midday. I'll put my men onto it and see what
they come up with. Thanks for the tip, by the way.''

Yardley replaced the receiver and returned to his leather
chair. "It seems, gentlemen," he said, "that the Russians

have given the President an ultimatum. They will abandon the SALT talks permanently and catch the first plane home if we don't hand Rabinovich back."

Lyle whistled. "That must be some illegal economic activity he's involved in."

"Precisely," Yardley said. "The Secretary of Defense believes he can stall the White House for a few hours, so we've got until noon tomorrow. By the sound of it, they're getting ready to throw Rabinovich to the wolves."

Ross's face registered instinctive anger, but Lyle remained relaxed and unemotional. He'd seen this sort of thing before: men sacrificed for a fashionable theory, or a negotiating advantage that sometimes turned out to be real and sometimes illusory. Anyway, there was no point getting worked up about it.

"Goddammit, that's a disgrace!" Ross exclaimed.

Yardley stared at him coldly and added after a pause, "But of course, there's nothing to stop us having a word with him before the decision is made, and if what he says is important, it could sway the White House."

"Jesus, it had better!"

The Director's voice was icy with distaste. He hated his men taking moral stands. It was bad for efficiency, and it wasted time. "May I remind you, Mr. Ross," he said, "that you are an employee of this Agency and subject to its discipline. I know you don't have a military background like Major Lyle or our other agents, but that doesn't excuse you from conforming to our standards. You know what they are. You've been through our training at Fairfax. You've heard the lectures. You've signed on. Now buckle down for Christ's sake! You're not omnipotent. You don't know the whole picture, only one small part! And your job is to deal with that small part as best you can, without making waves. Do I make myself clear, mister?"

Clive Lyle's eyes were focused on some distant part of the room.

"Yes," Ross said grudgingly.

"Yes?" The Director worked himself into a rage. To hell with careful handling "Yes what?"

"Yes, SIR."

"Again! Say it again!"

"Yes SIR!"

"That's better, Mr. Ross. Now do you think you're good enough to handle this assignment?"

Ross, stung, replied softly. "Of course, sir."

"Then get the hell out of here and do it!"

Lyle broke in, "What's the location of the safe house, General?"

"Ah." Yardley returned to his desk and found a piece of paper in a drawer. He handed it to Lyle who read it and gave it back.

"Thank you, General," Lyle said.

"You may go."

As the two agents left the office, Lyle was aware of his comrade's barely suppressed anger. In the outer office, Yardley's secretary, Lucy, gave Ross a moist-eyed smile that he did not return.

Lyle put an arm around Ross's shoulder in the corridor. "Don't let it worry you, David," he sympathized. "Yardley does a number like that from time to time. It's happened to all of us. That was a pretty mild example, actually. You didn't even get his lecture on teamwork. Consider yourself lucky."

"Yeah." Ross was not convinced.

"And he's right. It's not up to us to make moral judgments. We just carry out orders."

"Bad luck for Rabinovich, then. He'd have had as much chance in Nazi Germany. A lot of people there just carried out orders. And I seem to remember the Nuremberg trials had something to say about their moral responsibility.''

"Yeah.'' Lyle was thoughtful, "That's true. It's a pretty murky area. But I guess the bottom line is this: do you believe the people you work for are basically decent and honest?''

"No,'' Ross replied.

Lyle began to laugh and punched him on the arm. "That's my boy,'' he said. "Come on. Let's go see if we can save Rabinovich from the KGB.''

The CIA safe house was in the Maryland countryside, set inside acres of trees and shrubs and surrounded by a six-foot wall. A gatehouse controlled the only entrance, and although scaling the wall would present no problem for an intruder, the grounds were crisscrossed with electronic devices. These alerted the security detail if anyone came within range who lacked the special metallic identification badges that the equipment could "read" and thus override the alarm.

Lyle and Ross presented their DIA authorizations at the gatehouse and waited until the security men had received telephone confirmation to allow them in.

They drove up the winding road to a large house of white-painted brick with green shutters. One man waited for them at the front door, his hands behind his back and his face wooden. He watched as they parked and walked toward him. "Parking spaces are provided at the rear,'' he said.

Lyle glanced at Ross and raised an eyebrow, remembering Yardley's order to keep things cool. "You don't say,'' he said. "Looks like you've got everything organized just fine.'' To Ross he said, "Stay here and talk to our friend while I move the car.'' Then unable to resist the temptation, he added, "Do you think I should lock, or is it safe to leave it open?"

He met the hostile gaze of the CIA agent with his most charming smile before turning away. Ross stood silently for a few seconds, sizing up the other man. They were almost the same height: he judged he had perhaps an inch advantage, and they were probably both around two hundred pounds.

"I'm David Ross," he said, extending a hand.

"Special Agent Hughes." They shook hands hard but briefly, then Hughes looked away, clearly unwilling to give more than the absolute minimum.

"Quite a place you've got here," Ross said conversationally.

Hughes grunted, so Ross tried again.

"How's our friend Rabinovich?"

The CIA man shrugged. "Who's he?"

"Are you in charge here?" Ross asked.

"No," Hughes said.

Ross walked a few feet farther on, looking around to see what security measures he could spot. In the distance a handler walked a black dog through a grove of trees, but otherwise there was nothing apparent. It was a hot, sunny day.

Lyle returned and seemed to have decided to be briskly businesslike. "Let's go," he said.

They passed into a wooden-floored entrance hall, which was sparsely finished and then into a large, slightly more comfortable living room.

"Wait here," Hughes ordered. He disappeared through another door.

The agents looked around in silence. Clearly, no one lived in the house for any length of time. The furniture was functional, and only the minimum effort had been expended on decor. The bookshelves were virtually empty, except for some old dog-eared paperbacks and a pile of gun and sports magazines.

After several minutes a lean, bespectacled man in his early forties came into the room, followed by Hughes.

"Your identifications please?" he asked without preliminaries. Lyle and Ross handed them over and watched as they were scrutinized.

"I am Dean McClellan," the man said finally. "I am responsible for looking after Mr. Rabinovich." He tried to keep his tone neutral while making his meaning plain. "Nothing here is done, or undone, without my stated approval. I take it General Yardley made that clear to you?"

Lyle, recognizing there was no advantage in meeting the offered confrontation, turned on his considerable charm. "We're not here to step on your toes, Mr. McClellan," he said. "Of course this is your show, and personally I wouldn't have it otherwise. From what we've seen so far, it looks pretty damned efficient."

McClellan unbent slightly. "Well, we think so," he said.

"David Ross and I are a bit superfluous, I guess. But we've been sent here to see if we can help out, and I hope we can. How's Rabinovich?"

"Mr. Rabinovich is fine. He's still on ice as you probably know."

"Of course." Lyle decided not to say that was all about to change. "He must be pretty nervous."

"So would you be in his position."

"I guess so. Can we see him?"

McClellan looked reluctant. "I don't suppose I can stop you. Well, you might as well have a look at what security we've got on him. That's what you're here for."

"Thank you. We appreciate that."

McClellan led the way up the stairs, with Hughes taking

the rear. An armed guard was in position in the corridor just beyond the stairwell, and Lyle noticed closed-circuit television cameras positioned flush against the ceiling.

"Where're the monitors for the cameras?" he asked.

"They're in one of the rooms downstairs," McClellan said. "You can see them later if you want."

A door at the end of the corridor was locked. McClellan rapped on it once . . . a pause, then twice more. Lyle glanced at Ross and rolled his eyes. The Boy Scouts were back in town. There was the sound of a key being turned, and the door opened to reveal a hefty young man with a revolver on his hip.

Beyond him, Rabinovich was sitting on the edge of a bed, eyes shifting nervously from one to the other as he tried to determine if this were good news or bad. An air conditioner hummed faintly.

"How you doing, Mr. Rabinovich?" McClellan greeted him with a heartiness that rang obviously false.

"When will someone speak to me?" the Russian asked plaintively. "I wait and no one comes."

"They'll be along real soon," McClellan replied. "I don't know exactly when. Everyone's pretty busy at the moment."

Rabinovich's shoulders sagged, and his face looked incredibly tired. David Ross felt a sharp pang of compassion. He remembered that exact expression on the face of a Soviet professor his family had befriended when he was a boy. The professor had defected on impulse while in Finland but, once committed, could not go back. His wife and children were left behind in the Soviet Union, and he had neither seen nor heard from them again. It was as if the earth had opened up and swallowed everyone he had ever known and loved up to that point when he changed his political allegiance. A sad man, tired and defeated—just like Rabinovich. They both knew they had been beaten by the system.

Ross spoke quietly in Russian. "Have courage, my friend. There are people working on your behalf."

Rabinovich's mouth opened in surprise and alarm, as if he had been confronted by the KGB. McClellan turned angrily to Ross. "I didn't give you permission to talk to him," he snapped. "What did you just say?"

"I told Mr. Rabinovich to have courage," Ross replied. "He's not a prisoner, and this is a free country. I can talk to him if I wish." McClellan was no more than 5 foot 9; so Ross was able to look down at him and with his big and obviously fit body, command attention.

McClellan's tongue licked across dry lips. "This is our show, Ross. I though I made that clear."

"I'm not disputing that," Ross replied. "But it's not exclusively yours. We've been sent along to babysit, so that's what we're going to do. We take our orders from General Yardley, and he takes his orders from higher up. If you don't like it, I suggest you get on the phone and sort it out with the White House. Major Lyle and I will leave when we're instructed to do so by General Yardley and not before. Do *you* have any questions?"

There was a silence while McClellan glared furiously at Ross. Rabinovich sat on the bed, looking astonished and scared.

Finally McClellan turned away. "Mr. Hughes," he said "remain here with these . . . gentlemen. I'll be back as soon as I can."

The CIA guard locked the door behind him and pocketed the key. He stood waiting, his right hand on the butt of his pistol. Hughes, beside him, seemed uncertain what he was supposed to do.

Ross crossed the room to Rabinovich.

"Don't be frightened of me," he said. "I prefer to

speak to you like this in Russian because our friends here have long ears."

"You are Russian," Rabinovich said numbly. "I can hear it from your accent. You are from Moscow."

"I had a good teacher, but I am American. I hope you will trust me. Now listen carefully. The Soviet Union has threatened to abandon the talks unless you are handed back to them. They say you are guilty of economic crimes." He paused. "My government is considering its position."

Ross didn't realize it, but he'd said exactly the wrong thing: one sentence that would irrevocably alter the course of his life—and Lyle's. The certainty of welcome to the United States, with which Rabinovich had embarked upon his defection, had given way to a chilling uncertainty. This grew while the CIA kept him on ice, and his imagination worked ceaselessly. Now his fears had been confirmed outright by the young man before him. He realized he needed urgently to reassess his position, to see if there was some way he might yet save himself.

Rabinovich whispered, his voice stricken, "Will they give me back?"

"Perhaps," Ross said. "Unless there is good reason for them to do otherwise."

"What reason?"

"The information you have on the Soviet neutron program. You are a scientist, a member of the Academy. There is much you must know. What can you give my government to make it worth their while to abandon the talks?"

From the door, Hughes snapped, "That's enough now, Ross. You've had your chance to say hello, so shut up."

Ross ignored him, staring intently at Rabinovich, trying to persuade the Russian to speak. "There is not much time," he urged.

"How much time?"

Ross decided to tell the truth. "Probably until midday tomorrow," he said. "The decision will be made then."

Rabinovich sat in silence, considering his predicament. Ross studied him, schooling himself not to get too close to this man, whose portly body suggested an ample standard of living, but whose eyes were frightened and beaten. If you looked into them, you could see the story of his life written there.

"If I tell you what I know, what is the guarantee that your government won't hand me back once they possess the only thing of value I have?" Rabinovich asked.

Of course, there was no guarantee, but Ross could hardly admit it. So instead he said, "We don't operate that way." When he saw the faint flicker of black humor and disbelief in the other man's face, he added defensively, "Your comrades want you. They also want a ban on neutron weapons, yet they are prepared to give up that far greater prize if you are not returned to them. This means you must have information that is very important." He looked shrewdly at the Russian. "Tell me," he asked, "what will the KGB do if they get you to Moscow?"

After a moment, Rabinovich replied thoughtfully, "That depends. Naturally they will interrogate me. Sometimes they use torture, and sometimes they use drugs. With me, I think they may take the more civilized course. I am, as you say, a member of the Academy. But if I have told the Americans anything of importance, they will execute me as a spy and a traitor. If I have not, they will send me to prison—until I die, if I am unlucky, but perhaps only for a few years if they need my professional skills later." He paused and stared at the American. "So you see, comrade, I may still have something to lose."

Ross exhaled audibly. Rabinovich had a point. "But unless you tell us what you know—or give some idea of the information you have to offer, you will leave my government no option but to send you back," Ross argued. "It is done with most defectors. Think of it like this: you are coming to us as a salesman. If you expect us to buy your wares, you must at least show us a sample. Is that not fair?"

"Yet if I do, and you decide not to buy, I will be killed," Rabinovich countered.

"And if you do not, you will be sent to certain imprisonment, probably in a labor camp, and you may die there—a lot less pleasantly than if the KGB shot you."

Rabinovich sighed. "We are talking in circles, comrade."

There was a series of sharp knocks on the door— McClellan's code—and everyone turned to watch the guard let him in. To the surprise of Ross and Lyle, he had become relaxed and courteous.

"I've had a talk with my superiors," McClellan said from just inside the entrance, "and they've clarified the situation. As far as we're concerned, the two of you can take complete responsibility for the security of Mr. Rabinovich. We don't believe there's any point fighting among ourselves."

"Does this mean the CIA is withdrawing?" Lyle asked warily.

"Only so far as this floor is concerned," McClellan said with a faint smile. "The house and the grounds are still CIA property, paid for out of our budget, and ordinary security will operate as usual. But the safekeeping of Mr. Rabinovich himself becomes a Defense responsibility. If you think you'd like to take it on, of course."

Ross and Lyle exchanged glances. It was exactly what they wanted. "Thank you, Mr. McClellan," Lyle said. "We accept that responsibility."

"So be it. Would you like a weapon?"

"Uh, yes. That would be useful."

"Mr. Howe." The young guard braced himself. "Hand

over your gun to Major Lyle.'' The guard did so with obvious reluctance. Lyle extracted a Walther PPK short-barreled semi-automatic pistol from the holster and checked to see if it was loaded. In a pouch he found an extra clip containing eight rounds. He nodded and buckled it on.

"Would Mr. Ross like one?" McClellan asked. He addressed his question to Lyle: obviously he hadn't overcome his antagonism to the point of actually talking to the more aggressive Defense man.

From across the room, David Ross said, "Might as well, seeing as you're handing them out."

McClellan gave the order to his guard. "Well, gentlemen," he said "he's all yours. If we can assist you in any way, please let me know. Otherwise, we're stepping aside. Dinner will be brought up here at eight. You want it for the three of you?" With the suspicion of a smirk, he added, "Of course you might like to bring in your own food. Please feel free to do so."

"That won't be necessary, Mr. McClellan," Lyle replied. "I'm sure the CIA's capable of providing a meal." He went on hastily, "An excellent meal, I mean. We'd be glad to accept your hospitality."

McClellan nodded and led his men out of the room. As a parting gesture, the guard handed over the door key.

When it was locked behind them, Ross and Lyle stared at each other. "Christ, what do you make of that?" Ross asked.

"Sounds like McClellan made a telephone call to complain about us and had his ear chewed off. One thing you can say about Yardley, when he needs to pull strings, he knows exactly the right ones to go for."

"It's pretty impressive." Ross smiled at Rabinovich. "Well," he said, "we're in charge of you now, and that makes us happy."

"Those men were CIA?" Rabinovich asked.

"That's right."

"And who are you?"

"We're from the Defense Intelligence Agency."

"Ah. Like the GRU* in the Soviet Union. The GRU hates the KGB, just as you hate your comrades in the CIA. I find that very interesting. It seems our countries are similar in many ways."

"Not too many, I hope," Ross said. Then to Lyle, "I've told Mr. Rabinovich the score. He's got until midday tomorrow to give us at least a sample of what he knows about the Soviet neutron program, or we'll hand him back to his Embassy."

Lyle raised an eyebrow. It was a lot more than he'd have disclosed in the circumstances, but he supposed David knew the Russian mind. Anyway, it had been done, and there was no point arguing about it.

"Well, Mr. Rabinovich," Lyle said, "what about it?"

The Russian looked from one to the other before replying earnestly: "My friends, you have been speaking frank with me, and I speak frank with you. Something is happening, and I do not trust it. I escape from my comrades to tell you news, and no one comes to listen to me."

"We're listening," Ross said.

"Until you," Rabinovich acknowledged. Then, apologetically, "But who are you? Of what importance in the deliberations of your government? You see, I have no wish to spend my years in a labor camp in Siberia or a hospital for those with mental sickness. I have no wish to die. You look at me, and you see a frightened man. But I am frightened also about the United States. I think it is not the country some comrades talk about. America is the same as the Soviet Union, yes?"

* GRU—Soviet Military intelligence, the Glavnoye Razvedyvatelnoye Upravlenie.

"No," Ross said firmly.

"Not the people, perhaps. Not the money, the economics. But the government, ah! That is the same. Let me ask you, my friend," he said to Ross, "about this case concerning me. It is a moral question, is it not? Your government knows the KGB may torture and kill me if they send me back, yet still they do it. So are they not then responsible for what is done to me, just as the KGB is, as the Soviet Government is? Is it not your President himself who is torturing me and shooting me?"

Ross caught Lyle's eye. He didn't think there was any way around that, short of a dishonest semantic smokescreen of the kind politicians erect instinctively, rather like a threatened squid knows to spurt a cloud of ink and dart away to safety in the confusion.

"Personally, I think you're right," Ross said. "America would have to share the moral responsibility."

But Lyle tried to counter the argument. "Let's look at it from the other side," he invited. "Let's imagine, Mr. Rabinovich, that you're the President of the United States. After years of trying, you've finally got the Soviet Union around a table to discuss seriously the limitation of strategic arms—intercontinental ballistic missiles, stockpiles of nuclear weapons, that sort of thing—in exchange for banning the neutron bomb. Now the world is going to reap considerable benefits from that. No more useless billions spent on arms. But then suddenly a member of their delegation wants to defect, and the Soviets threaten to scrap everything unless you hand him back. What do you do? On one side of the scale, you've got a single defector, and on the other, tens of thousands of lives saved or enriched because arms money can be diverted to socially important uses. How about that?"

"I think," Rabinovich said after a short silence, "I would consider the following points: One, does not the

Soviet Union have to weigh the same things in the balance—this single defector against the many thousands? And if they believe the defector is more important, what does that tell me about how sincere they are? And two is a moral issue which concerns democracy, but not communism. At least, that is my view. If the democracy does not care about the single man, can it truly care about the mass of the people? All the ugly things that happen in my own country do so because the state concerns itself with the mass and stamps on the individual as if he was a bug.''

Ross grinned at Lyle. ''Well, Clive?'' he asked.

''Governments don't always do rational things,'' Lyle replied. ''They may just think it's a matter of principle, getting you back. Unless of course you know something they don't want us to find out, because if we knew, we wouldn't be interested in the talks anyway.''

Lyle stared steadily at Rabinovich, challenging him, until the portly Russian nodded gravely, ''That is the news I bring,'' he admitted at last. ''Something to anyway stop the talks.''

''Then you should tell us,'' Lyle insisted, ''or you will be sent back and we'll never know.''

Rabinovich sighed. ''It is not easy to decide,'' he said. ''I am gambling with my life. I have until tomorrow, is that not so?''

''Yes.''

''Then it is best if I think about what to do during the night. In the morning we will speak again.''

The agents glanced at each other. Short of giving Rabinovich a dose of truth drug, there was nothing they could do. Lyle thought perhaps they might try the drug in the morning, if the Russian was still holding out; and he'd ask Ross to explain, as they pushed the needle in, just how the Americans were different from the KGB.

"Okay," Lyle said with a shrug. "We'll talk again later."

A knock on the door—the CIA code again—brought the guard with a spare Walther and ammunition for Ross, and he buckled on the gunbelt. Later, Lyle went to inspect the rest of the security in the house, including the room where the closed circuit television cameras were monitored. It seemed a good enough operation. He made a telephone report to Yardley, who was well pleased with the arrangements.

Two men brought in steaks, french fries, and a couple of Cokes each for dinner, but otherwise the CIA left them alone.

There was a pack of cards in the room, so Ross and Lyle taught Rabinovich some games, and they played for matches until about eleven o'clock. On the basis of which of them had won the most the agents organized the night routine, although it was going to be difficult to get any sleep at all. Rabinovich had a bed but there was only one easy chair and a straight-back. They debated briefly asking the CIA if there was a spare stretcher somewhere but decided against it as a point of pride.

Ross took the first three hours. He drapped a towel over the lamp to dim it and turned off the overhead light. The room was bathed in a dull, warm glow. The Russian donned a pair of pajamas that had been provided for him and slipped under the covers, while Lyle made himself as comfortable as he could and closed his eyes, trying to relax completely, if not to sleep.

Ross sat, deep in thought. With the coming of night, sound carried more easily, and he became aware of floorboards creaking in the corridor and of voices, too low to make out, from the room directly below.

Rabinovich seemed to be asleep. At least his breathing was deep and steady, and he was not tossing about. It was a wonder he could rest at all, Ross thought, not knowing whether or not he was a condemned man.

Time began to drag. Lyle sprawled in the easy chair, unmoving except for the slight rise and fall of his chest. A few strands of sandy-colored hair, flopping over his forehead, stirred in the light breeze from the air conditioner. Ross studied his partner. When Lyle was like this, there was just no way of telling how strong he really was or what a complete shit he could be. There was certainly nothing in his peaceful face at that moment to suggest he was dangerous. Apart from a few wrinkles around his eyes, which might have been laugh lines on someone else, and the faint white of a small scar down the side of his cheek, he had no distinguishing features. Lyle was good looking in a conventional way, but he would not stand out in a crowd. Only the way he moved suggested that he was in complete command of his body. But it was his eyes more than anything that signaled he was a man to be reckoned with. They were very light brown, and if he was really angry, they became lighter, with a hint of yellow, like an animal's.

Ross thought the air conditioning might be too cool for the sleeping men, and he crossed quietly to turn it off. The switch didn't work, so instead he adjusted the thermostat. He settled back in his chair to wait out the last section of his shift.

Outside on the grounds, the rising of an almost-full moon cast a glow over the lawns and the driveway, which heightened the blackness of the shadows around the large shrubs and among the trees.

Apart from occasional subdued rustlings of small animals moving through the grass, there was silence. The infrared beams of the electronic devices sliced across the ground, invisible to anyone not wearing special glasses.

There was a spill of light from the windows of the gatehouse where two CIA guards sat at a wooden table, complaining about their pay.

An ambulance drove carefully along the perimeter road toward the entrance. It doused its lights and pulled over to the curb before it came in sight of the gate.

Inside it, Lappa checked his watch and saw that it was four minutes to one. Beside him, Nikitin moved uneasily, tense as he always was immediately before an operation. In these final minutes, he found it difficult to keep still. He squeezed his hands together until his taut muscles trembled or rubbed his arms with unconscious absorption or shifted in his seat. Lappa knew that once they got under way Nikitin would be as cool as the best of the KGB. It was the waiting he didn't like.

Two other Russians, dressed in the white uniforms of hospital medics, sat in the back of the ambulance, surrounded by the paraphernalia of emergency resuscitation equipment.

There was silence in the ambulance as the minutes passed. Finally Lappa said, "Comrades, it is time."

The engine coughed into life, the headlights illuminated a section of the curb and some of the road, and Lappa drove the ambulance carefully toward the gates. Nikitin sat quietly now.

They stopped at the entrance, and Lappa turned off all but the parking lights. One of the CIA guards came out toward them while the other watched, framed in the doorway of the gatehouse. Lappa and Nikitin walked forward, shoes crunching on the loose stones. They pulled out their wallets and flashed identifications. The guard took his time inspecting them, comparing the photographs with the faces of the men who squinted in the harsh glare of his flashlight.

"Anyone else with you?" The guard gestured to the ambulance.

Lappa gave a signal, and the two Russians in white came out to show their cards.

Time passed slowly. The CIA man at the gatehouse shuffled his feet and yawned. The one checking the identifications seemed to like keeping DIA agents waiting, and read every line. Lappa and Nikitin appeared uninterested in the process, remote and arrogant, studiously ignoring the guard.

When there was nothing more on the cards he could possibly check, the guard said, "Wait here," and returned to the gatehouse with the documents. He phoned the main house, asking to speak with McClellan. The Russians stood in a patient group outside.

McClellan apparently had to be awakened but was in a good temper when informed that four more DIA agents wanted to come in.

"Have you checked their IDs?" McClellan asked.

"Yes, sir."

"Are they okay?"

"Yes, sir."

"Then let them in."

The guard strolled back to the gate, pointedly taking his time. He returned the documents, comparing once again the photographs with the faces.

"Let's have a look at the vehicle," he said. Wordlessly, the Russians led him back and opened the rear doors. He peered inside, flashing his light around. Lappa took a cigarette and struck a match. The glow from the flame illuminated eyes without expression.

Finally the guard shrugged and walked away. The Russians climbed back into the ambulance and waited for the gates to be opened. As they drove through, Lappa offered the CIA guard a laconic salute.

*   *   *

In the locked room on the second floor of the safe house, Clive Lyle stirred and looked at David Ross, stiff and uncomfortable in the upright chair.

"How you doing, David?" he asked quietly, so as not to wake Rabinovich.

"Fine. Did you manage to get some sleep?"

"Yeah. Want me to take over now?"

Ross checked his watch. "No, it's just after one, so you've got another hour."

"Okay." Lyle closed his eyes again and squirmed slightly in the chair before settling down. Faintly from outside came the sound of an approaching vehicle.

Ross walked quietly to the window and drew back the curtain, but apart from a brief flash of headlights catching a section of hedge there was nothing to see. The driveway was on the other side of the house.

Ross stretched to ease the muscles in his back and shoulders before returning to his seat. Christ, it was getting to be a long night.

Several minutes passed.

Ross felt a faint tickling in the back of his throat. He coughed quietly into his hand to clear it, but it grew stronger, medicinal, reminding him sharply of hospitals. His arms felt heavy and it was hard to focus his eyes. He tried to call out "Clive!" but his body would not respond.

Ross was aware of the floor coming up to meet him, but no pain when he hit it, and then he was unconscious.

When he awoke, the sun was shining through the fabric of the floral curtains. Someone was banging on the door— not the knock . . . knock knock code of McClellan, but the side of a fist thumping the wood.

Ross rubbed his eyes. What the hell was going on?

"Okay! Okay!" he shouted, and whoever was outside stopped banging.

Ross found he had difficulty walking, as if he was badly hung over, and his head felt muggy. He reached in his pocket for the door key, but it had gone. He checked the other pocket. Where in God's name could it have gone? Perhaps Lyle had it. Lyle was asleep in the chair.

Then he saw Rabinovich's bed and it was empty.

3

The two agents sat stiff with embarrassment on the chairs in front of the desk of General Lyndon Yardley. The DIA Director stared across the mahogany expanse with an expression close to contempt.

"I don't need to tell you," he observed, "what this makes us look like?"

"No, sir," Lyle said.

"No, sir," Ross said.

"I had the Director of the CIA on the phone an hour ago, supposedly to commiserate, and he sounded as if he'd just inherited a million dollars. He was gleeful, gentlemen!"

Lyle's face was pale. Shit, they'd never live this down, not if they lived to be a thousand. It was a tale instructors would tell to frighten new recruits at Fairfax, and when those guys graduated as agents, they'd keep a watch for Lyle and Ross. If they were still there.

"You'll have my resignation today, sir," Lyle promised although it was the last thing he wanted to do.

"And mine," Ross said.

"Major Lyle, Mr. Ross, I don't want your resignations!" Yardley raged. "I want Rabinovich!"

"Well, do we have any idea where he might be?" Lyle asked quietly.

Yardley stared dispiritedly at his fingernails and they heard him sigh. "He's halfway to Moscow."

"Are you sure, sir? Because if not . . ."

"I am sure, Major Lyle. The Russians had a plane standing by to take their delegation back. As you'd expect. Rabinovich was with them. He checked through passport control. He went like a lamb. He was in the air about an hour before you two sleeping beauties woke up. We lost Rabinovich, and we lost the SALT talks. Although frankly, as far as I'm concerned, losing the talks is the only cheering bit of news."

Yardley expelled air through his lips in an audible puff. "What a day! What a day for the Agency!" He sat back and regarded his two men. "I have to prepare a report for the Secretary of Defense to submit to the President. What have you clowns got to tell me that will serve, in some small way, to mitigate the . . . the enormity of what you've done?"

"Do you mind if we smoke, General?" Lyle asked diffidently.

Yardley waved his arms. "Why not?" he said, "I can't imagine it will adversely affect your performance."

Lyle pulled out a pack and offered it to Ross, who took a cigarette. He hardly ever smoked, but felt he needed something. They lit up. Ross's mouth was dry and tasted terrible. He had to have something to drink.

"Do you think it would be possible to get some coffee, sir?" Ross asked.

"Coffee, too? Yes, why in God's name not?" He pushed a button, and after a moment the far door opened. "Lucy," Yardley said, "these two heroes would like some coffee. And so would I."

The Director let them sit in silence before he said, "Well? What do you have to say?"

Lyle began. "I really don't know exactly what happened, General. They blew in some gas—under the door, or maybe through the air conditioning. Neither of us heard a thing."

"You wouldn't have, Major Lyle. You were asleep."

"No sir, I was not. I was trying to sleep. Mr. Ross was actually on watch. I'd just spoken to him a few minutes before. I knew it was gas as soon as it hit my throat."

"But you didn't do anything."

"There was nothing I could do. By the time it registered on my brain, I couldn't move or talk. You know how these things work."

Yardley, who had once been in the field himself, actually did know. He grunted.

Coffee, which had been brewing in the outer office, was brought in. Lucy tried to remain studiously neutral, serving the Director, then Lyle, and finally Ross, who smiled gratefully at her, causing her to blush.

The hot drink made Ross feel better, and he stubbed out the half-smoked cigarette. The kidnapping of Rabinovich had been going futilely around in his mind since the sickening discovery that morning, and the more he considered the facts he knew, the more he felt something was gravely wrong.

"Okay," Ross said. "I'd like to go through the whole thing from the beginning. The Russians arrive at the safe house in an ambulance at one A.M. Right?"

"Right," Yardley said.

"They present DIA identification cards, which the men at the gatehouse accept."

"Right."

"The guards wake up McClellan who says 'Let them in.' They drive toward the house. A couple of them go around to the window of the room where Rabinovich is held, and blow in gas through the air conditioning unit.''

"How do you know that?'' Yardley asked sharply.

"Because I'd have heard them coming along the corridor. The floor's wooden, and it creaks.''

"Not necessarily. They might have walked along a part that doesn't creak.''

"It's an old house, General,'' Ross said. "Believe me, the floor creaks. Anyway, we can check it easily enough, because there ought to be some signs on the ground below the window. Whoever did it would have had to be hoisted up, or use a ladder, to get to the air conditioner.''

"But so what?'' Yardley remarked. "They put you out of action pretty effectively.''

"So the CIA let in an ambulance full of Soviet agents, let them drive up to the house, don't notice a couple of them peel off and go to the exact window where Rabinovich is being held and blow in gas. Then they let them in the front door—and they admit all four were there—and allow them to wander up the stairs, without escort, but carrying a stretcher so obviously they were going to bring someone out, and there're no prizes for guessing who. Yet no one thinks to ask McClellan if this is okay. Hell, those guys didn't even want us talking to Rabinovich a couple of hours earlier, but suddenly they're turned to stone when some alleged DIA men come to wheel him off the premises.''

Yardley was taking an interest now. Perhaps things didn't look so rosy for the CIA after all.

Ross finished his coffee. "Don't forget,'' he went on, "the two of us were only responsible for security on the second floor. All the rest was CIA territory. So the Russians walk along the creaking old corridor—four of them, not one man avoiding the noisy bits—and they let themselves in the door to Rabinovich's room, which has a special security lock, with their own key.''

''How do you know it was their own?''

Ross shrugged. ''The CIA haven't mentioned giving anyone a key. Check it with them, but I'll bet they didn't. Anyway, it would be a bit strange for DIA men to arrive in the middle of the night and ask for one, when their buddies were already up there. If they were genuine, all they had to do was go knock on the door and Clive or I would have let them in.''

Yardley digested this information and liked what he heard so much that he asked, ''Would you care for some more coffee, David?''

Ross smiled slightly. At least they were winning the Director back to their side. It wasn't looking like such an unmitigated disaster. ''Yes please,'' he said.

''Clive?''

''Thank you, General.''

''Go on, David, go on,'' Yardley urged.

''Two things we need to check: one—is there proof they blew the gas through the air conditioning, and two—did the CIA give them a key? If the answers are yes, and no, and I'm pretty sure they will be, we start getting to the heart of the matter. Who told the Russians the location of the safe house? Who told them the exact location of the room? Who told them the air conditioner would be on? And shit . . .'' Ross remembered trying to turn it off during the night, '' . . . who disconnected the switch? I had to lower the thermostat because I couldn't turn the thing off.''

He paused while Lucy poured him another cup, leaning close. ''And who gave the Russians a key to the room?'' Ross asked. ''It's not easy to pick that lock. They couldn't have been sure we'd still be asleep if they'd taken the time to get in by themselves.''

Lyle had recovered a lot of his color, and now he was

looking angry, his eyes a definite yellow. "Anyway, what happened to all the CIA security on the ground floor?" Lyle demanded. "Who was monitoring the closed-circuit TV? Those guys must have worn masks when they came into the room because of the gas. Why weren't they seen?"

"And who provided the Russians with DIA identification?" Ross added.

"Well, they could have done that themselves, David," Yardley pointed out. "The rezidenturas in New York or Washington could have made those up."

Lyle doubted it. "In a time span that short? Could our Embassy in Moscow issue four KGB cards in six or eight hours?"

"Yes, if they were geared up in advance."

"Which the rezidenturas here weren't. But we could in Washington, couldn't we, any day of the week?"

"Oh yes," Yardley said.

"And so could the CIA."

Yardley fell silent.

"Don't forget," Ross pressed their advantage, "that this was a CIA safe house. If anyone knew the layout, it was the CIA. If anyone had a spare key to Rabinovich's room, they did."

"Gentlemen," Yardley said at last, "it's beginning to look as if we were betrayed."

"Why? The question is why?" Lyle said.

"A political decision," the Director ventured. "The CIA wouldn't have done it without strong backing. As I told you, a lot of people in Washington weren't anxious to hear what Rabinovich had to say. They didn't want anything to harm the talks."

"But they *have* been harmed," Lyle pointed out. "The Soviets caught the plane out with Rabinovich."

"Ah yes," Yardley agreed, "but the truth is, they haven't said the negotiations are canceled. They've merely said they're adjourned. Once they find Rabinovich didn't tell us anything, they'll be back—wait and see."

"Christ, it is a dirty game," Ross said. "Unless, General, this is one of the little pieces of the puzzle I shouldn't make any moral judgments about?"

"Don't push your luck, David," Yardley said. "You're not out of the woods yet, you know. Betrayal or not, you still lost us a valuable defector. You were sent to do a job, and you failed to carry it out. That is inefficient. And dangerous."

Ross was silent. It was true, of course. There were no second prizes in their line of work, and if the Russians hadn't made it a peaceful operation, he and Lyle would now be dead. The thought of a Soviet agent going through his pockets and removing the security key while he lay unconscious was not a happy one. And both of them, drugged by the gas, had also been given injections to keep them asleep until morning so that Rabinovich would be out of US jurisdiction by the time the alarm was raised. The injection ampule could just as easily have contained a poison or a curare-based drug that paralyzed the respiratory system, and they would have died noiselessly. As it was, the only possible aftereffects were tetanus and hepatitis, and immediately after they got back to headquarters Yardley had ordered them to report to the DIA hospital for booster shots. He wasn't taking any chances on the standards of hygiene practiced by KGB agents in the field.

"What do we do now?" Lyle asked.

"Immediately, of course, I'll put in a formal complaint about the CIA's behavior," Yardley said. "I'll have a couple of men check out the area around Rabinovich's window and make sure those idiots downstairs didn't just hand the Russians a key. And then I'll give them hell." He studied his manicured fingernails and found nothing there to distress him. "But this isn't the end of the matter," Yardley went on. "Not by a long shot. It's true we've lost Rabinovich, and we won't get him back But I want to know what it was he had to tell us. There's something happening with the Soviet neutron program that isn't right, and I want to find out what it is. The CIA is in the pockets of the politicians, as usual, but I like to think we act for the people. Those two things aren't necessarily the same, David, not at all."

Yardley addressed himself directly to Ross. "A politician worries all the time about re-election. To him, survival is primarily a personal matter, and he looks at it in spans of a few years. But when this Agency thinks of survival, we think of the United States, of the whole free world and our time scale is forever." He stared at the new agent to see if he showed some sign of understanding what was the equivalent of the DIA Creed but there was nothing to be read on the young face. Still, at least he wasn't looking amused. "So," Yardley continued, "that's going to be your assignment from now on. Both of you. Find out what the Russians are hiding about their neutron program. Check through all the intelligence reports that have come in over the last three or four years. There may be a clue somewhere that we've missed. Find out where there are Soviets, visiting or based anywhere in the free world, who might be able to give us the information we want, if we got to them. I want you to pull out all the stops on this."

"I could go into Russia if you wanted," Ross offered.

"If necessary I will send you," Yardley said. "And when we succeed in this task, gentlemen, as we must," . . . and here he smiled for the first time, "then we'll wipe this blight off the DIA's record. We'll have our revenge."

4

It was like waking into a nightmare. First, sound drifted into his consiousness. He held his breath in disbelief at the remembered voices, and they stopped. He listened carefully, but heard silence. He decided it was a fantasy and tried to banish it from his thoughts.

Then there was the realization that although still in bed, he was also traveling. The vibration was soothing until the noise of the motor changed and lessened, and soon he felt bumps as if he was being taken over rough ground. The vehicle shifted into a lower gear.

Viktor Viktorovich Rabinovich opened his eyes cautiously, not at all convinced he was awake, and saw below his feet two dark shapes swaying slightly with the movement. They passed a lighted area, and the reflection through small frosted windows made the corners of the shapes come up white.

Behind his head, a man coughed.

Rabinovich tried to raise himself, without success. He tried again and felt his fingers curl. At least there was something he could move. His toes and feet too: those moved. And he could lift his head.

He did so, staring fearfully at the silent dark shapes,

malevolent presences, angels of death, vultures waiting for the dying to lie still so they could begin their tearing feast.

The shapes moved slightly, this way and that.

It began as a low, tentative sound, building quickly, followed by a gasp for air. Then Viktor Rabinovich roared, a full-throated primal cry, carrying with it the deepest instincts of survival and a man's worst sweating terrors. The shapes launched themselves at him. A strong hand struck across his face, but the roar would not be stifled. The hand hit again, jerking his head with its force, and he began to sob and moan, for he knew.

"Welcome back, comrade," Lappa's voice, dry and amused, said.

Rabinovich began trembling uncontrollably, his body held fast on the ambulance stretcher by restraints. It was useless trying to explain his defection, or apologize, and he did not make the attempt. He lay shaking, wishing he could be brave, but seeing ahead unknown torments stretching to infinity. He clenched his teeth in an effort at control.

The vehicle was stopping, bumping over something. The interior light came on, and he saw the two men in white at his feet, hunched, ready. Lappa, behind his line of sight, ordered, "Give him the injection."

One of the men opened a medical chest and extracted a syringe. He filled it with a colorless liquid from an ampule while the other men knelt on Rabinovich's chest to keep him down while he undid one of the restraints and exposed an arm. The needle jabbed roughly into a vein and Rabinovich cried out in pain, trying to pull away.

"Hold still, can't you!" the man snapped. He removed the needle and tried again. The drug surged into Rabinovich's bloodstream.

After a few moments, fear vanished replaced by numbness and acceptance.

"Shouldn't we dress him now?" he heard Nikitin ask,

also out of sight. "We'll be at the airport in twenty minutes."

"I think you're right, comrade." Lappa replied. To the others he said: "Make him look respectable."

They unfastened the straps that they no longer needed and stripped off his pajamas. Rainovich lay in plump alabaster nakedness in the harsh light, watching dumbly. He even tried to help as they pulled on his trousers, which they'd taken from the bedroom. The men treated him as if he was an inanimate object, neither looking directly at him nor addressing him. He might have been a tailor's dummy. He lacked humanity. Lappa and Nikitin were the same, ignoring him as if he did not exist.

The ambulance moved on, Rabinovich sitting heavily on the stretcher, and before long they came into a well-lit area.

As Rabinovich stepped carefully from the vehicle, he saw the lightening sky. It was nearly dawn. He thought: By midday, I must decide what to tell the Americans.

It was really rather funny, and if it hadn't been for the drug, he might have laughed. Lappa and Nikitin flanked him, standing close, but they knew he would not run.

They walked him slowly through the fresh, chill morning air into the terminal building where Fedor Fedorovich Konev and the other members of the delegation waited in a silent group. They glanced at Rabinovich only long enough to establish that he was there before he became invisible to them, too.

Everyone moved forward through a doorway. Their passports were checked. Rabinovich looked into the face of the immigration officer, wondering vaguely if he should say something. This was his last chance. But there seemed nothing to say and, even if he spoke, no one who was prepared to listen.

He passed through the check. They walked along corridors for what seemed like a long time, until suddenly they were in the Ilyushin itself, moving down the aisle to the rear. He took the last seat at the window, and Lappa buckled his belt. Then everyone left him alone.

There was a remote, dreamlike quality to events. He heard the engines, saw the lights move as the jet was pulled back from the terminal, and soon they were on the runway. The thrust pushed him into his seat, and when abruptly the wheels left the land in which he had once placed his hopes, the drug stopped Rabinovich from feeling sad or betrayed.

It wore off gradually as they crossed the tip of Greenland, leaving inside him, palpable down in his stomach, a sick hopelessness. He became acutely aware of his body and how vulnerable it was, how easily injured.

Lappa came and put him in handcuffs, not because of anything he had said or done—indeed, he was sitting in appalled stillness—but because he knew how long the injection lasted and they didn't want any trouble.

During the long hours of the flight, they offered Rabinovich neither food nor anything to drink, although farther forward in the cabin he could see stewardesses with trays and bottles. Rabinovich was not hungry, but the pressurization was making him dehydrated and he began to crave a glass of water. And worse, his bladder filled, badly needing release. He wanted to call out to one of the KGB men sitting up front, but found he lacked the nerve. He tried to catch someone's eye, yet even those who walked past him to the toilets at the back ignored his stammered attempts to get their attention. He was, of course, totally invisible to the cabin staff.

The fullness of his bladder gradually became not mere discomfort, but actual pain. Rabinovich was unable to move at all without giving small involuntary gasps. The hours dragged on.

Finally the urgency of his predicament became so great that he shouted: "Comrade! Comrade!"

A few heads turned to look, and Lappa detached himself to walk to the rear. He held the back of a seat for support and leaned forward. "What is it?"

"Please, comrade. I must go to the toilet urgently." Rabinovich's unshaven face was pale with distress.

Lappa laughed at him: a genuinely amused sound. "The New York water again?" he asked, and went away still chuckling, leaving Rabinovich sick with pain and humiliation. Halfway to his own seat, Lappa stopped and came back. Rabinovich's heart leapt with gratitude. Lappa leaned so close, the prisoner could feel his warm breath. "If you piss on the seat, you bastard," he warned, "I'll rub your face in it."

Rabinovich slumped, defeated. He had no doubt Lappa would carry out his threat. And that was only the start. Soon he would be off the aircraft, out of the presence of civilians, and the KGB would have him to themselves. His mind refused to think beyond that, and he closed his eyes, trying to sleep so he could forget the pain for a while and praying—even praying—for the Ilyushin to reach Moscow.

The jets droned monotonously; time was suspended.

Rabinovich was almost beyond caring when the engine noise changed and they began their descent. His forehead sweated, his fists were tightly clenched. The rumblings of lowering flaps and undercarriage vibrated through the plane, and Rabinovich waited in anguish for the thump as they came to land, fearing that for him it would be the final straw. But the pilot brought the Ilyushin down as lightly as if the concrete was a natural extension of their flightpath, rather than a change of elements. Instead, it was the reverse thrust and the hard braking that pushed Rabinovich's stomach hard against his seatbelt, causing him to roll his head and whimper through his parched mouth.

When they came to take him off, Rabinovich could scarcely pull himself out of his seat, and he walked with such pain and difficulty that, just as they reached the exit, Lappa pushed open a door to one of the toilets.

"Get in there," hc said curtly, "and hurry it up."

Rabinovich's handcuffed hands scrabbled frantically at his trousers even before he was inside. He leaned with relief against the bulkhead, and as the pain decreased and the pressure slowly subsided he heard Lappa's voice outside, explaining. "I didn't want him pissing in our car."

At the end Rabinovich was panting.

They drove him through perimeter security at Sheremet-yevo Airport, and he felt not so much calmess as dumb acceptance. Lappa and Nikitin sat on either side of him, with another KGB man and a driver in front. No one spoke.

It was dusk when they entered the sprawl of Moscow. The wide avenues, eight- or ten-lanes, were crowded with taxis, trucks, and buses, and Rabinovich watched them passively, wondering when, if ever, he would again see such pleasing, ordinary things.

They reached Dzerzhinsky Square, two blocks from the Kremlin, and passed the old gray stone building, which before the revolution belonged to the All-Russian Insurance Company and which is now part of the KGB complex. But even then Rabinovich felt no fresh stirrings of terror.

The car turned into a side entrance, down a ramp into a basement, and parked. Rabinovich was escorted to an office where his few personal belongings were taken from him: a watch, a ring, his wallet containing some rubles and a few dollars. They were listed on a form, with many copies.

Lappa and Nikitin left, and he was alone with the new guards. They kept him waiting a few minutes before leading him along corridors, through gates with increasingly tight security, and finally into a cell.

At least a dozen pairs of eyes looked back at Rabinovich as he stood uncertainly in the entrance. He was pushed forward by one of the guards, and the door was slammed and locked behind him.

The cell was perhaps 10 feet by 20 feet, and its walls which had once been white were now gray. It was illuminated by bulbs recessed behind glass covers in the high ceiling. There was one bed on which three prisoners sat, staring at him. The others were sitting or lying on the cement floor, also staring. And, chillingly, every one of them was crippled. Some had stumps for legs or arms, or both, wrapped in filthy, pungent bandages. Others had disfigured limbs which had been broken and not properly reset. Rabinovich saw rough wooden crutches propped against the walls or lying on the floor next to their owners.

His knees began to shake.

When the CIA wanted to keep Rabinovich on ice, they locked him in a room with a taciturn guard. The KGB, with the same object in mind, made sure he had people to talk to.

By the time they came for him the next morning, Rabinovich felt he stood at the gaping edge of hell. A lifetime of humiliations and minor persecutions, of hearing stories about what went on in KGB dungeons, of fighting the cruel, lumbering system with the only weapon nature had given him—his mind—and believing at the end that he understood Russia and that if the worst happened (as it now had) he would be given special treatment because he was a member of their sacred Academy—all these things became meaningless in the face of this reality in the Lubyanka.

Rabinovich's nerves were strung so tight he needed only

a touch on his flesh to make him cry out. He even thought longingly about his wife, Vera, and their daughter, Irina, forgetting the years of hate and bitterness that had once so soured everything, but which now appeared desirable beyond any words he could possibly find to utter.

They took him out of the Lubyanka and along corridors, painted light green, of the adjoining KGB building. Boots and shoes clattered on the parquet flooring.

Rabinovich walked, regretting the wasted time, forever lost, and the growing estrangement from his daughter so that finally neither she nor her mother could find anything courteous or affectionate to say to him. And what would they feel when they heard he had been brought back in disgrace as a traitor? That he was being held in this place?

Regret at not seeing them again was swamped by the thought of what would happen if he did. More bitter words, scorn no longer half-concealed but shouted for all to hear. Public shame.

They took him through a hallway, and up some stairs. One of the guards knocked at a door and when a voice called out, swung it open.

Rabinovich stood, bright-eyed with fright, on the edge of a carpeted office. A KGB officer in his mid-forties, with curly black hair and the faint scar of what had once been a hare lip, regarded him from behind an old battered desk.

"Come in, Rabinovich," he invited. He waited until the prisoner was standing uncertainly in the middle of the room before saying, "Sit down, please."

Rabinovich was not expecting politeness, and it flustered him more than the blows and shouts of his imaginings.

He sat diffidently on the edge of a chair. The man behind the desk pulled out a file and opened it, reading papers in a leisurely fashion, looking at photographs. He wrinkled his nose at one. "This isn't a very good likeness," he observed, glancing over.

The KGB officer selected two documents: Rabinovich's foreign travel passport and his internal passport. The first had only the Soviet and U.S. immigration stamps in it. The second contained within its fourteen pages a detailed personal dossier. Under the entry for his ethnic origin, where other Soviets had their region of birth noted down, was written Yevrey—Jew. The officer scrutinized his employment history, marriage details, and draft status.

At last he dropped the internal passport on the desk and looked into the prisoner's eyes.

"Do you know what the Fifth Chief Directorate of the KGB does?" he asked.

'Unfortunately not, comrade." Rabinovich was quick and respectful, trying to please.

"It is responsible for ridding the motherland of subversive political dissent," the man said. "It has a number of sections. I am in charge of this one. It is called the Jewish Department."

"Yes comrade, I see." Rabinovich ventured a sycophantic smile.

"I am Mikhael Pavlovich Rogov. I want to help you."

"Thank you, comrade."

"So you must tell me the truth. Why did you try to defect?"

"I was mistaken, comrade. Misled by anti-state elements." Rabinovich launched earnestly into his explanation. "Others had told me . . ."

Rogov cut him short. "I don't want excuses," he said impatiently. "Save those for later, when you need them. I want to hear facts. Nothing more. I think now perhaps is the time I should make myself clear. Everything you say to me in this room will be checked. We will check from many sources, but one of them will be from you yourself.'' He looked directly into Rabinovich's eyes. ''That will be when you are interrogated.'' He paused to let the import of his words sink in, and he could see from the prisoner's face he understood what was meant only too well. ''If we discover you have been lying to me, or hiding something—however small it is—you will suffer badly for that. Do you understand?''

Rabinovich nodded numbly.

'So let us start again. Why did you try to defect?''

''I wanted to live in the United States,'' Rabinovich said haltingly, confessing an awful sin. ''I was going to tell them about the neutron program.''

Rogov seemed unperturbed. ''And did you tell them?'' he asked.

''Oh no! No, comrade!''

Rogov stared hard at him. ''Remember the interrogation, Rabinovich! Remember the punishment you will suffer for every lie. I can assure you it will be very terrible. You will cry to me and ask me to let you die.''

''I swear on my mother's grave! I told them nothing!''

''Why not? That's what you defected to do, isn't it?''

The whole story came tumbling out, every detail Rabinovich could remember. When it was finished, Rogov laughed as if he had been listening to a classic among comic anecdotes told by a master. The sound was so infectious that Rabinovich found the corners of his own mouth twitching with the drollness of his tragedy, while his eyes beseeched understanding and forgiveness, knowing that finally there would be none.

Rogov packed the documents back into the file and returned it to his drawer, still smiling. And his amused expression hadn't changed when he said, ''You'll go for interrogation now.''

Rabinovich felt his bowels soften and he stared pleadingly at the KGB officer.

"I hope for your sake," Rogov observed, "that you have told me the truth."

"Yes, comrade," he said sadly. "I have."

Rogov dismissed him. Rabinovich turned and went to the door. As he opened it, the guards waiting in the corridor fell in on either side of him, and they retraced their journey, down the light green corridors until they crossed the security gate that marked the end of the parquet flooring and the beginning of the Lubyanka, with its horrors and desolation.

But Rabinovich was not led, as he expected, into a torture room. Instead, he found himself taken to the underground car park and pushed into the back of a KGB car.

They drove into the sunny streets of Moscow where Rabinovich gazed enviously at those who, however regimented and unsatisfactory their lives, at least still had them to lead.

There were steel gates, guarded by armed sentries, leading to the old stone building. But as they turned in, Rabinovich sagged with relief. His membership of the Academy had done it! It had swung the balance! The building was the Serbsky Institute of Forensic Psychiatry. He would be interrogated with merciful drugs, not with blows and rods and electricity. Thank God, thank God.

Rabinovich was led in. An Institute employee escorted the KGB and their prisoner to the special diagnostic clinic where the mental disease of political nonconformity was treated.

Six men waited for him in a room, and although two wore the white coats of doctors, all were members of the KGB.

Rabinovich flinched at the injection.

The cell—the appalling, hopeless room with two high windows and its population of tortured maimed, and half-mad inmates—confronted him once again. The eyes stared unblinking to determine where he had been hurt and whether he could still walk. When they found him unharmed they seemed to accuse.

Rabinovich had no wish to speak to any of them again or hear more of their stories and warnings. He sat with his back to the wall and avoided their gazes. He closed his eyes, pretending to sleep.

They left him alone. They had seen this sort of thing before, and some even remembered doing it themselves.

5

They forgot him. Rabinovich waited through interminable
weeks, steeling himself for the summons to another interrogation, or perhaps to his death. Each time boots echoed
in the corridor outside the heavy locked door, the cell fell
silent in case the guards were coming for one of them.
Twice a day the footfalls were heard to be accompanied by
a dull clanking of tin plates and mugs, and relief swept the
room like a discharge of electricity. The men fell upon the
food—thin soup with a few potatoes in it, hard pieces of
bread—jostling, almost fighting among themselves. A prisoner with a crippled leg battled for two portions of everything so he could feed a young friend with the brown eyes
of a child and stumps for arms, who stayed close by him
through both days and nights, sometimes nuzzzling against
the man's back, like a lover, desperate for warmth.

Rabinovich ate little. That was not unusual: he was still
new. He had neither suffered physically, as the others had,
nor made the bitter descent down a rung or two of humanity's ladder. He still believed he was better than they were,
and different.

But he listened as they did when the door at the far end of

the corridor crashed open, its noise echoing, and the boots coming near; and like theirs, his heart fluttered in panic.

Sometimes once a day, sometimes twice, and sometimes not at all, the boots grew loud and stopped. The key was pushed into their door and the prisoners' eyes looked from one to another. Which of us? The door opened, the guards shouted a name, and in the silence a figure rose, mesmerized, to make its way to whatever nightmare waited.

An hour later, or two, or eight, the guards would return the man, moaning, sobbing, inarticulate; and when they had gone, the others would hear the sounds of pain, grateful it was not them.

But they never called Rabinovich.

Apprehension rose in him until he reached a state of damp-palmed terror. Each time the guards arrived, he thought they had come for him. Every time he was left alone he knew that, statistically, the chance of him being next had improved. In his mind, it became a certainty. Through the long nights, he found it hard to sleep on the concrete floor, and when he did doze, he had appalling nightmares.

His weight dropped sharply until his filthy trousers were baggy on him. The others wore rough prison uniforms of a scratchy weave, but Rabinovich had been allowed to keep his own clothes and did not know why.

Early one morning they came for Shvarts, the man who fed Kopytov, the young prisoner without arms. Kopytov watched with an expression of dread as his friend limped over to the guards; it was as if he was making the journey himself. While Shvarts was away, he sat pale and motionless, staring fixedly at the door, willing a safe return. Breakfast came and one of the others tried to feed him, but he waved it away with the stump of an arm and his eyes never left the steel of the entrance. Kopytov radiated such intense nervous energy that they all became charged with it. Some tried to talk to him, to take his mind off the vigil, but he refused to answer. The cell settled down to wait for Shvarts's return.

He came back after several hours, apparently unharmed, but his face was pale. He resumed his position next to Kopytov, who fired nervous questions at him. Shvarts replied in such a low voice that Rabinovich could not hear the words, only the reassuring tone. Soon Kopytov leaned his head against the man's thin arm and relaxed in relief.

Late that night, when the cell was dark and quiet, except for the moans of a few who slept and dreamed, Shvarts gently extricated himself and limped cautiously to where Rabinovich lay against the far wall.

Rabinovich was not asleep and watched him come.

"Viktorovich!" Shvarts whispered, using the patronymic The man's mouth was only inches from his ear as he knelt, and his bony hand touched Rabinovich's shoulder.

"Yes? What is it?"

"Sssh. Softly. I must speak to you."

Rabinovich struggled to sit up.

"Will you help me?" he heard Shvarts hiss.

He nodded. "If I can."

There was a long silence while Shvarts tried to find the words. His hands clasped Rabinovich's arms, kneading them abstractedly. At last he whispered, "Tomorrow I am to die."

Rabinovich turned to stare directly at the dark shadow of his face. He opened his mouth to speak, but nothing came.

"Today was my trial," Shvarts continued. "They will shoot me in the morning." There was no emotion in his voice, beyond earnestness.

"My friend, that is terrible," Rabinovich whispered at last, and the hands gripped him hard, as if to reply: thanks.

"I am worried for Otto Ilyich," Shvarts said, referring to Kopytov. "When I am gone, it will be hard for him."

"Yes."

"Will you help him, Viktorovich?" Shvarts asked. There was a silence as Rabinovich's heart sank. "Please help him," Shvarts urged. "After I have been taken, tell him that I will not return. See he gets his food. Be kind to him."

Rabinovich found himself nodding.

Shvarts patted his shoulder. "I hope things go well for you," he whispered and made his way silently back to the other end of the cell.

They waited for dawn. When it was growing light, Shvarts caught Rabinovich's eye and held it for a moment. He was scared.

They heard the guards coming, and no one except the two of them knew it was not to bring breakfast.

The door crashed open.

"Shvarts!" a voice ordered, and the cell fell silent. Those expecting food retreated to the walls to make space for the one who had been summoned.

Shvarts limped slowly out, without saying a word to Kopytov, or looking back at him.

The steel door slammed shut.

On the bed, Kopytov sat silent and staring, his vigil resumed.

Rabinovich thought he was going to be sick.

The KGB workday begins at nine, and it was shortly after this time that Mikhael Pavlovich Rogov, head of the Jewish Department, was driven in his official car along the belt highway outside Moscow toward the large modern building that since 1972 has housed most of the KGB's First Chief Directorate—the section responsible for foreign operations.

Rogov was met at the entrance by a young captain and escorted to the fifth floor conference room. It was comfortable and well-appointed, with a green carpet, a large rectangular wooden table and upholstered chairs. On the wall at the far end was a stern portrait of Feliks Dzerzhinsky, the founding director of Cheka, the first security apparatus of the Soviets. Beneath this sat the head of the first Chief Directorate, Igor Vladimirovich Gorsky, a fastidious man, thin and upright, as if a metal rod ran down the back of his general's tunic. His eyes were bright blue, and his hair, now white, was close cropped.

"Welcome, comrade," Gorsky said. "I think you know everyone here."

Rogov looked around nodding.

The head of Directorate S, which was the Illegals Directorate, sat on Gorsky's right. General-mayor* Alexei Vasilevich Sumskoy was in his late thirties, a handsome man, strongly built with straight dark hair and arrogant eyes. He was said to have a large appetite for alcohol and for women other than his ballerina wife. Suraskoy's Directorate selected, trained and ran KGB agents living abroad under false identities: the illegals.

On the other side of Gorsky was Colonel Leonid Dmitrevich Panin, whose Special Service II, the Counterintelligence Service, had penetrated foreign security organizations including, at some key points, the CIA. There was a sluggish look about Panin, but Rogov knew not to underestimate him. Several had tried, to their cost. The fifth Directorate, in Dzerzhinsky Square, knew all the stories, and a colleague of Rogov's had even been present in the Lubyanka basement to witness the execution of one of those who had unsucessfully confronted him.

All Panin's movements seemed slow, as if he were

---

* Equivalent to a U.S. brigadier general.

running at half speed. He was grossly overweight, which partly accounted for the impression, and the ponderous way he talked further accentuated it. But Panin missed nothing and forgave nothing. He was almost bald, except for a fringe around the sides and back and a few long strands coaxed over the dome of his big head. His eyes were black and shrewd, and they darted constantly, focusing on faces, documents, objects, in a restless search.

The fourth and last man at the table, Colonel Yuri Andreyevich Zhikin, smoked nervously and looked as if his hair needed washing. No one much liked Zhikin, but he survived as head of Department A, the Dezinformatsiya Center, because he was good. Zhikin got results. The Disinformation Department was not to be underestimated either, and many senior KGB officers owed Zhikin at lease a debt of gratitude for launching swift campaigns to cover up embarrassing messes left behind by their agents in foreign parts.

Zhikin's main task, however, was to plan clandestine campaigns designed to influence the decisions of foreign governments. He had been the brains behind coordinating international opposition to the neutron bomb, which had brought Washington to the point of agreeing to its ban. Zhikin knew how to use people. Over the years his own agents in the West had worked their ways into positions of respect and responsibility in universities, colleges, student bodies, trade unions, even churches. They in turn manipulated the opposition that naturally emerged to almost any policy concerning the Soviet Union—and particularly to the concept of a new nuclear weapon.

Disagreeable though Zhikin might be as a man, with his lank blond hair and nicotine-stained fingers, to his face everyone tried to pretend otherwise. KGB officers never knew when an operation for which they were ultimately responsible might backfire and an urgent summons to Zhikin provide the only chance of salvaging their reputations.

It was a high-caliber meeting, Rogov thought, as he greeted the men. Gorsky, Sumskoy, Panin, and Zhikin between them wielded considerable power.

Rogov took a seat on Sumskoy's left and waited for Gorsky to open the meeting.

He did by pulling out the transcripts of Rabinovich's confession in Rogov's office and of his subsequent interrogation under drugs. "We've all seen these, I think," Gorsky said. "Does anyone have any doubts he is telling the truth?"

Everyone shook his head.

Panin offered, "Our agent Feliks in the CIA says the tapes of conversations in Rabinovich's room showed he did exactly what he said: he told them he would think about his position overnight."

Gorsky nodded approvingly. "Good," he said. "Now we must proceed to the next part of the campaign. Comrade Zhikin has been giving the matter his consideration."

Yuri Andreyevich Zhikin stubbed his half-smoked cigarette into an ashtray with such nervous force that it split and he had to extinguish separate bits of smoldering tobacco with the side of the filter. Immediately he lit another. The others waited patiently. Zhikin always seemed to be taken by surprise, even when he was well prepared to speak.

Finally he bit his lower lip and looked around anxiously. "Comrades," he began, "we have established that the Americans know nothing significant about our neutron program. Therefore there is nothing to prevent us sending our delegation back to New York. Our position is that we postponed, rather than canceled, the SALT negotiations. The United Nations Secretary-General has requested our return although there has been silence from Washington. But I think we can interpret that silence as consent. I can make arrangements for certain Western newspapers to renew their campaign in favor of the talks, and we will be able to respond positively to this."

Zhikin drew deeply on his cigarette, and ash fell onto his trousers. He brushed it onto the carpet. General Gorsky flinched.

"Nevertheless, we face a problem," Zhikin continued. "As we know, the Defense Intelligence Agency has consistently opposed the ban on neutron weapons and thanks to the Armenian, their suspicions have been deepened. We will have to fight the DIA."

Panin, of Counterintelligence, hunched his shoulders, while his eyes darted over the faces of his other colleagues. "Why, Yuri Andreyevich, should we fight the DIA?" he asked. "They are already outmaneuvered. The ban on neutron weapons will now be a political decision, not a military one."

"Yes, yes," Zhikin agreed, "but the DIA has its own access to the media, and if they wanted to, they could embarrass us over the Rabinovich affair."

"They've never used the media in the past, except for getting information," Panin pointed out.

"Not as far as we know," Zhikin said. "But if they were sufficiently angry with the politicians, and worried, they might decide to strike back. It is a risk we should take into account, that is all."

Panin shrugged. "Then take it into account," he said.

Zhikin warmed to his subject, as he always did after a minute or two, and his face became more animated. "The next thing I must know is about Rabinovich. What has happened to him?"

"He is in the Lubyanka," Rogov answered.

"Has he been tortured?" Zhikin asked directly.

Rogov smiled slightly. Most other men would have used

a euphemism. "No, he has not been tortured. I spoke to him once, and he was interrogated once under drugs at the Serbsky Institute. That is all."

Zhikin nodded enthusiastically. "Good," he said. "Very good. Now my plan. We build up Western enthusiasm for a resumption of the SALT talks. That will take, say, a fortnight. Then we announce we will be returning immediately, and we send back our delegation."

"Minus Rabinovich," Panin said, in what began as a grunting laugh and ended abruptly.

"No," Zhikin said. "Rabinovich should be there."

His comrades stared at him. Panin shook his head slowly. "That is not possible." The others stayed silent, waiting for the rest.

Zhikin resumed. "We need Rabinovich," he argued. "If the DIA tries to make trouble, there the Armenian will be, large as life, disproving everything they claim. It will strengthen the hand of the American President and all those who want the talks to succeed. They will be able to laugh at the DIA. It will be evident that our negotiators left New York not because one of their number tried to defect with dangerous information about our neutron plans, but because of certain . . . minor problems which needed consultations in Moscow. Now these have been completed, and they are back—all of them."

"Until Rabinovich escapes again," observed Sumskoy, head of the Illegals Directorate.

"I think the KGB could make sure he did not escape again," Zhikin said. "Could they not?"

No one was prepared to dispute that statement.

"But anyway, let us consider Rabinovich's state of mind," Zhikin resumed. "What is his view of the Americans?" He reached across the table. "May I have the transcripts, please, comrade General?"

Gorsky slid them up the table, and Zhikin quickly found the passage he wanted.

"This is what Rabinovich said during interrogation at the Serbsky Institute. Question: Were you surprised that the Americans did not welcome you? Answer: I was shocked. I had escaped from my comrades and I had important news to tell the Americans about our neutron program, but they would not listen. Then they handed me back. Question: But surely you trust them, Viktor? Don't they represent freedom and justice? Answer: No more than the Soviet Union does. The governments are the same. They treat people like pawns. There is no morality in Moscow, and there is none in Washington. The Americans only pretend to be different."

Zhikin laid the transcripts on the table. "Will Rabinovich try to defect again?" he asked rhetorically. "I don't think so. All we need him to do in New York is sit with our team at the negotiations and appear smiling when the photographers come. Do you think," he inquired delicately of Rogov, "that Rabinovich could still be persuaded to smile?"

Rogov laughed. "I think, comrade, if I told him he was going to be freed from the Lubyanka, he would find difficulty stopping smiling."

"Then I rest my case."

"But we told the Americans the Armenian was guilty of economic crimes, did we not?" Panin persisted.

"We did, and if they ask further, we will say that a thorough investigation left him without a stain on his character. He had been falsely accused."

Panin grunted disapprovingly.

Beneath the grim portrait of Dzerzhinsky, General Gorsky stirred. "Well, comrades," he said "let me hear objections to this proposal."

"There are two facts I think we should weigh," Colonel Panin observed. "Even if Rabinovich does not want to defect, and even if the KGB is protecting him, the possibility exists that the DIA will mount an operation to kidnap him. They know he has something to say. They'll want to find out what it is. Whatever his state of mind, they will use drugs, just as we did.''

"But surely," General Gorsky said, "if we expect such a thing, we should be able to prevent it. Is the KGB powerless against the DIA?''

Panin lowered his head as if about to charge. "Of course not," he replied. "But we are on their territory, not on our own. There may be moments, particularly in public, when Rabinovich will be vulnerable. I mention this merely as a possibility.''

"And how high a rating do you give this possibility?" Gorsky asked.

"A low rating," Panin conceded. "But I should like us to remember it is a possibility.''

"We shall remember it," Gorsky said, "and take appropriate steps. And what is your second point?''

"Rabinovich is a traitor. He should not be allowed to get away with his crime.''

"At the moment he is more useful to us unpunished," Zhikin replied. "I make no claim on him after that. What happens once the treaty is signed and he is back in Moscow is of no interest to me. . . . Although," he added after a short pause, "it is vital that he believes we have decided not to prosecute him. It will be an incentive for exemplary behavior in America. He mustn't imagine he will be returning to the Lubyanka.''

"Oh no," Rogov said. "Of course not.''

Rabinovich waited four hours after Shvarts had been taken until he was certain it was over. Kopytov had not moved his eyes off the steel door for an instant, not even when breakfast arrived. He was like a faithful dog, awaiting the return of its master.

Neither Rabinovich nor Kopytov ate. Rabinovich rehearsed in his mind what he would say to the young man, how to break the news gently. He had not done such a thing since the death of his own mother, but that had been different because it was long expected. And no one had been in a position of utter dependence on her.

When he felt he could postpone it no longer, he went across to the filthy bed where Kopytov sat, motioning one of the others to make room. Kopytov showed no sign of noticing he was there. Rabinovich put out his hand toward the young man's shoulder, but found he could not make the contact. It was repugnant, like touching a corpse. Kopytov sat, frozen and wretched.

Rabinovich tried again. His fingers managed lightly to graze the rough prison jacket and then went tentatively forward until they met the hardness of bone.

"Otto Ilyich?" he said softly. There was no response. Rabinovich tried again. "Otto Ilyich, do not grieve for your friend. He is free now."

There was a slight movement of Kopytov's head, showing he had heard and was listening, but his eyes did not waver from the door.

"He came to me last night," Rabinovich explained haltingly, aware that in the crowded cell, others were listening too. "We spoke before dawn, when you were asleep. He asked me to tell you when it was over." Rabinovich ran out of words. He found his hand automatically rubbing and stroking the bony shoulder, as if to salve the pain. Then it came hissing out in a rush, "Yesterday was his trial. He was sentenced to be shot. His execution was this morning. Be glad for him, Otto. At last he is free."

Around them, there rose voices as prisoners heard and

passed on the news to those who had been out of earshot, and in the confines of the cell, a wave of sound grew. But at its center there was a core of utter stillness. Kopytov had not moved, and it seemed he had ceased breathing.

Rabinovich felt tears flooding his eyes, and without thinking, he put his arms around Kopytov and hugged him, whispering fiercely, "Be glad, Otto, be glad! He is free!"

In the distance, the door leading into the corridor crashed open, but the prisoners did not hear it above the noise filling their cell. It was only when boots halted outside and the key turned in the lock that the volume diminished quickly and settled into an uneasy, scared silence. Kopytov stared unblinking at the door, willing Shvarts to be there when it opened. All eyes turned to the entrance.

Two guards, pistols drawn because of the noise, stood in the doorway. A quick glance reassured them there was no danger.

"Rabinovich!" the leader called.

Mother, it had come!

Rabinovich's fingers dug hard into Kopytov's arms, and he found himself paralyzed. Half-hidden by the young man, his instinct told him to stay, in the futile hope that they would not see him and would go away.

"Rabinovich!" The voice was harsher, more commanding, and it released his limbs.

He patted Kopytov in a spasmodic movement and rose numbly to his feet.

At last Kopytov spoke, a small, drained voice. "Shall I be glad for you too, Viktorovich? Will you also be free?"

Rabinovich stumbled, terrified, to the door.

6

It seemed to David Ross and Clive Lyle that they were drowning in a sea of paper. Five years of agents' report intercepts, and expert assessments of Soviet neutron policy by themselves added up to an extraordinary number of documents, before public sources like Radio Moscow or transcripts of official speeches were even touched.

When first they visited the DIA registry to see what was available, Lyle spoke for both of them when he looked at the relevant shelves and exclaimed softly, "Holy shit!"

There were several hundred files to go through, none of them thin. The information they contained was supposed to include every report about, and reference to, the enhanced radiation weapon that had reached the DIA or the CIA, or been picked up by cryptographers at the National Security Agency, the biggest government installation in the Washington area.

Ross knew the NSA well. He had worked there as a consultant before assuming his present role, and it was an impressive operation. Billions of dollars worth of computers processed intercepts from more than 2,000 NSA positions around the world and electronic espionage was practiced in its purest form, while elsewhere in the Operations Building men eavesdropped on Soviet conversations thousands of miles away. Ross trusted NSA information rather more than reports from CIA men in the Soviet Union and elsewhere. The printed page never told you the really important information—such as how much pressure Langley had been putting on a particular agent at the time he came to write and whether he was trying to get them off his back by presenting an unchecked piece of gossip as the truth. Or worse still, if he was just making something up.

DIA reports, on the other hand, were considered relatively free of this failing. Yardley, in his years as Director, had scrupulously avoided pressuring his men in the field, regardless of what noises were being made at him by the Secretary of Defense or the President of the United States. Yardley was a military man who neither liked nor particularly trusted politicians although he voted Republican in the belief that this party contained fewer certifiable maniacs. Yet no President—Republican or Democrat—could make him respond if he considered the pressure unreasonable or jump to their command if he believed the order wrong. Yardley was prepared to be fired first. This was a policy that made some enemies—but even more friends, because it depended on him being right, and he usually was.

The DIA took care in the selection and training of its officers, and it followed their personal and private lives in detail. Everyone knew—because they were told so during training and had to sign a "no objection" form—that their homes would be subject to bugging, their telephones tapped, and their mail opened. They knew, too, that Yardley would hear within hours who they had slept with and whether that person was of any significance. Within their limited DIA family, there were almost no secrets—but almost no restrictions or recriminations either. Because they were called upon to do extraordinary things in their work, Yardley did not mind what his men and women did in their own time, providing they kept themselves healthy, security tight, and aware that simply because he knew everything, they were immune from blackmail.

So DIA reports were certainly a step up from their CIA rivals.

Yet for all that, there was not much new to be learned.

It was well documented why the neutron bomb had caused the Soviets to be overcome with concern for mankind's suffering. Their own massive arms buildup over more than twenty years had mostly been centered on the European theater. More than 20,000 tanks in the Soviet-controlled Warsaw Pact forces were deployed for use against Western Europe—well over half of them in actual Russian units.

NATO forces, by contrast, could field only one-third of this tank force. If it came to war, short of a super-power nuclear conflict that devastated major cities and killed hundreds of millions, the Soviets would be well ahead. They could push quickly from Czechoslovakia and East Germany into Western Europe, and the only thing guaranteed to stop their inexorable progress—again short of a major nuclear conflict—was the neutron bomb.

Huge invisible doses of radiation would penetrate the armor of enemy tanks, and the crews would suffer massive damage to their central nervous systems. Within 400 meters of ground zero, the dose level of fast neutrons and hard gamma radiation would be more than 8,000 rads.* The men just outside the immediate, devastated area of impact would go into convulsions, and their hearts would fail. As distance from ground zero increased, so it would take longer for the crews to die.

Ross found a statement by Herbert Scoville, former

* A rad is a unit of dosage of whole body radiation.

deputy director of the CIA saying he believed enemy troops receiving even ten times a lethal neutron radiation dose could still continue to fight effectively for about half an hour, and would die only a day or so later.

But die they would and the fact that the Soviet Union was advancing with 20,000 tanks against NATO's 7,000 would be an advantage quickly lost.

"What an awful weapon," Ross said in disgust as he read a report detailing the effects of a U.S. neutron bomb test on pigs.

"Almost all weapons are," Lyle said. "You've never been in a war, David, so you haven't had the chance to see what goes on. Is the neutron bomb worse than napalm? Is it worse than those things the Soviets have been using in Afghanistan where a bomb explodes sending out a million sticky balls which bond onto people's skin, or clothes, and can't be pulled off? And then they burst into flame. How about that?"

"Christ almighty! What kind of people invent such stuff?"

"People who want to win wars," Lyle said.

Ross shrugged. "It makes you think about the human race, doesn't it? I reckon we're crueller now than we ever were."

Lyle lit a cigarette. "Want one?" Ross shook his head. "I don't know about that," Lyle said. "We're bigger, sure, and we can kill everyone on earth a hundred times over. But crueller? Suppose we were living in medieval days, and we were attacking a castle. What sort of reception could we expect? Hell, I'll tell you: a vat of boiling oil poured on our heads, that's what. Now you want to spare a thought for what boiling oil can do to a man, how it would just peel away his skin? He'd scream a long time before dying."

Despite himself, Ross laughed. "I guess the thing to do is make sure it's your side who's doing the pouring."

"These days," Lyle said, "it's trying to see no one does the pouring."

"But what I don't get," Ross said, "is why the Russians are making such a big deal about the neutron bomb. I understand about us wiping out their tank force in twenty-four hours, but as soon as I reach that point, I don't understand any further. Neutron bomb or not, if the Russians invade Western Europe, they're surely heading for a world war, and its inevitable that whichever side starts losing is going to want to press the big nuclear button. Why does Moscow imagine we'll settle for seeing our NATO allies overrun by their tanks? Why the hell do we think Moscow'll watch their T-72s and all the other expensive armored junk grinding to a halt over Europe with their crews puking their hearts out and dropping dead, and then just sit back and shrug it off? Surely they'd have to go on, they can't pull back. And we'd have to go on, too. It's credibility as much as survival, if you can separate those two things, and I'm not sure you can."

Lyle shook his head. "No," he said "I don't agree. This whole campaign's actually being waged with an eye on the next decade, not this one. Things are changing. We're now entering an age where it's going to be physically impossible for the Super Powers to fight a thermonuclear war."

"Bullshit," Ross replied.

"Not bullshit. There's a NASA film floating around here somewhere, restricted viewing only. I'll try to get hold of it. Then you'll see what I mean."

Lyle went off to set about proving his point, and Ross spent the rest of the morning absorbed in the details of intercepts.

One of the things that became apparent was that the

claims about Russia reluctantly going into neutron production only in 1981 in response to Reagan's announced
American program were no more than propaganda. The
Soviet Union had in fact started neutron weapons development in 1976, shortly after U.S. army and government
nuclear scientists began to work on a miniature version of
the neutron bomb, suitable for the battlefield.

The intercepts showed Ross that when the U.S. developed the W70-3 one-kiloton neutron warhead for the army's
Lance missile, the Soviets were putting together a similar
device, code-named Cutlass. And by the time the United
States had designed the W-79 eight-inch shell to carry the
same size enhanced radiation warhead, Russia was also
working on its own artillery delivery system. The details
were not spelled out, but the thrust of the program was
clear enough.

After lunch, Lyle took Ross to one of the DIA viewing
rooms. As they waited for the video to be run, he handed
Ross the photostat of a 1981 letter, written to UN Secretary-
General Waldheim by the Soviet Foreign Minister Andrei
Gromyko, proposing a ban on all weapons in outer space.

In it, Gromyko complained that the existing international agreements on the peaceful use of outer space for-
bade only weapons of "mass annihilation."

"As a result of this, the risk of militarization of outer
space has been maintained and recently increased," Gromyko wrote. "The Soviet Union believes this cannot be
tolerated. It is in favor of keeping outer space clean and
free of any weapons for all time."

Ross handed back the photostat as the lights dimmed
and a picture flashed onto the screen.

"You'll see why Gromyko wants that ban in a minute,"
Lyle said.

A transport aircraft from Edwards Air Force Base was
shown high above the Mojave Desert. From the editing,

they could tell there was a camera on the ground, and another in a plane flying a parallel course. A man appeared in the door of the transport and dropped into space, followed by a second, and a third. The camera on the ground tracked their plummeting figures until parachutes blossomed behind them.

"That's the whole crew," Lyle said. "They left the bird on auto."

The camera picked up an F-15 fighter closing in, before focusing back on the transport. For several seconds, nothing happened.

Suddenly the plane disintegrated in a ball of flame, a wing breaking free and scything through the air while fuel blazed intensely and torn metal melted. The pieces plunged to the desert floor.

"Jesus!" Ross exclaimed. "What happened there?"

"The F-15 knocked it out with a high energy laser," Lyle said.

The next sequence was taken in space and showed a satellite hovering, apparently motionless, in the blackness. "The camera for this was on the Columbia shuttle," Lyle said. "They've got the laser firing control on board too. Just watch."

One second the satellite was there, the next it was a collection of pieces of junk, spinning lazily into the void.

The screen went blank. Ross was impressed. He had never seen a laser in action like that.

"Which means we've got ourselves a science fiction-type deathray," Lyle said taking a cigarette as the lights went up. "The Russians have too. We know they've been experimenting in space, and they've killed more than twenty of their own satellites with lasers."

"If that's the case, why do they want to ban weapons up there?" Ross asked.

"Mostly to stop us from going to the next stage and

developing space lasers capable of knocking out ballistic missiles before they ever get to target. We're probably only six or seven years away from a system like that. I don't myself see how they can believe we'll agree to having our hands tied behind our backs like that. Although," Lyle added thoughtfully, "they're doing pretty well at the moment with the campaign against the neutron bomb. So maybe there is hope for them."

"But if we do keep going," Ross said, "and we both get lasers in space which do their job efficiently, it'll mean . . . hell Clive, you're right. So long as we can protect the weapons satellites, there couldn't ever be a thermonuclear war! After 1990, both sides might as well stop making nukes because there won't be any way of delivering them."

"Right on the button. The beams can be fired from the ground as well as from space as we saw, but the trouble with the ground is that cloud and haze tend to weaken a laser, so space is the prime place. And don't forget a laser moves at the speed of light so its computers can make it attack dozens of missles, one after the other, in a matter of minutes."

Ross laughed. "That makes World War Three quite a different proposition."

"Doesn't it? Not that it'll be pleasant, or that fewer people will die in nicer ways than the other world wars but at least when it's over, we won't have destroyed everything. We might even win. And that's why the Russians are worried about the neutron bomb. Hell, it's not even really a bomb, is it? It's a shell, or a short-range missile. So if they're going to be restricted to conventional means of fighting, they don't want unconventional ones destroying their first line of attack—their tanks."

"But if that's true, what the hell's the President doing, talking about banning neutron weapons?"

"I wish I knew, buddy," Lyle said.

"I wish we had some idea what it is the Russians are hiding from us. We know they've got these things themselves, so what was it Rabinovich wanted to tell us that would stop the talks?"

They rose to leave the viewing room, and retrieved a batch of files from the registry where they had been lodged for safety during lunch.

Lyle and Ross worked until 5:30 without coming up with any ideas. "Hey, are you and Elaine doing anything tonight?" Lyle asked as they were leaving.

"No, I don't think so."

"Well, there's a guy down the block who's giving a party . . ."

"No thanks, Clive." Ross was apologetic. "I don't think it's our sort of thing."

"Come on, David. It's open house so there's no problem about the two of you turning up. I'll phone and let him know in advance if it makes you feel better."

"Well, you know we don't get out much . . ."

"Yeah, and I think it's about time you did. Just because you work for the DIA doesn't mean you have to live like hermits."

"Are we living like hermits?" Ross seemed amused.

"Well, you will be if you don't start getting out," Lyle said. "You're in a new town, you need to set up a circle of friends. Otherwise you're going to be pretty unhappy here. Not so much you, because you've got your job and you'll move about a bit. But Elaine. What's she going to do with herself if you're away for three months? Her work's not enough. Who's she going to talk to?"

"I guess so," Ross said neutrally, not knowing how his wife would react to the idea of going with him into a room full of strangers and having to talk to them. She'd been avoiding situations like that since they came to Washington and was really only comfortable among people they both knew. "Listen, I'll ask her how she feels and give you a call."

"Do that. Tell her they're nice folks, and anyway, I'll be there." Lyle scribbled the address on a piece of paper as they rode the elevator down. "Eight o'clock," he said firmly, handing it over.

"Yeah, well I'll call you."

But Lyle could detect a social lie when he heard one, and he made sure his MGB got home ahead of David's car. He was on the phone to Elaine before Ross had even parked.

"I hear we're going out tonight," she said as Ross stooped in the hallway to kiss her on the cheek. "I've just been speaking to Clive."

"Lyle doesn't waste time, does he?" Ross was slightly irritated. "What did you say?"

"That we'd love to come."

"Would we?" Ross asked. "We don't have to if you'd rather not."

"Well, would you rather not?"

"I don't mind," Ross said cautiously. "I'd be happy spending an evening at home or going to a movie maybe."

"What's the matter, kiddo?" Elaine teased. "Don't you want your friends to see who you're married to?"

"Hey, don't say things like that," Ross protested. "You know it's not true."

"Yes, I know." She smiled. "You need a drink." As she walked through to the living room, she added, "But Clive's got a point. We can't shut ourselves away here. I realize it's been my fault, but we've got to get out and meet people. I've got to get out and meet people. Do you realize, I don't even have a friend here I can complain to about you?"

Ross grinned. "Why don't we keep it that way?"

"Not a chance. How was your day?" she asked as she mixed the martinis.

"Not bad. Yours?"

"I've got a commission to advise on computer purchases for the FBI." She couldn't stop herself smiling.

"No kidding? That's wonderful! Congratulations." Ross kissed her.

"I don't know why it came to me," Elaine said, trying to be modest. "I've never done any work for the feds before. But it's interesting, and it'll keep me busy. I'm going to have to do a bit of traveling though—find out what their present computer setup does and what facilities they'll need in the future."

"They came to you because you're the best," Ross said.

"Better than you?" She touched his chin, feeling the rough stubble of beard.

He grinned. "Well, neck and neck. Anyway, I'm out of the race."

They relaxed together for an hour before showering and changing for the party. As the time approached to leave, Elaine felt apprehension building inside her. David, who knew how self-conscious she had become about their age difference, was aware of this tension, but there was nothing he could do to help beyond being as supportive as possible.

They walked the few blocks to the N Street address Lyle had given them, arriving at a quarter after eight. Clive was obviously watching the door because he appeared beside the host to greet them before Ross even had the chance to say who they were. Elaine was standing slightly behind her husband and Lyle caught her biting her lip.

"Glad Elaine persuaded you to come, David," Lyle said cheerily. "I'd like you to meet Brian Stewart, a friend of mine who's our host tonight."

Ross shook hands with a brown-haired man in his late twenties who had blue-green eyes and a beard and mustache that were slightly sparse but probably still growing.

Brian Stewart showed no flicker of surprise when Ross said, "And this is my wife, Elaine," urging her forward with a large hand. Lyle had obviously briefed him.

"Hi, Elaine," Stewart said. "Come on in and meet the others."

This was the moment she had been dreading. Ross took her hand as they entered, and she was acutely conscious both of this and the looks he received. David dwarfed Elaine by several inches in height, and by his sheer bigness. He might have been a football star, for there was nothing about him to suggest a sedentary life or slackening muscles, only a strong, confident presence.

Elaine hated the calculating way women, and some men, were sizing up her husband, and then her: the older sparrow with the prize peacock. She could see them wondering why. It's love, she explained to them in her mind. We're together because we're in love. Isn't that funny?

The overhead light was so bright she knew it wasn't going to flatter her in any way. At least her hair was okay and still dark, thanks to her hairdresser.

She tried to focus on one person at a time. There was a man with a preoccupied expression who didn't see her any more clearly than she saw him. She smiled. And a couple of smartly dressed girls in their early twenties, one of them quite a bit overweight, and she smiled again. A tall, well-built black man in very expensive clothes said, "How you doing?" and shook her hand; with him was a beautiful redhead who had to be a model or an actress. Faces, more faces. Names she couldn't remember a second after they'd been announced. Elaine felt her smile straining and her forehead wrinkling with the effort. David's reassuring bulk was beside her, and she could hear him making the necessary small talk while she trailed after looking, she was sure, ridiculous. Then they came to a very pretty girl—surely not more than twenty—with long, shining auburn hair, almost no makeup, and a tan that could have advertised California, who was riveted, just riveted, on David, with her voice unmistakably signaling her interest. Brian Stewart said, "And this is David's wife, Elaine." The girl turned to her and looked momentarily stunned. Then she smiled brightly. "Hi!"

When they had moved on to the next couple, Elaine quite distinctly heard her say, "Oh my God!"

Elaine couldn't help it, the flush mounted in her cheeks until they glowed pink and hot. Her throat went dry. She longed for David to squeeze her hand and wished she had not come.

Clive Lyle was either a mindreader or he had been watching from across the room and had seen her distress because the next thing she knew, he was ushering her off to a sofa, putting a drink in her hand, and talking cheerfully to her and another couple in their group. She was grateful for a seat and a drink. Lyle offered her a cigarette, which meant he'd provided three of the things she urgently needed. The fourth was something to divert attention entirely from herself, and he gave her that too, by telling a story about the mayor of New York which, even in her humiliated state, sounded funny. The others rocked with laughter.

David had been absorbed into a crowd near the bar, and she could see him smiling, at ease and enjoying himself. She prayed he hadn't heard the girl's remark. Gradually the flush left her cheeks and when she put the cigarette to her lips, her hand hardly shook at all. She began to relax.

Lyle brought her another drink, and she managed to talk to the others without her voice sounding strained. She even made a joke and was grateful when they laughed.

But the fact was, she felt out of place. It wouldn't have been a problem if she'd been there by herself, on her own terms, but as the older wife of the handsomest young man in the room she was arousing natural curiosity.

When the others went to help themselves to the buffet dinner, Elaine waited a few minutes, Lyle with her.

"How's it going?" Clive asked, regarding her with affectionate eyes.

"Thanks for your help," she said. "I mean it."

"Thanks for coming. It is important. And this is the worst bit, getting to know new people. It's downhill all the way from here." He stubbed out his cigarette. "Have you met anyone you think you might like?"

"There seem to be some very nice young people," Elaine said. "But Clive, they are young."

"Jesus, I'm young. You're my friend."

Elaine chuckled. "You're different, Clive."

"How old do you feel? Now answer truthfully."

"You really want to know?"

"Yeah. I really want to know."

"Clive," she said, "in my heart I'm the same age I was when I first fell in love. Twenty-two." Elaine smiled. "A long time back. Isn't that funny? My body gradually got older, young men got younger, and so did a lot of the people I was working with in computers. But somehow I felt I wasn't changing at all, almost as if I was caught in some kind of time-warp. And I feel it now. Hell, I feel as young as David looks: younger."

"There's nothing wrong with the way you look," Lyle said. "You're a pretty woman, attractive. There are a lot of girls here who'd be lucky to have your charm and poise. That's all stuff that's got to be learned, and some people never make it."

Elaine leaned forward to pat Lyle's hand. "You're very

good for my morale,'' she said. ''Now let's have something to eat.''

As she helped herself from a table laden with delicious-looking food, Elaine noticed David talking animatedly to the pretty, sun-tanned girl who'd made the cruel remark. He obviously hadn't heard her. Elaine felt suddenly less hungry.

David Ross was intrigued with Julie Klein, and not only because she looked like a slightly less feline Lauren Bacall, but because she told him she was a poet and spoke two more languages than he did and had taken up parachuting as a hobby.

''You're kidding,'' he laughed.

''It's true.'' Her lips twitched in a challenging smile. ''Come out sometime and I'll prove it to you.''

''I might just do that.''

''Just give me a call,'' she said. ''I go most weekends.''

Ross was impressed. ''Do you really do that? Now tell me why.''

And she did, going through the usual reasons of adventure and excitement, to more thoughtful ones: that it was a way to personal freedom, not shared by most of society, and that in doing it, she created closer bonds—almost family—with the other skydivers. Ross knew exactly what she meant. It was in microcosm the world of the DIA.

''What do you do, David?'' Julie asked.

''Oh me?'' He felt embarrassed after her colorful disclosures. ''I work for the government.''

''Doing what?''

''I'm an accountant. I look after departmental budgets.''

''That sounds interesting,'' she said politely.

''Like hell it does.''

''You look like a football player. How do you keep in shape?''

"I work out in the gym."

"It had to be something like that. What sport do you play?"

"None actually. Not since high school."

"Try sky diving," Julie Klein advised. "After adding up those columns of figures, it'll be something to get your adrenalin going."

"I might do that," Ross said. "I just might." He wondered what Yardley would think of the idea. He'd try it out on the Director sometime. "How do you earn a living?" he asked.

Julie smoothed the hair away from the side of her face and said with a secretive half smile: "I don't. I've got a rich daddy. I don't suppose I'll ever make money writing poetry, but that's what I do with a lot of my time. I write, and I read other people's work." She paused. "I can see you thinking 'lazy bitch,' but there really isn't anything else I want to do, and as I say, I don't have to go out and get a job."

"Actually, I think you're very lucky," Ross said. "You've got financial independence, and you're using the free time it gives you. That's not an easy combination to bring off. What sort of poems do you write?"

She looked particularly feline. "Mostly erotic verse," she said, watching for his reaction.

The corners of Ross's eyes crinkled. "Sounds interesting," he said. "I'd like to see some."

"Maybe I'll let you one day." Their eyes met and held.

"Yeah," Ross said, "I'll look forward to that." He became conscious that his voice had gone slightly softer, and that there was an edge to it. Then he remembered Elaine, and thought Oh Christ, I don't want to get into anything like this; and he glanced around guiltily to see where she was. But his wife had her back to them and was deep in conversation with another couple.

Julie Klein turned to see where Ross was looking, and when she turned back, her face had become neutral and her tone a little distant. "Your wife seems very nice," she said. "Where did you meet?"

"At college. We were studying together."

"Jesus! I've heard about mature students, but . . . oh, sorry."

Ross felt himself flush. "I was a student. Elaine was lecturing."

"Oh yes, of course." She paused, and he hoped she was going to back off. But that was not Julie Klein's style. "Why did you two get married?" she asked.

Ross felt the first stirring of resentment. "I married Elaine," he said, "because I loved her. I still love her."

"Good for you," Julie said. "I only ask because you're quite a find—good looking, well-built, charming, intelligent. A lot of girls must have wanted you. I guess they did. You could have had your pick."

"I did," Ross said. "I picked the one I loved."

Julie Klein rolled her eyes as if it was too much for the mind to comprehend, and Ross found himself explaining— although he despised himself for doing it: "Anyway, she was younger when we met."

"Yes," said Julie. "I imagine she must have been."

Clive Lyle appeared at their elbows. "Can I join you good folks?" he asked. Ross, relieved to see him, made the introductions. Then he watched Julie Klein do an instant appraisal of Lyle and approve of what she saw.

Maybe Julie had had a lot to drink, or maybe she wanted to score a point, but she said casually, "I've just been throwing myself at David here, and he tells me he's still in the middle of an o-o-old love affair. Maybe I should throw myself at you, Clive. I seem to be free after the party."

Lyle didn't miss a beat, nor did his smile flicker. "No sale," he said.

She frowned, unused to striking out twice in a row. "Why not?"

"You're the wrong sex," Lyle said.

Julie Klein stared at him, not knowing whether to believe him. "Tonight really isn't my night, is it?" she murmured. "Would you excuse me?"

The men watched her walk off and join a group as far away from them as she could get. They grinned at each other.

Ross asked quizzically: "Is that true about you, Clive?"

"Not necessarily," Lyle said cheerfully. "I just thought she needed a putdown and you a breathing space. Brian warned me about her when she was making her pitch for you."

"Was it that obvious?"

"Well, she could have lit fireworks, but otherwise it was pretty plain. Brian tells me she's trouble. Behind that beautiful facade lurks a spoiled kid who'll kill to get her own way."

"I guess she's written the two of us off."

"Me she has. Women never try to reform fags these days. I'm not so sure about you. How's Elaine doing, by the way?"

"Uh, fine, I think."

"Maybe you'd better go make sure," Lyle suggested. "She wasn't feeling too happy earlier."

Ross went to join his wife, feeling vaguely that he ought to have stayed closer to her, been more protective. But then, if she'd wanted help, she could equally easily have stayed close to him.

Across the room, Julie Klein watched the Rosses together, then sought out Lyle again. He was at the bar helping himself to a beer. "Hello again," she said.

Lyle turned, slightly surprised to find her still friendly. "Hi," he replied. "Are you okay for a drink?"

"Yes thanks. Is that beer yours?"

"Mmmm. Usually I drink crème de menthe frappés, but they don't seem to have any."

Julie grinned. "Look," she said, "I really don't care if you're gay or not. That's your business."

"Thanks." He raised his glass in salute.

"I was behaving badly back there. I wanted to say I was sorry."

"No need to apologize," he said. "It was a nice offer."

"It's just that I was thrown by David." Her voice became confidential. "You know what I'm saying? I mean, how does a spectacular-looking guy like that get mixed up with a woman . . ." she glanced over her shoulder, " . . . like that."

"Elaine's great," Lyle said. "And she's a friend of mine, so don't knock her to me, please."

"Oh, I wasn't putting her down," Julie protested, conscious of making her moves badly. "I'm sure she's perfectly sweet. Honestly, I've only spoken to her for about three seconds. But, oh Jesus, how can I explain what I mean without sounding like a Grade A bitch?"

Clive watched steadily, refusing to help.

"Look, it is unusual, isn't it? Older men with younger women, that I see around. Plenty. But a young man married to an older woman—that's a rare event. Even in California it's rare, unless the man's gay, or a gigolo. But David isn't either."

"No," Lyle said.

'So? What's the answer? Is she very rich?"

Lyle put down his beer. He wanted to tell her to go to hell, but he knew it would only make her more determined to get answers, and it was better she heard the authorized DIA version from him. "No, David didn't marry for money. He's got more of that than she has. He married because he loved her."

"But why?" Julie persisted. "He could have had almost anyone he wanted."

"Listen, he did have almost anyone he wanted. From what I hear, he did more screwing in college than studying, mostly with women your age. And when he'd had them, hc married Elaine."

"A mother fixation?" Julie wondered aloud, ignoring the implied slight.

"Gays have mother fixations. If you want amateur psychoanalysis, try a father fixation."

"I get it," Julie said, realization dawning. "An Oedipus complex."

Lylc watched her, bemused, but the explanation seemed satisfactory. He was saved from further discussion by Brian Stewart.

"Clive, there's a telephone call for you."

Lyle took it in the bedroom. A minute later he left the apartment without a word to anyone. His MGB was parked a short distance down the block, and he drove as quickly as he could to DIA headquarters.

Lyle was in Yardley's office no more than fifteen minutes before returning to the party, deep in thought.

When he walked in, Julie Klein was back talking to Ross. He could see she wasn't a girl who gave up easily. Lyle interrupted without apology. "David, I need a word."

Lyle led him far enough from other guests for them to talk safely. "I've just been to see Yardley," he said. "He tells me the Russians are on their way back."

"The talks are on?"

"Yeah. And guess who's coming with them?"

"I don't know. Tell me."

"Rabinovich."

"That can't be true," Ross said.

"It is true. They get in tomorrow. We've had it confirmed from Moscow that he's with the party. We don't know where they'll stay in New York, but it'll probably be the Soviet Residency. We don't see them risking a hotel. They're going to have the lid down tight."

"Mmmm. I'll bet."

"Which doesn't help us very much." Lyle lit a cigarette and looked seriously at his comrade. "Yardley wants him, David. He wants us to take Rabinovich."

7

A battery of press and television cameras greeted the Soviet delegation as it emerged from the Ilyushin at Kennedy Airport. At the foot of the stairs, Fedor Fedorovich Konev read a prepared statement.

The Soviet Union, he said, was determined to do all in its power to see that mankind was pulled back from the brink of madness and mass annihilation. The Soviet leadership and people welcomed the growing realization in the West that the neutron bomb, "the most inhuman type—a cancer bomb," should be totally outlawed.

Behind him, the Russian delegation applauded warmly, Rabinovich louder than anyone.

He kept his eyes fixed firmly on Konev, not daring to glance around. Lappa was close on one side of him, Nikitin on the other. Rabinovich would not have had it any other way. He was glad of their protection and, yes, even of their company. As had been pointed out to him so straightforwardly by comrade Rogov at the KGB headquarters, there were serious dangers in New York. Defense agents, warring with the CIA, might try to kidnap him and use torture or drugs to extract Soviet secrets. When they had done that, Rogov said, they would undoubtedly kill him as they had killed others. But further, if the Soviet Union was able to secure his return, they would not take such a lenient view of his conduct in future. The fact that he had spoken under drugs would not be considered a mitigating factor.

It was Rabinovich's job to ensure he was never in a position where he might be vulnerable to the Americans. He was to stay close to the comrades charged with his security and to report immediately if he noticed anything suspicious. He was, of course, never to go anywhere alone, and he was to obey orders implicitly.

If he behaved responsibly as a good, loyal Soviet, he would be able to return to his laboratory at the Dubna Atomic Center, and Rogov could guarantee the allocation of a high-quality apartment for his own personal use, separate from the one occupied by his wife and daughter.

Rabinovich was overcome with relief and gratitude. He had learned a harsh, bitter lesson, both in the United States and in the Lubyanka, and he could scarcely believe the Party was prepared to offer him a second chance. He wondered if he had not been unfair to them in the past. Because he had been carried away by appearances, perhaps he misjudged them.

There had to be reasons for everything, he told himself, and it was not given to him to know what they were. One had to have faith. And surely in the end the system worked. There was justice and humanity. He himself was proof of this.

There was little room in Rabinovich's rationalizations for the tormented men with whom he once shared a cell.

Rabinovich was determined to be an exemplary member of the delegation, a credit to the Party, and as small a target as possible for the Defense Intelligence Agency, which he now saw clearly to be a ravening wolf, waiting to pounce if ever he strayed from the safety of his familiar flock.

When Konev concluded his remarks and stepped toward the leading vehicle in the fleet of Embassy limousines drawn up on the apron, Rabinovich hastened toward the third car, allocated to him in the final briefing on the aircraft, Lappa and Nikitin close behind. They got into the back, Rabinovich between them. He smiled conspiratorially at Lappa and received an answering grin.

Everyone was being so kind considering what he had done. Konev had hugged him when first they met after his release and enquired solicitously about his health. Konev said the comrades never had any doubts about his true loyalty, that it had been a regrettable misunderstanding, and they were relieved it was over so they could all get back to work.

The motorcade moved off, past the airport perimeter security and toward New York. The delegation would have a day of rest before resuming negotiations in the United Nations building under the chairmanship of the Secretary-General.

David Ross and Clive Lyle watched the arrival ceremony on television at DIA headquarters, and recorded it on video tape. Neither of them was able to spot Rabinovich, and there was some doubt he had come at all until they took the cassette and ran it through one of the special DIA machines. This threw the picture up onto a large screen, and apart from being able to slow down or freeze action, it could zoom in on some particular area.

Lyle and Ross studied the faces of the Russians coming down the stairs without recognizing Rabinovich. They stared long and hard at a frozen view of the entire party gathered on the apron. There were sixteen Soviets, eight of them official delegates: the number they expected. They discarded those they recognized—Konev and his deputy at the talks, three of the KGB—and zoomed in on the rest, face by face. Halfway through, Ross was about to move off one man when Lyle said sharply: "Hold it, David. Have another look at that guy."

They stared. "It's him," Lyle said.

"You're joking, Clive. He's short and he's got dark hair, but that's all. Rabinovich is a plump little guy."

"Rabinovich *was* a plump little guy," Lyle said. "A lot's happened since then."

Ross inspected the picture minutely, going up to the screen to see if that helped but the figure blurred into indeterminate lines so he moved as far away as he could get and leaned against the wall. Almost a minute passed before he said: "I think you're right. Where did all that flesh go?"

"I guess they had him on a diet."

'Some diet!'' Ross was appalled.

"We've got to get a better picture. I'll put someone on to getting hold of all the news agency stills, and we'll try to blow something up from that. I doubt anyone will have a close-up of him. He isn't important enough."

Ross thought for a moment. "What do we know about their movements, Clive. Any itinerary?"

"Yeah, in the office. It's provisional, though, and full of gaps."

"Well, let's take a look. If they're going to have a press conference before the talks, we might get in there and see what Rabinovich looks like in the flesh—what little he's got left."

Lyle was uncertain. "Well, maybe if we keep a good distance from him it would be okay," he said. "We don't want the KGB heavies seeing us around. Security's going to be tough enough as it is."

Lyle had a point. But nevertheless they needed to identify their quarry positively before attempting a snatch.

Photographs were certainly helpful, but nothing could beat an on-the-spot identification.

Back in the small, impersonal office they shared, they studied what was known of the Soviet schedule. There was a "photo opportunity" in the UN building before the first round of talks in two days' time and a dinner hosted by the Secretary-General the evening before that. The agents put their feet up on their desks and stared at each other. "Okay," Ross said. "Tell me. How're we going to do it?"

"I haven't a clue. Have you?"

"No."

"They're staying in the Residency, so that's out. The KGB is thicker around there than nuns at St. Peter's. They have to move him to the UN most days, so in theory we could do it somewhere on the route."

"But that'd make it a straightforward kidnap. There'd be a world war."

"Yeah. So we can't do that either. The conference chamber is out for the same reason. But maybe somewhere in the UN building would be okay. The thing we've got to aim for is Rabinovich vanishing into thin air, so the Russians don't know if he's tried to defect again or what."

"Maybe they'll take him out somewhere. Sightseeing, or to a restaurant."

"I wouldn't count on it," Lyle said. "That's how he got away last time."

"Well hell, they can't just drive him between the UN and the Residency for as long as the negotiations go on, can they? It could be months."

"They can do exactly as they please. The KGB is in charge, and there'll be top security around Rabinovich. He's not in any position to complain."

"Clive," Ross asked, big hands behind his head, "suppose Rabinovich doesn't want to come across."

"What the hell are you talking about, David? Of course he wants to come. That's why he tried to defect, isn't it?"

"Sure. But a lot's happened since then. See what he looks like? And why isn't he in Siberia somewhere? I don't like it."

"Maybe it's just for propaganda," Lyle suggested. "If they drop their token Jew, people are going to start asking questions."

"Not if they replaced him with another Jew. They could say he was sick."

"I guess so. Well, I don't know what the answer is. We'll find out in the end."

"You hope."

"We'd better," Lyle said. "We don't only want Rabinovich. We want revenge."

"So Yardley keeps saying."

"Not only Yardley. I say so."

"Yeah, I suppose I do too." But Ross wasn't sure he did.

Neither of them had been in the United Nations building for many years; so they went there in the afternoon and walked around familiarizing themselves with the general layout. Security seemed lax, except for the floor where the Secretary-General's offices were situated. Apart from that, people were able to move freely without questions being asked.

They made no attempt to enter any area occupied by the Soviet delegation, but they saw how things were on floors above and below and presumed the layouts would be similar. They could check that easily enough on the official plan of the building.

The photo session at the resumption of talks was to take place in the conference chamber itself, and the agents had to show special authorizations before being allowed in to check it out.

It was a large room, with windows on one side and a view out to sea. A table capable of seating about forty had been prepared. Sound was muffled by the thick royal blue carpet and the heavy curtains covering three of the walls.

On entering Lyle and Ross found themselves in a clear section of the room, uncluttered by furniture. Presumably the cameramen would crowd into this section, with a few perhaps being allowed around the narrower sides to shoot from a different angle. If he and Ross were to come in behind the main throng and keep to the back, there was a good chance the KGB wouldn't spot them, particularly if they waited until the television lights were switched on before entering. It was difficult for anyone to see behind their glare. And of course, once they'd had a minute or so to inspect Rabinovich, they could leave, well ahead of the others.

"What do you think?" Ross asked as they strolled down the corridor to the elevator.

"I think we can get a look at him okay, but I don't see how we can take him. Do you?"

"No." Ross paused. "How about when he goes to the toilet?"

"No good," Lyle said. "They'll have someone with him the whole time. Anyway, I reckon they'll use the johns inside their own area. They're not going to grub around with the public."

"So where does that leave us? We can't do it at the Residency, or when he's in a car, or in the UN building."

"Not if we want to make it look like a defection."

"Which we do."

"That leaves us," Lyle confessed, "at a dead end. Still, we'd better go back and dig up the floor plan. It might throw new light on things."

But when they had studied it, it became clear that the UN building could only be used to snatch a target who wasn't under heavy security and who would use the facilities, particularly the cafeteria, in an unsuspecting, casual way.

They went to see Yardley, to explain their predicament. Sometimes he came up with a good idea. But the Director frowned over the floor plans, considered and discarded all the alternatives they had covered, and could offer no further help.

"You're just going to have to keep at it," Yardley said. "Rabinovich will be here several weeks. Follow him. See if their security relaxes. Something will turn up. And if it doesn't, your job is to make it turn up."

The Russians did not stir from the Residency throughout the following day, but in the evening they went in convoy, with police motorcycle escort, to the Secretary-General's dinner.

Lyle watched them leave, and Ross saw them arrive. They were out of the limousines and into the entrance so swiftly it was barely possible to decide which one was Rabinovich, let alone get a good look. Only Konev paused at the doorway and turned to wave for the cameras.

It was hardly better at the end of the dinner.

The following morning, the two agents, armed this time with CIA accreditation—a guise they regularly adopted because everyone was used to Langley and CIA IDs drew little comment—went to the UN building for the photo session, taking with them a photographer, under orders to get as many different angles as he could of Rabinovich.

The photographer entered with the first surge of journalists, but Lyle and Ross waited in the corridor until the television lights were on. Then they slipped in the back.

The delegations were in their seats, with the Secretary-General at the far end of the table. Everyone wore suitable expressions of solemnity. Konev was in earnest consultation with one of his aides, while the others stared straight ahead. Rabinovich had been placed two seats down from his delegation leader.

Behind them, on chairs against the wall, sat the Soviet "advisers," most of whom were KGB. They were the ones peering into the milling ranks of cameramen and TV producers, trying to see beyond the glare of the lights.

Ross stared at Rabinovich for several seconds, comparing him to the remembered portly figure. Rabinovich's cheeks were sunken. Even his neck looked scrawny. There was no sign that he had ever had a double chin. But it was his eyes that gave Ross definite stirrings of unease.

Ross remembered how it had been in the safe house: that same look he recalled from childhood. Eyes that reflected not only what was going on in the mind at that moment—fear, anxiety, despair—but that told of the past, of persecutions and suffering endured over years.

All that was gone from Rabinovich now. His eyes had ceased to mirror his soul.

What have they done to you? Ross wondered and felt fresh anger at the betrayal by politicians, some of whom were now sitting calmly opposite Rabinovich, and by the CIA that had carried out their orders.

He felt Lyle nudge his elbow. They pushed their way out into the corridor and headed back for the DIA and a conference with Yardley.

It was decided the agents should not risk hanging around the UN, as their chances of being seen by the Soviets were unacceptably high. The job of shadowing the Russian delegation and trying to find a weak link in its security would be passed to another DIA team. However, Yardley insisted that Ross and Lyle concentrate on surveillance away from the UN.

"You can't have others doing all your dirty work for you, Clive," he admonished. "Anyway, it'll be a good

opportunity for David to practice streetcraft. You can over-
see it and tell him if he goes wrong.''

"He won't go wrong," Lyle said. "You saw his marks
from Fairfax.''

"That may be," Yardley replied testily, "but I still want
you both to put in some groundwork. If the time comes,
you're going to have to give me a plan to make KGB
security collapse, and you're not going to work that out
sitting on your ass in the office.''

The days settled into an unchanging routine. At ten in
the morning, Mondays to Fridays, the Soviet team, their
guards and KGB chauffeurs, drove with a New York
police motorcycle escort to the United Nations where they
remained, either in guarded offices or the conference hall
itself, until it was time to return at four.

Except for Konev and two senior aides, the others did
not leave the Residency again until the talks the following
day. The exceptions were the weekends, when there was
usually one excursion—a dinner with the Ambassador of
another Eastern bloc country or a national day reception.
Whatever the function, security remained unwaveringly
tight.

The negotiations dragged on. The Soviets were haggling
about the reduction of their main nuclear capability, particularly intercontinental ballistic missiles, and were holding
out against American proposals for mutual inspections of
sites. Considerable time was spent with Konev flatly denying the USSR had anything like the nuclear force ascribed
to it by Washington.

This was a tactic which went beyond bluff or time-
wasting. In fact, the Soviets were concerned to see if they
could goad the United States into disclosing details. Would
the chief American negotiator finally, in despair, have to
place on the table satellite photographs of missile sites or
convoys to prove his point? If so, it would provide a useful

opportunity to inspect the latest Western spy technology. Or would no documentary proof be forthcoming, strongly indicating that their information had been received from agents in place in the Soviet Union? And would a pattern of such examples emerge over the long weeks to reveal, on analysis, that all the sites in question were controlled by one overall command, or supplied by another, and that the American agent could therefore be found among twenty or thirty people in certain identifiable headquarters?

It was a complex puzzle, one on which the Soviet team worked after hours at the Residency and sent details back to Moscow for simultaneous inspection there.

They were, therefore, in no particular hurry to save the world from looming annihilation, a prospect on which they had much to say in public.

Lyle and Ross followed the tortoise progress of the talks, interested mainly in what it revealed about the time scale available to them for picking up Rabinovich. The longer the talks lasted the more likely it was KGB security would relax and give them the chance they needed.

They watched from a distance and continued to work systematically through the Registry files on Soviet neutron capability. No solution to either problem suggested itself.

Ross became bored and anxious. His regular workouts in the DIA gym with Lyle no longer satisfied him. He craved action. He found himself thinking about Julie Klein and the invitation to go skydiving.

It happened fortuitously that Elaine Ross had to travel to New York, Chicago, and Los Angeles to discuss computer requirements with FBI department heads and that she would be gone at least three weeks.

Ross was sorry to see her leave, but all the same, there was an undeniable stirring of excitement in his stomach at the prospect of making a jump. Seeing Julie again would be okay, too, although he remembered Clive's warning about her. He'd make sure he kept his distance.

Ross knocked on Yardley's door one afternoon.

"Come in, David. What can I do for you?" the Director asked. "Let's go sit where we can be comfortable."

They settled themselves in the armchairs, and Yardley summoned coffee.

"I wanted to clear something with you, General," Ross said.

"Sure. What is it?"

"How would you feel about me taking up skydiving?"

Yardley did not hesitate. "First class idea," he said. "A good character builder. You need a medical first though. When was your last?"

"Three months ago."

"You'll have to have another before they'll let you strap on a parachute. Go speak to Peter Barry at the hospital. He'll sort you out."

Ross knew Dr. Peter Barry very well indeed—a suave, middle-aged man, with thick silver hair and expensive clothes, and a great doctor, which was why the DIA employed him.

"May I ask, David, why you've suddenly hit on skydiving?"

"Well, actually I met someone at a party who does it," Ross explained. "They suggested I try it."

"A man?"

"Uh, no, General. A woman."

"I see. All right, just don't get carried away by any macho rubbish. Skydiving is the same as everything else. It's safe as long as you do as you're told and remember you're a beginner. This girl—who is she by the way? . . ."

"Julie Klein, General."

"Klein? Hmmm. Don't know her. Well, presumably she's been parachuting for a while, so she'll be jumping higher and delaying longer than you will. If you want to get into her pants, and I suppose you do''—Ross began to flush—''for God's sake don't fall into the trap of trying to show off. It's the quickest way of breaking your neck. You're a presentable young man, and that ought to be enough for any girl. Do I make myself clear?''

''Yes, General,'' Ross mumbled, wondering whether he should set the Director right on his intentions toward Julie Klein but not quite being able to get the words out.

When Ross had gone, Yardley called his secretary in.

Lucy Sherman had been with him ever since his appointment to the DIA. In fact, he had taken her over from the previous Director. As far as appearances went, she was entirely wrong for the job, which in a perverse way made her the ideal candidate. She wore too much makeup, and it was too bright for a woman in her early fifties. If she told someone, in her pure Brooklynese, that she was a cashier at a delicatessen, they would have found no reason to doubt this. Yet to Yardley she was beyond price. The most sensitive secrets passed across her desk in a routine day— some deeply personal, some cruel, some vital to national security—and she handled them all without fuss or visible emotion. Her loyalty was beyond doubt, although Yardley implicitly doubted it every week, when he received from a separate section the latest surveillance reports and monitoring from the apartment in which she lived with her car salesman husband and a selection of cats.

Now she stood before the Director, notebook in hand.

''It looks,'' Yardley said, studying his fingernails, ''as if David Ross might be getting himself involved with someone named Julie Klein. See if we've got anything on this person, Lucy, and have a check run on her.''

There was a special place in Lucy Sherman's heart for Ross, and Yardley knew it. But he also knew the iron discipline to which she kept, and he was not surprised when her only response was a neutral "Right away, General."

Later that afternoon she brought in a file, marked JULIE ANNE KLEIN, which contained a few magazine clippings and a typewritten sheet: the results of preliminary research which she herself had done before the first security reports could be compiled. She laid it on his desk, with a fresh cup of coffee, and left without a word.

Yardley studied the photographs.

Julie Klein was certainly lovely. Ross knew how to pick them. *Vogue* had photographed her at the opening of a New York art gallery, in company with some prominent painters. The caption described her first as the daughter of Martin Klein, who owned a string of racehorses and a department store chain and then as a poet.

The second was a tearsheet from an arts magazine, which profiled her first as a poet and second as the daughter of Martin Klein. She had just published privately a book of verse, and the article provided a sample of her talent that Yardley hoped was not representative. It took him a few lines to realize it was a description of her vagina. Yardley wondered what her father thought when he read it. For his own taste, he found it frankly repulsive and decided he had little respect for her imagery. He was glad he had no children, especially not daughters.

He hoped Ross knew what he was letting himself in for.

Lucy's own research contained the girl's date of birth, address, the fact that her apartment was owned by her father, and that there was no record of her ever having held a job.

David Ross, meanwhile, had excused himself from another session with the neutron files and presented himself to Peter Barry at the DIA hospital where a medical certificate was made out and signed in ten minutes.

Ross felt exultant and on the way home that evening,

drove past the address Julie had given him at the end of the party.

She was right about being a rich man's daughter. It was a very expensive building, and she had the penthouse. As he slowed down, he wondered whether he should take a chance on her being in but decided it would be better to phone.

His own apartment seemed empty without Elaine, who had flown off that morning. He opened a can of beer and drank it sitting in an armchair, flicking idly through a news magazine. When he had finished, he went to the telephone.

"Julie?"

"Uh-huh?"

"I don't know if you remember me. David Ross? We met at Brian Stewart's party a week or so ago."

"Oh, yes. Hi." She didn't sound particularly enthusiastic, but Ross was not to know that a slow grin was spreading over her face as she settled herself in a chair.

"You were talking about going skydiving."

"That's right. You want to come along?"

"Sure. If that's okay."

"That's fine," Julie said. "I was going Saturday morning. How does that sound to you?"

The weekend was two days away: it couldn't be better. "Perfect," Ross said.

"Do you want to go in my car?"

"I'll pick you up if you like."

"You remember where I live?"

"Yes. I remember."

He could hear the warmth in her voice now. "Good." And then, more formal, "Will you be bringing your wife along?"

"No, she's away for a while." There was a silence at the other end while Julie tried to think of some suitably neutral response. She didn't want to scare him off.

"That's too bad," she said finally.

"What are the chances of my making a jump?" David asked.

"Would you like to?"

Ross was enthusiastic. "I'd love to."

"We'll have to go Sunday as well then. They'll do ground training the first day."

"That's fine, as long as you don't mind."

"Oh, no," she said. "I don't mind the least bit. Pick me up at . . . uh, seven o'clock Saturday. It'll take us an hour to get to the club, and they like beginners to start early."

"See you then," Ross said.

When she put down the phone, Julie Klein threw back her head, ran her fingers through thick, auburn hair, and could hardly stop smiling, while Ross, in his apartment, smashed a fist into the palm of his hand in jubilation. It would be good to get the blood moving again.

Next morning, Ross asked Yardley for permission to take the weekend off. It would be his first break since the arrival of the Soviet team. Once the Russians' routine had become established he and Lyle had spent weekdays in Washington on their research, and Saturdays and Sundays practicing what Yardley called "streetcraft" in New York, which usually meant hanging around the Residency, staying out of sight.

Yardley agreed readily. Lyle could handle the New York end by himself and have time off later. There was no point running both men into the ground at this stage. The talks looked set to continue for weeks, and it would probably only be toward the end that Soviet security would begin to relax. Yardley hoped that when it did, it would leave them enough time to snatch Rabinovich and discover the neutron secret—and enough time, if warranted, to abort the negotiations.

*   *   *

David Ross was outside Julie Klein's door prescisely at seven.

She opened it wearing a flimsy bathrobe. "Sorry," she apologized, inviting him in. "I overslept." She headed toward her bedroom on bare feet with pink painted toenails. "Make yourself comfortable. There's some coffee ready. I won't be long."

Ross felt uncomfortable, an intruder in this expensively furnished apartment, with a lovely, half-dressed girl disappearing into the next room. Seeing her like that made his mouth dry, and he wondered automatically what Elaine was doing.

He helped himself to coffee and settled on the sofa. A copy of the *Washington Post* was on the table beside him. He picked it up and read the latest prognosis on the SALT talks.

Julie emerged within five minutes, relaxed and looking stunning in designer jeans and what purported to be a man's rugby shirt. Ross could see the outline of her nipples. He averted his eyes.

"Let's go," she said and led him quickly out into the corridor. He presssed the button for the elevator while she locked the apartment.

As they drove toward the small airfield where the club had its headquarters, Julie provided a flow of interesting and occasionally perceptive anecdotes about the people he would be meeting and how she came to take up skydiving.

"As soon as I heard free-falling was better than orgasm—I mean, wow!" She smiled happily. "I thought, that's for me."

"And is it?" Ross asked.

She grinned. "Depends how good your orgasm is," she said, and for that Ross had no answer.

There was no sign in her conversation of the barbs he had noticed on the night of the party, and although he

remembered Lyle's warning that she was a rich kid who'd
kill to get her own way, Clive might have been talking
about a different girl from the one who was with him on
this bright, cloudless morning. Ross wondered if she hadn't
been harshly judged. He found himself relaxing in her
company, responding to her jokes with genuine laughter.
Best of all, she didn't seem to take herself too seriously,
and there was no sign at all that she considered Ross
anything other than a new acquaintance, a recruit for the
club.

The airfield was off the main road, and she directed him
to a rutted dirt road skirting the perimeter. Half a mile
farther on, they reached a gate, beyond which were a
hangar and a brick building with a porch running the
length of the front. A handful of people were gathered on
the grass.

Ross could see a few turn to watch them arrive, but
there was warmth in their greeting. And when they heard
he wanted to jump, he was quickly absorbed into the
ranks.

The man who taught beginners was named Pete Grethel.
He was younger than Ross—around twenty-two. There
was a calm assurance about him that made him a natural
instructor. Ross had come across the type many times.
Fairfax was full of them.

There were four other men and three girls, two of whom
Ross decided were either girlfriends or groupies, but anyway, non-jumpers. The third girl, Sue Collins, was due to
make her first descent that morning.

Pete Grethel introduced her to Ross. Sue was plain,
overweight and beginning to feel nervous, surreptitiously
wiping her palms on the back of her jeans.

"Come up in the Cessna with us, David" Grethel invited. "See what it looks like from there. It's a static line
drop of course, so there's nothing for Sue to do except

enjoy herself." He smiled confidently at her, ignoring the fact that enjoyment was far from her thoughts. "You don't mind if David watches, do you?"

"That's okay," Sue answered with a quick smile. "Just as well if he comes. It'll probably take the two of you to pry my fingers loss and throw me out."

"You're going to be fine," Grethel assured her.

Julie had wandered off toward the clubhouse, and Ross noticed she was crouched beside a young man packing a chute on the clubhouse porch. Her arm was flung casually across his shoulders.

The man was in his early twenties, like most of them, and Ross could see how muscular he was from the thickness of his neck and the clear definition of his biceps as he sorted the canopy lines. There was no doubt he was also extremely handsome: brown hair, thick, straight, and well-cut; dark eyebrows that extended far toward his temples; and serious dark eyes. Julie said something to him, and he glanced in Ross's direction. Ross could see a scar in the center of his lower lip, almost a cleft, which made him even more striking.

Ross felt strangely annoyed, and, without knowing why, slightly cheated.

While Sue went to get ready, Grethel showed Ross the swing where later he would practice landing rolls.

"How soon can I jump?" Ross asked. "Julie said maybe tomorrow."

"You need a medical certificate," Pete Grethel replied. "Rules, I'm afraid. Once you've got that, you just need a few hours of ground training and you're off."

"I've had my medical," Ross said.

"Have you brought a piece of paper?"

"Yeah."

Ross handed it over, and Grethel studied it briefly. "Government doctor," he remarked.

"I work for Uncle Sam."

"Doesn't everyone in Washington?"

"Just about."

"Okay, well that settles everything. We'll get you ground trained today, and you can jump first thing tomorrow if you like."

"That'd be great."

"Let's go to the clubhouse and see if we've got gear that'll fit you."

By the time they returned to the clubhouse, Sue was on the porch in a faded red jumpsuit and black boots, starting to look very scared.

Grethel gave her a hug as he passed. She tried to smile but said nothing.

The storeroom smelled not unpleasantly of sweat. When they were out of hearing of the others, David remarked, "Sue's not looking too good."

"Oh, she'll be fine. A lot of people are like that before their first. Wait till you see her afterward." He picked out a large blue jumpsuit with ROTHMANS emblazoned on the back. "Here, try this."

While Ross changed, Grethel hunted through the spare boots. Most of them were old, obviously army surplus.

"You'll also need a crash helmet," he said, "but I won't bother about that till you gct started."

They went into the main clubhouse area, Ross feeling conspicuous and awkward. He heard Julie say, "Don't you look smart!" and as he turned, he saw her sitting with the man who'd been packing the parachute. Ross went up to them, trying not to look embarrassed.

"Hi," he said, and Julie introduced them.

"David Ross, this is Andy Marcus." The young man rose to shake hands.

From the door, Pete Grethel called, "Come on, David. We're ready to go."

"I'm going to watch Sue," he apologized to Julie and Andy. "See you two later."

Some men were wheeling a Cessna out of the hangar. Grethel had his arm around Sue, giving her last minute encouragement. When this was done, he loaded David into the back seat of the plane first; himself—as despatcher— next and finally the girl, sitting at the opening where a door had once been mounted.

She put on her crash helmet, and her expression was private and preoccupied. Grethel attached the end of her static line to a fitting inside the Cessna and tapped her shoulder to make her look around and check that it had been properly done. Grethel grinned and gave the thumbs up signal. She returned the sign, but not the smile.

Ross began feeling nervous for her and wondering how he would react when his turn came the next day.

The propeller of the Cessna began revolving laboriously until suddenly the engine caught. The pilot spoke to the control tower, opened the throttle, and they bumped off across the grass onto a taxiway. A group of people had gathered on the porch to watch. Ross noticed that Julie Klein and Andy Marcus were not among them.

The noise and vibration increased as the engine was tested at the end of the runway. Then, after the pilot had been given takeoff clearance, the small plane gathered speed and the ground dropped quickly away.

Ten minutes later, bumping through mild turbulence, they reached 2,500 feet. Pete Grethel leaned close to Ross, shouting above the noise.: "Our DZ—that's the drop zone—is just ahead over there." He pointed through the window, and Ross could make out, in the center of a field, a small orange cross with an arrow beside it, indicating the direction of the wind. Half a dozen cars were parked nearby and some tiny figures moved around, looking up as the sound of the engine grew louder.

"Why don't you use the airfield?" he shouted back.

"Not allowed!" Grethel leaned forward and exchanged a few words with the pilot. They crossed the DZ and banked around in a wide turn.

After two or three minutes, they banked again to begin their run-in. Grethel put his hand firmly on Sue's shoulder and shouted, "Get your feet out!"

Her face was ashen, but she moved automatically. The Cessna droned on, Grethel craning forward to see how far they were from the DZ. He spoke to the pilot again. Abruptly the engine cut, and in the sudden silence, Grethel ordered: "Get out!"

Sue sat frozen for a second but then she lumbered up, one foot on the step, and snatched forward at the strut. She was entirely outside the plane, her knuckles showing white as she gripped the metal.

"Go!" shouted Grethel.

She fell like a stone. The Cessna banked sharply so they could watch her, and instantly the static line went rigid, then slack as her weight pulled it free of the parachute. The drogue flared, the chute blossomed.

"Beautiful!" Grethel cried.

They circled while the girl floated over what looked to Ross suspiciously like power pylons, toward the DZ. She hit, rolled, and the canopy slowly collapsed.

"That's all there is to it," Grethel said.

When they got back to the airfield, Julie, Andy Marcus, and a third man Ross hadn't met, were waiting their turn.

"Are you jumping now?" Ross asked.

"Yes. We're going to try a link-up from 7,000. You going out to watch?"

Ross looked at the instructor. "I don't know," he said.

"Sure," Grethel replied. "I wanted to show you the DZ anyway. And you ought to have a look at these guys landing, so you'll know what not to do."

"Up yours, my friend," Julie said.

Grethel had an old Land Rover parked in the back, and as the plane taxied away, they bumped over the rough road toward the highway. "The DZ is about three miles from here," Grethel said. "It would be great if we could use the airfield, but there's too much traffic. So we've negotiated the use of a field."

"Were those power lines I saw near the DZ?" Ross asked.

"Yeah, high-tension cables."

"Isn't that dangerous?"

"Only if you hit them." Grethel smiled mirthlessly. "No one has so far."

Ross fell silent. What a strange place to use as a DZ, he thought, but he presumed they knew what they were doing.

The Land Rover turned onto a dirt track, in worse repair than the one leading to the clubhouse, and in the distance they could see a group of people watching the sky as the Cessna climbed in wide circles.

Grethel parked beside the other vehicles and went immediately over to Sue, whose face shone with triumph. Grethel lifted her off the ground and swung her around whooping, but he didn't have to ask any questions because she spoke compulsively, recounting everything that had happened, everything she'd thought, from the moment she boarded the Cessna.

"Congratulations," Ross smiled, warmed by the infectiousness of her spirits. "It looked just fine."

Ross walked around inspecting the area. The high-tension wires were about 500 yards from the DZ. He could see why they couldn't move farther away because the spot they'd chosen was about equidistant from two other hazards— the main road to the north, and a rocky hill to the east. Over to the west he glimpsed a fence, presumably demarcating someone else's property where skydivers were not welcomed.

Ross squinted into the sky, toward the sun, looking for the Cessna. Grethel joined him.

"That Sue," he chuckled. "The greatest day of her life."

"You certainly seem to have a convert there," Ross said.

Grethel looked at him wryly. "Sue? Oh hell, no. I don't suppose she'll ever jump again."

"Why not?" Ross asked.

"Oh, I don't know. A lot of people try it once and never again. It's a big thrill, and that's it. They did it for a dare maybe, or they want to prove to themselves they can get up there and bail out, but that's all they want. I'll bet you a dollar that's the end of Sue."

"Okay, you're on." They shook on it.

"We'll see. I've just got a feeling about her. Now let me tell you a couple of things you need to know." Grethel went over the procedure for exiting and the theory of skydiving. "The idea is," he said "that you assume a starfish position, like this." He stood legs apart, back arched, arms up symmetrically. "That puts the center of gravity somewhere around your solar plexus, and you fall in a stable position, face down toward the ground. It takes about twelve seconds to reach terminal velocity."

"How fast is that?"

"About 120 miles an hour. If you're stable at that speed, you're riding on a cushion of air, so you can maneuver, track across the sky, that sort of thing. That's what those guys coming out of the Cessna are going to do."

He checked the position of the plane. It was beginning its run-in.

Ross had a sudden image of Julie Klein crouched in the doorway, with far below a toy landscape of browns and greens, rectangles and squares, houses and sheds the size of matchboxes with thin strips of road along which vehicles seemed hardly to move. It really was something to launch yourself into the emptiness separating the Cessna from that.

They saw the tiny black figures drop from the plane, one after another, fast, even before the sound reached them of the engine throttling back; three dots, half the size of small buttons, ranged in a line against the blue sky. Grethel's voice in his ear, "You'll see the starfish position as they get nearer. They'll be reaching terminal velocity now, so watch for them tracking into position."

Ross noticed that two of the figures had moved closer together, but the third was still some distance away.

"It's more difficult than it looks," Grethel said. "They're dropping so fast any movement has an exaggerated effect."

"So how do they link up? Hey look, two of them have done it."

"I see. The third's trying to come in now. What you do to move any big distance is to assume the delta position—arms and legs swept back, and backside raised: you can just make out that guy doing it now—then you move laterally as well as vertically. Understand?"

"Yeah."

"But the danger is collision. If you're not careful, you could cannon into one of the others."

"Jesus, that must be bad."

"It is. The speeds are so great skydivers can knock each other out."

"What happens then?" Ross turned briefly to stare at Grethel.

"If they regain consciousness when they're high enough," Grethel said, "they open the chute and land with a headache." There was no point spelling out what would happen if they did not. "Okay, see that third guy, he's back in the starfish position. What he'll be doing now is grabbing handfuls of air,'' he demonstrated with his hands, ''and inching forward. They haven't got too much time left to make the link-up.''

They could see the figures clearly. The space between them narrowed gradually until at last they linked, and fell like a star toward the earth.

''That's pretty good,'' Grethel said. ''I guess we'll try for a four tomorrow.''

The skydivers split apart, tracking away from each other.

''It's time to open the chutes, so they need room,'' he explained.

Two drogues and parachutes blossomed almost simultaneously, and they watched the third plummeting figure. The drogue burst out, followed by the chute. It seemed to bloom as the wind rushed to fill it and the descent slowed. But something was wrong: it had only half-opened. Ross stared uncomprehending.

Grethel's voice, calm in his ear, ''What's happened there is that a couple of lines have tangled around the canopy.'' They saw the figure being swung around in a spiral, falling faster than the others. On the ground, the spectators watched transfixed.

Grethel continued, ''Now the best procedure for this is to cut away the main canopy—ditch it altogether—and open your emergency chute. But you have to have height for that, and I don't think that guy has it. So the emergency chute is on his stomach. He puts his left hand over it, pulls the ripcord with his right. The canopy presents itself to him as a pile of laundry on his belly. He takes it in both hands and throws it in the direction he's spinning.''

As they watched, the figure seemed to be doing just that. But the wind caught the emergency chute immediately, and it flared up at the side of the main canopy.

And tangled.

The figure continued spiralling around, the descent scarcely slowed.

After a pause, Pete Grethel admitted, "I don't know what I'd do now."

They watched in silence. Ross felt a sickness in the back of his throat. It might be Julie. There was no way of knowing. But whoever it was, it was hard to look at, and impossible not to.

The figure braced for impact, feet and knees together, as the ground came up. There was a puff of dust as it hit, and Ross, Grethel, and the others began to run.

A breeze filled a section of canopy and threatened to blossom it and drag the figure along the ground. There was no discernible movement.

The first people to reach the spot pulled the lower rigging line to collapse the chute entirely, while Ross and Grethel knelt beside the skydiver. Ross's Fairfax training had included emergency first aid and instinctively he took command.

"Help me turn her over, gently now," Ross ordered in such an authoritative voice that Grethel obeyed.

But it wasn't Julie.

Thank God, Ross thought.

The face was Andy Marcus, teeth gritted in pain, eyes closed, his nose and part of his cheek grazed and bleeding.

Ross's hands fumbled with the release straps, but it was unfamiliar equipment and he didn't want to waste time. "Get this stuff off him, Pete," he said.

When it was clear, Ross's hands moved expertly, testing for breaks. Andy Marcus's breath was coming in gasps. "Andy, move your toes," Ross said. "Can you move them?"

The head nodded slightly. From the corner of his eye, Ross noticed Julie running up.

"Is he okay?" she asked anxiously.

Ross ignored her, too busy with his checks. He removed the crash helmet and lifted Marcus's eyelids to check the state of his pupils. They seemed fine, responding quickly to light. "Raise your arms, Andy," Ross said. He could do that too. His breath was a little easier. "Get his boots off," Ross said and immediately Grethel was working on one, and Julie Klein on the other. Andy Marcus's breath hissed in pain.

"Which foot hurts?" Ross asked.

The words were forced out. "The left."

"Okay. Take it easy with that boot, Pete. Get the laces out before you try to slide it off."

When it was done, Ross gently removed the sock and inspected his foot. "I don't think anything's broken," he said at last. "You'll need an X-ray to make sure." The ankle was becoming puffy. "I guess you've got yourself a dandy sprain though. You must be made of rubber or something," he said cheerfully. "Try to sit up." The young man struggled into a sitting position.

"Oh, man," he said softly, "it doesn't feel like rubber."

Ross went around to his left side. "Okay now, stand. Lean on me."

Marcus rose slowly, careful to keep his sprained foot off the ground. When he was up, a smile spread over his scraped face, blood and dust caking one side. "What do you know," he said in disbelief. "I made it after all."

Julie threw her arms around him, and he winced. "Easy now, I'm a bit sore."

"I reckon you're okay," Ross said, "apart from being winded and hurting your ankle. You should be good for another jump in a couple of weeks."

"Who the hell packed your chutes, Andy?" Grethel asked.

Marcus began to laugh. "I hate to admit it, but I just

did, the main canopy, not the reserve. I don't know who did that.''

"Remind me never to use one of yours.''

"I got down, didn't I? You know what they say: if you can walk away from it, it's a landing.''

They got Marcus to one of the cars, and a couple of club members drove him to the nearest hospital for a checkup. Ross noticed Sue standing on the fringes of the crowd, the euphoria she had felt after her first jump changed into something more thoughtful. There goes my dollar, Ross thought.

He joined Pete Grethel, who looked at him with new interest. "Thanks for the help, David,'' Grethel said. "Are you a doctor?''

"Hell, no.'' Ross cleared his throat slightly. "I'm an accountant, actually.''

"Bullshit!''

"No, really. That's what I do with my days.''

"So how did you learn that stuff?''

"Well, I've knocked around. You know how you pick things up.''

Grethel grinned, half believing him. "Yeah,'' he said. "I guess.'' They walked toward the Land Rover. "You do the accounts at West Point, maybe?''

Ross laughed. "No, nothing like that. Never been in the army.''

"You could have fooled me.''

Ross, wanting to move the conversation to less personal matters, asked, "Do you see that sort of thing often?''

"Luckily no,'' Grethel said. "That's a freak. But these things happen sometimes. Now I guess I'd better show you the landing rolls, Mr. Accountant. You've just seen how important they can be.''

As Ross suspected, Grethel proved a thorough, good teacher, and he gave David what in club terms was a hard time—far more and tougher work than he required of others—but by Fairfax standards it wasn't much. Grethel made him practice the rolls over and over until he had them right. It was more than just overcaution, given impetus by the Andy Marcus incident. Grethel was testing Ross, seeing how far he could push him, what his level of fitness was, how good his reflexes, how developed his self-discipline.

Ross took it without complaint or comment. Indeed, it had not occurred to him it ought to be any other way. He felt the tightness of sets of muscles that had been underused as Grethel pushed him high on the trapeze and he dropped/hit/rolled on the hard ground.

They went at it for three hours without a break—so long that other members of the club, Julie Klein included, came out onto the porch to jeer at Grethel. But he ignored them, content for them to watch the progress of his new pupil.

Ross was extraordinary. He responded instantly to commands and seemed to lack fear. If his body hurt, and by that time it did, he gave no sign. He had attained a high degree of proficiency, and Grethel was prepared to give the others a show.

"Okay, Accountant," he said softly, "We're going to go through the six basic rolls to show our friends what they ought to have been doing for the last couple of years. You ready?"

Ross nodded.

"Get up there."

As Ross hung from the trapeze bar, Grethel gave him a hefty push. "Backward roll to the left!" he shouted, then waited until Ross's body was arcing toward the ground. "Go!"

Ross dropped, absorbing the impact along the side of his left leg and diagonally across his back, completing the movement by springing back to his feet.

"Get back up!" Another push, another order. A perfect forward right roll, a lot harder than he would normally expect to encounter.

When the six had been done, there was a chorus of appreciation from the porch and a scattering of applause.

Grethel slapped him on the back. "Not too bad," he acknowledged. "You can jump after lunch if you want."

Ross felt his stomach knot. He wasn't ready for it, not so soon. But he said: "Sure."

"Let's go see about a chute for you."

When they reached the clubhouse, Julie gave him a kiss on the cheek. "David, that's fantastic!" she said. "You're a natural!" David felt inordinately pleased.

Ross was to use Sue's parachute—the one allocated to all newcomers. Regular jumpers had their own personal chutes, and after a discussion, Grethel said they might as well eat first and pack it afterward.

Some of the women had brought sandwiches and pizza, and with beers and soft drinks from a small refrigerator, they had a friendly, relaxed meal. Except for Ross, who wasn't hungry—the same sick feeling he experienced before a mission. Yet, now as then, it was necessary for him to behave normally, force himself to eat, so no one would be aware that a battle was taking place inside him, and his nerves were tightly strung.

Before they had finished, Andy Marcus arrived back at the clubhouse with the men who had taken him to hospital. He limped in, his ankle tightly strapped, but he was smiling and in good spirits. A narrow escape is one of the more euphoric things that can happen in a person's life. The scraped part of his face, where dirt had been ground into the flesh, was painted with a reddish-brown substance, and Ross noted that it didn't do much to spoil his looks.

Julie Klein immediately went to get him a beer and something to eat, totally forgetting Ross. So he turned his attention to Sue, happy on the thin carpet nearby, and began asking about her job and her friends. Yet through it, Ross was constantly aware of Julie and Andy together. He tried to pick up their conversation without his attention straying too far from what Sue was saying. He wondered if they were sleeping together, and thought: well of course they are—what do you expect?

When lunch was over, Grethel took him out to the porch and spread Sue's rough-packed parachute on the cement floor, explaining as he sorted the lines the theory behind it and what had probably gone wrong with Andy Marcus's canopy. Grethel worked neatly and methodically, carefully checking every stage of his progress.

"You've got to make sure you keep a clear tunnel up the center of the chute," he explained, "so the wind can get in there and bust it out of its sock."

"If you don't?"

"Then it doesn't open. It'll trail behind you like a bundle of laundry. That's the time to go for your emergency pack. But don't worry about it. Your chances of a malfunction are a lot less than of being hit by a car crossing any street you care to name in Washington. Statistically, that's true. Anyway, more people die in the United States being kicked in the head by mules than parachuting."

Ross laughed. "Is that what your insurance company says?"

"Listen," Grethel said, "I'm gonna live to be a hundred." He closed up the pack and fitted the static line release mechanism. "When you fall, the weight of your body will pull this out, and it'll open behind you like a dream. There's a guarantee on this one. But as the airlines say, international safety regulations oblige me to tell you what to do if it doesn't. Now when you jump, you go into the starfish position," he demonstrated again with his body arched, "and you count One thousand . . . Two thousand . . . Three thousand . . . Four thousand—look over your shoulder, see what's happened to the chute— Five thousand . . . Six thousand, and if it hasn't opened by then, go for the ripcord on the emergency pack. Pull it as far out as your arm will stretch. Don't mess around. You're only going out from 3,000 feet so you don't have a lot of time, not if you want to see the beautiful view. Any questions?"

"Yeah, one. What happens if I find I'm coming down into those high-tension cables."

"Well, judge it so you don't. Either run with the wind, and float over them, or else turn into the wind so you land before you reach the pylons."

"If I misjudge? Or the wind changes?"

"Well then the procedure is this: you put one foot over the other and lock them, keep your knees together, and you try to thread your way through the lines."

"You're joking!" Ross said. "How the hell can you thread your way through anything when you're falling twelve feet a second?"

"And you say: 'Our father, who art in heaven.' "

"Oh, piss off." Ross began to laugh despite the tension within him.

"Come on. Time to go. Have you bought your ticket?"

"I'll go do it now." Ross went into the clubhouse to find the secretary and pay for the hire of the chute and the lift in the Cessna. Handing over the money seemed the final act; he wondered if he looked as nervous as Sue had earlier in the day. He could see her watching from across the room. He smiled, feeling sure it came out as more of a grimace. Julie called from the door, "Hey, David, I'm going out to the DZ now. Good luck."

"Thanks." His palms were sweating, and he had the terrible sensation that he would soon be sick. He walked onto the porch.

Pete Grethel supervised strapping the parachute onto his body. The webbing came around the back, between his legs, clipped onto the harness at the front and was pulled tight. The emergency chute snapped into place on top of that.

Ross felt as if he was carrying a refrigerator on his back. Not that it was particularly heavy, merely cumbersome and restricting. The crash helmet muffled sound isolating him from the others. Grethel gave the thumbs-up sign and an encouraging smile, and they walked out toward the Cessna 172 where the pilot waited.

Sitting with an empty space where the door had been increased Ross's feeling of unease, and a few minutes later, as he watched the ground falling away, he thought: The next time I touch that, I'll be coming straight down.

It seemed to take very little time to reach 3,000 feet. There was more turbulence than during Sue's early morning jump, and it added to his queasiness.

Ross checked twice more that the static line was properly attached to the fitting inside the cabin.

Ahead was the DZ, and Grethel was craning forward to check the wind direction. They banked and went around for the run-in. Ross found himself breathing deep and slow, his chest pushing against the constriction of the harness.

"Get your feet out!" Grethel shouted to him.

Ross held the side of the seat and the rim of the door frame. There was a metal step for passengers and he sat with his left foot on that, the other trailing back. He could feel the wind whipping strongly against his legs. Below was a road and fields. But Christ, he thought, they were a long way down.

The Cessna's engine cut, the plane began to glide.

"Get out!"

Ross took a deep breath and swung himself around and out, gripping the metal strut. He was exposed now and totally vulnerable. He looked sideways into the cockpit at Grethel.

"GO!"

A ferocious blast of air hit Ross as he began his plunge, and involuntarily he screamed "Jesus!" One thousand . . . Two thousand . . . Three thousand. The chute bloomed, the webbing straps dug hard into him, pulling him up short.

Ross hung suspended.

A long way away he could see the Cessna, gliding down, circling so Grethel and the pilot could watch how he was doing.

It was all very quiet: almost a cathedral hush. He seemed not to be falling at all. Ross pulled the right hand toggle of the chute and he swung in that direction; then tried the left. The DZ was a good distance ahead of him. He had to reach it. Grethel had despatched him well ahead of the marker, so he could ride with the wind and turn against it, with room to maneuver over the hazards, particularly the pylons. Ross looked down to locate them. He could see the ground coming gradually closer and realized the quiet calm of the ride was deceptive. He had some fine judgments to make now. Ross decided to run with the wind until he was sure he would be able to float over the high-tension cables and then go in backward.

He looked down. He was directly over the pylons, with perhaps three or four hundred feet to spare. It was difficult to judge heights. He angled the chute so he headed directly toward the landing marker, then turned into the wind to cut his speed.

The earth came up quickly. Ross locked his ankles and

his knees, slightly flexed in the landing position, and pulled his forearms into the side of his chest. He hit and rolled. The air emptied from the canopy.

Ross felt the tension drain from him, to be replaced by an extraordinary feeling of accomplishment, a surge of adrenalin loose in his body, with no place to go.

People ran up, shaking his hand. Julie Klein was around his neck, kissing his cheek. He was vaguely conscious of perfume and the softness of her skin. It was hard to stop grinning.

"David!" Julie cried. "That was fantastic! A bull's-eye first time."

Ross looked around. They were standing near the edge of the orange marker. "Did I hit it?" he asked.

"Did you hit it? My God, right in the center. Now don't tell me it was beginner's luck. I could see you maneuvering."

Ross put an arm around her shoulder. "Yeah," he said, "I aimed all right. I just didn't know if I hit. The ground comes up pretty fast right at the end. You know what I mean?"

Ross rough-packed the chute and loaded it into one of the cars for the journey back to the clubhouse. The euphoria stayed with him, and although he tried to stop himself talking too much as Sue had done, it was difficult. Julie sat next to him in the back, and they laughed and joked a lot.

He watched another couple of lifts leaving, enjoying the conversations and stories, and feeling relaxed: at peace and exultant—a potent combination.

When the sun went down, everyone gathered at the clubhouse to pack away the gear and get the beers out of the fridge. Pete Grethel made sure they all had drinks, then called for silence.

"Tonight," he said, "we've got to celebrate David and

Sue's first jumps and initiate them into the fraternity of skydivers.'' There was applause as he walked ceremoniously to a cupboard and opened it with a key. "Which means it's time to introduce them to one of our founder members and club mascot, Sam. Now Sam here, as you all know, holds the club record for the longest delayed first free fall.'' He brought from the shelves part of a human skull, missing the lower jawbone. "Five thousand feet to zero, without goddam pulling his ripcord!''

There was a ragged cheer. Someone opened a couple of cans of beer and gave them to Grethel who carefully filled the head of the skull, making sure nothing frothed over. It took almost two pints.

He held it aloft, careful not to spill a drop. "Ladies first,'' he said. "Come on up here, Sue. You've got to drink this, and you've got to get it all down in one go.''

She gave a cry of protest, but no one would accept a refusal. They pushed her forward, until at last she took the skull, shuddering, and sipped as much as she could. They let her off before she had got through more than half.

The skull was refilled.

"David! Come on up here!''

Ross, grinning at the bizarreness of the ceremony, grasped the skull firmly. He carefully turned an eyesocket toward him and poured, gulping the beer as fast as he could, not pausing for breath, while the others whistled and cheered. He felt his stomach distend and it became difficult to swallow, but he forced himself until every drop had been finished. There was a big round of applause. Ross saw spots in front of his eyes.

Then they seized him: all the other men in the club, except Andy Marcus whose sprained ankle ruled him out, but who shouted encouragement from the side. They turned Ross, unprotesting, onto his face, while four held his arms and legs and bounced him into the air, up and down. As he went up, the others hit him on the back with the flats of their hands. The beer fizzed and frothed in his stomach. Ross, who could have stopped them at any time, was having more fun than he could remember.

They let him down, to more cheering, and he got unsteadily to his feet, gasped, and ran for the door.

When he'd got rid of the beer, he came back to renewed applause, and Grethel presented Ross and Sue with their club badges: an embroidered skydiver, falling in a stable position over a blue delta flash.

Later, heading back to Washington with Julie Klein, Ross thought it one of the finest days of his life. He relaxed in the front passenger seat, with a pleasant buzzing in his head from the beers. Traffic was not very heavy, and they made it into the city in good time. Julie had suggested that she drive because she'd had less to drink, and Ross was content to let her.

When she pulled up outside her apartment, she cut the engine and asked, "Would you like a cup of coffee? Or a nightcap? Or something to eat?"

It didn't occur to him to refuse.

He stood in the kitchen while she fixed dinner. She told him about herself and her family, revealing relationships and tensions in an unforced, often amusing way. She didn't ask David to talk about himself because that risked his wife rising like a specter between them.

When the food was in the oven, she asked if he felt like a shower, and he said he did, half expecting her to join him as he stood under the hot spray in the luxurious guest bathroom and half wanting her to. But as he discovered when he emerged, his hair tousled and wet, she was in her own bedroom, taking a bath.

Ross walked idly over to the bookshelves and inspected her reading tastes. There was a wide range, although mostly anthologies and the collected works of poets through several centuries. A slim brown volume, which he almost missed was entitled *Me*, and when he pulled it out, he saw she was the author.

This would be the erotic verse. Ross took it over to the sofa. At first, he felt uneasy at what she had written, then found himself becoming interested, and finally stirred. He became very still when, toward the end, he found a poem, entitled "Andy" and knew it must be about her and Marcus. He read it carefully, twice. It was the sexiest of them all. It would be, of course.

As he got up to replace the book, he saw Julie standing in the doorway. She had changed into a loose silk dress, through which the contours of her body were apparent, and she was watching with a half smile.

"Well?" she said. "What do you think?"

Ross tried to return the smile, but had to force it. "What about? Your dress or your poetry?"

"My poetry."

"It's pretty sexy," Ross admitted.

"Good. But you didn't like it. I can see from your face."

"Yes, I did like it." He paused. "Actually, I did—rather a lot."

"But?" she persisted.

Ross held the book and looked at it. *Me*—by Julie Klein. "I see you've written about Andy," he said.

She laughed. "Oh sure. Andy and I are old friends. We've been going together, off and on, for more than a year."

"Are you dating?"

She looked at him curiously. "You mean, are we sleeping together?"

"I guess so."

Julie came into the room and took a seat near him.

"You sound like an old man," she said, amused. "Andy and I are friends. He fucks other people, and so do I. It's not serious. We're not jealous of each other. Sometimes we meet up, and if we do, it's great. Afterward he goes his way, and I go mine." She put her head slightly to one side, regarding him affectionately. "It's not a happy-ever-after situation I want, David," she explained. "I'm too glad to be free. Why would I change that?"

"I don't know," Ross said replacing the book. "I guess I've never met anyone like you before."

"Fine," she said. "That's the way I like it. Now let's eat."

Julie kept the conversation easy during dinner, and the inhibitions Ross felt about Andy Marcus passed.

It was eleven by the time they had cleared the plates and brewed coffee.

Julie glanced at her watch. "Why don't you stay over?" she invited. "We can go back to the club in the morning, if you want."

Ross cleared his throat slightly. He heard himself say, "Thanks. I'd like to," and then he was committed, just as he had been earlier when he paid his money and knew he was going to have to jump.

The curtains were ajar, and when the moon rose it cast a glow into the room. Ross was sleeping lightly, and it woke him. He lay still, remembering where he was, automatically checking to assure himself nothing was wrong, and then turning to look at the girl.

He could see the shine on her hair. Her skin was clear and when he touched it, very soft. She breathed easily. There was a faint scent of her perfume and the lingering smell of their love.

Ross ran a hand down her spine. She did not stir. Her face was turned toward him, and he studied the fineness of her features, the shape of her nose. With the tip of a finger, he touched her mouth and her lips moved automatically, closing over it.

He'd never had a girl like Julie, for whom sex was entirely pleasure, without any hint of obligation, who used her extraordinary body as it pleased her, and made sure it did please her, and him.

He felt content. Then he saw she was awake, her green eyes watching. Ross moved toward her.

"Wasn't that better than free falling?" he murmured. She smiled.

Clive Lyle stood in a doorway fifty yards down from the Soviet Residency in New York, on the other side of the street. It was ten o'clock Sunday morning, and he had been in position for three hours.

He unlocked the door and went into the room from which he mostly maintained his watch. Saturday had been a waste of time. The only people to emerge from the Residency were Russians based in the States. Lyle wondered what the hell the negotiating team was doing with its time.

He settled into a chair, set a distance from the window, and scanned the entrance. If this was what Yardley called practicing streetcraft, he didn't know what he was talking about.

It was a dull, overcast day, and it looked as if it might rain later. He wished he had Ross for company, someone to take over now and then to relieve the monotony. But Ross was out breaking his neck. Good luck to him, Lyle thought. Anything was better than this.

There was light traffic in the street: nothing to interest the DIA.

Two men in dark suits turned the corner and walked toward the Residency. Lyle lifted the binoculars to his eyes and studied them. One he recognized as a Soviet cryptographer, and therefore KGB, and the other was a Second Secretary, probably also KGB. They were part of the Residency's regular traffic, meticulously charted by the DIA teams who watched on weekdays and familiar also to Lyle and Ross from their weekend duties. Lyle noted the movement in a small logbook. One never knew when a pattern would emerge and suddenly pieces of a puzzle would fit together.

He watched idly as the men walked up the Residency steps. Suddenly, Lyle leaned forward straining for a better view. They'd halted at the door, and there was movement beyond—people coming out. They were still in shadow; so it was impossible to recognize anyone. He stared intently.

The cryptographer stood aside, and Lyle rose slowly to his feet, unable to believe his luck: good luck, because it lifted the monotony, and bad because Ross was not there to help, and he needed him.

The emerging group was made up of members of the SALT talks delegation: not Konev or his deputy, but some of the others. At the rear was Rabinovich.

Lyle scanned the street for Embassy limousines, but there were none. The group must be going for a walk.

He focused on the faces, recognizing three KGB guards. Lyle waited to see the direction they were taking, and they made it easy for him by heading his way. He stood back from the window, paying particular attention to the known KGB. They were alert, watching to see if anyone was following, and scanning ahead not only for who was approaching, but also in case there were alleys or entrances that needed a preliminary check. They glanced into the interiors of parked cars.

Lyle waited until they had passed his position and turned the corner before leaving the room. He walked briskly to where he had parked his car: a yellow cab. As soon as he had the Russians in sight again, he pulled up to the curb and watched.

They didn't seem to be going anywhere in particular, just strolling. The delegation members chatted and looked about like tourists; and the KGB observed like professionals.

Lyle never parked closer than 150 yards, relying on the ubiquitous nature of yellow cabs to allay any suspicions. He was lucky finding places to park, sliding in behind other vehicles, and only once in thirty minutes was it necessary for him to drive past the Russians and circle the block.

He felt relaxed and in control, and when the game changed abruptly, he completely failed to realize it.

Perhaps Lyle wouldn't have made the mistake had Ross been with him working the usual DIA surveillance routine, although Yardley would never have accepted that as an excuse.

A few minutes after Rabinovich and his group left the Residency, another two Russians emerged and followed the same route, to see if they could detect American surveillance.

Lyle hadn't expected that, and while he watched his rearview mirror, it was mainly for other traffic, rather than for pedestrians.

The two Soviets quickly realized what was happening, and moved in to assess its significance.

One of the Russians, carrying a small, black, man's satchel, hurried up to the yellow cab and leaned in the open front window. Lyle saw the figure and turned to look. A camera nestling inside the bag, its tiny lens built into the leather, began photographing him.

"I want to go to Kennedy Airport," the Russian said. His accent was indeterminate: mid-European American— one of a few hundred thousand similar sounds in the New York area.

Lyle shook his head. "I'm busy."

"But it's very important! I'll miss my plane!"

This was one of the drawbacks to using a yellow cab. Occasionally you had to fight off people who refused to see the Hire light was off.

"Look buddy, can't you see? This cab's already hired," Lyle said. "Go look for someone else."

The Russian retreated, his job done.

Lyle lit a cigarette and glanced around to make sure the man had gone. He was glad to see him walking away. He turned back to study the group ahead.

If Lyle had watched the Russian a few seconds longer, he would have had his second chance to realize the advantage had slipped from him, because another cab cruised past, looking for business, and the man who urgently wanted to get to Kennedy ignored it. Instead he headed back for the Residency, leaving his comrade to watch Lyle.

Viktor Rabinovich, unaware of the almost invisible espionage game being played behind him, was relaxed and cheerful, glad to be out in the open. His fears of kidnapping were evaporating. Everything had gone so smoothly, with each day a model of normality, that it seemed absurd to do more than leave the KGB to take their routine precautions.

Rabinovich was feeling much better. He had put on a lot of weight and was again wearing his old clothes rather than the small new wardrobe provided for him by comrade Rogov in Dzerzhinsky Square.

As they walked along, Rabinovich made frequent comments about the unnecessary consumer items with which many Americans burdened themselves—at the expense, he pointed out, of decent accommodation and jobs for millions of black Americans and other underprivileged groups. He drew attention to the moral decay evident everywhere.

They walked for almost an hour before returning to the Residency, entering the familiar hall with its massive portrait of Lenin and its ornate furnishings.

Rabinovich headed for the library, where he had been studying American publications dealing with nuclear and defense matters and finding several things of interest for his own field of research at the Dubna Atomic Center. But before he reached the door, he heard Lappa's voice.

"Yes, comrade?" Rabinovich asked turning.

"You're wanted now," Lappa said abruptly.

Rabinovich frowned. Lappa's manner seemed to have changed. It was noticeably less friendly, and there was an official edge to it. He wondered anxiously what he had done wrong.

Rabinovich followed the KGB officer down the corridor to the rooms occupied by senior security personnel—an area ordinarily out of bounds and guarded day and night by plainclothes men. He hunted anxiously through his memory for anything he might have said or done which could have caused offense. Perhaps he was too outspoken in his public comments about capitalism? No, it couldn't be that. Had he said something to anger one of his colleagues? Maybe he was just talking too much and ought to keep his own counsel.

He felt a prickle of fear. Or perhaps they had changed their minds and decided to send him back to the Lubyanka!

By the time Rabinovich was ushered into a room at the end of the corridor, his mouth was dry and his face strained.

"Sit down, comrade."

A man in casual Western clothes, his back to the window and his face half in shadow, was in charge. Rabinovich could tell nothing from his tone.

He hesitantly took a chair, aware of Lappa directly behind him and two other officers, whom he knew by sight, standing at a bookcase looking at a series of photographs.

Rabinovich waited fearfully.

I am General-leytenant* Kirichenko," the man at the widow said. "I am in charge of security at this Residency."

"Yes, comrade," Rabinovich answered. "In what way can I help the esteemed KGB?"

Kirichenko smiled. "We have been very pleased with you, Viktor," he said "so far." Kirichenko let silence fall. "I want you to look at some photographs and tell me if you recognize the man in them."

Rabinovich was handed the file and opened it carefully, making sure he disarranged nothing and left no messy fingerprints.

Considering the conditions in which they had been taken, the defintion of the pictures was excellent. Clive Lyle's face stared enquiringly out of some, belligerently from others.

Rabinovich's eyes widened. "It's him!" he cried.

"Where do you know him from?" Kirichenko asked.

Rabinovich felt overcome with embarrassment at having to talk once again about his attempted defection. He said hesitantly: "At the house, when I so mistakenly . . . stupid . . ."

"Yes, yes," Kirichenko said. ""That is all behind you now. This man was at the CIA house, was he not?"

"He came with one other—a big agent, very tall, who spoke excellent Russian."

"What was the name of this man in the photograph, Viktorovich?"

"I think he was . . . yes, he was called Clive. I don't know his family name. The other man was David."

* Equivalent to a U.S. major general.

Kirichenko took the photographs and studied them himself.

"This is a very dangerous man, comrade," he said. "His name is Clive Lyle, and he is, as you know, an agent with the Defense Intelligence Agency. You were told before you left Moscow that the DIA might try to kidnap you and that you should be vigilant yourself and cooperative with those responsible for your security."

"Oh yes, comrade. And I hope you have found me so," Rabinovich said eagerly.

"Indeed we have," Kirichenko acknowledged. "But this very morning, while you were walking, we found this man Lyle following you."

There was a sharp intake of breath from Rabinovich. "I swear to you, comrade," he said, "I didn't see him."

"No, Viktor, I am sure you did not see him. He was in a car, some distance behind. We just wanted you to confirm the identification and show you that the need for vigilance is stronger than ever. They want you, Viktor. I think they will try very hard to get you."

"What shall I do, comrade?" Rabinovich asked anxiously, knowing a kidnap by the DIA could mean his death. "Shall I return to Moscow?"

"Perhaps," Kirichenko said. "We will send a message home, asking their advice. In the meantime, it is best that you do not leave the Residency."

"Of course," Rabinovich agreed. "I will follow your orders to the smallest detail."

"I'm sure you will, Viktorovich. You may go now. Thank you for your assistance."

Kirichenko watched as Rabinovich respectfully took his leave and hurried away.

He turned to the others. "Armenian dirt," he growled. Then businesslike, "Come, we have work to do, comrades. We had better get on with it."

8

There was one change in the attendance at the morning meeting. Rogov of the KGB's Jewish Department was not needed, and his place in the First Chief Directorate's conference room was taken by a small, balding man with a lined, impassive face.

His name was Anatoli Dmitrevich Sanko, and everyone treated him with caution. Even Gorsky, the titular head of this KGB empire, deferred to him.

Sanko was a man who never raised his voice. Even his gestures were kept to a minimum. If anything surprised him, it was absorbed and evaluated entirely inside his brain. It was partly his imperturbable nature that made people afraid, and partly the knowledge of what his job entailed; but most of all, it was because Sanko had direct family links with the upper echelon of the Central Committee, and therefore enjoyed not only political patronage, but protection. He was a killer, whose father-in-law was one of the three most powerful men in the land.

Sanko ran the Executive Action Department of the KGB, known as Department V, specializing in *mokrie dela*.*

* Literally ''wet affairs'': the spilling of blood.

Department V also had the theoretical ability to sabotage the transport and communications facilities of foreign nations, and paralyze public utilities. It maintained its own foreign networks, separate from the other arms of the KGB. Sanko ran his own agents, his own illegals. Occasionally, if he needed to hire a professional gunman, he did so, using appropriate cutouts and making it almost impossible, if something went wrong, for responsibility to be traced back to him.

The handsome Alexei Sumskoy, in an upholstered chair on Sanko's right, was responsible for training and running the bulk of KGB agents living abroad under false identities, yet even he had no idea of the strength or extent of the illegals network operated by Department V. Sumskoy felt uncomfortable next to Sanko, and tried to hide it by becoming more unapproachable himself.

Igor Vladimirovich Gorsky, thin and upright beneath the portrait of Feliks Dzerzhinsky, tried to maintain some sort of balance between respect for the family power Sanko possessed and the fact that he, Gorsky, was still in charge. It was a tightrope he never managed to stay on for more than a few minutes.

When Gorsky smiled, he smiled first at Sanko. If Sanko proposed a line of action, Gorsky never had a word to say against it. If others felt strongly opposed, it was for them to declare themselves.

Yuri Andreyevich Zhikin was totally unnerved by the head of Department V, although Sanko treated him exactly as he did the others, with quiet courtesy. Zhikin had been known to light a cigarette feverishly at a meeting while another one, hardly smoked at all, smoldered in an ashtray in front of him. Zhikin avoided Sanko's eyes when he could, even though there was nothing malevolent in the man's gaze. Sanko's look was guarded, but that was all. There were others in the KGB whose eyes when angry turned to pools of blankness, and anyone could see there was murder in their hearts: and yet Zhikin could cope better with any of them. He was never able to explain to himself his reaction to Sanko.

He sat across the table, chain-smoking, spilling ashes, and fidgeting miserably. A small pad in front of him was filled with anxious doodles of thick, aggressive arrows, pointing skyward, which he then boxed in with intricate patterns of squares, triangles, and flowers. A fine film of ash covered the paper.

The fifth man, sitting beside Zhikin and looking disagreeably at the mess spreading inexorably toward him, was Colonel Panin, who led the Counterintelligence service and who was a formidable enemy for those whose family connections did not reach quite as high as Sanko's.

Gorsky opened the meeting by outlining the events in New York the previous day.

"It doesn't surprise us that the DIA is still interested in the Armenian," he said, mostly for Sanko's benefit. "In fact, we anticipated it, which is why security precautions have been at their high level. I have called you together, comrades, to review the position. Our resident in New York reads significance into the fact that the agent seen following Rabinovich was the man Lyle. He is, as we know, a senior DIA operative, and he along with another man, Ross, was with Rabinovich when we got him back. The question the rezident raises is whether we should now take advantage of the opportunity which has presented itself."

Zhikin broke in nervously. "The talks are going well, so why don't we just withdraw Rabinovich? We've made our point. We can say now he is not well, and fly him out."

Panin, a sluggish figure whose eyes darted from one face to another, said, "But if we do, we lose an opportunity to inflict damage on the DIA."

"Sooner that than lose the talks," Zhikin observed,

scratching abstractedly at an arm. "Sooner that than have the capitalist media reporting the KGB has been engaged in gang warfare with American agents in Manhattan, while their governments talk about reducing tension."

Sanko spoke softly, but the effect could not have been more electric if he had shouted. "Can we not have it both ways?" he asked, and everyone became still. "You, Yuri Andreycvich," Sanko said, addressing Zhikin directly, "you are skilled at this sort of thing. Surely it is possible for us to deal with Lyle without harming the talks. Ross too, if they are still a team. It would be in our interests to get rid of both these men, and after all, in this case it is not we who are the aggressors. It is they. They are the ones seeking to kidnap a member of our delegation. Is that not true?" He glanced around for assent and received it immediately. "So if any blame is to fall, it should fall on them." He permitted himself a mirthless smile. "We can make sure it falls on them. If they attack one of our negotiators, it will then be up to us to decide, in the glare of publicity, whether the talks should be abandoned, and we will delight the world—will we not?—when we put the aggressive American action to one side in the interests of all mankind. Yuri Andreyevich, your Department could surely give us that victory."

Zhikin stubbed a cigarette into the cluttered ashtray and blew through his lips. "Yes," he agreed. "As long as it is clear that the Americans are at fault. And that must be clear from the beginning. It's very difficult to recover a lost advantage."

"We will make it clear," Sanko promised. He turned his attention to Panin. "From you, Leonid Dmitrevich, I need detailed information. I must know the DIA surveillance routines."

Panin hunched his shoulders, and his eyes flickered from Gorsky at the head of the table to Sumskoy beside him and back to Gorsky. He seemed unable to focus on Sanko. "I will reinforce our men at the Residency," he offered diffidently. "I will put our best officers onto following and observing Lyle and any others involved."

Sanko shook his head slightly. "That is not what I want, comrade Colonel," he said. "I don't want the KGB involved at all." He looked directly at Panin, forcing him to meet his gaze. "Naturally I have the greatest respect for your officers," he added formally, "but I don't want to risk them being seen by the DIA. I want the Americans to feel secure and unobserved because they will be unobserved. At least by us."

"So then?" Panin asked.

Sanko replied, "I think we might make use of your excellent contact in the CIA, Leonid Dmitrevich. Let him do our work for us."

Panin stared for a moment, uncomprehending, but at last he gave a gruff bark of laughter. "Why not?" he agreed, as the plan became clear to him. "Our agent Feliks is well placed for this. He can suggest to the Director that the DIA is once again determined to wreck the talks. And that after all is not a lie. He can get a watch put on them which will confirm their surveillance of Rabinovich, and he can report back to us."

Zhikin began to smile, and Gorsky looked particularly pleased.

"That is precisely what I want," Sanko said. "When we know how the ground lies, we will be able to make the appropriate plan."

"The CIA will make it easy for our men to be waiting for Ross and Lyle, that I promise you," Panin said.

If it had been his nature to reveal his feelings, Sanko would have looked pained. The head of Counterintelligence still didn't understand.

"That is not what I want," Sanko said. "Our men will

not come into direct contact with them at all. I want to use Rabinovich as bait, like a goat tethered to a stake. I want them to take that bait, by themselves. And when they do, let them find it poisoned.''

If Yardley was angry at having let Ross take the weekend off, it was more than offset by the realization that at last, the Soviets were relaxing their guard.

He called the agents to his office for a conference, and instructed them that in future Ross and Lyle would be on permanent weekend duty. Now that Rabinovich was being allowed out, there were unacceptable risks in having only one man responsible for surveillance.

''I know this cuts into your, uh, other activities, David,'' Yardley said, remembering the Saturday monitoring he had seen earlier, ''but that can't be helped. From now on, you'll be in New York from Friday night to early Monday morning. If Rabinovich is starting to wander around, we need to see if we can find a pattern. Bear in mind that you might have to call in reinforcements. I want to hear some sane, practical proposal for taking Rabinovich without causing an outcry. It ought to be relatively easy. After all, he does want to defect.''

''I wish I believed that, General,'' Ross said. ''If it is true, why would they let him back? Why would they let him walk around town? Why relax security? It doesn't make sense.''

Yardley brooded a moment. ''Well, whatever the case,'' he said finally, ''take him first and sort it out later. But for God's sake, make it look like a defection, even if it isn't.''

Lyle could see Ross on the point of arguing, so he said quickly, ''Yes, sir,'' and stood up to leave, adding, ''If you don't mind, David and I ought to get back to our files.'' Ross caught Lyle's eye and saw in it an unmistakable warning. He followed reluctantly.

"What was that about, Clive?" he asked in the corridor.

"I could see you were about to launch into another debate on morality. I didn't think I could take it on a Monday morning."

"I guess I might have, at that."

"There's no point. Yardley's right. We do have to get Rabinovich, whether he's willing to come or not. A lot hangs on it."

Ross shrugged. "Revenge."

"I don't know why you've gone so cool on the concept of revenge, David. It can be a pretty noble ideal, particularly in a job like ours. You'll learn that for yourself one day, I guess."

"Is that what happened to you? Did you discover the nobility of revenge after you joined?"

Lyle's face became impassive. "Don't mock. No, it was something I'd always felt, but working here reinforced it. And don't forget the other reasons for wanting Rabinovich—the main ones. He knows something about the Soviet neutron program that'll stop the talks, and if we stop the talks, we prevent a neutron ban . . ."

"And if we do that, we head off the possibility of a nuclear war in the next decade. Yeah, I know," Ross conceded.

"Not only the next decade, but forever. That's not a bad prospect, is it? Even if it means Rabinovich goes to the wall."

"I guess."

They turned down the corridor toward their office. "Now tell me about skydiving. How did it go?" Lyle asked, and could see from the look on Ross's face that the neutron files were going to have to wait.

The agent known as Feliks received his orders on Tuesday night.

Colonel Panin of KGB Counterintelligence considered Feliks so important, so highly placed within the CIA, that all communications with him, except in times of gravest national emergency, were carried out using Gammas: the so-called "one-time pads" to which the Soviets entrust their most important secret messages.

A Gamma pad is no bigger than a postage stamp, yet it contains up to 250 pages, with dozens of five-digit groups printed on each page. For every Gamma issued to an agent, a duplicate copy exists in Moscow. When a spy has used one page, he destroys it, usually by burning. The attraction of Gammas is that every page of every pad is unique and is used only once. The system is regarded as 95 percent secure, which in these days of sophisticated electronic espionage is an enviable rate.

The Gamma Panin sent to Feliks was carried by a Soviet courier and lodged with one of the two KGB rezidenturas in New York. From there, a separate Gamma instruction to the agent who ran Feliks in the United States gave details of its delivery.

Feliks received two copies of *The New York Times* on Wednesday morning, an apparent mistake in delivery. On one of them, a page was partly torn. He searched it for the clue.

That night after work, Feliks went to a movie theater and watched a Goldie Hawn comedy. He sat on the aisle, making sure there were vacant seats farther on. Shortly after he'd settled down, the lights dimmed: and a few seconds after that, someone tried to squeeze past in front of him. Feliks rose to make more room, and the man thanked him. The Gamma changed hands as they crossed.

Feliks had seen the film before, but he stayed to the end. Then he went home and began work, deciphering.

On the basis of his instructions, he decided not to make

a direct approach, but instead to tip off legitimate political contacts.

By noon on Thursday, the Director of the CIA had received telephone calls from two congressmen and a senator, which he regarded as sufficiently serious to summon an informal meeting of his senior aides.

The meeting convened in the Director's office at Langley: an imposing room, not quite as big as General Yardley's in Washington, with a desk that was merely large, rather than the DIA kingsize model. Size and trappings are how bureaucracies signal relative importance.

Of the three who took seats around the Director's desk only Feliks knew why they had been called.

"These Defense bastards may be having another go at wrecking the SALT talks," the Director began bluntly. He outlined the telephone conversation and reminded his officers—although he scarcely needed to—that the politicians who raised the alarm were among the CIA's best friends on Capitol Hill. Their concern should therefore be taken seriously.

"At this stage," he said, "all I want to do is find out what's going on. There's no point asking Lyndon Yardley because he certainly wouldn't tell me. As you all know, we're not on the best of terms since his boys lost Rabinovich." Glances were exchanged, and smiles too. "So we're going to have to find out for ourselves. I want to know who they've got on the surveillance, where and how they work. I do not, repeat do not, want any member of this Agency intervening. Not yet. I want us to stay out of sight. I expect daily reports. Any questions?"

There were none. By early afternoon, the existing CIA presence in the United Nations building had been reinforced and was at work trying to uncover the identities of the Defense team that would inevitably be there. This was more difficult than they expected because the DIA men were carrying CIA identifications, as well as routine UN documents, and they were happy to present both on proper demand, because they were perfect replicas.

There was nothing to report to Langley at the end of that day, and it was not until after lunch on Friday that someone thought to compare the number of CIA agents assigned to the UN with the actual headcount, and found a disparity of three men. After that, it was a matter of elimination.

The CIA Director was outraged that Yardley should have given his men Langley accreditation. He suppressed with difficulty his first instinct to complain immediately to the president. He would save that for later.

On Saturday morning, when Ross and Lyle arrived at the building near the Residency to resume their surveillance, CIA agents were already in place along the street. Video cameras with telephoto lenses had been set up on rooftops on either side to monitor and record all movements.

Clive Lyle parked one vehicle—another cab, this time black—around the corner while Ross found a space for his Avis rental car just outside the building they used. They went inside and waited.

Just after lunch, Rabinovich again left the Residency with four KGB officers and three other members of the delegation and set off for a thirty-minute walk.

Ross followed on foot, while Lyle went to get the cab. If it became necessary for them to join up later, it would be a simple matter for Clive to put on the "For Hire" light, and Ross to flag him down.

For the watching CIA, it did not need an analysis of the videos to pinpoint the Defense base. Two agents spotted it immediately, and on their instructions, a cameraman took an excellent series of 35mm photographs of David Ross walking casually along the street after the Russians.

On Sunday, the KGB provided another opportunity.

Rabinovich and his group were taken in two Embassy limousines for a drive around the Central Park area. After twenty minutes, they returned to the Residency where they let off one passenger from each car: but not Rabinovich.

Lyle, thinking the outing had ended, was already parking his cab, while Ross walked down the street to observe them disembarking. He was surprised and thrown to see only two men get out before the limousines moved off again, and he turned back, trying not to hurry but nonetheless moving at a fair speed to alert Lyle. The CIA, observing from top floor windows, laughed loudly.

On Monday, there was no sign of Lyle and Ross.

Agents watching air traffic movements reported they had caught the early morning shuttle to Washington.

That night, Feliks had a drink in the almost deserted bar at the Algonquin Hotel, sitting at a table in the alcove. There was only one other customer: a man doing a crossword puzzle and drinking whisky.

Feliks finished his martini, paid for it and, after the waiter had cleared the table, left silently.

The man with the crossword moved over to the alcove, and while he pondered an apparently difficult clue, he had little trouble locating the Gamma fixed to the underside of the table.

By ten o'clock, the KGB had decoded the message and the first pattern of DIA movements was before them. It seemed very satisfactory.

David Ross went directly to his own apartment that Monday evening, having finished for the day. There was, at last, the feeling that something was moving, that the Russian defenses were being lowered. Soon they would be able to consider specific plans for snatching Rabinovich. Best of all, there was no sign that the talks were drawing to a close. They seemed as far from a conclusion as ever.

He and Lyle would be able to take their time, and make sure the plan they came up with represented the best possible option.

Yet Ross felt tense and caged. He hated the emptiness of the apartment, where everything was exactly as it had been when he walked out days earlier; and there was no expectation of Elaine returning for another couple of weeks.

Ross would have liked to phone Clive, to invite him over, or go around there: at any rate, to spend time with one of the few men he was cleared to talk to freely. But Lyle had mentioned having a date. Ross wondered idly who he was seeing.

He threw away a pint of milk that had gone sour in the refrigerator and fixed himself a drink. He put a record on the stereo, but Bach neither soothed nor provided mental stimulation. There was nothing he particularly wanted to read. He turned on the television and switched through eight channels, before banishing the picture in disgust.

Then he did what he had in his heart been wanting to do all along. He showered, changed, and drove to Julie's apartment.

Ross didn't telephone. He hardly felt it necessary any longer. Until Friday when he left for New York, he had spent every night there, barring the Monday when he made a half-hearted effort to stop falling into a routine.

But he had not slept well that night, and on Tuesday when he phoned, heard her voice, and remembered what they were like together, his resolution cracked. Hell, they only had a short time before Elaine got back, and it was ridiculous not to make use of every moment.

Ross pressed her doorbell and waited. When Julie opened it, she was obviously pleased to see him. She put her arms around his neck, kissed him, and led him in. And that was when he saw Andy Marcus, relaxing in the living room.

"Hi Dave," Marcus said cheerfully.

Ross felt a pang of jealousy. How long had Marcus been there? All weekend?

Julie, who was sensitive to atmospheres, understood immediately what Ross was thinking and decided to ignore it. David knew the rules: if he faced a psychological block, he would just have to get himself over it.

She made it obvious by the way she held his hand and kissed the side of his head when he sat down that she and Ross were more than friends, but this was mainly for Ross's benefit. Andy Marcus knew the score.

"How's the ankle?" Ross asked, trying to keep things on an even level while he got used to the situation.

"It's still sore to walk," Andy said, "and you should see it when the bandages are off. Oh man, it's black and purple and green. But they say it'll be okay in a couple of weeks." He grinned at Julie. "It hasn't cramped my style too badly otherwise."

"Andy has to make love with his feet hanging over the end of the bed so his ankle's clear of the action," Julie explained, dispelling any doubts Ross might have about what had been going on during the weekend. This was the take-it-or-leave-it method she used when she was running two or more men at the same time. But she found herself increasingly hoping David Ross would not be put off, and she watched for his reaction.

Ross managed a smile, which showed he was trying: a good sign. She kissed his forehead.

"What can I get you to drink?" she asked.

"A dry martini, please."

"How about you, Andy?"

"I guess I could take another beer, thanks," Marcus said. Then to Ross, "We missed you at the club this weekend. There were some good jumps."

"How many near misses?" Ross asked, doing his best to be friendly and relaxed.

Marcus laughed. "None. Not even a scratch. Julie said you had to work."

"Yes, that's right. I was out of town."

"Bad luck. You coming next weekend?"

"I'm afraid not. I'm going to be tied up Saturdays and Sundays for a while yet."

Andy looked shrewdly at Ross. "Don't mind me asking this, Dave, and please don't feel uptight about answering: but have you given up on the club? A couple of jumps enough for you?"

Julie, preparing the drinks at the bar in the corner, waited for his reply.

"No, I haven't had enough," Ross said. "Not nearly. Hell, I've only just started. I've still got my first free fall to do, and that's four jumps away. But this thing's come up, and I don't have a choice."

"I thought you government guys worked regular office hours," Marcus commented.

"Well, normally we do. But when there's a panic on, they act like they own you. That's what's happening now. It couldn't have come at a worse time really." He smiled at Julie. "I was pretty close to finding out whether there's something better than a really spectacular orgasm."

Marcus took him up on the remark. "From what Julie tells me, you'd need to go out from about 100,000 feet and snort coke to get the same effect."

Ross was washed by conflicting emotions. First, pleasure at receiving a compliment of that sort from a man he still considered a rival; and second, unease because Julie had been discussing him in those terms. Ross asked, "What have you been saying, Julie?"

She brought him his martini. "The truth," she replied. "Only the truth. You'd have been proud."

"Didn't your mother ever warn you about kissing and telling?" Ross tried to keep his tone light.

"My mother never discussed kissing," Julie said, "or anything connected with that subject. But Andy wanted to know about you. You know how you guys are about each other." She deepened her voice, pretending to mimic Marcus. " 'How big is he? Is he bigger than me?' " Andy roared with laughter. "So I thought it fair to tell him. After all, you knew about Andy from my poem, didn't you?"

"I'm glad you're staying with the club, Dave," Marcus said, changing the subject. "I'll be back to normal soon, and once you've got a few free falls under your belt, we might try a link-up."

Ross was pleased. "I'd like that. I don't know when it'll be, though. Maybe a while yet."

"Well, whenever it is, I'll be there."

As the evening went on, Ross found himself relaxing completely, growing to like Marcus, and no longer minding about him and Julie—genuinely not minding. He was learning an entirely new type of relationship. He liked it, because within its easy structure he could move at will. It didn't threaten his relationship with Elaine, because it wasn't in competition. Julie didn't have marriage as a goal, nor did she need the permanency of living with any one man. She wanted Ross when he had the time and the inclination, and Andy. And probably others, too, for all he knew.

Ross nevertheless regretted that Andy was at her apartment that night because it seemed to rule out the possibility of him staying over, especially as Andy was making no move to leave, and it was getting late.

Ross finshed his drink and rose to go. "Goodnight, you two," he said. "I've got to be getting along now."

Julie raised an eyebrow. "Why?" she asked. "I thought you were going to sleep here."

Ross caught Marcus's eye. "Well," he said uncertainly, "isn't Andy . . .?"

"Oh, Andy's staying." There was a silence while Ross thought about that. "You don't mind, do you?" Julie asked. "Does the idea shock you?"

"Uh, no," Ross said, reluctantly.

"Scare you?"

"No."

"Well then?"

Ross stared at the two of them. "Stay, Dave. It'll be good," Marcus said.

"I guess I might as well," Ross said.

Julie smiled at him as pleased as if he'd just passed an important test.

General Lyndon Yardley frowned over the latest batch of reports and monitoring contained in files on his mahogany desk. David Ross's personal dossier was being constantly updated and cross-referenced. The newest addition was Andrew Charles Marcus.

There was nothing about Ross's friends to give the DIA cause for concern on security grounds, and personal morals were of no interest to Yardley. Ross, Lyle, and all his other agents had to sort out that aspect of their lives for themselves without interference.

But the general area of health was very close to the Director's heart. He was prepared, in consultation with Dr. Peter Barry at the DIA hospital, to turn a blind eye to a moderate intake of soft drugs on an occasional basis, just as he didn't mind agents getting drunk, infrequently and on their own time, even though both these circumstances were potential matters of security concern. The thought of a maudlin, loose-tongued Ross, for example, talking to strangers about how he came to join the DIA, or his first

assignment inside Russia, would be very serious indeed, a
case for instant dismissal and possibly sanctioning which,
in Agency parlance, meant death. But Yardley believed,
and so far he had not been proved wrong, that his men
were sufficiently aware of the seriousness of their calling,
and of the stakes involved, to keep their mouths shut on
professional affairs when, to everyone else, their defenses
were down. It was when the drugs became harder that
Yardley took a more serious view.

Lucy opened the door to his office and announced, "Dr.
Barry's here, General."

Yardley looked up. "Good. Bring some coffee, please."

Peter Barry walked in, looking expensive in a well-cut
gray suit and silk tie. "Good morning, Lyndon," he said.
"How are things?"

"Not bad." Yardley waved toward the chairs at the side
of the office. "Make yourself comfortable. I'll join you in
a minute." He packed most of the files into a desk drawer,
which he locked, before going across, carrying Ross's
dossier.

"What's the problem?" Barry asked.

"David Ross."

"Oh?" Barry had a personal interest in the new agent.
"How's he settling in?"

"Pretty well, on the whole. No trouble at home that I'm
aware of. His wife's moving around at the moment, working on some FBI computer scheme we were able to set up
for her, so she's keeping busy."

"I'm glad to hear it."

"And David's making the necessary adjustments. He's
going to be a fine agent, no doubt about it. But . . . well,
take a look at this and tell me what you think."

Yardley extracted the monitoring from Julie Klein's apartment the night before. Attached to the front was a synopsis
and analysis, and Barry read carefully through this first

page. Yardley thought he saw the glimmer of a smile at one point, but then his face became impassive. When he was finished, he found the passage that interested them both, and read it carefully.

"Well, what do you think?" Yardley asked, when the doctor had placed the documents on the glass table in front of him.

"I tend to agree," Barry said. "It sounds as if they were using cocaine. It's a pity the bug missed that critical section. Isn't that typical of modern technology? But whatever it was, Ross took some."

"I don't like it," Yardley said.

"No, nor do I. It doesn't have to become a habit, but it is the sort of thing we should watch."

"What do I do? Call him in and give him hell?"

"You could. It wouldn't do any harm."

"Except I don't particularly want him to know we're in her bedroom."

"But he does know that, Lyndon. All our people know they're liable to surveillance. For God's sake, I know it."

"Yes, but only in principle. It's one thing being aware of the possibility, and another to know specifics. I guess I don't want to cramp his style. Do you understand that?" Barry nodded. "Ross is still finding his feet. He's getting used to the way we are, and to what he's becoming. There's a lot he has to learn. He needs to develop Defense instincts. He'll get there, I'm sure, but he has to do it by himself. So until he's really ours, I don't want to seem to be busting into his life more than I have to. And the question I want to ask you is this: do I have an alternative?"

"Well, you could wait and see if he did it again. It might have been a one-shot."

"It's a gamble, though, isn't it? How long does it take to get hooked on cocaine?"

"It varies with individuals, but it's certainly more than a

couple of times. Some people claim to be occasional users for years without becoming addicted, although I don't know about that.''

There was a knock at the door, and Lucy arrived with a tray of fresh-brewed coffee. Yardley sighed as he stirred his cup. "I wish I knew the best way to handle him. I'd have him in for a man-to-man talk if I thought it would help, but inevitably there's a certain distance between us.''

"Then why don't you have a word with Lyle and ask him to handle Ross?''

"That's not a bad idea," Yardley said. "I guess Clive might be able to do it.''

"Lyle's been around quite a bit himself, if I remember," Peter Barry said.

"Indeed he has," the Director replied, a fraction grimly.

After the doctor left, Yardley sent for Lyle and spent the best part of an hour with him. Clive had already gathered that his partner was sleeping with Julie Klein although not from anything David had said. A series of facts made it inevitable, starting with Ross going to the same skydiving club as Julie while his wife was out of town and coming into the office most mornings looking pretty pleased with himself. In isolation, these meant nothing, but taken together, there wasn't a jury in the world who, having looked at Julie Klein, would fail to convict. And that was without seeing, as Lyle had done in the showers after their workouts, the nail marks on Ross's back, and the fading bruise of teeth just above his collarbone.

The news about Andy Marcus was a surprise though. While his face remained impassive, because Yardley was scrutinizing him with care, Lyle grinned inwardly. Still, he could see what the Director meant about the coke. That was a bad scene.

Lyle replaced the documents on the huge desk and waited for Yardley to say what it was he wanted.

Back in their own office, Clive asked Ross over for dinner that night. He felt if they were relaxing after a few drinks, they might get around to a personal discussion: an old-time bull session. But Ross declined. He had other plans for the evening, and Clive had a fair idea what they were.

"Then come and have a drink before you go out," Lyle insisted.

So Ross went home shortly after five, showered and changed before going to Lyle's.

They drank beer while in the background the Rolling Stones performed loud enough to jam any but the most sophisticated listening devices. Clive kept the conversation low key and personal. He spoke first about himself, often amusingly, telling Ross about the people he got involved with, and his difficulty at the beginning in believing his job could run parallel to his private life.

Ross listened, intrigued, and laughed a lot. What an extraordinary guy Lyle was, he thought; made more so by his total confidence and lack of concern for what others thought of him.

The conversation turned to skydiving, with Ross bemoaning the fact that he was having to delay his first free fall.

"How's Julie?" Clive asked, taking the opening that was presented. "Do you see much of her?"

"Oh yeah, a bit," Ross replied vaguely. "I remember your warning, Clive, but she's a lot nicer than that. Really."

"I'm glad to hear it." Lyle refilled their glasses. "Tell me about her. What's she like?"

Ross sketched her character as he saw it, and spoke about her family. "Did you know she writes erotic verse, Clive? It's really something."

"Yeah, I've read some." His voice was neutral. "Are you gonna be starring in her next slim volume?"

"Christ, I hope not!" Ross was startled at the idea. It certainly hadn't occurred to him. "I mean, she knows I'm married, so she wouldn't do anything stupid. She's not a dumb kid."

Lyle noticed Ross wasn't denying sleeping with her, which was a good sign. He pressed on. "She seems to be a hell of a woman. She sleeps around quite a bit, as you know."

"Don't we all?"

"Yeah, we do. I'm not pointing a finger, you understand. I could hardly do that." He smiled disarmingly. "I'm just saying I guess she could teach me a lot."

"Well, you had your chance, Clive."

"And I blew it. I know. Maybe I'll try again sometime after you two have split up. If you split up."

"Hell, try when you like. There's nothing between Julie and me except friendship and sex."

"That sounds like a lot, Dave."

"Ah, it's not like that. She doesn't make demands. As you say, she sleeps around, and she likes it."

"Is she going with other guys right now?"

Ross paused. "Someone from the club," he said finally. "Name of Andy Marcus. A hell of a nice man."

"So how do you feel about that? No jealousy?"

Ross shrugged. "At the beginning, yes. But not now. That's something Julie's taught me."

"Marcus," Lyle said thoughtfully, as if trying to recall. "I think I've heard of him. Big, looks like a film star."

"That's him."

Lyle had eased the conversation around to the point he wanted, and he moved in to do Yardley's business. "Marcus had better watch himself," he said.

"Why?"

"The word is he's on the cocaine trail. That can be a

bitch. If the Feds don't pull him in, he'll be lucky to keep his physical and mental shape."

"How did you hear that?" Ross asked.

Lyle was evasive. "You know how people talk."

"Come on, Clive. You can do better than that."

"Marcus snorts coke. True?"

A pause. "Okay, true."

"And so does Julie Klein."

Ross inclined his head; maybe.

"And so will you. If you haven't done it already."

"Jesus, they only do it occasionally, along with a couple of million other Americans," Ross said defensively. "It's a harmless social thing, like marijuana. Haven't you ever smoked marijuana?"

"Sure, lots of times."

"Have you snorted coke?"

"No, never."

"Why not?"

Lyle lit a cigarette, using the pause to add weight to his reply. "Because if I did, my job would be on the line. Yardley and Peter Barry think cocaine's the start of a bad scene, and it's not good for the health of their people. They don't care about dope, as long as you use it occasionally, when you're off duty. And of course, as long as you keep your mouth shut."

"Well, Yardley knows I'd never say anything about my work."

"He does know that," Lyle replied seriously. "Otherwise you'd be dead."

Ross grimaced. "I guess so."

"But if you were taking coke, he'd be worried about your health. He'd take you off active operations, put you onto a desk. And if that didn't work, he'd kick you into the street. Or me. Or anyone."

"Shit. Even if you did it once?" Ross was worried.

"No, not if you only did it once. If you tried it again, you might be in trouble."

Ross was overcome by a strange sensation, the realization that Lyle had been reading him like a book. What exactly did Clive know? And how?

Ross took a gulp of his beer. "So this is an official warning," he said, keeping his voice steady.

Lyle shook his head. "No," he said. "This is a talk between friends about a hypothetical case. Listen, let me spell out some things to you. We're pretty close, the two of us. I like working with you. I'm relying on you to save my life at some point. And that's not bullshit. You know the sort of thing we do, the risks we run. I love you like a brother, you bastard, and I don't want to be paired off with some other guy because Yardley kicks you out. Now the fact is, you're hanging around people who snort coke, so it's a fair presumption that at some point, they're going to offer you some. David, you don't need that stuff. But the DIA needs you. I need you, for Christ's sake. Do you hear what I'm saying?"

"Yeah," he said, "I hear, Clive." Then after a pause: "You know, don't you?"

"I only know what you tell me," Lyle said.

"Okay." Ross looked away for a second, and then back. "I did snort coke." Lyle held his gaze while he made his confession. "I did it once, last night. I won't do it again."

"What was it like?" Lyle asked.

"It was pretty good actually," Ross said. "I mean, I could live without it, but it made the evening something spectacular."

Then Ross told Lyle exactly what had happened, everything Clive had read in the monitoring in Yardley's office, and a lot of things that would have had to be seen.

"You going back tonight?" Lyle asked.

"Yes. Elaine's away until the end of next week, and I don't want to waste any time."

"I can understand that." Lyle went to change the record. "What are you going to tell Elaine?"

"Oh Christ, nothing!" Ross said, alarmed. "Nothing at all. As far as I'm concerned, it's just a physical thing with Julie. It doesn't affect my marriage. I guess it would hurt Elaine badly if she knew, and I don't want to do that."

"I think that's smart," Lyle said. "But remember what I said about Julie Klein?"

"Yeah?"

"Well, I say it again, David. Keep your relationship with her, and Andy, and the whole gang in one pigeonhole, away from your wife. And watch Julie, watch her like a hawk. I don't want to badmouth the girl you're going to be sleeping with tonight, but I must tell you, as a friend, that the reputation she's got around town isn't only for her performances between the sheets. It's for what she does out of them. That girl's like an unexploded bomb. Okay?"

Ross didn't believe a word of it, but he appreciated Lyle's concern. He finished his beer and went off to meet Julie and Andy, aware that he had official approval for everything he did, barring the coke, which really was the least important. It was a good feeling.

The KGB let Ross and Lyle draw nearer their quarry.

The next Saturday, Rabinovich, Lappa, and Nikitin—just the three of them—left the Residency at 10:30 and strolled away from the building where the DIA maintained a watch.

From upstairs windows along the street and from rooftops, the CIA continued their monitoring, logging Lyle's and Ross's movements for the Director at Langley, and backing it up with videos.

The Russians walked about fifty yards and stopped. A discussion followed. It seemed as if they had forgotten something. Nikitin returned to the Residency.

That left just Lappa and Rabinovich on the sidewalk, the most relaxed security they'd seen yet.

"Look at that, Dave," Lyle said. "We could almost take him now."

"Yeah. Except Yardley wants it easier than that. A defection, remember."

"The way things are going, maybe he'll have it too."

Ross grunted.

On the sidewalk, Lappa smiled at Rabinovich. "Don't worry," he said. "You're safe with me. Nothing will happen."

"I hope you're right," Rabinovich replied. "I feel someone's looking at me through the sights of a rifle."

Lappa laughed. "Trust me, comrade. Just stay close and do as you're told."

"I will," Rabinovich said. "Don't concern yourself about that."

Lappa offered him a cigarette, but the scientist shook his head and nervously smoothed his thinning black hair. After five minutes, Nikitin returned, and the three resumed their walk.

It was Lyle's turn to follow on foot while Ross went to fetch the car.

They stayed too far back to be able to tell anything of Rabinovich's state of mind. Even when he turned sideways to look into a store window or, unable to restrain himself, glanced back toward them, they could not see how pale his face was, or that his forehead was sweating.

Lappa and Nikitin kept an easy pace. They made routine security checks, the sort of things the DIA would expect, and neither caught sight of the cab, or Lyle. But they were confident the agents were back there somewhere, and that even further behind were the CIA.

They broke their walk at a coffee shop where they took a table near the rear. They placed Rabinovich with his back to the plate glass windows onto the street, making him feel even more wretched and vulnerable.

Lyle saw them enter the shop, and reported to Ross via a small two-way radio, whose microphone was the top button of his open neck shirt.

Ross parked the cab where he could monitor the entrance while Lyle went to see if there was a service alley in the rear, through which the Russians might exit. There was none. Lyle fell back to wait.

Inside, Rabinovich had been persuaded to order cheese-cake, but it stuck to his tongue and the dry roof of his mouth and he nearly choked. He washed it down with coffee so hot it almost scalded him, and then he waited miserably for the KGB to take him home.

After fifteen minutes, they retraced their steps, walking near the yellow cab, in the front seat of which Ross sat, apparently indifferent, reading a newspaper. He watched them through his rearview mirror until they'd turned the corner, with Lyle strolling after them on the other side of the road and a reasonable distance back. Then he started the engine and drove around the block to resume his part of the surveillance.

Rabinovich returned to the safety of the Residency, weak with relief, and slumped into a chair feeling drained. He wanted to go to bed and sleep.

"You did well, comrade," Lappa said, patting his shoulder. "You can rest now."

But the following day, they went out again, this time to a cinema. Rabinovich sat in the darkness between Lappa and Nikitin, remembering the other Times Square cinema on that terrible day, a hundred years ago, it seemed.

The KGB men guffawed beside him, while Rabinovich, rigid and unseeing, wondered if the Americans were moving in to strike.

In fact, Clive Lyle, a less distinctive figure than Ross, had walked in soon after him and taken a back seat against the wall.

Ross waited in the street, in case the Russians came out the side exit. If they did, Lyle would not follow them. With the corridors and staircases, it was too easy an ambush.

When the movie was over, Rabinovich and his escorts left through the front entrance and returned to the Residency.

"How did you like the film, Viktor?" Lappa asked cheerfully as they walked along the street.

Rabinovich felt so miserable, he could hardly reply.

General Yardley read through the reports compiled by Lyle and Ross while the agents waited patiently on the leather chairs.

Ross stared at the painting of giant redwoods on the wall in front of him, wondering if the unease he felt so strongly was part of the tension he could expect every time an assignment reached this decisive stage.

But instinct told him it was not that. The problem was Rabinovich.

Something was wrong. The Russian had gained weight since returning to New York, so presumably whatever pressure was on him in Moscow had been removed. But why was he back? Perhaps, Ross thought, he had been lying in the first place when he said he knew a secret sufficiently devastating to abort the talks. Even so, he had tried to defect, and the Russians considered that a grave crime, tantamount in some cases to treason, and punishable by death.

Yet there Rabinovich was a couple of days back, watching a movie with the KGB. It made no sense.

Yardley put the report on the glass table. "So?" he invited.

"I think, General," Lyle said, "we're getting to the stage where we ought to reinforce at weekends and take our chances at a snatch. They're becoming casual, which is what we want. Of course, we can't expect they'll ever let Rabinovich out on his own, but they might let him out of sight for a minute, and that's the chance we have to look for. We need to be ready to move the moment that happens."

"That sounds right," Yardley said. "David, I take it you agree?"

Ross avoided his eye. "I guess so," he said.

"That sounds less than enthusiastic," the General reproved. "If you've got any reservations, now is the moment to speak. We want to consider every option before we commit ourselves."

"No, Clive's right," Ross conceded. "That is the way we'd have to play it. My reservations . . . well, they're more basic than that. I've said it before—I don't trust this whole setup. I think it stinks."

Yardley had seen the monitoring of Ross's views on Rabinovich, apart from what the agent had said to his face. "Are your instincts based on your view of the morality of our action, David?" he asked.

"No, sir," Ross replied. "I accept that we need to find out what Rabinovich has to tell us." He smiled fleetingly. "Even if he goes to the wall."

"Well?"

"It just doesn't feel right. I can't tell you why because I

don't know myself. I realize that isn't very satisfactory, but you asked, and I've told you.''

"What about you, Clive? What do your instincts say?''

"With all respect to David, I don't think it matters—not if we do the snatch right. I agree there is something going on, and God knows what it is. We won't find out until we've got Rabinovich under drugs. We haven't heard anything from our guys in the Soviet Union that helps us, I take it?''

"I'd have told you if we had,'' Yardley said.

"Sorry,'' Lyle said. "I know you would have. The question David's really raising is this: are the Russians setting us up for something?'' He looked at Ross. "Maybe, but I can't see what's in it for them unless we really blow it and they can make propaganda capital. But it's up to us to see we don't. We've got to have enough men in position so that if they let Rabinovich off the leash for thirty seconds . . .'' Lyle clicked his fingers ". . . we take him. He disappears. That means we need to hang loose. We can't make elaborate plans for anything specific because we won't know how it's going to happen until it happens. Of course, there are basic scenarios to work on. And we have to be ready to stage a diversion of some kind, make it hard for the KGB to get after Rabinovich. We might need the extra time.''

"David?'' Yardley asked.

"Yes, sir, I agree. It's our only hope. We've got to be smarter and more flexible than the Russians. We know the dangers. I guess we should be able to do that okay. We're on home ground after all.''

They analyzed the logs of Rabinovich's movements, but there were no conclusions to be drawn. The routes taken had all been different, and so had the purposes of the excursions. They decided to deploy DIA agents at points around New York and when the Soviet intentions became clear on any day, order them to converge at a particular spot, prepared for the kidnap. Lyle would lead, with Ross his number two, and the team would maintain radio contact.

They also agreed on the ground rules. Once they were committed to action, they would not, under any circumstances, abort the kidnap. If it came to a shootout, Rabinovich was their only chance of salvaging something from the mess—he and the secret he claimed to know. If it was good enough to prevent agreement on a neutron ban, the end would justify the means. If it was not, the DIA would be in the worst trouble in its history.

"I don't have to emphasize how important it is that we carry out this operation quickly and cleanly," Yardley said. "We don't want to end up looking like the CIA."

As Rabinovich's cooperation was not assured, they agreed that he was to be immobilized to ensure a combination of silence and speed in getting him away.

With a map of New York spread in front of them and different colored lines tracing the various routes the Russians had taken during their weekend jaunts, they tried to identify places likely to be visited in future. The Soviets had driven around Central Park but might be inclined to walk there later. They wouldn't visit the Statue of Liberty for ideological reasons. A festival of Russian films was showing near Carnegie Hall, and they might attend some part of it.

Yardley arranged to assemble the DIA team for a preliminary briefing the following day before flying to New York for an inspection of the areas allocated to them. By the weekend, they were to have a good working knowledge of streets and alleys, unconventional escape routes, and places they could safely hide.

Ross immersed himself in the details of the planning, aware that their only hope was to be swift and clean as Yardley wanted and, in the end, to be right.

He forced the unease from the forefront of his mind.

Membership of the KGB meeting in the first Chief Directorate's conference hall had dwindled to three. It was no longer necessary for Gorsky to preside because the broad policy outline had already been agreed. There was also no reason for Sumskoy's aloof presence as the illegals he ran in the United States were not involved, at least not at this stage.

The impassive Anatoli Dmitrevich Sanko took the chair beneath the portrait of Feliks Dzerzhinsky, with Panin of Counterintelligence on his right, and the nervous Zhikin, with his brilliant ability to manipulate and sow the seeds of misinformation, on his left.

Sanko's voice was so quiet the other two had to lean forward to hear. He called first for a report from Panin on surveillance near the Residency and then on Zhikin to say what stage the talks had reached.

"Everything is running smoothly, comrade," Zhikin told him, brushing away ashes that had somehow dusted the table. "As you know, the negotiations are progressing slowly, but it is our decision that this should be so. I see no sign of a cooling in the American attitude toward a neutron ban."

Sanko nodded. "Good. I think we're ready for the final stage. We've exhibited the bait, and we know Ross and Lyle have been sniffing after it. Soon they will want to take it, and we must dictate the pace on this, too. Comrades, I have a plan. Please listen closely, and if there is anything that seems to you a miscalculation or an unreasonable danger, I ask you to speak now. You should know, Yuri Andreyevich," he said to Zhikin, "that I welcome constructive criticism at this stage. I don't care if every component of my plan is taken apart and studied with the utmost intensity. If I am persuaded that something is wrong—or even better, that the whole thing will not work—you will see me at my most happy, and I will speak of your virtues whenever I get the chance. However," he added, scrutinizing Zhikin's face, "it is later that I become less tolerant. If anything goes wrong, I need only hear a comrade say 'I knew it would,' and I ask myself: if he knew, why did he not speak? Is he for us, or against us? I can, in those circumstances, be an uncomfortable adversary. I mention this, Yuri, because we have not worked together before, and these are things you ought to know."

Zhikin fumbled for a fresh cigarette.

"So we understand each other," Sanko said. "That is good. Now when you hear my plan, you will be able to speak freely about its demerits."

Sanko sketched out what he had in mind. Then he went through it again, in detail. When he had finished, he sat back. "Well?" he asked.

Panin's eyes flickered from Zhikin to the Dzerzhinsky portrait over Sanko's head and finally, reluctantly, to Sanko himself. "It is good," he admitted. "I find no quarrel with it."

"Yuri?"

Zhikin drew deep on his cigarette, seemingly lost in thought. They waited expectantly. "It is not good," he replied at last. "The plan is brilliant."

"Then we are agreed," Sanko said. "I shall send out the appropriate orders."

Clive Lyle recognized the voice on the telephone although the man hadn't identified himself.

To someone listening in, the conversation would have been smooth and easy, with no reason to read anything into it beyond the fact that two obviously good friends were arranging to meet for a drink and didn't find it necessary to specify where: obviously a spot well known to them. There was a bit of good-natured bantering before the connection broke.

When he left his apartment, Lyle took care to ensure he was not followed. He made the rendezvous well in time and, taking a booth at the back, ordered a beer.

He had known Steven Dibelius for a long time although they met only occasionally. Dibelius wanted to join the DIA, but it was unlikely he ever would; not formally, at least, although his security credentials checked out and he had served as a Marine officer in Vietnam. But Dibelius had first been recruited by Langley, and there was an unwritten Defense law banning sideways transfers.

Although Dibelius knew this from the beginning, he tried anyway. He'd heard Lyle's name and sought him out to see if there was any way around the rule. Lyle consulted with Yardley and reported that there might be, under certain conditions. For several months, without Dibelius fully realizing what was happening, Lyle became his case officer, running him as a Defense mole within the CIA and giving him all the care, encouragement, and attention that would have been his had he worked for the KGB itself. As far as Yardley was concerned, it was sometimes only a matter of degree anyway.

When Dibelius finally caught on to what Lyle had done and realized there had never been any hope of him joining, he became very angry. It took all Lyle's powers of persuasion, physical as well as mental, to convince Dibelius that he was, in all but name, a Defense man whose territory was the tangled and sometimes infiltrated corridors of Langley. That was his assignment, until the end of his career.

Dibelius eventually accepted the situation.

Within the CIA, his was a rising star, and both Lyle and Yardley were pleased with the information he turned over to them. Unfortunately for the DIA, Dibelius had been on an assignment in Europe when the KGB took Rabinovich from the Maryland safe house or there would have been a good chance of him hearing about the planned treachery.

Lyle spotted Dibelius as soon as he walked in and waved at him. They shook hands. "Good to see you, Steve," Lyle said. "What'll you have?"

"A beer, I guess."

Lyle placed the order and looked across the table.

Dibelius was a rangy man but very strong, as Lyle knew from the settling-in days of their professional relationship when Dibelius launched an unexpected attack as a means of expressing disappointment at what seemed then like a double cross. Dibelius's features were sharp and his eyes watchful. DIA security checks showed he was not particularly successful with women, not interested in men, and that he had no close friends. He was a loner.

"What brings you to Washington?" Lyle asked.

"This and that," Dibelius shrugged, waiting until the waitress had served his drink and pushed fresh bowls of olives and peanuts onto the table.

Lyle maintained silence until she was out of earshot. There was no one in the next booth. He raised an eyebrow. "Okay, let's have it."

"We've got an operation on," Dibelius said. "I only heard about it a couple of days back, and I thought I ought to drop in and see you. It could be the usual pickle factory bullshit, in which case I'm wasting your time, but you'd better be the judge of that. We're doing a big surveillance number in New York."

"Oh? Who's the target?"

"You are. You and David Ross. They think you're planning to snatch this Russian guy, Rabinovich, and the Director's about to complain to the President."

*   *   *

Lyndon Yardley had already received Dibelius's report and was discussing the implications with Lyle and Ross when the Secretary of Defense called on the secure telephone to ask what the hell was going on.

"Yes, sir," Yardley said. "We're watching these bastards every step of the way." He glanced at his agents and grimaced. "Oh no, that's ridiculous. Why would we want to do a thing like that? Now if Rabinovich decided to defect again, that's a different matter. Naturally, we'd want to make sure the CIA didn't just hand him back . . . Well, don't you want to hear what he has to say? I sure as hell do . . . Of course it might be bullshit, but we won't know that until we've heard him out. It's his First Amendment right, isn't it? You want to deny him that? . . . Listen, don't worry. If he did defect and it turned out he wanted to tell us about the potato harvest, I'll take him back to the Soviet Embassy myself . . . Yeah, well thanks for letting me know. You know what these Langley guys are like. Sometimes I wonder whose side . . . okay, okay, . . . Well, reassure the President. He has no cause for concern, I promise you."

Yardley hung up, expelling his breath in a puff of exasperation and worry. "That, gentlemen," Yardley said flatly, "means my job's on the line. If you fuck up, I'll be out of this office in disgrace within twelve hours." Yardley almost never swore, and the effect was considerable.

"We'll do our best, General," Lyle promised.

"Yeah, I know you will," Yardley said. "It had better be good enough. There's a lot riding on this operation, Clive—not just my job, because the Chiefs of Staff will see to it the President appoints a fine successor, but the entire Agency. Can you imagine how it will be if we have Congressional committees rifling through our files, imposing restrictions, appointing watchdogs . . . ?"

The red scrambler phone buzzed again. Yardley returned quickly to his desk. They could see his fingers scratching slowly in the spiky gray hairs: the Director's only nervous habit. The Secretary of Defense was back on the line.

". . . No, no problem. What can I do for you?"

Yardley's hand froze on his head and he listened, unmoving, for what seemed a long time. At last he said, "Well, I'll be . . . How long did they say? . . . They didn't mention Rabinovich specifically, did they? No, of course they wouldn't . . . Okay, thanks for letting me know."

When he hung up, Yardley stared at Ross and Lyle with a peculiar expression.

"The Soviets have called a temporary halt to the talks," he told them. "They're going back to Moscow at the beginning of next week. Konev says unofficially that there'll be changes in their team when they come back. No details, of course, but no prizes for guessing who.

"That means," Yardley continued, "it's this weekend or never. How do you feel?"

"We feel fine," Lyle said. "If they give us even half a decent chance, we'll take Rabinovich. You have my word for that, General."

"That's good enough for me," Yardley said.

Saturday came.

Lyle and Ross reached the building near the Soviet Residency shortly before dawn, unseen by the CIA, who had not expected them so early and who, although in place, were not yet watching efficiently.

Elsewhere in Manhattan, a team of more than a hundred DIA men and women took up their positions and awaited orders.

It was hard to tell exactly when the sun rose because the

sky was heavy and threatening, and only a dismal light leaked through.

Lyle and Ross shared sandwiches and a thermos of coffee at around eight. While they were eating, the first big drops of rain began to fall. They stared at each other in disbelief. It was all they needed.

Then it poured.

Within minutes, the street was awash, and it was impossible even to see the building opposite. Rumbles of thunder and the noise of the rain made conversation difficult. The morning darkened. Street lights came back on.

"Shit," Lyle said. "If this keeps up, I wouldn't give two bits for the chances of anyone leaving the Residency."

"We wouldn't be able to see them if they did," Ross pointed out. "You think I should go stand where I can watch the door?"

"Are you volunteering?"

"Sure." Ross picked up a raincoat, buttoned it tight, and raised the collar to stop the water running down his neck. Lyle tossed him a hat.

The rain was almost like a physical assault, battering him as he hunched his shoulders, soaking the legs of his trousers below the raincoat and seeping into his shoes. Ross's feet were squelching in water before he got to the Residency.

Even from the edge of the opposite sidewalk, it was hard to see more than an undefined dark hulk of the Soviet building. Ross glanced up and down to check for traffic before stepping off the curb. Gutter water gushed over his feet and, in seconds, no unprotected part of him had escaped a thorough soaking. He splashed through another torrent on the other side.

Ross stood a few feet from the Residency, peering in. He could just make out the front door.

Had the rain suddenly cut off, like a tap being turned, Ross would have found himself staring at Lappa, who was

looking from a hallway window at the streaming, impene-
trable grayness that separated them.

Lappa cursed with low and malevolent peasant invective
that continued for many seconds without repetition. Nikitin
watched silently farther back in the hallway.

At last he said, "It's not so bad, comrade. This rain is
too heavy to last."

"Huh!" Lappa snorted derisively. "It will pour the
whole weekend. And then where will we be? Answer that,
comrade. Would you like to send the message to Moscow
telling them their big plan has been rained off?"

Nikitin lit a cigarette. "Luckily," he said, "that is not
my responsibility. Nor is it yours."

That was true. Lappa felt slightly mollified. "Anyway," he said, reluctant to abandon the disagreeable mood
which so suited the vile weather, "I want to be finished
with the whole thing. I tell you, when the Jew is gone, I
will drink so much vodka even you will be surprised. If I
have to smile at him for another day, or look at his stupid
face, or say 'Don't worry, comrade; trust me, comrade,' I
think I'll . . ."

Lappa caught Nikitin's warning movement and stopped
abruptly. They stared to the side, down the corridor. Someone was coming, but the lighting was too bad to be able to
make out who. The person turned into an entrance farther
down, and there was the faint sound of a door closing.

Lappa shrugged. "You know what I mean, anyway."

"Yes," Nikitin acknowledged. "I know what you mean."

Lappa checked his watch. It was a few minutes before
8:30, the time designated for the briefing. "We'd better
go," he said. "Comrade Kirichenko's mood will be no
better than mine, I guarantee it. We'd better not be late."

They walked along the corridor and flashed their passes
at the plainclothes men guarding the entrance to the security wing.

General-leytenant Kirichenko's office was bathed in warm yellow light, a pleasant change from the unrelieved gray and black everywhere else on this miserable morning. Kirichenko was not in an evil temper as Lappa had predicted, but sat at his desk, relaxed and confident.

Two other KGB men were already there.

"It seems that one of our comrades has been held up by the rain," Kirichenko said. "No matter, I will brief him separately when he comes. Now, according to the weather forecast, the storm will be over soon, and we can expect a sunny afternoon. So this is only a temporary setback which will make our Defense friends still more eager to get their hands on Rabinovich."

Lappa, who had no faith in weather forecasters, capitalist or progressive, gave a derisive grunt, and Nikitin nudged him to be quiet.

Kirichenko crossed to the wall where a large map of the Manhattan area had been pinned onto a board. A route had been marked in red, and Kirichenko indicated it with a wooden stick.

"This is where we are going," he said. "When the weather improves, you will be given a thirty-minute warning. I will speak to Rabinovich myself, and we will make him ready. Comrades Lappa and Nikitin will travel in the limousine with the Armenian, which means you other two, with our missing comrade, must leave fifteen minutes earlier to be in place."

Kirichenko went through the details, pointing out exactly where the DIA should be given the opportunity for the snatch.

When he had finished, he handed the stick to Lappa, and ordered him to repeat what was to be done. Lappa flushed: he hated this sort of test, but Kirichenko was famous for it. After Lappa had gone through the plan, the others dutifully stepped forward for their turns. At last Kirichenko was satisfied.

"Now we must wait for the weather to clear," he said. "I will call you when we are ready to move."

The meeting broke up, with no sign of the storm diminishing. In fact, if anything, it seemed to be getting worse. Lappa peered out of the hall window and found it impossible to see more than a few inches ahead. The Residency was an island in a sea of lashing gray.

On the sidewalk, with cold water seeping higher up the legs of his trousers, David Ross waited, hunched and motionless.

He splashed through the water and across to the other curb, not bothering to hurry because there was no way he could get wetter than he was.

The Residency was only just visible from this distance, but he would be able to tell if anyone stepped more than a few feet beyond the door.

Ross glanced at the sky. It was the color of slate although there was a patch of lightness where the sun was trying to break through. Gradually the storm eased, and Ross pulled back progressively toward the sanctuary of the room where Lyle, hot coffee, and a change of clothing waited.

The first car arrived at the Residency, with a Second Secretary driving. A few minutes later, two men hurried by on the other side of the road, but Ross could recognize only one of them: a cryptographer. The other was short, built like a wrestler, with wavy blond hair, wet with rain. Probably a KGB guard. He hadn't seen him before.

It looked as if it would soon be business as usual. Clive should be able to monitor everything from the window.

Ross unlocked the door and went in. The room was warm and so dry it seemed almost an alien environment.

Water flooded off his hat and raincoat, and his shoes tramped puddles along the carpet.

Lyle had an electric heater on and a towel ready, but there was no other light in the room. Ross stripped off his clothes, rubbed warmth back into his skin with a towel, and dressed quickly.

Lyle poured him a cup of coffee. "Anything?" he asked.

"Not much." Ross told of the arrivals, and Lyle noted them in the logbook.

They settled down to wait. It drizzled for another two hours before finally stopping, and just before noon the sun broke through.

Lyle and Ross ate more sandwiches for lunch and speculated on the chances of Rabinovich and the others venturing out. It did seem to be turning into a reasonable afternoon, and with the freshness of a newly washed Manhattan, the prospects had to be fair.

Inside the Residency, General-leytenant Kirichenko took a light lunch and watched the time. When it was 2:30 he summoned the men assigned to the Rabinovich operation and ordered them to get ready. Three prepared to leave immediately. Lappa and Nikitin went to the library to fetch the bait.

Rabinovich, who had been delighted with the morning's storm because it represented safety, watched the improving weather with apprehension. Now that the sun was shining, his spirits were at their lowest.

He was not surprised to look up from his book and see the guards in the doorway.

"Comrade Kirichenko wants you," Lappa announced.

Rabinovich rose, the now-familiar dampness breaking out in the palms of his hands. He followed them into the security wing.

Kirichenko greeted Rabinovich with cordiality and motioned to the chair directly in front of his desk. The scientist sat, a pathetic mixture of unease and dependence.

"You are a fortunate man, comrade," Kirichenko began, regardng Rabinovich with kindly eyes. "The Central Committee, whose benevolence you have already tasted, has decided there is work you can do for them."

"I am at the disposal of our comrade leaders," Rabinovich said, wondering: What can it be?

"It has not been easy for you these past few weekends, Viktorovich," Kirichenko observed with understanding and apparent sympathy. "I know that. You were not told our purpose in taking you to places where you felt you were at risk. In fact, all the time you have been quite safe. Apart from our comrades here," he nodded at Lappa and Nikitin, "there have been many others in the streets, unknown to you, ensuring you came to no harm."

Rabinovich was relieved. If only they had told him earlier . . .

"But now to the matter at hand. We know that the agents Lyle and Ross are still following you. We believe they will try a kidnap before this weekend is over."

"Rest assured, comrade, I will do nothing . . . I will not leave the Residency at any time . . ."

"The Central Committee wants you kidnapped, Viktor," Kirichenko said, and heard the sharp intake of breath. "Do not be alarmed," he went on. "We will get you back, unharmed. This is my personal promise. We want to demonstrate to the world the true nature of the Americans: show what warmongers they are. And we want to make it easier for us to extract concessions at the talks. These are noble objects, are they not?"

He looked inquiringly at Rabinovich, who felt obliged to nod, without enthusiasm.

"So here is your opportunity to repay the debt you owe the motherland for your earlier . . ." Kirichenko seemed to hunt for a neutral word ". . . actions. You understand what I mean?"

"Yes, comrade," Rabinovich said sadly. He wouldn't have had a choice anyway, but now he also had a moral duty. "I will do whatever you wish."

"Excellent," Kirichenko approved. "It will not be too bad, Viktor, so cheer up. It is in fact a very simple plan. You will leave shortly with your two comrades here, and drive to Central Park. It is very beautiful at this time of year, particularly after the rain. You will like it. At a certain point, a . . ." again he seemed to search for the right word ". . . diversion . . . has been arranged. When it happens, you will leave the comrades and go off by yourself. Walk around the park. That is when we can expect the Americans to move in. But they will be gentle with you, Viktor. After all, first they want to talk to you, do they not? But at an appropriate moment, before they do, we will come and bring you home." Kirichenko smiled. "That's all there is to it."

"But, comrade, how can you be sure of reaching me before . . . of course, I will tell them nothing! But if they use drugs?"

"We know that." He motioned to Lappa, who lifted what looked like a padded waistcoat from a chair and brought it over. "This," Kirichenko said, "is what you will wear under your shirt. It is a bullet-proof vest, for extra security. I don't think you'll need it, but we don't want you harmed, so the Central Committee has issued appropriate instructions. Now in this vest is a small radio device. In a moment, I will show you how it operates. It tells us exactly where you are so we can come and rescue you. It's powerful, but I regret that the life of the batteries is not very long, and once it is switched on, it cannot be turned off. Do you understand?"

"Yes, comrade."

"Good. Now your instructions are these—listen carefully, Viktorovich, because I will ask you to repeat them in a moment. If the Americans take you, you must not resist. Go with them. Wait until the agents Lyle and Ross are there, and when they are, and only when they are, you switch on the homing device. The Central Committee wants these two particular criminals caught red-handed. They are very important, very dangerous men. When we have exposed their deeds to the world, they will be neutralized. Repeat your instructions, please."

Rabinovich did so.

"That is good," Kirichenko said. "Now, how do you activate the homing device?" He took the jacket from Lappa and spread it carefully on the top of the desk. "You can see that there are two wires, ending in cufflinks. These wires will run down your arms, under your shirt."

"I don't have a shirt that can take cufflinks," Rabinovich broke in.

"I know that, Viktorovich," Kirichenko said. "I have brought one for you." He smiled charmingly. "You see, we think of everything. Now to start the homing device, you touch one cufflink against the other. It's as simple as that. Immediately, the radio signal is transmitted, and we will pinpoint your position. But do not touch the links until you are ready to start the device. I repeat, the batteries last a limited time only, and they cannot be switched off. So if you want to be rescued rather than interrogated and later killed by the Americans you must not make a mistake about this."

"Yes, comrade. I understand."

"Good. Now Viktor, remove your shirt, and we will fit the vest."

Rabinovich fumbled at his buttons, suddenly remembering the time in the ambulance when Lappa and Nikitin had seen his pyjamas stripped off. He felt a chill of humiliation. His white chest and stomach, virtually hairless, shone in the yellow glow of the lamps.

Kirichenko placed rubber covers over the cufflinks, in case they should accidentally touch, and Rabinovich was helped into the vest.

It was surprisingly heavy, weighing several pounds, and it laced across the back. Rabinovich held a cufflink in each hand, while the shirt was pulled on. Lappa removed the rubber cover from one link and fastened it in place, while Nikitin saw to the other. Then Lappa buttoned the front of the shirt.

"Well," Kirichenko smiled, "that looks all right. How does it feel?"

"Heavy," Rabinovich said.

"Such is the price of safety, Viktor. Now I think you're ready, so I wish you good luck. I will see you back here later this evening. Perhaps you will join me in bottle of excellent vodka which I've kept for a special occasion."

"I would be honored," Rabinovich said, flattered despite his apprehension.

Kirichenko watched Lappa and Nikitin follow the Armenian out into the corridor and was well pleased. The Defense agents would not be able to resist bait so temptingly placed. And when they took it, it would be the end of Rabinovich and Ross and Lyle, and no doubt others, too.

The vest was not bulletproof. In fact, a bullet striking it would almost certainly detonate any one of the dozen packages of explosives sewn in as "padding." The ideal method of detonation was for Rabinovich to touch the metal cufflinks together and complete the circuit. The alternative was for the KGB to send out a radio signal that would have the same result. This would be done anyway within five minutes of Rabinovich's capture, presumably while he was being transported.

The effect would be devastating. The Armenian would cease to exist, his body pulverized into pieces so small that those scraps the Americans could find would have to be lifted up with teaspoons, or scraped off with knives. Anyone traveling with him, or in a radius of ten yards, would also be destroyed, with damage decreasing beyond that point.

In Moscow, Zhikin of the Dezinformatsiya Department was waiting, ready to pour out a stream of outrage at the kidnapping and murder by American agents of a Soviet peace negotiator and to order his well-placed contacts in the West to take up the matter themselves.

It would be hard for the American President to defend himself in the coming crisis. It would be impossible for the DIA to do so.

In the gloomy hallway of the Soviet Residency, Rabinovich stood, stiff and scared. Lenin regarded him from the wall.

Lappa peered out of the window to see if the limousine had arrived. "We might as well wait on the sidewalk," he said. "Give them time to see what we're doing."

Nikitin nodded and opened the door.

It was a beautiful, clear, hot afternoon.

Rabinovich stepped outside.

"He's coming!" Lyle said.

He depressed the transmit button on his shirt front and gave the day's code word for action. "All stations, blind man. Blind man."

A hundred DIA agents on the radio net heard the order and prepared to move.

A Soviet Embassy limousine turned into the road, heading toward the small group waiting outside the gate.

"David, get the cab. Pick me up outside," Lyle ordered.

Ross left quickly. Lyle watched the Russian car stop and Rabinovich and his two bodyguards get in. He saw Lappa glance up and down the street.

Lyle was at the front door before the limousine pulled away, and a few seconds later, Ross drove a black cab around the corner. Lyle waved to flag it down.

The CIA, from their top floor position, logged and filmed the departure.

Lyle, in the back of the cab, spread out a map and radioed the streets they were taking toward lower Manhattan. As they passed points at which DIA operatives were stationed, he gave instructions for them to move in behind the Russians.

At Central Park, the limousine slowed, looking for a place to pull in. "Jesus!" Lyle exclaimed. "This couldn't be better."

Ross fought back apprehension.

Rabinovich and his guards left the car. Ross slid the cab into a space some distance behind while Lyle gave the all-stations order to converge. Within fifteen minutes, at least half their team should be in the Park itself, with the rest not far behind. As each pair of agents arrived, they would check in by radio, giving Lyle and Ross details of their position and a running indication of the force available.

Central Park had its usual quota of joggers, lovers, cruisers, and families enjoying the feel of grass and the sight of trees. The Russians moved among them.

As he walked, Rabinovich's fear resolved itself into a numb feeling of sickness, deep in his stomach, an inability to focus on anything.

He was vaguely aware of others, of horse-drawn carriages clopping slow on roads, of people selling ice cream and balloons, of children's voices as they passed, but everything seemed to disappear in a haze. He was afraid. Rabinovich did not want to look, to see what was coming.

Lappa and Nikitin hardly spoke to each other, and when they did, it was a terse exchange.

Rabinovich began sweating, not only the sweat of fear but of heat, too, because of the thick vest covering his chest and stomach. He said nothing. There was no point.

Lyle and Ross, working separately and keeping well apart, shadowed the Russians, while through their hearing aid receivers, DIA agents began checking in. There were now thirty in the Park, spread out, anticipating where the Russians were heading and sometimes being in position before they arrived.

Rabinovich passed so close to two of them that they could see his flushed, miserable face and the sweat beading his forehead.

Ross stayed well behind because he was known to Rabinovich and probably to the guards as well and would be easiest to spot. However, when the Russians stopped to buy ice cream cones from a vendor, they doubled back at an angle, heading straight for him. There were big shrubs and some trees nearby, so Ross was not worried. He moved back a few paces and watched.

Lappa and Nikitin were eating their ice cream, apparently casually, while Rabinovich's melted unnoticed in his hand, creamy liquid dribbling down the cone. It was as if he was unaware he had it.

And then, without warning, it happened.

Two men, walking briskly behind the Russians, closed the gap. As they drew level, they said something to the guards to attract their attention and, as they turned, the men produced guns. The KGB and Ross registered the threat at the same moment. The Russians were being mugged!

There was the beginning of an argument, voices raised, and Lappa shouted, "Run, Viktor! Run!"

Rabinovich moved, hesitantly at first, ponderous and looking over his shoulder to determine if this was it, if he should keep going, until he saw a pistol crash down on the side of Lappa's head and the guard's body sagged, beginning to crumble.

Rabinovich took off, as fast as he could.

Ross shouted into the radio, "Two, move now!" and he ran, powerful and swift, after the fleeing Russian. In the distance he could see others on a course to intercept Rabinovich, Lyle among them.

Ross was closing fast, breathing easy, legs pumping, feet splashing through half-hidden pools of rainwater in the grass. But as he ran, it hammered in his brain: There's something wrong, there's something wrong.

But what was the use? They'd started the kidnap and couldn't abort.

What is it?

Ross was so close he could hear the sobbing of Rabinovich, part effort, part terror.

Ross thought: The mugger—I know him! Where have I seen him before?

Rabinovich heard Ross behind. His speed faltered. He stopped and turned, a trapped animal, eyes frightened. A hundred yards away, Lyle closed in.

Ross pulled from his pocket the injection ampule. Rabinovich watched passive, panting, making no further effort to escape, until he saw the plastic cap coming off the needle. He jerked as if an electric current had coursed through his body. In the next instant, there was blank acceptance on his face.

Where have I seen the mugger? Where did I see him?

Lyle, with them now, seized Rabinovich's left arm tight, holding the unresisting hand for the injection.

"Come on, David!" he urged. "Move for Christ's sake!"

Two other agents ran up.

But Ross had frozen, the needle an inch from the purple, protruding veins.

Rabinovich's confused brain began to function, to remember Kirichenko's orders. Ross and Lyle were both there. He drew his right arm across, to touch the cufflinks and activate the homing signal. He should do it now, before he was given the drug.

Rabinovich's movement was awkward and obvious. Lyle thought he was about to break free, and twisted his left arm violently. Rabinovich gave a high-pitched cry.

"Jesus, David! Move, you bastard!" Lyle snarled.

The needle touched skin, about to penetrate.

Then Ross pulled back. His hand fell to his side. "No," he said.

"You fucker!" Lyle screamed. "Reuben, do it! Move!"

"Leave him alone!" Ross said, his voice calm but authoritative.

Again Rabinovich's free hand edged across, tentative, seeking contact, the links no more than two inches apart.

Reuben pushed forward, wasting no time, pulling an ampule from his pocket, popping off the plastic cover.

Ross's arm swung out, the side of his palm smashing hard into the agent's ribs. Reuben grunted in surprise and pain at the attack from his own side. His feet slipped in the wet grass and he fell.

"Leave him alone!" Ross shouted, angry now. "Can't you see! It's a setup!"

He knew who the mugger was!

Lyle's eyes were furious, the yellow of a tiger's.

Rabinovich's right cufflink edged nearer. He concentrated on the small remaining gap. One inch, no more. He had to touch the pieces of metal and his duty was done. The comrades would come. But his shirt cuff had twisted in Lyle's grip.

"Two men mugged the guards back there!" Ross yelled desperately, hating the way Lyle was looking at him: the look of a killer. "One of the muggers was KGB! Don't you understand, Clive? I saw him going into the Residency this morning! Short guy, wavy hair, built like a wrestler. God, don't you see! It's a setup!"

Reuben, back on his feet, was circling warily, waiting for an order to attack, but Lyle, uncertain now, did not give it.

Ross, taking advantage of his indecision, focused on Rabinovich. There was something about him, too, something he'd noticed when the Russians walked nearby. His chest was too bulky.

Rabinovich's fingers fumbled to find the second link, to pull it into position and make contact. His face strained with the final effort.

Ross ripped open Rabinovich's shirt front, exposing the padded vest. "What the hell's this, Viktor?" Ross demanded. "What's this you're wearing?"

Lyle found a pressure point on the scientist's wrist and squeezed to hurry the answer.

Rabinovich screamed in agony. His right hand jerked back with the pain. "A vest!" he cried. "A bulletproof vest!"

"The fuck it is," Ross said in disgust. "Take a look at that, Clive."

Lyle felt and prodded with his free hand at the thick material, the hard, putty-like substance beneath. "That wouldn't keep out the rain." Lyle looked around swiftly, making his decision. In the distance, he thought he could see Lappa and Nikitin.

"Let's get out of here," Lyle ordered. Then, savagely, "Go on, Rabinovich! Fuck off!"

Lyle, Ross and the others walked away, leaving the Russian alone and bewildered, staring after them. Something had gone wrong, and he didn't know what. He didn't even know if it was his fault.

As they went, Lyle spoke into his button microphone, giving the unthinkable order for an abort.

Rabinovich hesitantly made his way back to where he had left Lappa and Nikitin. He was soaked with sweat, his arms ached and his heart pounded painfully.

Lyle and Ross walked in silence. Ross was glad to see the yellow had gone from Lyle's eyes, and that his expression was neutral. Ross was sure he'd done the right thing, but at the same time, he knew Lyle bitterly disapproved. And he realized he wanted Lyle's approval almost more than anything in the world.

They pulled out into the afternoon traffic.

"Better head for the airport," Lyle said. "No point hanging around here. Yardley'll want to see us."

"Okay."

The silence extended. Ross wondered if he should break it by further explanations or justifications but, Christ, Clive knew the score. He'd seen the vest, whatever it was. He'd been told the mugging was a fake. And he'd noticed, because both of them turned to look as they left the Park, that Rabinovich was returning to the KGB. What more did he want?

"Pull over there," Lyle said when they reached a fairly clear stretch of road.

Ross did what he was told. He cut the engine and turned to face his comrade. They stared at each other for several seconds before Lyle began to speak.

"There's a law in the DIA," he said, "that if ground rules are set for an operation, you stick to them. The rule in this case was that once the kidnap started, we wouldn't abort, not under any circumstances. We'd take Rabinovich and trust that what he had to say vindicated our action. You broke that law, David, and I just don't know what Yardley's going to say about it."

Ross shifted uncomfortably, about to defend himself,

when Lyle continued, chillingly, "You might be looking for a new job tomorrow. I might be too. I don't know how he's going to take it. Sometimes he plays strictly by the book, and he can be a bastard."

Lyle saw that Ross had turned pale, but there was something else in his look too: defiance. "For my own part," Lyle said, "there was a point back there when if I'd had my arms free, I'd have killed you. Why were you screwing us up? Some new moral scruple? Jesus, I just didn't know. If I hadn't been holding Rabinovich, you'd be dead now. Not only the kidnap and the lives of our guys, but Yardley and the DIA itself were at stake. Shit, you can't just ditch rules like that, Dave! No one ever has before."

Ross turned and stared through the windscreen at the traffic flashing by in both directions. There was a great emptiness in his stomach. At the time, it had seemed that he was doing the right thing, but now he wasn't so sure. There was nothing he could think of to say.

Lyle touched Ross's cheek gently with his fist. "But I guess I owe you," he said. "We'll probably never know for sure what it was, but that vest wasn't bulletproof. I reckon it was a booby trap: explosives maybe. Rabinovich sure as hell didn't know, so they obviously thought he was expendable." Lyle shrugged. "What can I tell you? I said I was counting on you to save my life, and I guess you did. Thanks, Dave."

"That's okay," Ross said. "Any time."

"Yeah. We'd better go see Yardley."

Rabinovich wept in Kirichenko's office. The vest and shirt had been taken from him, and he sat in his trousers on a chair in front of the desk.

The interrogation had gone on for more than an hour, its

tone unrelievedly hostile. Visions of disgrace and a return to the Lubyanka flooded Rabinovich's mind.

"What did you tell the Americans, you traitor!" Kirichenko demanded.

"Nothing! Nothing, comrade!"

"You lie! You will pay for every lie!"

"It's the truth!"

A fist hit the side of his head, smashing into his ear. There was an explosion in his brain, and he grabbed at the desk to stop himself falling. A buzzing started loud in his ears, and they burned as if seared with intense heat. "It's the truth! I swear it!" Rabinovich cried.

But the interrogation did not stop.

What happened? What did you do? Who was there? What happened? What did they say?

And back always to the question that was also an accusation: What did you tell the Americans?

At last, two men held Rabinovich while the Residency doctor administered an injection. After he had passed out, grateful for that relief, the questioning resumed.

It was over fairly quickly.

"Take him back to his room and put him to bed," Kirichenko ordered.

"Is he under arrest, comrade?" a guard asked.

Kirichenko shook his head. "No, but bring in Polozok, and stand by."

The time elapsed between carrying Rabinovich from the General-leytenant's office and returning with Polozok, the stocky KGB man whom Ross had identified as one of the muggers, was about five minutes. During that time, Kirichenko did some hard thinking. Orders for the operation had been signed by Colonel Panin although the plan did not bear his mark. There was obviously someone behind Panin—Zhikin, of course, but beyond him even.

Kirichenko had the uneasy feeling it might be Sanko of Department V.

And now all of them were waiting for news of their big victory. Kirichenko's heart sank. He could provide a reason for the failure—the idiot Polozok and his unbelievable lapse in security—but he did not have an excuse. It was ultimately his responsibility, and even making Polozok pay for his mistake would not relieve him of that. Something had to be salvaged from the mess, and Kirichenko needed a clear idea of what it should be before the coded signal went to Moscow.

"You wanted me, Comrade General?" Polozok was standing just inside the door.

"Come in. Stand over there." Kirichenko indicated a spot in front of his desk. The guards took up positions at the rear.

Kirichenko stared at Polozok, almost as if he had never seen him before. Had the man been six foot three, he would have had the body of a god. As it was, he was five foot six, and the muscles had been compressed into the available space. Polozok bulged sideways.

"What happened?" Kirichenko asked abruptly.

Polozok went through his version of the mugging, which coincided with what both Nikitin and Rabinovich had said. Lappa had not yet contributed. He was sedated, under the care of the Soviet doctor after this musclebound ape smashed the butt of a pistol into his temple.

Kirichenko listened, impassive. "You were late this morning," he said. "Why?"

Polozok seemed puzzled. "It was raining."

"I know it was raining, you buffoon," Kirichenko snarled. "Why were you late? How did you get here?"

"The car broke down," Polozok replied stiffly, then added as an afterthought: "Comrade General."

"So what did you do?"

"It was only a few blocks. We pushed it to the curb and walked."

"Did you see anyone?"

"No, comrade. There was no one about. It was raining, as I said."

"No one? Are you sure?"

"Quite sure," Polozok affirmed.

Kirichenko looked at the guards. "This man is under arrest," he said crisply. Polozok's eyes widened in disbelief. Kirichenko told him. "You are charged with criminal negligence in your duties as an officer of the KGB, thus destroying a major counterintelligence operation against the United States. You are to be kept under guard in the security wing, pending your return to Moscow."

The guards moved forward and stood one on each side of Polozok.

"You fool," Kirichenko said contemptuously. "This morning you walked right past an American agent. He saw you then, and he recognized you again this afternoon when you hit Lappa. You want to know why the operation failed? It failed because of you. He saw you, and he knew."

"It is not possible," Polozok whispered.

"Take him away," Kirichenko ordered.

He was alone in his office again. He could put off the signal to Moscow no longer.

Kirichenko switched on his desk lamp and a warm glow flooded the polished wood.

He pulled a pad toward him and began writing, seeking exactly the right combination of professionalism, regret, competence and, most important, suggestions for the future —plans, decisive and good—which would find favor with Panin. And with Sanko. Oh please God, with Sanko.

*   *   *

It seemed that Yardley was carved out of granite. He sat so still behind his desk, his eyes focused, unmoving, on some distant point behind their heads, scarcely blinking, that Ross wondered if he was really listening. Lyle knew he was. This was Yardley at his most dangerous.

He had not invited the agents to sit. He had not asked them to be at ease. They stood rigidly at attention.

Ross could see, reading upside down, that both his and Lyle's personal files were on the Director's desk.

Yardley was aware that they had aborted the operation well before they landed in Washington and he was waiting for them in his office. Night had long fallen, and most of the corridors of the building were quiet. Yet Yardley was there, and so was his secretary, Lucy. She was in the other office, expecting them. There was no sign of coffee, nor of her usual welcoming warmth. She found it hard to meet their eyes.

Lyle touched Ross's shoulder before they went through and gave a pat of encouragement. But they did not look at each other either.

Lyle had been in charge of the operation, so when they came to attention before Yardley's desk and Lucy closed the door behind them, the Director said merely: "Well, Major Lyle?"

Lyle told his story, simply and fairly, without embellishments.

When he had finished, ending with the word "Sir!", Yardley did not shift position, or move his eyes. "Mr. Ross?" he said in that same remote, neutral tone.

Ross told what had happened. He described the scene in the rain near the Residency when the stocky Russian walked past. He told of Rabinovich sweating, of the ice cream melting in his hand. Then the mugging, and how, as he closed in on the fleeing scientist, he realized it was a KGB setup. He described the bulky vest Rabinovich wore.

At last, Yardley's eyes shifted to look at his two agents. "You didn't know about the vest, Mr. Ross, at the time you disobeyed Major Lyle's order to administer the injection?" Yardley asked.

"No, sir. Only that one of the muggers was KGB and that it was a setup. I did know Rabinovich was wearing something bulky under his shirt. I didn't know what it was, though."

"And you still don't know, do you?"

"It wasn't a bulletproof vest, sir."

"A booby trap, you think?"

"Yes, sir."

"You didn't consider rendering Rabinovich unconscious, in compliance with your orders, and trying to get the vest off him? And then taking him away?"

After a slight pause, Ross admitted, "No, sir. I didn't think of that. There . . . there didn't seem time."

"Why not? The KGB weren't closing in on you, were they? I mean, it was a setup, wasn't it?"

"No, they weren't closing in, sir. And yes, I guess we could have removed the vest. Or at least, had a look to see if we could." There was silence. Ross began to feel resentful, that he ought to be less defensive. "But with respect, sir, what if we had tried, and the Russians expected that?" he asked. "What if it was a bomb and we detonated it by mistake? There'd be a few dead DIA men, and a dead Soviet negotiator. It wouldn't have looked too good."

Yardley stared at Clive. "Major Lyle, what is your opinion of this?"

Lyle met Yardley's gaze. "I thought at first Mr. Ross was wrong," he admitted. "At one point, I'd have killed him if I hadn't been holding Rabinovich. He knows that. But now, sir, considering all the facts, I think he was right. I'm grateful to him."

"What about ground rules, Major Lyle?" Yardley asked.

"What about orders? Are these not the foundations on which the military is built?"

"Yes, sir," Lyle replied. "But I guess there should be exceptions to every rule, even military ones. I think this was one of them."

Yardley grunted.

"Permission to speak, sir?" Ross asked.

"Go ahead, Mr. Ross."

"With respect," David said, making what he knew would be his final submission before Yardley decided their fates, and putting as much force as he could behind his words, "the DIA is not a mirror image of the army. It can't be. We're a special service, and everyone here knows it. I realize if I'd been wrong in thinking it was a setup, I'd have endangered us all. The KGB would have closed in. Major Lyle and I might be dead now, as well as a lot of others, and you, sir, could be looking for a job. But I wasn't wrong. We were taking Rabinovich on their terms, KGB terms, and if it's good for the KGB it's got to be bad for us. Not only for the Agency, but for America. If we'd gone on with the kidnap, just because of the ground rules, we'd be no better than those guys in the First World War who went over the top because they were ordered to and died for no purpose. Cannon fodder, nothing else. We're not cannon fodder. We're experts, specialists, all of us. We've got skills and minds, and we use them. We exercise judgments. Okay, we lost Rabinovich today, and you may think that makes it twice. I don't like losing any more than you do, General. Nor does Major Lyle. But I don't think today was a defeat. The first time the KGB took Rabinovich back, yes, that was different. It was humiliating. Today wasn't like that. They didn't take him back: we gave him back. We rejected their bait. And I think that's pretty good, sir. I'd do it again in the same circumstances. I know my job's on the line, and Lucy's waiting out there with my letter of resignation." Ross was becoming heated now, fists clenched so hard the knuckles showed white. Lyle was rigid and impassive: the trained army man. Yardley watched without comment.

"This Agency was becoming my life," Ross said. "I was growing to understand what it was doing, and why. And I guess I'm as close to Clive as I've been to any man. We work well together. But I'll sign that letter, sir, if that's what you want. I won't feel I'm leaving in disgrace, whatever you may think. Today wasn't by the book, I know. Jesus Christ, it may not have been a victory, but it wasn't a defeat either. At least we're living to fight another day." Ross shrugged. "Well, maybe Major Lyle's living to fight another day. I guess I'm not. That's all I have to say," he concluded. "Sir."

Yardley pressed the intercom button on his desk and spoke to Lucy. "Come in, please, and bring the letters."

Letters. The muscles in Lyle's jaw knotted and he held himself straighter and tenser than before. Yardley was throwing them both out. Lyle wanted to look at Ross, but he couldn't move. He could feel David standing as tense and stiff as he.

Behind them, they heard the door open, and Lucy came into their line of vision with a folder which she placed before the Director. Then she left, not looking at either of the agents.

Yardley drew out two typed sheets of paper and laid them side by side. He read them thoughtfully.

"Major Lyle," he said, "have you anything further to say?"

"No, sir," Lyle's voice was quiet.

"As you no doubt realize," Yardley said, "these are your letters of resignation from this Agency although in Major Lyle's case, not from the army as well. His is a request to be returned to active duty." Yardley met Lyle's eye, then Ross's. "You have placed me in a difficult position, gentlemen, and I was prepared, as you see, to get rid of you both, with immediate effect."

There was a silence, during which Lyle and Ross stopped breathing.

Yardley picked the letters up and stacked them one on top of the other. "However," he added, "I recognize there is force in what Mr. Ross has said. In one operation out of a thousand there might be a case for ignoring ground rules and disobeying a direct order, potentially endangering us all. I guess this was it."

There was the sound of paper being torn, and they saw Yardley slowly rip the letters in half. "I should be surprised, though," he said, "if another occasion such as this arises in either of your careers. Please bear that in mind. Especially you, Mr. Ross. Now get out of here. I want you back on duty Monday morning."

"Yes, sir," Lyle said.

"Thank you, sir," Ross said.

When they were out in the corridor, Ross's whoop of joy carried into the Director's sanctum, and he smiled wryly. He locked their personal files into his safe, fed the ripped letters into the shredder, and went to say goodnight to Lucy.

She was packing up too and looked at him particularly warmly.

They went to Lyle's flat for a celebration drink, feeling both euphoric and wrung out. It had been a close thing.

It was late when he left, and Ross was more than a little drunk. He was half way to his own apartment when he remembered it would be empty. Elaine wasn't back for another week. Well, Julie then, he thought.

He pushed heavily on her bell, hearing its faint sound in the distance. He knew he'd had too much beer, but he hoped she wouldn't mind. He rang for what seemed like a long time.

The door was opened by Andy Marcus, obviously pulled out of bed, wearing only a pair of shorts and a bandage on his ankle. His fists were clenched, and he looked prepared for trouble.

When he saw Ross leaning against the door frame, grinning inanely, he shook his head, bemused. "Jesus Christ," Marcus said. "You sure pick your moments."

"Jesus, you started without me! You bastard!"

"Jesus nothing. You know what time it is? Oh shit, come in."

Beyond, inside the apartment, Ross spotted Julie Klein in a nightdress at her bedroom door, coming to see what was going on.

"Hi!" Ross called out and she looked exasperated, and pleased, and very beautiful. He hadn't realized she owned a nightdress. Marcus locked the door and followed him in. Ross was aware of Andy standing close as he bent to kiss Julie on the mouth. Andy's hand touched his shoulder and rubbed his hair affectionately.

Julie pulled away. "Aargh," she said. "Too much beer. Go brush your teeth, David."

"What brings you back so unexpectedly?" Marcus asked.

"Job's over," Ross said. "I'm a free man again."

"Fantastic! Does that mean you're coming to the club tomorrow?"

Ross hadn't thought about it, but yes, that's what it did mean. He cuffed Marcus delightedly on the head. "Free fall coming up soon," he promised.

Ross showered and brushed his teeth while Julie made coffee for all of them, and by the time they sprawled over the king-size bed, he was feeling a lot less drunk.

It was great to be back among friends, relaxed, no more

hanging around New York. Lovely Julie, hair shining against the white of the linen.

"Feel like some coke, Dave?" Andy swung his feet onto the floor, about to go to the dresser.

Ross shook his head. "Not me, thanks. You go ahead if you want."

"Didn't you like it?" Marcus asked, surprised.

"Sure, it was fine. I'm not going to repeat, though. I can get my highs other ways." His fingertips stroked down Julie's body.

"How about you, Julie?"

"No thanks, Andy. Not tonight."

"I guess I'm outvoted." Marcus lay on the other side of the girl. "Okay, Dave," he said, "let's see how you get your fantastic high."

Ross showed them.

Elaine had tried telephoning the apartment several times over the past week, but there was never any reply. At first she presumed David was busy with whatever assignment had been occupying his mind before she left, but later she wondered if he'd been sent out of the country. She debated how to find out; whether in fact she should try to find out. She didn't want to call Yardley, and anyway he probably wouldn't tell her anything over the phone. But she might be able to get some clue from Clive Lyle. Lyle answered on the fourth ring.

"Hey," he said cheerfully. "How are things, Elaine? How are you?"

"Everything's fine. I'm having such an interesting trip, Clive. I'll tell you about it when I get back."

"When's that?"

"Next Sunday. Listen, I've tried to call David all week, but there's no reply. Have you seen him? Is he out of town?"

Lyle became cautious. "Well," he said, "he has been pretty busy, not all of it in Washington."

"Oh, I see."

Lyle gathered she was thinking about David's work, rather than his play.

"Well, that's fine. I'm sorry to bother you like this. Do you think he'll be around next Sunday?"

Lyle was determined to make sure he was. "I reckon he will be. All other things being equal, of course."

They spoke for a few minutes, and when she hung up, Elaine went to bathe and change for dinner. She was being taken out by some senior FBI men who had long passed the point of talking computers with her and had found a lot to say on a dozen different subjects, some of which had nothing to do with police work.

But there was not a morning when she woke, or a night when she went to bed, that Elaine did not think of David and wonder what he was doing. During the day, too, he surfaced regularly in her consciousness. She had sent off a stream of postcards, which were probably piled up in the apartment.

When she had dressed, she inspected herself in the mirror. With her fingertips, she smoothed her skin back, eliminating the lines around her eyes.

Is that better? she wondered. Younger?

She let herself out of her room and took the elevator to the downstairs bar. To hell with the wrinkles. She felt happy, happier than she had for some time. Everyone accepted her as she was, and found her amusing, interesting company. When she got back to Washington, she'd just have to make sure people there did the same. How ridiculous to care what they thought, as if she was acceptable only as an extension of David, comparable in looks and age.

The trip had been good for her. She felt she was winning back her self-esteem.

The three men in the bar saw her enter and immediately rose to greet her. She walked over, feeling she was among friends.

The tension around the table was so great that Zhikin didn't dare smoke nor, curiously, did he want a cigarette. He sat mesmerized, wondering which of the assembled comrades would be the first to explode, and fearing that when blame was apportioned, some would fall on him.

He remembered describing Sanko's plan as "brilliant." He could hardly believe he had ever done that. Brilliant. Although it was.

There was an unusual grimness in the manner and features of Gorsky. Obviously, the Politburo had been demanding explanations. The head of the First Chief Directorate sat ramrod straight, and more tense than Zhikin had ever seen him.

Blame had to be fixed, but where? Not on Sanko, whose plan it was, because of his close links with the comrade leaders. On Panin then? His men had wrecked the operation. But he was powerful, too.

Zhikin could almost feel the anger and indignation radiating from Panin's ponderous body, while his eyes flicked around, contemptuously, daring someone to make him the scapegoat. He could still fight, and they knew it.

Only two men at the table were outwardly calm. Alexei Sumskoy of the Illegals Directorate had not been involved and was able therefore to keep his emotional distance. It wasn't his battle. And Sanko of Department V.

Who could say what was going on in the mind of the man whose brainchild the Rabinovich operation had been. His face was impassive and his eyes offered no clues. Panin was a rattlesnake who made a noise before striking, enabling countermeasures to be attempted. Sanko gave no warning at all.

Gorsky opened the meeting. "I assume," he said, "everyone has read the deplorable message from New York."

Everyone had.

"So we know why the operation failed. Does anyone have anything to say?"

There was a long silence. This should be Sanko's moment, or Panin's. Gorsky glanced from one to the other, waiting for an explanation, or an accusation, or at least a suggestion for something he could tell the Politburo in the report they had demanded.

But it was Zhikin who spoke first although he himself could scarcely credit it. He heard his voice, which he imagined was talking privately in his head, and then he saw the others turning to stare at him. Zhikin was saying, "I hope this doesn't degenerate into the usual shouting match. A search for scapegoats isn't going to help anyone."

Gorsky's mouth almost dropped open, and Sumskoy looked incredulous. No one ever said things like that. Not in the KGB.

But in Sanko's face, there appeared a small spark of amusement, and Zhikin, whose heart lurched painfully when he realized what he'd done, took comfort and plunged on.

"It was a good plan," Zhikin argued. "It's a pity a small breach in security was enough to destroy it." He paused, suddenly needing a cigarette badly. He fumbled for his pack. "It was a small breach, as I said, and so there is only a small lesson to be learned from it." A match flared and he inhaled deeply. "Can we not agree to leave it at that, and consider what we should do next about the Americans?"

Panin grunted. "Well spoken, comrade."

Sumskoy glanced bitterly at him. Panin wouldn't have been so prepared to forgive and forget if it had been someone else's mess. He'd have wanted blood.

"Well, Yuri, what do you think we should do next?" Sanko asked.

Zhikin shrugged, glad that some of the tension had gone. "First, the SALT talks. There's no reason for them to adjourn now. I think our comrade leaders might order a two- or three-day break, but it isn't necessary to bring the team home. A neutron ban is our first priority, and we should go for that goal, without long breaks."

"What about Rabinovich?" Sanko asked.

"I don't care about Rabinovich," Zhikin said, "and we can be sure the Americans don't either. They know he's poisoned bait. He might as well stay in New York and come back when the talks have succeeded. There's nothing to be gained by bringing him back early."

"And the DIA?" Sanko asked.

"That's not my province," Zhikin replied. "You must decide what you want to do and how to do it. I'm only urging that we look forward to victory, not backward to retribution."

Sanko nodded, and Gorsky, seeing this, took his cue. "There is, perhaps, force in what you say, Yuri," Gorsky said. "Naturally, some punishment has to be meted out. The blame clearly lies with the Residency, and particularly this fellow . . ." he consulted a paper, "Polozok. He is being brought back, and I will recommend he be reduced in rank and posted to some, uh, remote and unpleasant part of the motherland."

"If such a thing exists," Sanko murmured.

"What?" Gorsky asked, suddenly uncertain.

When Sanko's face remained impassive, Gorsky went on, "Furthermore, I shall sternly reprimand General-leytenant Kirichenko for the disgraceful lapse in security and warn him that any future failures will see him joining Polozok, wherever he ends up, and at the same rank. I think we need go no further than that."

Sumskoy could hardly believe his ears. He had been at KGB post-mortems before, some of them involving his own Illegals, and all concerning operations of considerably less importance; and never once had those directly or indirectly involved escaped so lightly. Not a word of criticism against Panin and Sanko! It wasn't fair.

"And now," Gorsky said, content that the chapter was satisfactorily closed, "let us turn to the future. Kirichenko in New York is anxious to mount another operation, striking direct at the DIA. What are your thoughts on that, comrades?"

"I agree," Sanko said. "That Agency represents our biggest threat. We should hit at it selectively."

Panin grunted assent, and his eyes rested on Sanko. "How selectively?" he asked.

"Lyle and Ross," Sanko replied. "They should be killed."

There was a murmur of approval.

Sanko picked up a briefcase from beside his chair and snapped it open, pulling out some typewritten sheets of paper. "These are abstracts from our dossiers on Lyle and Ross. For much of the information in them we must thank Colonel Panin and his agent Feliks. The CIA can be a useful ally." He gave Panin a wintry look. "Lyle is the more difficult of the two. I think we must take him when he is alone, and we must act from a distance: a remote-controlled bomb, perhaps, or a sniper. Something of that sort. I have not made the final decision. But Ross," he dropped the papers back into the briefcase and shut it, "Ross will be easy. He is learning parachuting. In such sports, accidents happen. Unfortunate malfunctions of equipment." He shrugged, "I think Ross will be unlucky."

"When will you do it?" Zhikin asked.

"I have not decided. We need not hurry, but there is no reason to delay either. Two weeks, perhaps, to prepare the ground. We must strike at both men simultaneously if we can. We don't want the death of one alerting the other."

"Well, as long as they're far away from the Soviet negotiators when it happens, I don't think it raises any international problems," Zhikin said.

"They will be far away," Sanko promised. "Leave it to me."

Ross made his third static line jump on the Sunday: his first using a dummy ripcord, fitted to get him used to the idea of pulling something to deploy his chute.

The canopy opened before he'd got the ripcord handle out of its housing, and he found to his agony that a webbing strap, coming up between his legs, had trapped one of his balls. The jerk that halted his plunge was like a blow with a fist. Ross cried in pain and fought to free himself, thrusting his thumbs under the straps and pulling down to relieve the pressure while he wriggled and twisted.

At last he took his hands away gently and found the pain had eased to a bearable pitch. He pulled at a toggle and swung in a circle, orientating himself. Shit, he was getting low! He hadn't realized how much time had elapsed while he got his balls unjammed.

The power pylons were away to the west, with the DZ beyond them. Ross was badly off course. There was a cross wind, and he had to head into it, which cut his forward speed. He drifted toward the power lines, trying to calculate if he had enough height and speed to get across. He decided he did not. He swung around to go in backward and land this side of them and so failed to notice those on the ground running to change the wind direction arrow.

A stiff breeze had sprung up, blowing him faster toward the high-tension lines.

When Ross looked over his shoulder to see how good his calculations had been, he felt a tingle of fear. He was heading straight into the middle of the wires.

You put one foot over the other and lock them, keep your knees together, and you try to thread your way through. And you say "Our father, who art in heaven . . ."

Ross pulled on the right-hand toggle to swing the parachute around. His only option was to run with the wind and hope to Christ he had enough height and speed to clear the cables. And if he didn't . . . well, maybe Grethel hadn't been joking after all. Maybe it was possible.

Beyond the pylons, he could see people running toward him and a couple of cars starting up. His hands began sweating.

He could see details on the pylons now, the cables sagging under their own weight, the ceramic cones. Ross instinctively pulled his legs up, feet locked, hands gripping the rigging lines.

He was on top of them, then he was over, and suddenly he hit the ground with an impact that knocked the breath from his lungs, even as he rolled to distribute the shock up the side of his legs and across his back.

Ross lay on the ground, panting and sore, unable to believe his luck.

"You okay, Dave?" A hand grasping his shoulder, an anxious voice. He sat up, looking at the gathering crowd, and began to laugh.

It was strange. At the end of it all, the payoff still came: a surge of fulfillment. Ross got to his feet and limped around to begin rough-packing the chute.

"What the hell happened up there, Dave."

"Why do you think I'm limping?" he asked. There

were general expressions of sympathy. It had happened to others too.

Ross unzipped the front of his jumpsuit and felt himself gingerly. One of his balls was a little tender, but otherwise he seemed in good shape.

He caught the eye of the girl who had jumped that first day at the club. ":What're you looking at, Sue?" he asked.

"Your expression," Sue said. "As if you weren't sure what you were going to find down there."

"Well, I didn't know if there was anything left to find. But I guess I'll live."

"I'm glad to hear it."

Ross went to join her, leaning against the front fender of her car. He felt exhilarated, really good.

"Why don't you jump any more, Sue?" he asked.

She shook her head emphatically. "Not a chance. Once was enough. I don't want to get tangled in any power lines."

"Hell, that was my own fault. If I hadn't been so concerned about my sex life, I'd have been over those things at five hundred feet. Didn't you like jumping? Didn't you feel great afterward?"

"Oh, sure," Sue said. "It's a wonderful thing to have finished doing. Other than that, it's a little hard on the nerves."

"Ah, come on, Sue," Ross said. "I've got a dollar riding on you."

She looked surprised. "How come?"

"Pete Grethel said he didn't think you'd jump again. I bet him a dollar you would."

"Bad luck, Dave."

"Think about it anyway," Ross said. "Maybe you'll change your mind."

"No way," she said. "I've got too much imagination for this sort of thing."

"Haven't we all? What do you think I'm going to be dreaming about tonight? Power lines, that's what."

Sue glanced speculatively at him. "From what Julie tells us, you don't have a lot of time to dream."

Ross grimaced. He wished Julie wouldn't discuss him with others. He picked up his parachute. "You going to give me a ride?" he asked.

Julie was in the air when they arrived at the clubhouse, but she'd heard all about his jump by the time she got back. She came over, full of concern, and sat close, stroking his hair and behaving in a proprietorial way. Ross found himself becoming restive.

"Jesus, it wasn't that close a shave, Julie," he said finally, after he'd caught Andy's amused eye.

"It's your balls she's worried about," Andy said. Everybody laughed.

Ross remembered Lyle's warning to keep Elaine well away from the skydivers. How right you are, Clive, he thought.

Julie kissed his hand, laughing with the others, and her fingers rested on the inside of his thigh. She sat relaxed, signalling to everyone: This is my man. At least, that was what Ross thought she was signalling, before he remembered that her philosophy was sexual freedom and no ties.

Later in the afternoon, while David was listening to skydiving stories from Grethel and some of the others, Julie took Marcus aside.

"Listen," she said, "I want Dave to myself tonight. Okay?"

Marcus shrugged. "Sure. No problem."

"You're a doll. I'll call you, okay?"

Marcus watched her rejoin Ross, thinking David could be in for a hard time. Julie wanted most what she couldn't have, and that, in Andy's experience, was married men who weren't planning on leaving their wives.

When evening came, Marcus had fixed himself up with one of the club groupies, so Ross and Julie returned alone to her apartment.

Julie busied herself in the kitchen, while Ross lounged around, sipping champagne that she'd produced from the refrigerator.

She went out of her way to be captivating. There was mischief and laughter in her green-gray eyes although sometimes Ross thought he glimpsed sadness too. Ross wondered if she was ever lonely. But if she was, presumably she immersed herself in her poetry. Or phoned Andy, or one of the other single men she knew who were freely available.

They ate by candlelight.

"I'm glad Andy's not here tonight," Julie said. "Aren't you?"

"I guess so," Ross agreed. "But we had some good times."

"Yes, we did. I like Andy," she said. "But sometimes I feel I need a break."

"Yeah?"

"I wanted to concentrate on you exclusively for a bit."

Ross grinned. "Sounds sensible."

"I'm glad you approve."

She cleared away the plates, stooping to kiss him on his cheek.

"I'm going to be sorry when all this is over," Ross said.

She was out of sight in the kitchen, so he didn't see her stop and stand very still. "When all what's over?" she asked. He could tell nothing from her voice.

"Well, Elaine will be back next weekend, so we won't be able to see each other so much. I'll miss not staying over with you. I've never known anything like it before. But I guess you have, a lot."

Julie returned with the main course. "Not as often as you think," she said. "Hardly ever, in fact."

Ross was flattered. "Well, that's nice to know. Do I get the Good Housekeeping Seal of Approval?"

"You do," she smiled.

After dinner they shared a shower, and later their love-making was intense to the point that Ross, exploding into her as she shouted David, David my darling, felt his pleasure nudging the edge of pain.

He lay, tension gone, muscles relaxing, sweat pooling between their bodies. He kissed her eyes and found them wet. It took a long time for his erection to subside, but when it did, Ross was already asleep.

She lay awake, wondering about her next move.

Clearly, they needed new orders, so Ross and Lyle went to see Lyndon Yardley shortly after nine on Monday.

The Director had put behind him their traumatic Saturday night meeting, and gestured toward the comfortable chairs at the side of the office, while he finished his telephone call.

He joined them two minutes later, with the folder containing their weekly reports and summaries on Rabinovich and what little they had gleaned from the neutron files.

"We have to press on," Yardley said, settling down and spreading the papers before him. "I take it neither of you thinks there's any point in having another go at Rabinovich?"

Ross shook his head, and Lyle said: "Not unless we're prepared to make it a straight kidnap and live with the publicity."

"No," Yardley replied. "We're nowhere near that point and probably never will be."

"In that case, sir, I'd advise against it. They're waiting for us and it'd be suicide. Let's leave Rabinovich alone."

"Which brings us back to these files," Yardley said. "I've had another look at your reports," he shuffled through some papers, "and frankly they don't tell me a great deal."

"We're only about a quarter of the way through the Registry material," Ross pointed out. "We'll keep looking if you wish."

"I don't see what else there is to do," Yardley observed. "We have to assume the Russians have something vital they don't want us to know, and the whole question of a neutron ban probably hinges on it. I believe Rabinovich on that. So we can't give up. Keep at those files, gentlemen. They're our only hope."

"What about lifting someone other than Rabinovich?" Ross suggested.

Yardley raised a quizzical eyebrow. "Who did you have in mind?"

"I don't know. One of the other team members. Konev, maybe?"

"The delegation leader? Out of the question," the Director said.

"Well, aren't there other Russians—not connected with the talks—who might be useful to us?" Ross wondered. "Perhaps somewhere in the Eastern bloc. What about me going into Russia and doing the job there? That ought to be possible."

Yardley looked thoughtful.

"We'll keep a look out for a likely target inside the Soviet Union," the Director agreed. "See if one of our people over there's able to come up with a bright idea."

"Meanwhile, back to the files," Ross said.

"It looks that way," Yardley replied. "Do you want me to assign anyone to help you with the research?"

Ross glanced at Lyle, then said, "I don't think so, sir. If anything does turn up, it's bound to be hard to recognize. Someone coming in fresh would really need to start at the beginning. Maybe we've already picked up a dozen clues without knowing it, and we only need one more for them to fall into place."

"Okay," Yardley said. "Then you'd better get on with it."

Allowing for the time difference, Anatoli Dmitrevich Sanko began his morning at the KGB's Department V a couple of hours after Lyle and Ross had called it a day and returned their files to the Registry.

Moscow was still cold. Summer seemed a long time coming, but then it did every year. Some people now blamed the Americans for the bad summers and the Chinese for the long winters, and that was as good an explanation as any.

As he arrived, Sanko nodded impassively to his assistant, Jovan, who saluted and took his cap and coat.

"Good morning, comrade General," Jovan said. "The report is on your desk."

"Thank you, Jovan. Bring some tea, please."

Sanko entered his bright, modern office and took his seat. To his left were four telephones of different colors. Behind and to the right was a wall safe, connected to a sophisticated alarm system. It had to be opened within twenty-five seconds, using both a combination and a key, or the safe automatically sealed itself and the alarm sounded. Sanko had been caught out once, and when the armed guards burst in, they found him with his hands up to avoid being instantly shot and an expression of such cold annoyance that the guards spent much of their time apologizing that he should be so inconvenienced. Sanko, as everyone knew, was a dangerous man.

On his desk stood a leather photograph frame with a portrait of his wife, an overweight woman with a jolly expression. Beside it, in ornate silver, was a picture of his father-in-law relaxing at a Black Sea resort with other Politburo members. The few people in the Department who had seen that photograph were awed by it. Four of their leaders, including the comrade President himself, were shown in swimming costumes, their bodies old and sagging as they waded, ankle-deep in the sea, grinning at the lens. Imagine them paddling, just like factory workers! Everyone knew about the photograph, even if they hadn't been into Sanko's office.

Sanko opened the file that awaited him and scanned it quickly. The report from his chief representative in the United States was disappointing.

Although it would be easy to deal with Lyle, Department V had no one there with the expertise to sabotage Ross's parachute. It was simple enough to cut through rigging lines, but the equipment had to be properly re-packed afterward so that it wouldn't look as if it had been tampered with. The report recommended that an expert be flown in from elsewhere.

Jovan brought a cup of tea, black, with a slice of lemon.

"I'm looking for a man," Sanko said, almost to himself while Jovan waited alert and listening, "from this Department, who speaks good English, if possible with an American accent. He must be an expert at parachuting, and in particular, he must know how to pack a parachute. He must be able to arrange it so a parachute malfunctions."

"Right away, comrade General," Jovan said.

While he sipped his tea, Sanko considered the problem of Clive Lyle.

Lyle's car could be booby-trapped quickly and easily.

Explosives mounted on a magnetic base could be snapped onto the metal underside simply enough and detonated by remote control. Similarly, a sniper—or even two snipers firing from different angles—could eliminate Lyle with ease, particularly if they were working in the dark, using night sights.

While Sanko was mulling over the matter, Jovan returned with printouts from the Department's own computer, which for security was linked to no other network, not even within the KGB.

"There is no one, comrade General," he announced.

Sanko raised an eyebrow. "No one in Department V who knows about parachutes?"

"No one whose English is good. There are several men able to do the job from a practical point of view. One speaks French and German, another is Italian. We have a Ukrainian, and the rest are Russians who specialize in East European languages." He handed over several sheets.

"A pity," Sanko murmured, flicking through the printouts.

Jovan stood quietly, awaiting further orders. He had thick ginger hair and the calm freckled face of a farm boy. He was one of the few who did not fear Sanko, and that was because he followed instructions to the tiniest detail and was totally loyal: qualities he knew the man appreciated above all others.

At length, Sanko said, "I want to see General-mayor Sumskoy. Ask him to step into my office."

"Yes, comrade General."

Sanko's request was in the form of a Royal command, and although Alexei Vasilevich Sumskoy was about to conduct a meeting of his own Directorate S, the Illegals Directorate, he immediately canceled it. He did so, however, with ill grace, swearing loudly. Then he took the elevator to Sanko's floor.

Jovan showed him in.

"Ah, Alexei," Sanko looked up from his desk. "It's good of you to spare the time. Please sit down."

He indicated a chair immediately in front of him.

"Comrade General," Sumskoy replied formally, careful to keep his feelings under control now that he was in the lion's den.

"Would you care for tea?"

"Thank you, no."

"In that case, let us get to business. As you know, I am about to order the elimination of the American agents, Lyle and Ross." He stared at the darkly handsome face before him. "I thought you might be able to help."

Sanko outlined his requirements, and Sumskoy agreed to see if he could provide someone.

Sumskoy had no alternative, of course, but still it would be to his credit if one of his own Illegals was able to help the great Sanko.

He used a secure line to call his own assistant, and then, relaxing, agreed to a renewed offer of tea. It was a rare experience for him to be in the position of supplier, rather than supplicant, and he found he enjoyed it.

In due course, Jovan arrived with more printouts, which Sanko, by a gesture, indicated should be given to his visitor. Sumskoy appreciated this courtesy. He had not imagined the head of Department V would be so sensitive.

Sumskoy scrutinized the papers. "It does not look," he said at last, "as if we have a man who can help you."

He tore one page along the perforations and handed it across the desk.

"But there is a woman," he added.

"A woman will do perfectly," Sanko said.

9

Sophie Johnson was a single. In Soviet espionage terms, this did not mean she was unmarried, although she was, but that she was an Illegal who worked alone. She was a member of an elite, sent into the United States while in her late teens knowing that, if convicted of espionage, the potential penalties against her included death.

Death was far from Sophie Johnson's thoughts as she prepared to leave for dinner. She felt safe. During her fifteen years in the country, she had virtually become an American, which meant she was no longer acting out a role.

It scarcely seemed possible that her name, at birth, was Nadezhda Chebrikov, or that her hometown was Leningrad. If anyone asked Sophie where she was born, she would say, without thinking, Kansas City, and that when she was too young to remember, her parents—now dead—had taken her to Chicago. She could describe the neighborhood where she grew up and the schools she attended. She knew the names of the teachers. She had, somewhere in her apartment, report cards and certificates attesting to many of the things she claimed. Sophie Johnson had come to believe in this other life. Even the anecdotes she told, learned by rote in Moscow, had taken on a life of their own. She embroidered them sometimes, as people do when they want to make a story sound better, or more amusing, and she now felt that they were true.

She had been lonely in Leningrad, with few friends. Her real parents were dead, and she had been an only child, so there was nothing vibrant in her memory to make her recall the winter city of the Tsars, and no family ties beckoning her back. In her heart, she was as American as any of the others who worked on Capitol Hill.

Once a month, however, or more often if circumstances warranted, she had a meeting with a man she knew as Trevor Prince, and to him she revealed confidences. He congratulated her, or complained, and once when she failed to provide a document he required, he threatened. That was briefly frightening and very unpleasant, but generally their relationship progressed smoothly.

Before coming to Washington Sophie had, on Prince's instructions, hitched herself to the star of a San Francisco politician. She worked in his office doing basic chores, but because she was efficient and clever, her status rose swiftly.

During this time, as a dare, she took up skydiving and found she liked it. She didn't tell Prince until she had completed twenty jumps because she thought he might stop her. When finally she confessed, she found he was interested only in the people she met, and not at all in her adventure although subsequently he did ask how she was getting on. The information went into her file. Sophie Johnson continued to free fall, enjoying the sport, the camaraderie, and the men she picked up through the club. She even won a couple of trophies in competition, and her photograph appeared in a skydiving magazine on the West Coast.

That picture, taken six years ago, showed a woman who would not age well. Sophie had been at her best during the unhappy teenage years in Leningrad, the point at which the KGB took her over.

In the photograph, Sophie looked jubilant. Anyone who sees a skydiver landing safely, let alone winning a prize, will recognize the expression. But behind the triumph was a face that was becoming less pretty and acquiring a hardness that careful makeup would not entirely hide. Her eyebrows were plucked, then as now, into questioning half-moons over light brown eyes. Her long black hair fell in waves. Lines started near her mouth, ending at her chin. Those lines had deepened over the years.

In another ten years, few men would give Sophie Johnson a second look, but at the moment she still had enough going for her in her face, fashion sense, and figure to turn heads. Her personality was breezy and no-nonsense, and she got on well in politics. The core of steel that the KGB had recognized and honed in Moscow had never been properly exposed to those around her, but it was there.

Sophie Johnson checked her appearance in the mirror before letting herself out of her fifteenth-floor apartment and taking a cab to the small restaurant.

She wondered what the problem was. Trevor Prince had never before called her at work, even when he had something urgent to say. The procedure for organizing a special meeting involved the delivery of an issue of the *Ladies' Home Journal* to her apartment—a magazine she didn't ordinarily read—which signaled that she had to go that night to whichever bar or restaurant they had arranged for their next routine rendezvous. This time, over the telephone, Trevor Prince mentioned a place she'd never heard of, and she'd been obliged to cancel a date. Clearly, something was on.

She found the restaurant without difficulty. It was more expensive and upmarket than she was used to going to with him. Maybe they were going to give her a bonus.

Prince was waiting at a table near the entrance and rose to kiss her on both cheeks.

He was at least five years older than Sophie, and his skin bore the faint pitted scars of a case of adolesent acne. His lips always seemed dry, and when they brushed against her cheek they rasped slightly. He had finely textured fair hair. His eyes were light blue and seemingly uninterested, although Sophie had seen them change when he was angry or emphatic, or wanted to make sure she understood the importance of a particular task. Prince reminded her of a snake.

"Lovely to see you, Trevor," she cooed. "What a surprise to hear your voice this morning! I didn't know you were in town."

"I just got in." His accent was midwestern. "I hope I didn't disrupt your plans."

"Nothing I can't reschedule," Sophie said, slipping into the seat beside him.

"What'll you have?"

"Scotch on the rocks." She opened her purse and extracted a small mirror which she quickly scrutinized her makeup. Satisfied, she turned to him with a smile. "How've you been?" she asked.

"Oh, pretty good."

The waiter arrived with menus, and they ordered. When he had gone, Sophie waited for Trevor Prince to give some indication of why he had called her because, other than business, conversation between them was hard work. But instead he began discussing movies and politics.

Sophie became restive. She wondered vaguely if this was intended as a social evening for personal motives. She'd never considered him in those terms before, and now that she did, it gave her a chill.

She kept her responses cordial but guarded, signaling that she wouldn't welcome a relationship closer than strictly necessary, yet knowing that if he insisted, she would have no choice. Prince could make life difficult for her in a thousand ways.

She noticed he selected an expensive Burgundy to go with their steaks, and her heart sank. In the years she had known him, he had always been careful with Moscow's money. Tonight he was sparing no expense.

Sophie glanced around to ensure they were private enough to talk and tried to steer the conversation onto business lines, which in her forthright way meant asking bluntly, "So, what's up?"

But Prince, lifting his wine glass in a silent toast, replied: "Later. When we leave here we'll have a little talk."

She bit her lip. He smiled. He didn't often smile, and it changed his face, making him seem not entirely bloodless and unattractive, although even as she registered this impression, she knew she was only trying to compensate for what was beginning to seem inevitable. She believed that soon she would feel the cool, dry hands touching her body, and taste the mouth with the hard, dry lips.

Sophie launched into a long dissertation on the Congressional hearings that were occupying her days, and this took them through dessert. He listened politely, asking occasional questions. It was nothing to interest the KGB, however, merely to fill in time.

After coffee, he called for his check and suggested they go for a drive.

Here it comes, she thought. She smiled at him as graciously as she could manage.

A couple of blocks from the restaurant, he unlocked a Lincoln Continental and held the door open for her. Sophie was surprised at the car: it upgraded his status. Maybe it was just part of his cover, but perhaps he was more important than she'd imagined. He started the engine, headed for Sheridan Circle and onto Massachusetts Avenue.

"Isn't it strange," Sophie exclaimed. "We've known each other for years, and actually I don't know very much about you at all."

Prince said nothing.

"For instance," she went on, "are you married? Do you have kids?"

After a silence, Prince replied, "I'm not married."

"Well, where do you live? Here in Washington?"

"Yes. I have an apartment."

"Is that where we're going?"

Prince glanced at her, and she saw him smile again. "Don't worry, Sophie," he said softly. "I won't touch you. You're not my sort." He could tell she didn't like that. "And I'm not yours either. No, this is business. We're going somewhere quiet for a walk. I'm going to hold your hand, but that's all. So just relax."

They turned down 17th and later into C Street, parking near the National Academy of Sciences. Prince helped her out and locked the car. Then as he said he would, he took her hand.

His own was hard and stronger than she had expected. It felt rough on the side of the palm.

Anyone who noticed them crossing Constitution Avenue toward West Potomac Park would have assumed they were lovers. They walked slowly toward the Lincoln Memorial reflecting pool, and Prince began to speak of the task she was now required to perform.

As he talked, Sophie became acutely conscious of his touch, its strength and coldness: a symbol of the organization that employed them both.

She'd never been involved in *mokrie dela* and wondered what it would be like to kill. In this case with David Ross, it would be easy. She'd be in the same emotional position as the pilot of a bomber, who'd be outraged if you gave him a machine gun and told him to massacre a school full of children, but who would, without qualm, release a load of bombs over a civilian area, destroying the same number of children, and be able to eat a good breakfast when he got back to base.

For her, killing Ross would be like that. She would be operating from a convenient distance.

"When do you want me to do it?" she asked.

"Soon," Prince said. They turned and strolled toward the Lincoln Memorial. "You need to join the club, find out how they operate. Get to know them, their procedures. When does Ross jump? Which parachutes does he use? Maybe he's got his own, in which case it'll be simple. When you know all that, call me." He pulled a business card from his pocket and handed it over. "When you do, I'll ask you out for a drink."

Sophie thought it over as they walked. If Ross's club was anything like the one she'd belonged to in San Francisco, security would be casual. There ought to be little personal risk. She didn't even have to be around when it happened.

Nevertheless, Sophie's hand had begun sweating and she tried to pull away, but Trevor Prince gripped her tightly.

He stopped and turned toward her, standing very close. She realized for the first time that he wasn't a desk man as she'd always assumed—the link between her and whoever in the KGB was in overall control—but a killer in his own right.

And that was quite an exciting prospect. Suddenly she found herself wanting him, hoping he'd make a move after all. She looked at him quizzically, but his face was in darkness and she couldn't see his eyes. Her hand brushed forward against the front of his pants to see if he was hard. He was not.

Prince said steadily. "Just business, Sophie."

Her arm fell to her side, and he released her. She felt as if she'd been cut adrift, and she stood on the grass rubbing her palms together and looking at the shadow of the man before her. "Yes, well it sounds okay," she said. "I'll join up and let you know how it goes."

"Good girl," Prince approved. "But make it fast."

They went back to his car, and he drove to her apartment. She invited him in for a nightcap, really wanting him to accept, but he shook his head.

She watched the Lincoln Continental pull away and turn the corner out of sight, before she slowly entered the building and waited for the elevator.

That had never happened to her before—personal repugnance for a man changing so swiftly to intense attraction. But then she'd never been given a *mokrie dela* order before. Maybe that made the difference.

The elevator arrived, and she pressed the button for her floor. Goddam, she'd really wanted him.

David Ross lay naked beside Julie Klein, trying to sleep, thinking: You can't win them all.

He'd used every trick and technique he knew, working over her body with care and tenderness, using tongue, mouth, teeth, fingertips to arouse her, but she lay indifferent. At one point, he'd wished he could lose his erection, but it throbbed almost painfully. He tried to talk to her, to find out what was wrong, but she wouldn't answer, and just shook her head. Maybe she simply wasn't in the mood for sex, but Ross felt it went deeper than that.

He knew the decent thing was for him to leave her alone and lie quietly beside her, but his own body was making urgent demands. He pressed himself against her stomach so she could feel how hard he was, and abruptly she reached down and guided him into her. She turned her face away. She was wet, but that was from him. Ross moved gently, deep long strokes, hoping to get a response. He thought of Elaine, who had never really liked sex, but at least put on a show of wanting to please him. Ross remembered that some prostitutes were like this. He began thrusting quicker, shallower, concentrating on pleasing himself and getting it over with as quickly as possible, yet when he came, convulsive and hard, slamming deep into her, he cried out at the sharp waves of pleasure and gripped her tight, calling her name. She remained limp.

Ross stroked her hair and kissed her face. He could feel the pumping of his heart. He stayed inside her, unwilling to pull out.

But after a minute, he sighed and rolled regretfully onto the cool sheet. Julie Klein might have been dead, except for her regular breathing.

Maybe she missed Andy? But if she did she only had to phone.

Ross thought back over the evening, to see if he'd said anything to offend her. But Julie was the sort of girl who let you know immediately if there was something she didn't like. She wasn't the silent treatment type.

It could be she was growing tired of him, and wanted a new man, different feel, muscles, technique, taste. She might just be bored, and this was her way of telling him it was time to move on.

Ross didn't understand. He'd see how she was in the morning. If her mood hadn't improved, he'd take it as a sign he should stay away for a bit. But hell, he only had a few days before Elaine got back.

Maybe she'd talk, in her own time, about what was bothering her.

He closed his eyes and tried to sleep.

Julie Klein stared into the darkness.

10

She usually found it a strain to get up this early in the morning, but when her alarm went off near her ear, Sophie Johnson was awake and alert as if sleep had been a mere closing of the eyes, with an unaltered state of consciousness; yet she knew it had been so deep she had scarcely moved.

The room was dark and filled with the anonymous silence of high-rise apartments in the pre-dawn. Suburban houses might have birds rousing themselves outside, and some might hear the sound of early traffic, but nothing reached the fifteenth floor.

Sophie walked on bare feet to the bathroom and prepared herself for the day. In twenty minutes, she was waiting for the elevator and listening to the low whine of machinery starting up, a noise daytime somehow suppressed.

She drove through the virtually empty streets and quickly out of the suburbs, heading for the airfield.

The day came upon her gently, with a calmness that made her at peace.

She'd plotted her route on a map, but it was simple enough to find the place. She slowed as she came near,

watching for signposts to the club, but even so she noticed
the painted wooden sign too late and had to turn around.

The road had grass growing high on both sides, and the
car's suspension skimmed over ruts. She could see the
airfield's perimeter fence and beyond it, in the distance, a
line of silver hangars and a small group of buildings
surmounted by a control tower. From a quick glance it
looked deserted, until a light plane droned across her path,
a hundred feet up and climbing through air so soft and free
of turbulence it was like velvet, and she realized there was
already functioning life inside.

She drove on, slower than the poor state of the road
demanded, giving herself a chance to inspect the area, see
whether any paths intersected, and what hazards she should
take into account. She made no attempt to hide her presence because on this first day it wasn't necessary.

The road followed the perimeter, and soon there was
another crudely painted wooden sign and an arrow pointing to the entrance. Sophie stopped the car and went to
inspect the metal gate. It wasn't locked, and she only had
to slide a bolt to let herself in. It was exactly like San
Francisco, where no one cared about security except around
the hangars, the valuable aircraft themselves, and the control buildings. Skydivers couldn't believe they possessed
things anyone else wanted and, broadly speaking, that was
true. Most of the members had their own personal chutes,
and took them home at the end of the day; while the
scrappy furnishings and bits of equipment in the clubhouse
would not justify the cost of the gas used in stealing them.
She slid the bolt and pushed open the gate.

Sophie drove toward the hangars until the road curved
and ended in a hard dirt area that was obviously used for
parking.

She got out, smelling the clean morning.

In the distance, an aircraft engine burst into life and settled into a drone.

The brick clubhouse was directly ahead of her: an old building with a tin roof and a long porch. It must originally have been an administrative office before the airfield was enlarged and its center of operations moved to a point parallel to the middle of the main runway.

The door was locked. Sophie peered through a window.

Unlined green curtains hung on rings and, beyond, the room was shabby. The walls needed a coat of paint because the white had peeled off in patches, revealing a duller color beneath. There were a couple of sofas, probably bought from a garage sale, and half a dozen chairs— some old and clumpy, others relics of the ugly Scandinavian designs of the sixties, with spindly legs at strange angles. The carpet, where it wasn't threadbare, had a pattern of forest leaves and twisted vines.

Two electric bulbs hung on cords from the ceiling, shaded with cheap plastic domes. There was a battered filing cabinet, a handpainted wooden cupboard, and a refrigerator, which was probably the only thing of slight value. The telephone was locked to prevent unauthorized outgoing calls.

To the left was a closed door. She walked around the building to look in the side window. As she'd expected, it was the storeroom. Jumpsuits in various sizes hung on hooks, and against the other wall there was a jumble of boots. A large padlocked cupboard probably contained the club chutes and crash helmets.

It all reminded her strongly of San Francisco, and Sophie smiled. She headed toward the nearby hangar.

The sun was getting high in the sky, and she stood at the cavernous entrance, staring in at the planes. There was a Cessna 172, a couple of Pipers, and—she could hardly believe it—an ancient Tiger Moth biplane. Owning one of those was like having a Model T Ford, only better. She could see a man in overalls walking around the Tiger Moth, inspecting it carefully.

Sophie walked toward him. "Hi!"

He looked up, a middle-aged man, almost bald. "Hi there. You looking for someone?"

"Yeah. What time does the skydiving club start up?"

He glanced at his watch. "You're a little early, ma'am. It's just after seven now. I guess they'll be around in an hour or so."

"Thank you," Sophie said, "I may as well wait."

She walked back to the clubhouse and sat on the low wall of the porch, smoking her first cigarette of the day.

They started arriving around eight o'clock. Sophie introduced herself and found the skydivers as relaxed and welcoming as they had been on the West Coast. No one had a key, so they chatted easily in the sunshine until the club secretary arrived to open up and the shabby room was transformed by the presence of young people who were friends.

Pete Grethel was among the early arrivals, and Sophie was presented to him as a new recruit.

Grethel watched her sizing up the men with an interest that was certainly healthy and wondered if she'd really come along just to get laid. But she said she wanted to jump, and that's what he'd teach her to do.

He gave her time to get to know the others and lose whatever initial nervousness she might have, although there was no particular sign of any, before taking her out to the trapeze swing and explaining the basics of skydiving. She nodded absently as he spoke, and he had the odd feeling she wasn't listening properly.

Grethel let it pass: actually having to do the rolls from the swing would sort her out.

When he told her she had to present a medical certificate before she could jump, she arched her eyebrows in disbelief.

"Oh hell," Sophie exclaimed. "I didn't think of that. I wanted to jump this weekend."

Grethel shrugged. "Sorry, that's the rule. But why not get your ground training out of the way today and tomorrow, and if you bring your certificate next Saturday, I'll give you a quick refresher and take you straight up."

The prospect of spending two days practicing what she could already do in her sleep was not a pleasing one, but Sophie knew for her own security she had to come in as a novice and therefore be beyond suspicion.

She smiled sweetly at Grethel. "You're the boss," she said.

"Yeah, well, let's go find you some gear, and I'll show you the six basic rolls."

Sophie Johnson loved the faint, stale smell of sweat in the clubhouse storeroom: the jock aroma she remembered from her years in San Francisco, and she sniffed appreciatively. Grethel, sorting through the jumpsuits, watched from the corner of his eye. If ever there was a woman who wanted to end up in bed, this was it. Like Sue, she'd probably be good for one jump, and the rest would be socializing and fucking; although Sue, plain and overweight, had had to settle for only the first of those.

He handed Sophie a faded red jumpsuit with LUCKY STRIKE emblazoned on the back, and the smallest pair of boots the club possessed. When she'd pulled them on, she followed Grethel back into the clubhouse.

It was filling up now, and half a dozen people were getting ready to drive out to prepare the DZ for the first drop.

"Sophie, here're a couple more members I'd like you to meet," Grethel said. "This is Julie,"—the women smiled at each other—"and David."

He had to be the handsomest man in the club, and she knew instinctively he was the target. Sophie felt her heart constrict. Of course, Trevor Prince wouldn't have bothered to tell her that; he'd let her find out for herself.

She held out her hand, and he shook it, strong and warm, not cold and hard like a snake.

"I'm Sophie Johnson," she said, wanting to be positive on the identification.

"David Ross. I hear you're going to jump."

"I sure am. But not until I can get the medical business sorted out. I'd forgotten about it, can you believe it?"

"Well, you're new—you couldn't know. Watch out for Pete, though," Ross warned. "He's a tough instructor. You might not want to go through with it when he's finished with you."

"Don't listen to Dave," Grethel said. "It'll be easy, wait and see."

Julie Klein watched, relaxed, having assessed the new woman and decided she posed no threat, even though she was looking at David in a way that made it clear she was interested. The problem Julie faced was not Sophie Johnson.

"I guess I'd better get ready," Ross said. "Pete's taking me up on the first lift."

"You want to come along, Sophie, see what it looks like?" Grethel invited. "It'll give you an idea of the procedure for exiting."

"Sure," she said. "I'd love to."

Ross, changing in the storeroom, fought his usual battle with himself, despising his damp palms and the nausea that was rising in his stomach. He dressed slowly, keeping his breathing steady and deep. He'd remembered to bring a supply of gum and he chewed a piece to keep his mouth from going dry. He had to do this jump well, not only because the last had been such a disaster but because this new woman would be in the Cessna, and he wasn't going to have her thinking he was scared. Maybe her being there would make it easier. Sometimes it was better to have an audience.

And that, in fact, was the way it turned out. Ross was calmer than he expected because he was under female scrutiny, and when the moment came to swing his body out of the Cessna and grip the strut, he felt remote and distant.

The order to jump came swiftly, and this time Ross had the dummy ripcord out of its housing before the canopy opened, and his balls were clear of the straps. He maneuvered easily over the power lines, and managed to land within the target circle, although not actually on the central cross itself.

Then there was nothing for him to do but to revel in the fantastic emotional payoff.

Ross was eager to get back to the club as soon as possible and talk Grethel into letting him do his fifth and final dummy rip in the afternoon. But no one was going back until after the next lift, so he hung around, feeling elated and at peace with the world, and watched an attempted three-man link.

At the airfield, Grethel was demonstrating landing rolls from a standing position.

Sophie forced herself to concentrate, making sure she gave him no cause to think she was anything other than a beginner. When she tried them herself, she was as awkward as she could be, not distributing her weight up the side of her leg and across her back, but falling almost straight onto her knees, then onto her hip and lying there, groaning. Grethel picked up her legs and pushed them across her body, completing the roll for her.

''That wasn't too bad,'' he said, ''but you've got to feel

it smoothly right along your leg and over your back." He demonstrated again himself. "Try it once more."

Sophie botched it a second time.

"That was a little better," Grethel encouraged, while she lay on the hard earth gritting her teeth because she knew she'd be bruised next day.

Gradually, Sophie allowed herself to improve, and at the end of half an hour, Grethel was genuinely complimentary.

"That's great, Sophie," he said. "You've really got the idea now."

She smiled at him, bright-eyed, playing her role to the hilt. These initial stages were as important as the final act: that was one of the basic lessons at the KGB school, where they expended massive resources in the preparation of an Illegal, but where the instructors were nowhere near as pleasant and sexy as this slim, fit young man with his neat brown hair and dark eyes—eyes maybe a little close together, but more interesting for that—and his sensitive mouth. Sophie had ruled out trying to get close to Ross, so maybe Pete Grethel was a possibility instead. She decided to make a pitch for him later and see what happened.

Grethel gave her a fifteen-minute break before she graduated to the trapeze. It was more painful faking mistakes from there, but Sophie felt obliged to let him watch a couple, and was gratified to see that the grit she exhibited in climbing straight back on and doing it over was increasing his respect for her.

By lunchtime, when David Ross and the others had returned from the DZ, she was doing everything perfectly. Grethel put his arm around her shoulders as they walked back to the clubhouse, so Sophie felt her performance had been an award winner.

During lunch, Sophie watched Ross whenever she could and spoke to him about his jump.

"David, it looked so exciting," she cooed, while Julie listened with indifference. "I couldn't believe how cool you were, like you were catching a train or something."

Sophie asked the usual beginner's questions: What's it like? How do you feel? Is it hard landing? And some less usual ones, in the same enthusiastic, slightly awed tone: have you ever used your reserve? Do you have your own parachute?

"Oh hell, no," Ross replied to this last question. "I guess I'll buy one when I've learned to free fall, but up till then, you and I get to share the club's spare."

"Can't David and I jump together?" Sophie appealed to Grethel.

"Not unless you bring your own equipment," Grethel said. "We're short at the moment, I'm afraid. Maybe we'll try to get a second chute fixed up in a couple of weeks, depending on how you do." Grethel was thinking there was no point paying good money for repairs until they knew whether Sophie Johnson was going to be a one-shot jumper, like Sue, or whether she was serious. He'd originally figured her as a one-jump woman, but after seeing her in action, he wondered if he hadn't underestimated her. She had a lot of guts, and she learned quickly. It was a pity about her medical. She was really ready to go.

After they'd eaten, Grethel took Ross and Sophie to watch him repack David's chute for the afternoon lift. It was a fine day, with a light steady wind, so there was no reason for them to put off Ross's final dummy rip, particularly as he wasn't going to be coming out the next day.

"You're not going to be jumping Sunday?" Sophie asked when she heard this. "That's too bad."

"I can't get away," Ross explained. "Family reasons." Then, because everyone else knew and there was no point keeping it from Sophie, he added, "My wife's coming from the West Coast."

"Well, that's nice for you," said Sophie, wondering maliciously where that left Julie. "I guess you'll be bringing her along to see your first free fall."

"Not a chance," Ross laughed, thinking what might happen. God knew what she'd find out. "I don't think skydiving's her scene. She'll expect me to break my neck, and if I knew she was watching, I might even do it."

Sophie gave him a "Shucks, you know you're wonderful" look, and tried to pay attention to Grethel's commentary on how to pack a parachute.

"I don't think I'd trust myself to do that!" she exclaimed, watching him. "What a terrible responsibility!"

"It's a pretty simple procedure, really," Grethel said.

"Do these things ever not open?" Sophie asked.

"The ones I pack always open. Isn't that so, Dave?"

"Sure is," Ross replied obligingly.

"Anyway, if you ever do get a malfunction, you've always got the reserve on your stomach. Just go for that, and you'll come down okay." Grethel turned back to his work.

Sophie asked Ross, "When will you be doing your first free fall, Dave?"

"Next Saturday, I guess. I don't want to put it off longer than I have to."

"Did I tell you you've got to buy beers for everyone that night?" Grethel asked, glancing up.

"Get in a big supply," Ross said cheerfully. "I'll be in a buying mood."

"Fantastic."

"Anyway, it'll be a double celebration, because Sophie'll have made her first jump, and she'll need to be initiated."

"What's this initiation?" she asked archly.

"Jump first, then see," Ross laughed.

"How many students have you got, Pete?" Sophie asked, filling in the remaining gaps in her knowledge.

"Just you and Dave at the moment," Grethel said.

That was fine. It couldn't be better, or easier. She just needed to make sure she stayed away next Saturday, or arrived after they'd scraped David out of the hole he made in the ground. She thought it would probably be better if she did turn up to be shocked, and sympathetic, and then leave. Even if the club was seized with a black, angry, show-must-go-on mood, and everyone lined up for jumps to exorcise David's ghost and prove it couldn't happen to them, there wouldn't be a student's parachute left. They'd have run out.

The core of steel, which she hadn't needed yet in her years as an Illegal, had taken over.

Sophie had been sorry, when first she met Ross, that it had to be someone like him; but now, perched a few inches away on the low porch wall, she felt no emotion at all.

"You work in Washington?" she asked Ross. "Not in politics, though, or I'd have seen you before."

"Dave's an accountant," Grethel said, his voice neutral, although she noticed he shot Ross a swift, amused look.

"That's right," Ross affirmed. "I work for the government. Departmental budgets, that sort of thing."

Sophie made the exclamation people deliver when they're not certain what response is appropriate.

Grethel finished packing and carefully threaded the static release into place.

"That's the last time you use this, Dave," he said. "Next week's the real thing."

"That's wonderful!" Sophie said. "God, how I envy you!"

*   *   *

Tony Kimber, born Alexander Volkov, was also an Illegal operating in the United States, although of a very different class.

Sophie Johnson had been trained basically as a spy for Directorate S and was ultimately answerable to General-mayor Sumskoy. Tony Kimber was a saboteur and assassin, and his boss was Sanko himself, the head of Department V.

Kimber's cover was as a door-to-door salesman, which gave him considerable freedom. As long as his monthly sales remained at a reasonable level, no one questioned how he spent his time. Even during those periods when Kimber's attention was focused chiefly on KGB activities, his sales record showed no significant deviation and often rose slightly, thanks to Sanko's budget. Only God knew what the KGB did with all those encyclopedias.

On this Saturday morning, Kimber was concentrating on a section of N Street in Washington, the area that housed both David Ross and his own target, Clive Lyle.

Kimber paused across the street from Lyle's building, and acquainted himself with the layout. It was an old apartment house, with one main entrance; at the side a ramp led down to a garage. Lyle drove a green MGB, a distinctive car, and it wasn't parked in the street. In any case, it was a reasonable assumption he'd have his own underground space.

Kimber had the fresh open face of a good-living American, with white, even teeth and clear brown eyes. His hair was clean and well-groomed, cut long so that it partly covered the back of his collar, and brushed over the top of his ears. He dressed conservatively—today, in a brown suit a couple of shades lighter than his hair. He had a smile that made women receptive to his sales pitch, and men, too, usually felt inclined to hear him out. Kimber's presentation had just the right combination of openness and diffidence. He wore a thin gold wedding band, so women, alone in their homes, were less reluctant to let him through the door. He looked safe and trustworthy.

Kimber was courteous, humorous, and a good talker, and he hated his work.

Every time he knocked on a door, or rang a bell, he had first to sell himself, and then his encyclopedias. It was like going on stage, doing the same one-man show twenty times a day. Each time the curtain went up, he was out there alone, with people who didn't know who the hell he was and often didn't care. If he hadn't been under KGB discipline, he wouldn't have stood it longer than six months, but now he was in his third year and there was no prospect of a change. Kimber acknowledged it was a good cover for his main activities, and he kept at it with charm and diligence, his mask securely in place.

Behind it, though, was the coldness that made him good at his other work. The selection of Tony Kimber to kill Clive Lyle was not a question of who from Department V happened to be available in the area at the time, but was the personal doing of Sanko himself.

Kimber, with his leather attaché case containing brochures, charts, samples and order forms, crossed N Street.

Against one wall of the foyer of Lyle's block there were separate mailboxes for each apartment, and he inspected these. Almost all had names, except Number 516, which belonged to Lyle.

That was a possibility. He could easily plant a bomb, set to explode when the small wooden door was opened.

Kimber went to the elevator and pressed the button. As he rode to the top floor, he examined the interior. He pulled open a small metal door labelled "Emergency" and inside the recess found a telephone for summoning help in the event of a failure. This offered another possibility.

The elevator reached the top, and Kimber began work.

The first two doors he knocked at didn't answer, but an elderly woman opened the third. He'd never sold anything to that age group before, but perhaps he'd be lucky this time and find she had both money and grandchildren. He gave her his nicest smile and went into his pitch.

Kimber was right. She wasn't buying. He took his leave courteously, thanking her sincerely for her time, and tried the next door.

When he had covered the top floor without success, Kimber took the stairs down and worked his way methodically through those apartments. A woman in her thirties seemed genuinely interested, so he left her with brochures and promised to return in the evening when her husband was home.

Number 517 was opened by a beautiful girl who invited him in and pressed a cup of coffee onto him. He went through his routine, although he knew she wasn't listening. She crossed and uncrossed her legs as she stared at him and sucked the tip of her painted finger.

Ordinarily, Kimber would have been prepared to put work aside and move on to other things—he ran across this sort of situation a couple of times in the average month and providing the women were okay, it helped break up the day—but not when he was starting an operation. Rather than desire, he felt irritation, which he was careful to suppress.

He finally got out, with the girl promising to think about the encyclopedias and inviting him around one evening to hear her answer.

Kimber rang Clive Lyle's bell and stood back so he could be seen through the door's built-in spyglass. In fact, Lyle was scrutinizing him on a television monitor kept in a cupboard in the hallway, well away from his front door—which was about as impervious to bullets as a stick of cotton candy.

He's not a Mormon, Lyle decided, they go about in twos. A salesman of some kind?

The bell rang again. Lyle was wearing only a pair of shorts, because he'd got up late. He closed the door above the monitor and went back to the bathroom. He wasn't in the mood for being sold anything.

Tony Kimber moved away.

He was ringing the next doorbell when he happened to glance back down the corridor and spotted the small, ceiling-mounted television camera. It was well concealed, and if he hadn't been trained, he'd never have noticed it.

Kimber was relieved when no one answered the door because he wanted to check the top floor again. He took the stairs and had a good look around, but there was no television surveillance there. He called the elevator and rode down two floors. Nothing there either.

It was obviously Defense apparatus, with the monitor inside Lyle's apartment. That was useful information. It ruled out an operation outside his front door because it would be too risky. Kimber knew he had to concentrate on other areas.

He went to the underground garage, and looked around.

In the corner was an office, and he could see a young man talking on the phone, facing away.

Kimber walked a few steps until a concrete pillar shielded him from the attendant's line of sight should he turn around. The garage was virtually full, but it was easy to spot Lyle's MGB.

Kimber saw that every space had painted on it the registration number of the vehicle authorized to be kept there.

The MGB was clearly visible from the attendant's room. This made life difficult but not impossible. Someone else would be on duty at nights, probably an older man, and during the low time of the morning, around four, he could be taken care of.

Outside in the street, Kimber strolled until he found a coffee shop and settled down to think how best to tackle the problem.

When he'd made his decision, he returned briskly and went straight to the door of 517, the apartment diagonally opposite Lyle's.

The girl opened it. When she saw him, she placed a hand on a nicely curved hip, and looked amused. "Why, hello again. I didn't expect you back so soon. Did you forget something?"

Tony Kimber stared, and smiled, but made no attempt to enter.

"I just wanted to say," he began, his voice soft and halting, "that I won't be free to come around until next Friday. Do you think Friday night would be okay?"

Her grin broadened.

"Maybe I can take you out to dinner? I mean," he said, "you don't have to buy the encyclopedias or anything unless you really want to. A no-strings dinner." The look on Kimber's face made it clear what he meant.

"Why don't we eat here?" she suggested. "I can fix something and we can, uh, talk. About your encyclopedias." She smoothed her hair off her forehead.

"That'd be fine," Kimber said, looking straight into her eyes. "I'd like that very much."

"Come around eight."

"I will, thanks." Kimber was about to turn away. "Excuse me, but I don't know your name."

"Lily."

"Lily. That's a hell of a pretty name."

"And you?"

"Tony."
"Okay, Tony. See you Friday."
"Yeah."
He gave her his warmest smile.

11

David Ross waited in the arrivals area for the San Francisco flight. It was late, so he hung around watching the steady stream of passengers.

Julie had spent the last few nights making up for her earlier coldness, and he felt he needed a decent night's sleep.

He hadn't made another arrangement to see her, and he thought he'd let things drift for a week until he did his free fall. Maybe afterward they could spend time together before he went home to Elaine.

At last, there was his wife, coming through the doors, smiling with pleasure when she saw him. Ross felt glad to have her back. Their sex life might not win prizes, but there was so much else they had in common it scarcely mattered.

He kissed her, noticing a new perfume, and also a new dress. "You're looking great," he said. "Welcome home."

"You're looking fine, too. I didn't know whether to expect you or not, but I'm so glad you could make it."

Ross took her suitcase and led her toward the parking lot. "I've been pretty busy with one thing and another, but it seems to have eased off now," he said.

During the drive home, she told him about her trip and the people she'd met, and it was clear Elaine had enjoyed herself enormously. They discussed the computer project and the preliminary conclusions she'd reached for the next FBI purchases. In their apartment, over pre-dinner drinks, Ross looked at the notes she'd compiled.

He handed them back, impressed. "These are really very good," he said. "You'll save them a couple of million bucks."

Elaine smiled. "I'm glad you approve." She reached for his hand. "I missed you, David."

"I missed you too," Ross said.

"What are we doing for dinner?"

"I'm afraid I didn't get around to any shopping," Ross said. "I was tied up till the last minute. So let's eat out."

Ross telephoned Germaine's, on the off chance they'd have a free table at short notice. "If you want Vietnamese food, our luck's in," he told Elaine. "There's a place on Wisconsin Avenue Clive swears by. They'll have a table in an hour."

"That's fine. I'll take a shower and get changed. Is it elegant?"

"It's pretty trendy from what I hear. An old Walter Cronkite watering hole, so be prepared to see famous faces."

Elaine laughed. "Sounds like fun."

Ross was gradually becoming aware of a change in his wife. She was relaxed and self-confident. She took his hand when they parked near the Washington Cathedral and walked the short distance to the restaurant. This time it was Ross who noticed the glances they attracted, and not Elaine.

They climbed the stairs to Germaine's, where a tiny Vietnamese woman greeted them. She led them past a pit of glowing coals on which shrimp and chunks of beef and pork were cooking, skewered on thin sticks of wood.

They ordered drinks in a small bar, and Elaine glanced around appreciatively. "Trust Clive to know where to go," she said. She caught the eye of a young couple nearby and smiled at them.

Later, they were escorted into an airy high-ceilinged room, decorated with large green plants. As they waited for their food, they played a surreptitious game of seeing whom they could recognize. That, more than anything, confirmed Ross's suspicion that something radical had happened to his wife during her three weeks away. Before, she'd been worried people were looking at her, at them. Now it was Elaine who was doing the watching.

It was an excellent meal, starting with *chai giao*—Vietnamese spring rolls—then mixed *sate*, the skewers of meat and prawns from the charcoal pit, and finally squirrel fish, a whole baked fish, flavored with ginger.

After coffee, the Rosses wandered back toward the Cathedral and their car, taking their time, enjoying the cool evening air. Elaine kissed him lightly on the cheek as they walked.

Ross hadn't meant to make love to her that night. In fact, he was looking forward to getting to sleep, so when he emerged from the shower, rubbing his hair with a towel, he was surprised to find her in his bed, waiting for him.

"I missed you," she said.

Ross went to her, touching the familiar skin and hair, acutely aware of the differences between Elaine and Julie, separated in his life by only a few hours. "I'm glad you're back," he murmured.

"So am I."

He felt her hands touching his body in a way he hadn't known before with her. Her lips gently kissing his chest, moved lower. For the first time, she was exploring him, as if she'd suddenly given herself the right to see what there was to find.

Ross lay on his back, wondering at the difference in his wife. He felt her lips on his stomach and her teeth gently tugging at the hairs. Her tongue. He wished desperately his body would respond. He concentrated on the sensations registering on his brain. Then he thought about Julie, her face and body, the things they'd done, but that didn't help either. He thought about Andy, a tangle of limbs, muscles and warm flesh. Ross tried to will himself into action, but he remained soft. Elaine's lips made this discovery and she worked patiently on him for several minutes, doing what she had never done before. At last she crawled back next to him, kissing his cheek and stroking his hair.

"I'm sorry," Ross murmured.

"It doesn't matter."

She stayed in his bed, curled close. Ross was soon asleep. He woke in the early morning, at last hard, and gently roused her to make love.

But that special moment had passed, the opportunity to move onto a new level in their relationship, to bring her to her own climax. Elaine had been ready, and Ross had wrecked it. He wondered if he'd get another chance.

When he was through, she held him close. He slept again.

When David left for work, Elaine checked through the apartment to see what needed cleaning, and what she had to buy. The refrigerator was virtually bare, and the cereals she had left in the kitchen cupboard were untouched. She looked into the laundry basket and found it crammed with David's dirty clothes. Whatever he'd been doing the last three weeks, it hadn't included a laundry service. She sorted the clothes and began loading the washing machine.

While it was running, she walked to a delicatessen and

stocked up on some basic items, then went to buy meat. She dropped off some of David's suits at the dry cleaners.

She was back before midday, in time to put a second load into the washing machine and transfer the first to the dryer.

Elaine ate a light lunch and spent the afternoon working on her report for the FBI. She hoped to complete it by the end of the week. She quickly became absorbed in her explanation of how best to overcome their problems, and why she was recommending particular equipment, and she didn't notice it was nearly six. The telephone rang next to her while she was halfway through a sentence which explained, with the minimum of computer jargon, a complicated technical point, and she picked it up without speaking immediately.

After a second, she heard a woman's voice say, "Hello? David?"

Elaine found her attention switched to the phone. "Hello? Oh, I'm sorry, he's not back yet. Can I take a message?"

But the line went dead.

Elaine stared at the receiver for a moment before shrugging and replacing it. She turned back to her work. What the hell had she been trying to say? The words no longer made sense. Her concentration had gone.

Then she glanced at her watch and saw how late it was. "Oh God," she murmured. She hurried to the kitchen to begin dinner, and a few minutes later, before she had got anything properly under way, Ross arrived home.

"Hi!" He put his arms around her and kissed her forehead. "Had a good day?"

"Busy." She told him briefly what she'd been doing.

"Lord, I'm sorry," Ross said contritely. "I should have sent all that stuff to a laundry. I just didn't get it together."

"It's not a problem," she said. "I had a look in your closet, and you've got enough clothes to last another couple of days, by which time you'll have the rest back." She bent over the table on which she was preparing the meat. "Someone phoned for you a while back."

"Oh? Who was it?"

"She didn't say."

Ross felt a stirring of unease. "Old or young?" he asked.

"Young, I'd say," Elaine offered, non-committally.

"You want a drink?"

"Oh, yes, please."

He was fixing martinis when the phone rang again. "Hello?"

"David?"

Jesus, it was her. "Yeah?"

"Do you hate me for calling you at home like this?" Julie sounded depressed.

What could Ross say? Elaine was in the next room, obviously able to overhear. "What's the problem?" he asked, brisk and businesslike.

"I miss you, I wanted to say hi."

Ross felt trapped, a fish on a hook. He also felt rising anger. "Look, I'll call you," he said. "Okay?"

Instantly, Julie hung up. Ross was left holding the receiver, uncertain what to do. Just putting it down, ending the conversation abruptly like that would sound suspicious. So he added, "I'll speak to Yardley and let you know. Goodbye."

He finished mixing the drinks.

"Who was that?" Elaine asked, taking her glass from him.

"Business," Ross replied shortly.

That was one advantage of working for the DIA. A lot of his life actually wasn't communicable, which meant the odd piece of unwelcome personal flotsam could conveniently be included in that category.

"Oh, I see," Elaine said. She lifted her glass. "Cheers."

"Cheers."

"How did your day go?"

"It was okay. Routine stuff, reading through files, that sort of thing." Ross watched her sticking slivers of garlic into the lamb. He said casually, "By the way, I took up a new sport while you were on your travels."

She glanced at him, interested. "Oh? What was that?"

"Skydiving."

"Skydiving! Good God. Whatever for?"

Ross explained how he felt about it and how far he'd got. When he'd finished, she said, "Well, if it makes you happy, I think that's wonderful. When are you going again?"

"I guess next Saturday. I'll do my first free fall then."

"Is it far away?"

"No, just over an hour's drive."

"Well," Elaine said, "perhaps I'll come along and see you jump. It's a long time since I've watched parachuting. I can't imagine what it'll be like knowing the person doing it."

She hadn't expected the silence that followed, but as soon as she noticed it, she kept busy, rubbing salt and rosemary into the meat, waiting for him to respond and resolutely not meeting his eye. If David didn't want her along for any reason, it was up to him to say so.

Ross stared at her bleakly, his heart sinking. His personal life had suddenly become complicated and messy. He'd been positive Elaine would want to keep away from the skydivers because of her sensitivity about her age, and that he'd have no problem keeping Julie and the others in their safe, separate compartment, well away from his marriage.

At last he said, "Actually, I'd rather you didn't come, if

you don't mind. If I knew you were watching, I think I'd get it all wrong.''

"Okay," Elaine agreed obligingly.

Ross offered an olive branch. "When I've got a few free falls under my belt and I feel more confident, I'll bring you over to meet the guys.''

"Sure," she said. "Say the word and I'll be there.''

Ross finished his martini in a gulp and felt the need for another. "How's your drink?" Elaine's was virtually untouched beside her.

"Oh, I'm fine at the moment," she said.

Ross went to get himself a refill.

Elaine, as she slid the tray of meat into the oven and set the timer, was aware that something wasn't right, although she hadn't yet put her finger on precisely what. She hated the role of the suspicious wife, and in any event, she didn't think she had enough information to justify it. There were a lot of secrets in David's life—she appreciated that—and maybe having her at the skydiving club next Saturday really would put him off his stroke, which she certainly didn't want to do. It was an unforgiving sport.

Ross was particularly attentive to her that evening, as if making up for something. After dinner, when she'd said goodnight, he came to her room and took special care trying to arouse her, looking for that elusive spark she'd shown the night before; and to both their surprises, Ross finally found it, felt his wife responding, moving beneath him, until suddenly she called his name almost in panic and cried out as the climax burst upon her, and a second later, on him.

Elaine lay trembling, holding him close, feeling the muscles on his back. In all their marriage, it had never been like that for her, and she'd never imagined it could be.

In the morning, she felt better and happier than she could remember for years. She hummed as she prepared breakfast, while David, having a boiled egg and coffee at the kitchen table, looked handsome and incredibly pleased with himself.

When he left for the DIA, she settled down to her own work and had no difficulty completing the final sections. The draft was ready by lunchtime, which for her was a record. A good sex life obviously improved efficiency.

She spent most of the afternoon reviewing the draft, interrupted only by the delivery of mail—mostly bills as usual. There was one letter for David. The envelope was of expensive paper, addressed in a firm, assertive hand-writing, using a thick-nibbed pen.

Elaine frowned, wondering who it was from. She put it on the hall table for him to find when he got home and was walking back to her desk when something made her look at the envelope again. She held it thoughtfully as if weigh-ing it, then lifted it to her nose and detected a faint perfume. Elaine wondered if she should open it and pre-tend to David she'd made a mistake, but she'd never pried into his correspondence before and she wasn't going to start now. She placed it carefully in a prominent position and returned to her work.

Elaine felt she needed to talk to someone. She thought of Clive Lyle, but quickly rejected him. Clive was a friend of David's, and it wouldn't be right to put him in the position of listening to her doubts and fears. If David was being pursued by some woman—and God knew it would be a strange world if at some stage or another he was not—or even if he had actually become involved, then the chances were Clive would be aware of it, and she knew him well enough to realize he wouldn't rat on a friend to anyone, least of all a wife.

But an idea formed in Elaine's mind: one that had been nudging at her consciousness for some time. She tele-phoned the DIA.

"May I speak to Geoffrey Howlett, please," she said.

After a moment, a woman's voice spoke. "Psychiatric unit."

"Is Geoffrey Howlett there, please? It's Elaine Ross."

"I'll locate him for you."

Howlett was on the line a few seconds later. "Mrs. Ross," he said. "Nice to hear from you again." His voice was friendly, and she remembered him with affection from the early days of David's DIA career when he had helped her over a bad personal patch.

"Hello, Dr. Howlett. Listen, I'm sorry to bother you, but I wonder if I could come over for some advice?"

"Of course. When would you like? Later today? I have a patient in five minutes, but I'll be free an hour or so after that."

Elaine checked the time. David would be back around then. "No, I'd prefer tomorrow if that's possible."

"Sure. How about the morning. Would ten o'clock suit you?"

"That would be perfect. Thank you very much."

When she hung up, Elaine went to her bedroom and inspected her face in the mirror. She was often doing that these days although she never learned any cheering news.

"How does an older woman keep a young and handsome husband?" she asked her reflection in a coy Jackie Kennedy voice, giving her prettiest smile; and answered wry and gruff, "With difficulty, my child."

She sighed. It was time for drastic action.

Elaine had put dinner in the oven before Ross returned. She heard his key in the lock but forced herself to stay in the kitchen, to give him time to find and read his mail. Perhaps he would tell her about it, or show it to her, so she could feel secretly ridiculous for her foolish fantasies.

It was a couple of minutes before Ross appeared, and when he did, there was no sign of the letter. Whatever it said, Ross seemed perfectly relaxed, and the evening passed without any sign of strain. David was so openly affectionate, she knew he intended trying to repeat the miracle of the previous night. It felt a little like being on honeymoon—one that actually worked—and after a while, even the niggling doubt in the back of her mind could not spoil it. She didn't ask Ross about the letter, and he volunteered nothing. It was as if it didn't exist, although she knew it must be there, in his pocket, and she was torn between wanting to read it and feeling fearful of what she might discover if she did. So Elaine concentrated on them, on the magical chemistry they had discovered which, apart from the joy it gave her, represented a new and unexpected weapon in her rather depleted arsenal.

The next morning she presented herself at the DIA's psychiatric unit a few minutes before ten, and sat in the bland, neutrally decorated waiting room, flicking through a magazine.

"Mrs. Ross."

She looked up to see Geoffrey Howlett smiling at her from the entrance to his office.

"Please come in."

Howlett stood aside to let her pass. Elaine liked him. There was a calmness about his manner, coupled with a quick, sympathetic understanding of issues. She had never moved into therapy with him, just a joint scrutiny of the options available to her at a time she doubted she had a place as an adjunct to David in his new role.

Howlett was approaching forty, and his looks were saved from being ordinary by the longest eyelashes Elaine had ever seen. There was a vigorous growth of dark body hair tufting from his collar above his tie, and below the cuffs of his white shirt. He wore no personal jewelry, beyond a plain watch, and his office was anonymous, lacking photographs, calendars, diaries, diplomas. There was just a clear desk, a large potted plant in one corner, a couple of comfortable chairs and a couch. Howlett dominated the room, by himself.

"How've you been?" he asked, settling on the other side of the desk.

"Pretty well. And David's fine. I suppose he's doing okay at the DIA although of course he doesn't talk about it much."

"But he enjoys it?"

"It has its ups and downs like everything else," Elaine said, "but on balance I'd say yes. I get the feeling he's very happy."

"So." Howlett placed his long and slender hands on the desk and scrutinized her. "What can I do for you?"

Elaine told him everything, even the sudden improvement in her sex life. She and Howlett had spoken about too many things in the past for her to have reservations now, and she trusted him to listen and respond sensibly. She talked about David's skydiving, the call from the girl, and the letter.

"Do you think David's having an affair?" Howlett asked.

"I think he might be, don't you?"

Howlett shrugged. "It's possible. David's an exceedingly handsome man, and in the ordinary course of events, he'll get occasional offers from women. But from what you tell me, it seems your own relationship's developing well. Now that's a good sign."

"I know it," Elaine said. "And I don't want to lose it."

"Tell me, Mrs. Ross, how would you feel if you discovered he was having an affair? Would you be able to carry on, or would you say 'that's it, that's the end?' "

"I think," Elaine answered after a pause, "I'd want to know how serious he was. Obviously, if David's in love with someone else, I wouldn't stand in his way. I can't fight for him as a woman in her twenties might. It would be absurd and embarrassing. I'd be in an impossible position.''

"But if he was just sleeping around?" Howlett asked.

"I guess I'd be hurt and angry, but I don't think I'd pack my bags. Or ask him to pack his.''

"Why don't you ask him? Have you thought of that?''

She smiled ruefully. "No," she said. "I'm afraid he might tell me the truth.''

"Well, what is it you want to do, Mrs. Ross? Is there anything specific, or is this just a general talk. As you know, I'm happy either way.''

Elaine stared at him for a long moment, summoning her courage. "There is something specific," she said finally. "I don't know if you're going to think me vain and stupid.''

"I won't think that," Howlett assured her, holding her gaze. "You're not vain, and you're certainly not stupid. You've had a hard couple of years, and I'm filled with admiration for the way you've coped.''

"Thank you." It came in a rush. "I wondered if I ought to have cosmetic surgery.''

"Why not?" he said. "What sort of thing did you have in mind?''

"A face lift. Get rid of these wrinkles around my eyes." Her fingers smoothed back her skin. "Something to make me look a little younger, more able to compete.''

"I think that's a fine idea," Howlett said. "There's no reason why you shouldn't make the most of your looks. Actually, you're a very attractive woman as it is, and not only because of your personality." Elaine began to demur, but he presssed on. "I mean it. I'm not just flattering you. There's no reason for me to do that. You've matured very well, very gracefully. But if nature can be given a little help, then you ought to consider it.''

Elaine felt relieved and grateful. ''You really mean that?''

''I really mean it.''

She smiled warmly at him. ''Thank you. It's exactly what I wanted to hear. Funnily enough, I used to hate the idea. I thought there was nothing worse than someone trying to cheat the years with surgery.''

''Like most things, cosmetic surgery can be a curse if wrongly used, but for you, I guess it'll be a blessing. You want me to call someone?''

''Oh, would you?'' She had been prepared to make her own inquiries.

''Sure. I don't know if you're aware of it, but the DIA has one of the finest plastic surgeons in the United States on its payroll. Our people sometime need a bit of work done on them.'' Elaine hadn't known that, although she could imagine the sort of thing it would entail: part of the dark, hidden side of Defense Intelligence. ''His name is Timothy Peal. I think you'll like him.''

''Will he mind doing a private job like this?'' Elaine asked.

Howlett smiled. ''This isn't a private job, Mrs. Ross. It's DIA business. Remember what you were told right at the beginning?—that we were here to help you and David make the necessary adjustments? We meant it. Whatever your problems are, we're here to sort them out.'' His smile broadened. ''We take care of our people, as you see.''

''That's nice to know. Thank you again.'' She looked anxious. ''Oh, one thing: I don't want David to know what I'm doing. I just thought I'd go away and come back a new woman. If he asks, I'll tell him, but otherwise not.''

"Some of our best work goes around unannounced," Howlett said philosophically.

He picked up his telephone and dialed. After a brief discussion with Timothy Peal, Howlett put his hand over the mouthpiece. "He's free now if you'd like to go down to see him."

"He's here? In the hospital?"

"Sure. A couple of floors away."

"Yes, please."

Howlett said into the phone, "That's fine, Tim, I'll bring her down right away."

Elaine returned to her apartment feeling both elated and nervous. She went to the mirror and stared at the familiar face which in a few days' time would be under Timothy Peal's knife, and out of post-surgical puffiness and bruising would emerge a new model.

She could be good in bed, and she could look younger. Those were the new weapons in her arsenal, to be added to the fact that David, bless him, still loved her and that they had a lot in common.

But if the day came she felt he really would be happier with someone else, Elaine vowed to bow out quickly and gracefully and avoid the deep hurt and wicked humiliation that otherwise would be hers.

The skydivers did not operate outside weekends, unless there was a public holiday, so Sophie Johnson could choose any night she liked.

She'd made her first jump on that Sunday, medical certificate notwithstanding. She clinched the matter by giving Pete Grethel a faultless display of the six basic landing rolls from the trapeze first thing in the morning, and when she'd finished, he stood with his hands on his hips, grinning at her.

"You're incredible," he said. "Just like David Ross, a natural."

Sophie beamed and kissed him on the cheek. She'd put on perfume that morning, and Grethel could still smell it. "It's because you're a fantastic instructor," she whispered, "and sexy too."

"Oh yeah?" Grethel raised an eyebrow.

Sophie had made her preliminary pitch, and Grethel's response was what she wanted. She felt his hand touch her waist lightly.

"I'll bet you say that to all the guys," Grethel said.

She shook her head. "A select few."

She moved away, brushing dust off her jumpsuit, and they walked back to the clubhouse. Grethel, who didn't have a regular girl at the moment, wondered whether to take her out to dinner that night and see where they ended up. Sophie wasn't bad looking, and she had guts. It would be interesting to find out what an older and obviously experienced woman was like in bed. But first things first.

"You look like you're in good shape, Sophie," Grethel said casually.

"Thank you, kind sir. I do my best."

"Hell, I don't mean your figure. Although that's not bad either." He glanced at her. "I mean your health. You're fitter than a lot of the beginners I see. Fitter than a couple of guys I could name at this clubhouse now."

Sophie guessed what was coming, but she let Pete get around to it in his own time.

"Oh, I'm fine," she said. "I've never had any problems."

"So how would you feel about doing your first jump this morning?"

A grin spread over her face. "You mean it?" she asked. "You'd let me do it?"

"I guess so," Grethel said. "As long as you haven't got

a weak heart or something like that. We really should have a certificate, but I reckon I can make an exception in your case. You're obviously ready."

Sophie flung her arms around his neck and was aware of hoots and catcalls coming from the clubhouse. "That'd be great, Pete! Thanks, thanks."

Pete broke away, laughing, "Hey, hey," he said, "this is the point you're supposed to get scared and serious."

"I'll do that later," Sophie promised.

Within half an hour, Sophie Johnson, the least nervous pupil Grethel had ever seen, exited from the Cessna like a professional and fell in the starfish position for the few seconds before her canopy automatically deployed.

Now it was after midnight on Wednesday, and Sophie's car was parked off the highway just short of the dirt road leading to the club.

She moved easily and quickly through the darkness, surefooted as a cat. The rutted road was clearly defined in the washed-out blue and grays into which her night vision goggles translated the world, with the perimeter fence bleached white and the hangars ghostly shapes far behind.

She'd had her jump that Sunday, then her initiation, and finally Pete Grethel, a lover of fumbling gentleness and almost unbearable sensitivity. Clearly he hadn't known many women because he was as willing a pupil with her as she had been with him, and he learned as fast. He'd come back for a second night, then a third.

Sophie remembered as she walked silently. Right now, he would have been warm and vulnerably sleeping in her bed if she hadn't pleaded an out-of-town engagement. Pete had promised to phone her at work in the morning.

It wasn't true love, but it was a lot of fun.

The road curved, following the perimeter fence, and ahead she saw the wooden sign for the club. She stopped near the entrance and fumbled in the pocket of her coat for a pair of thin cotton gloves.

She slid the bolt and pushed gently at the gate, opening it just enough for her to slip through. It hadn't squeaked that first day at the club, but she intended taking as few chances as possible.

Sophie squatted just inside the perimeter, looking and listening. There would be security around the hangars, although most were some distance off. The nearest hangar, with the club's Cessna and the ancient Tiger Moth, was the immediate source of concern.

When she was satisfied, she moved forward silently.

The clubhouse seemed smaller through the goggles, and strangely unimportant, as if long abandoned. She climbed the steps to the porch.

It took less than a minute to open the door, and as soon as she was in, she closed it quietly behind her.

There was less available light inside for the goggles to intensify. The pinpricks of stars that might have been visible from the small window were largely blotted out by cloud or curtain, and deep blue shadow covered much of the room.

But Sophie knew her way around and she headed immediately for the storeroom. The vision was better in there because the one window faced onto a clear part of the sky and there were no curtains.

She worked at the lock on the cupboard, coaxing the levers into movement. The shackle sprang free.

Sophie looked in. Rows of helmets were stacked on shelves, and beside them were the parachutes.

On the left was the main canopy she'd used on Sunday and which she had later watched Pete refold; and on the right the smaller packs of the emergency chutes. Grethel would pick up one of the two nearest reserves for use by

Ross, so it was also necessary for her to sabotage both these.

She took the main canopy into the club room and stood at the window, staring out. The airfield was quiet, seemingly deserted.

She laid the pack on the floor and knelt on top of it so she could ease the ripcord wire out of its cleats. She felt the tightly packed drogue and canopy straining to break free. She increased her weight on bulging areas and when the wire was clear, slid slowly off, transferring the lesser weight of her stomach and forearms to the tense bundle. Sophie eased away, letting the drogue pop out and the tension go.

The canopy was shrouded in a long white sock, which she pulled carefully to its full length. From the sock's narrow opening, the rigging lines, neatly laid and free of tangles, ran down to the harness.

Sophie took out of her pocket a piece of ordinary twine and tied it tightly around the lines, where they attached to the canopy itself, right at the mouth of the sock.

That was all she had to do.

When a drogue flares, pulling the parachute out behind it, the wind must rush up a clear central airway with enough force to bust the sock off the canopy, or it cannot open. If the airway is blocked and the rigging lines imprisoned, the canopy will stream behind a plunging skydiver in a long, useless package known as a Roman Candle.

Sophie Johnson repacked the chute neatly, threading back the ripcord that Ross would pull on his first free fall. She inspected the finished pack critically. It was perfect.

She laid it to one side and began work on the two reserves.

Three pieces of string were enough to end the life of David Ross.

Outside, a dog barked, then another.

She moved to the window and stared into an airfield of washed out blues and grays. She could see nothing.

She carried the reserves back to the cupboard, then the main chute, which she stacked carefully at the side.

The barking came closer.

Sophie shut the cupboard door and snapped the lock. She stared out of the window again.

There was a security guard with two dogs on a leash! She could see the animals yapping, straining.

And the clubhouse door wasn't locked! Oh shit shit. She fumbled at it, feeling panic rising but fighting it back. Getting in had been easy, so locking the door wouldn't be a problem.

It clicked shut. Sophie leaned against it in relief.

The beam of a flashlight passed over a window and briefly illuminated a peeling wall. The guard was still some distance away, judging from the dogs, so she moved cautiously to a window and sneaked a glance through half-closed curtains.

He was at the nearby hangar, checking. She could see he was armed but hadn't drawn his gun. One hand held the dogs' leashes, the other the flashlight. He moved out of sight, around the back of the hangar, and re-emerged after a couple of minutes to complete the circuit.

The dogs were Dobermans, muscular and savage, and there was both threat and excitement in their noise.

Sophie looked around to see where she could hide. There was nowhere totally protected from all possible lines of sight. She guessed the guard would try the front door first, and she hoped he'd be content with looking in the nearest windows. First she thought she'd stand against the door itself, until she realized her smell so close would inflame the dogs further, so she crouched behind a sofa as far away as she could get.

Because of her image-intensifying goggles, the beam of

the flashlight seemed radiant as it moved around. The room glowed with an unearthly light. The dogs worked themselves into a frenzy on the porch.

The light disappeared. She heard the door handle turn, the guard pushing against it hard, rattling the lock. She lay, her breathing shallow.

Does he have a key?

The door rattled again, the Dobermans howled. There was no way the guard would leave now. He'd call for reinforcements. He'd break down the door.

What could she do? Bluff her way out? Pull every political string she possessed? Name the Congressman she worked for, the Senators who owed her a favor? It wouldn't work; it was too late for that.

As clearly as if it had been that morning, the scene came back to her. The Soviet instructor was thin and balding. He had an American accent and no sense of humor. "If you're ever captured," he was saying, "you will not admit you work for the KGB. You will say nothing beyond your cover story. If necessary, you'll die saying nothing. That is why you've been selected, above others. We believe you have the capabilities, and beyond that, you have a duty."

How far away capture seemed then: how close now.

The rattling stopped. She could tell from the barking that the guard was moving around to the storeroom window. After a minute, she heard him coming closer again, circling the building.

She moved quickly to the other side of the sofa. The flashlight again, dazzling through the goggles. The dogs were still hysterical, but now she could hear the guard talking sharply to them—the first hopeful sign—and after a minute, the barking grew fainter.

Sophie Johnson lay limp and exhausted on the thin carpet.

At last she went to look out the windows, but could see nothing. The dogs were quiet.

It was time to get out. She locked the door after her and walked quickly and silently to the gate.

She closed it behind her and stripped off her gloves, cramming them into her pocket. The night was cool.

Now that she was clear, she felt calm again. It wasn't the end after all, not for her.

When Ross was dead, there would be an inquiry. The police would investigate and so would the DIA. Jesus, the DIA would know what had happened, but what could they do?

The security guards would tell them about the dogs late Wednesday night.

Everyone would be questioned, but Sophie would warrant the least attention. Her political credentials were excellent, and she was too new at the club to know how to sabotage anything.

In the end, the DIA would blame the KGB, that great, amorphous organization, and there the trail would run cold.

A few hours after Timothy Peal had given her the Friday hospital booking, with the operation scheduled for the following morning, Elaine told Ross she would be out of town on FBI business for at least a week.

"What the hell for?" David asked, faintly irritated. "I thought you'd done your report."

"Well, I thought so too," she said. "But they've got some new points they want to discuss. You know how clients are sometimes."

It was the first time she could remember lying to her husband, and she was surprised how easily the words came.

Ross felt inclined to protest further. They'd been getting

on so well recently he didn't want to take the chance of a separation spoiling their newly discovered personal chemistry before it had time to become properly established.

Then he remembered he'd be free falling on Saturday and, with Elaine away, on Sunday as well. He'd also have a chance to sort out Julie.

"I suppose," Ross agreed, "it can't be helped."

"No."

On Friday, a few hours after Ross had left for the DIA, Elaine packed a small suitcase and took a cab to the complex in which he worked.

She walked out of the elevator into the hospital reception area where a nurse sat behind a desk.

"Good afternoon," she said. "I'm Elaine Ross."

At seven that night, Tony Kimber rode the elevator to Clive Lyle's floor. In one hand, he carried his leather attaché case, in the other, a bunch of flowers. He'd just had a shower, and there was a healthy glow to his skin, a shine to his thick hair. He wore a dark suit, and his shoes were polished.

The door slid open and Kimber stepped out, walking confidently to Number 517.

The girl opened the door, wearing a long white shift, obviously very expensive, which strongly suggested the shape of her body. Kimber stood in the corridor and stared admiringly, making no move to come in. She looked unwaveringly back at him, a smile playing around the corners of her mouth.

"I wonder," Kimber said at last, "if I could interest you in something that might change your life?"

"Oh yes," she answered softly. "You certainly could."

David Ross sat at home alone, drinking a beer. When Elaine wasn't there, or wasn't expected back within a couple of hours, the apartment made him uncomfortable. He didn't know why. He hadn't felt that way about their home in Princeton. He'd been more self-contained then, happy to listen to music while Elaine was off on her own business, or read, sometimes watch television if there was a program worth seeing. But everything had been different then, starting with Ross himself.

The years before the DIA were remote parts of history, and it seemed extraordinary they had ever happened. Ross had become a new man, and he was still changing, growing as Lyle's world and Yardley's absorbed him more completely. He knew he had a long way to go before he was totally one of them: not physically so much, because the fighting and field craft aspects had been pretty well taken care of at Fairfax and maintained in routine weekly training. The final transition would be a mental and emotional one and would come through experience.

Killing, for instance, would be the biggest hurdle. He'd never taken a life although he had watched death. Yet how many times had Lyle killed in the course of duty? Some day he'd ask him.

What's it like, Clive? How do you live with yourself after you've done it? What do you dream about?

Ross thought he knew the answer to that question. Lyle probably didn't dream at all. He was amoral, and Ross was growing to be like him, becoming desensitized, learning to behave like a soldier fighting a secret war in a nation at peace. But while he made the transition, he wasn't happy with his own company.

Ross glanced at his watch and saw it was eight. He thought of calling Julie but had another beer instead. As he drank, he wondered about her, and why he had been so surprised when she began pestering him at home. God knew he'd been warned. But she'd seemed so content with her own life-style, so genuinely determined to keep clear of all permanent involvements, that Ross felt there had to be some explanation for her actions. If he could discover what it was, they ought to be able to come to an understanding for the future, although their meetings would now be less frequent than Ross had originally thought. Elaine was providing almost everything he needed now, except for the velvet, supple feel of a young woman. That he still had to look for away from home.

His resolution crumbled. He phoned Julie and listened disappointed to the ringing tone. She wasn't home. Ross stood uncertain, wondering what to do.

He dialed another number.

"Hi, Clive? It's David."

"Hi, Dave. What can I do for you?"

"Listen, I wondered if you'd like to come over for a meal or a drink tonight? Elaine's taken off for a few days, but there're some steaks in the icebox."

He could hear regret in Lyle's voice. "Oh hell, David, I'd like to, but I can't tonight. I've got company."

"Oh. Yeah, okay."

There was a pause during which Lyle recognized his colleague's disappointment, and Ross wished Clive would ask him over. At last Lyle said, "Dave, I've got a friend here, but I don't think it's going to be your sort of scene. If you feel it is, you're very welcome to come along and join us."

"Thanks Clive, but I don't want to intrude."

"It's no problem. Hey, aren't you doing your free fall tomorrow?"

He could hear Ross cheer up. "First thing in the morning. You want to come and watch?"

"No thanks, Dave. It's a little early for me. Maybe another time."

"Okay, sorry to have bothered you, Clive. Enjoy yourself."

"Thanks, I will. You too."

Lyle turned away from the phone and smiled at Brian Stewart. "How's your drink?"

Stewart sat relaxed in an armchair, hands behind his head, watching with steady blue-green eyes. "I could use another beer," he said. "Who was that?"

"David Ross. You met him at your party, remember? He came with his wife."

"Oh yeah. The older woman."

"Elaine. That's the one. She's gone away for a few days."

"He's not coming over?"

Lyle shook his head.

"Pity about that," Stewart said regretfully, stroking a neatly trimmed beard.

"Fuck you too," Lyle said, chucking him a frosted can, which he caught deftly.

"Ah hell, Clive, now this stuff's going to froth everywhere," Brian Stewart complained. He took it to the kitchen sink and lost almost half the beer opening it. He could hear Lyle laughing in the other room.

"Silly bastard," Stewart muttered.

Lily raised her wine glass to Tony Kimber, and her eyes sparkled at him over the crystal.

"That was . . . too much," she said breathlessly.

"Oh, I don't know," Kimber replied. "I thought we might try it again after dinner. Properly this time."

She giggled. "That wasn't properly?"

"I mean in bed. Taking it slow."

They were dressed again, and Lily had lit a dozen thin white tapers in a low metal holder. She looked beautiful in the soft light.

"What do you do, Lily? Tell me about yourself." Kimber

refilled their wine glasses, and his other hand touched her fingers.

"I'm in advertising," she said. "With JWT." Kimber didn't understand. "J. Walter Thompson," she explained. "I'm an account executive."

"Sounds good. What exactly do you do?"

Lily listed the products for which she was responsible. "I live in New York. I'm just visiting here."

Kimber's expression became a little strained. "You mean this isn't your apartment?"

"No. It belongs to my sister. She's in the hospital—due out the middle of next week. I said I'd come to hold her hand and get a break from the Manhattan madhouse."

"You're staying here alone?"

"I'm afraid so. My God, Washington's a boring town, isn't it? I know I wanted a rest, but I hadn't planned on a desert island."

Kimber laughed. "Oh, it's not that bad. Not after you've met a couple of people and found the right places to go."

She looked mischievously at him. "Well, there has been a certain improvement over the last hour or two," she conceded. "There had to be something about our capital city I wanted to remember, apart from endless hours at the hospital wondering what the hell to talk about. I feel I've been here a year."

"What's wrong with your sister? Nothing serious?"

"Gynecological problem," Lily said and offered no further explanation. "So, Mr. Kimber. Tell me about yourself. You're married, I see. Where does your wife think you are tonight?"

"I'm out of town on a sales conference. It happens from time to time."

"I'll bet it does."

"Hardly ever with anyone as nice as you."

She inclined her head. "Is that how you get rid of your encyclopedias?"

He laughed. "No, I only sleep with people who've already bought, or aren't going to buy, like you. I don't do it to clinch deals."

"Pity. You might break all previous sales records."

"I'm choosy who I go with."

"I'm glad to hear that. Do you want to open another bottle of wine? It's in the refrigerator."

When Kimber returned, she told him more about herself, growing up in Denver and moving to New York to get a job. "There's a guy at JWT who wants to marry me," she said, "but I'm not sure I like him enough for that. I went through a few months of loving him, but I guess I never completely liked him. I felt there was something in his background I'd discover when it was too late. I don't know what it is. Intuition, I suppose."

"What does your intuition tell you about me?" Kimber asked.

Lily laughed. "Well," she said, "when you rang my doorbell that first morning, and you stood there, the all-American boy, wearing your wedding band and your Pepsodent smile, with your encyclopedias and everything, I thought to myself: this guy's a phony."

Kimber raised an amused eyebrow.

"I thought: Behind the Mr. Nice Guy image lies a really sexy man. I guess I was right."

"Uh-huh. What else?"

"I thought . . ." She looked down at her glass. "I thought: I'll bet he's not even married. The band's there to fool housewives into letting him through the front door." Kimber's easy expression didn't flicker. "I thought . . . there's more to this guy than meets the eye. You know what I mean? I could see you were in shape, but hell, I didn't know what sort of shape until you had me down on the couch over there and were stripping down. You don't get a body like yours knocking on doors.''

"I work out," said Kimber.

"I'm sure you do. And your hands.'' She reached out and he turned them toward her. She ran her fingertips over them. "These are not the hands of an encyclopedia sales-man,'' she said. She touched the outside edges of his palms. "Look at that skin there. It's hard, almost like a callous.''

"Karate,'' Kimber explained. "It's my hobby.''

"You break blocks of wood, piles of bricks?''

"Something like that.''

"Dangerous hands. They scare me a bit. You scare me a bit. I guess that's what makes you so attractive. You aren't what you seem to be.''

"If you were scared, why did you ask me back? You don't know who I am. Maybe I'll strangle you and take your money.'' He smiled.

Lily shrugged. "There's not much to take. It wouldn't be worth it. No, I'm not that scared. I think you could be a dangerous man, but I don't think you're dangerous to me. There's no reason, unless you're a psycho. And my in-stinct tells me you're not.'' She looked him in the eye. "How am I doing?''

"You're doing fine,'' he said, "except for the wife. She's real.''

"You ready for dessert?''

David Ross walked along N Street to Scott Circle, then down 16th toward Lafayette Park, with the White House beyond it. He wandered slowly, passing time, waiting until he was tired enough to go home and to bed. Tomor-row was a big day.

He thought about Julie—whether she'd be back yet, whether he ought to call her now. He decided not to. New ground rules were needed before they went to bed together again.

He certainly didn't want to hurt Elaine, but he didn't feel bad about committing adultery. Adultery! What an old-fashioned word. Then he wondered, is it society that's changing, or is it me, because I'm working for the DIA?

Ross whistled softly to himself and headed for home.

Lily slept, peaceful and deep, one hand lightly touching herself between her legs.

Kimber eased gently out of bed and stood in the darkness on the carpet, listening to her breathing. It would be better if she didn't wake. He padded naked to the door and opened it cautiously.

It creaked.

Kimber stopped, listening. He heard her sigh and turn over, but almost immediately her breathing was again deep and even. The door was open enough for him to get through.

Silently he walked across the living room, aware of the position of the furniture and where he'd left his black attaché case. He carried it to the window and drew aside a curtain to give him enough light to see the combination locks. He worked quickly and calmly. They snapped free.

Kimber pulled out a pile of brochures and order forms and placed them on the floor.

He pressed the far edges of the case at a point near the locks. The false bottom, spring-loaded, lifted at one side and Kimber swung it open.

Beneath, everything was laid out in order. He took the first two items: a small gas mask, which he put over his face and attached with a band behind his head, and an unmarked aerosol can. He returned softly to the bedroom.

He closed the door behind him and it creaked again. He

moved toward the girl, pulling the pin from the top of the canister and depressing the lever. Gas hissed out.

Kimber, a bulky, motionless black shape, stood over Lily. She sighed again, as if in complaint, and then was silent.

The canister took several minutes to empty, but when it was done, he collected his clothes, let himself out into the living room and closed the door.

In that environment, the girl would remain unconscious for three hours. He switched on the lights and dressed.

It was three A.M. Kimber took out a package wrapped in brown paper and covered with plastic. He opened it carefully, exposing the explosive within.

Into this, he embedded metal detonator probes, making sure the thin wire aerial, which would pick up his radio signal, was hanging free.

The final item he removed from his case was a plastic bag of nails, nuts and bolts. Kimber put everything into an opaque carrier and went to the front door. He checked through the spyglass that the corridor was empty. It was unlikely anyone would be around this time of the morning, but you could never be sure. He left Lily's door unlocked and slipped out. He rang for the elevator.

Above him the machinery whirred, and he heard the elevator arrive at his floor. The doors opened. Kimber pressed the button for Lobby, and when the elevator was between floors he flicked the Emergency Stop button, prepared to turn it back on again if the alarm sounded.

The car jerked to a halt. There was silence.

Kimber opened the small metal door just below the operating buttons. The explosive fitted neatly over the handpiece of the telephone for summoning aid, and in front of it he placed the bag of nails and metal pieces—instant shrapnel, which, in the explosion, would tear a man to shreds.

Kimber closed the metal door and restarted the elevator. He went to the lobby and looked cautiously around before going up again to Lily's apartment.

There was cleaning to do now: his case to repack, the glasses, plates, cutlery to wash and dry carefully leaving no fingerprints. Kimber wiped the wine bottles, the table, the backs of chairs he'd touched.

It was almost five when he was through. From his case he selected another item. The injection.

Kimber put the gas mask back on and walked into the bedroom. He turned on the light.

Lily was lying on her side of the large bed, mouth slightly open. He lifted her arm, twisting it so he could see the crook where the best veins ran. Her skin was soft and milky colored.

Kimber's fingers wrapped around her upper arm and squeezed gently. She didn't stir. The veins stood out, delicate and blue.

He slid the needle in and pressed the plunger, then withdrew it and rubbed the pinprick spot with his thumb.

Kimber stood back to watch.

Lily's body began to twitch.

He saw a tremor in her hands; then her feet began to jerk, to dance, and her muscles jumped of their own accord. Her eyelids shot open and she stared, eyes bulging. Could she see him? Could she see anything? Her mouth gaped in a soundless scream and the flesh of her face trembled. Her arms began to thrash and so did her shoulders. Gradually her color changed from milky white to blue, and her movements subsided. She lay still.

The potassium that had stopped her heart, began to suffuse her body, almost impossible to detect in a post mortem.

Kimber left her where she was, glassy-eyed, staring into the far distance.

He wiped down the bedroom and door handles and returned to the living room.

He waited for dawn.

David Ross woke to the tight feeling in his stomach: the familiar fear that confronted him before every jump, a wall—getting higher and more difficult every time—that he had to climb before he could regain self-respect. A constant proving of himself.

He showered and dressed, then stared out the window.

It was a lousy, overcast day. He hoped it would be better at the airfield.

He forced himself to eat a bowl of cereal and drank two cups of black coffee.

He went to get his car.

Elaine felt hands beneath her, strong, secure, lifting her off the bed and onto a stretcher. Her eyes were heavy, and she struggled to open them. Two men in green coats were strapping her down. One of them saw her focusing on him and smiled.

"We're taking you up now," he said reassuringly. "Just relax. Everything's fine."

The ceiling began to move, sliding by: recessed tube lighting, acoustic tiles, doorframe; out into the corridor, lights every few feet and no sound except rubber shoes on the rubberized floor. A silent wait for the elevator. The doors rumbled open. Elaine was conscious of ascending two, perhaps three floors. Out into another corridor, another room. More figures, green-capped, green-gowned. People chatting casually around her.

The clinking of metal. Instruments, perhaps? Elaine couldn't tell. She tried to raise her head to look around but the effort was too much. A face came into view: Timothy Peal, smiling encouragingly.

"Good morning, Mrs. Ross. How are you feeling?" Peal asked.

"Dopey," she said.

"Excellent, that's just what we want."

Elaine was conscious of movement at the periphery of her vision, then Peal speaking again. "We're going to give you a couple of injections now. Just relax."

There was a sharp, sweet pain. She felt the needle, penetrating deep into her jaw, into the bone itself, it seemed, and she gave a gasp.

"Easy now," Peal soothed.

Another needle jabbed, a third, then a fourth which she hardly felt.

Sound lowered. Voices became background murmurings. It was impossible to catch more than an occasional word.

Someone, out of sight, took Elaine's hand and held it, gave a small squeeze of comfort and support. She squeezed in response. Thank you for holding my hand.

She heard a strange sound of scratching, as if a fingernail was being drawn down thick, heavily woven material. Then a tearing noise. Velcro? A ripping. Stout fabric torn along a seam.

They're cutting into my face, she thought idly. That's what it is.

There was no pain now. Yes there was; it was hovering somewhere just out of reach. She floated in a curious limbo, a dream world on the borders of which terrible things were happening.

She heard more tearing. The hand holding hers moved slightly, stroking her fingers. She concentrated on that: her anchor on reality, a contact almost spiritual, as if one of God's angels was comforting her.

A wave of pain washed across the border into her consciousness and was gone. She felt wetness on her face.

Was it blood? Or a cool saline solution? She increased her pressure on the hand and felt it answer, warm and alive.

Flesh was being drawn back from her skin. Sensations registered on her brain with no way of telling from where they came, or what they signified. Fingers around her head, near the temples, touched, held, pressed, but elsewhere there was numbness.

Peal's voice, soothing and careful, as if winning the confidence of a frightened child, "Clench your teeth please, Mrs. Ross."

The hand squeezed encouragingly. Elaine clenched.

"That's fine. Smile now— big smile. Let me see all your teeth."

Her jaw felt trapped in concrete. She forced it into action.

"Excellent. Try to whistle."

Her lips pouted into a rosebud mouth. She heard herself whistling the first notes of "The Star-Spangled Banner." O-oh . . . say . . . can . . . you . . . see . . .

Laughter floated into the netherworld where she swam along, and she heard low voices joining: ". . . by the dawn's early light . . ."

The warm hand rubbed hers.

Peal, obviously amused, "That's just wonderful, Mrs. Ross. Okay, relax."

What was happening to time? It passed at an uncertain speed. Had it been minutes, or hours? It was like a dream.

She heard herself ask, "How much longer?"

"Nearly finished."

She became aware of gauze being placed on her face, followed by cool liquid.

"Lift your head please, Mrs. Ross," Peal said in his calming voice.

Hands were there to help her. A bandage was wrapped

around her face and head, yards of it. "I feel like the Curse of the Mummy's Tomb," Elaine muttered.

"Think of it as a cocoon," Peal encouraged. "When you come out of there, you're going to be a butterfly."

"Or a moth," she mumbled.

"All my patients are butterflies," Peal said firmly.

The stretcher was moving again, out along corridors, into the elevator and back to her own ward.

It was done. Win or lose, she'd played her hand. She thought of David. Will he like me? she wondered drowsily. Will he stay with me longer?

She wished he was with her now, by her side, holding her hand. But he was out somewhere . . . where?

Skydiving. Oh yes, his first free fall.

She guessed it was over by now.

I hope you enjoyed it, my dear, she thought, and sank into sleep.

Ross walked into the clubhouse to find half a dozen skydivers sitting around, smoking, talking, and a couple of girls. No Julie.

"Morning, guys."

There was a muted chorus of greetings. Pete Grethel, coming out of the storeroom, said, "Hi Dave. Ready for your big jump?"

Ross's stomach was clenched tight, and he could feel his breakfast sitting high, threatening to come heaving out. "Sure," he replied. "Hope you've got a big supply of beer."

"We won't run short." Grethel sat next to Sue, who moved over to make room. Sue still came every week for the company, bringing pizzas and sandwiches.

"Actually," Grethel said, staring absently out of the window, "I don't know when you'll be able to go up,

Dave. That cloud's too low, I won't be able to see to launch you."

Ross felt a wave of relief. A reprieve, maybe?

"Hi, guys!" They looked around. Julie had arrived, more beautiful than ever. She saw Ross and came straight over, giving him an affectionate kiss on the cheek. Behind her was Andy Marcus. They'd obviously spent the night together.

Julie took Ross's hand. Whatever her problem had been earlier in the week, she seemed to have resolved it by herself. Ross felt sorry he hadn't phoned late the previous night. The three of them might have got it together without any fuss at all.

"I'm sorry about that trouble," Julie said. She meant the phone calls and the letter.

"No damage done," Ross said. Then, "Elaine's off for a few days."

"Hey! No kidding? Terrific!"

Ross felt uncomfortable. He looked around to change the subject and his eye fell on Sue and Pete sitting together. "What's this with you two?" he asked. "Sue, I've warned you about Pete. He's only after one thing."

She looked up wryly. "Oh yes? And what's that, Dave?"

Ross lowered his voice conspiratorially. "He wants to stop you doing a second jump. He wants to save himself a buck."

"Not true," Grethel objected. "I'd be glad to lose the money if I could get Sue into that Cessna with a chute on her back. How about it, girl? Sophie's going to be along for her second static line today. Why don't you keep her company?"

"Where's the company?" Sue asked. "You've only got the one chute."

"That's okay. I don't mind repacking. Mr. Accountant over there would win his dollar, and that would make him happy. Maybe we could get him to spend it on an extra beer tonight.''

"Go on Sue, what about it," Ross encouraged.

"Well, maybe. But not right away. I'll see how I feel later. You have your free fall, Dave. I'll think about it.''

There was an approving murmur. That was the closest they'd got to persuading Sue to reconsider. The talk moved on to the weather, aircraft, and the latest canopies on the market.

Outside, the sky was heavy. The Cessna's pilot arrived and joined the group. "The Met boys say the cloud's lifting slowly," he told them. "Around eleven, we ought to get in a couple of runs at 3,000 feet, but if you want to go higher than that, you're going to have to wait for late afternoon, I guess. Maybe tomorrow.''

Groans greeted this news. Ross felt like joining in. It looked as if his reprieve wouldn't last very long, and knowing that, he was anxious to get it over with. Waiting was the worst part.

He walked onto the porch and sat on the low wall, staring at the sky, willing it to clear.

Tony Kimber was in position by seven.

He sat on a chair, his head pressed against the front door, his eye near the spyglass. Beside him on a coffee table was the small radio transmitter which would send out the signal to detonate the elevator bomb.

Kimber had an excellent view of Lyle's door. When he walked out, they'd be separated by a couple of feet, and even with the distortion of the spy glass, Kimber would be able to have a last good look.

The corridor was deserted: no one came or went.

Seven forty. Kimber stretched and flexed his muscles; yawned; rubbed his jaw.

Up the corridor, a man and woman appeared. Kimber

watched them pass and go to the elevator. After a few seconds, it arrived, and the doors closed behind them.

There was occasional movement along the corridor, with people heading for work or going shopping.

Lyle's door stayed closed.

Kimber sat back briefly, flexing his muscles again. It was tiring and uncomfortable staring through that peephole. He sighed and leaned forward.

Suddenly the front door opened. Kimber's concentration became total. His eyeball almost touched the glass.

It was Lyle all right, by himself. Didn't look as if he'd shaved, just pulled on a sweatshirt and a pair of jeans. He wore moccasins without socks.

Lyle shut the door and walked to the elevator. The lights above the door showed it in the lobby. The numbers changed.

Two . . . Three . . . Four . . . Five. The doors opened. Lyle stepped in. Kimber watched him punch a button.

The doors closed.

Kimber picked up the radio transmitter, and leaned forward intently.

Shit! The elevator light had stuck at four! It couldn't be Lyle getting out. He'd have walked if he was only going one floor. There was no point detonating the bomb until the car was moving again. It should happen between floors. It would be most effective in a confined space. Especially the shrapnel.

Kimber waited tensely.

Inside the elevator, Clive Lyle glanced out onto the landing. Seven people were waiting: It was going to be a full house. He moved aside to give them room.

"Morning, Mr. Brooks, Mrs. Brooks," Lyle said.

The elderly woman looked at his chin. "Not going to work this morning, I see."

Lyle rubbed the bristles. "Not this morning," he said.

"Something more important than that. I forgot to get milk."

Lyle had known the Brookses for the five years he had been in his apartment, but he hadn't seen the others before. He figured they were visiting from out of town, staying with friends in the building. There was a woman in late middle age, her husband, and three teenage sons, tall and gangly. They avoided Lyle's eye.

Mr. Brooks pressed the button for Lobby, and the doors rumbled closed.

In Lily's apartment, Tony Kimber watched the light for the fourth floor go out.

His thumb hit the button.

Inside the elevator, the hand of God smashed out of the wall in a blur of lights and limbs, catastrophic noise, things slashing wildly through the air, eruptions, fountains of slick blood. The elevator buckled, became trapped between floors, shuddered, and stopped.

The explosion echoed in the corridors, and a concussion trembled through the walls.

Then there was a silence, deep and profound.

Tony Kimber closed his attaché case and let himself out of the apartment, heading for the emergency fire escape stairs at the rear.

Eleven o'clock. The pilot returned from the control tower. "Okay," he announced, "the cloud's up to three thousand five. If you want to do any jumping this morning, now's the time."

Ross reached into his pocket for a stick of gum. His mouth was dry and his hands damp.

"Sounds okay to me," Grethel said. "Okay, Dave, go get ready."

As Ross changed into the blue jumpsuit and laced the

Vietnam surplus boots, Grethel unlocked the cupboard to get the parachute and a reserve. He handed over a crash helmet. Here. This is your size, I think.'' Ross took it without checking. ''Thanks,'' he murmured.

Pete Grethel put a hand on his shoulder. ''Look, it's no big sweat today, Dave,'' he said. ''It's exactly like those five static lines, except you've got to give the ripcord an extra big heave to get the chute open. Pull it right out, arms extended as far as they'll go. After that, everything's routine.''

''I know.''

Ross followed him onto the veranda. Grethel hefted the parachute onto his back and Ross attached the harness.

''Watch out for your balls,'' Grethel reminded him.

''I haven't forgotten.''

''Okay, now here's your trusty reserve. You won't need it, but it's nice to know it's there.'' Grethel clipped it on. ''And we're ready. Let's go.''

Ross turned to follow Grethel to the Cessna.

In the clubhouse, the telephone rang.

Andy Marcus was nearest and lifted the receiver. ''Hello?''

A man's voice, terse and urgent. ''I have to speak to David Ross. Put him on right away.''

Marcus glanced out the clubhouse door. He could see Pete Grethel climbing into the back seat of the plane, with Ross on the taxiway, waiting to board. It seemed a pity to stop him now.

''You've missed him,'' Marcus said. ''He's gone to do a free fall.''

There was a brief silence. Then the voice said: ''Listen to me. It's imperative I speak to Ross as soon as possible. Can you ask the control tower to call the plane back?''

''Gee, I don't know,'' Andy said. He hesitated, watching Ross settle himself onto the floor in the Cessna's doorway, ready for exiting. The man sounded as if he meant business. "Who is this?"

"My name's Lyndon Yardley. Please tell Ross it's very urgent."

"Look, I'll see what I can do. Hold on, will you?"

The propeller turned sluggishly, once, twice. The engine burst into life. Marcus ran out the clubhouse, across the grass and toward the taxiway. He waved his arms to attract their attention. Ross saw him as he came close and leaned back to say something to Grethel.

Marcus reached the Cessna, shouting over the noise: "Dave! Phone call!"

Ross stared uncomprehending, the sound muffled by his crash helmet. Grethel leaned forward to hear, holding onto Ross's shoulders.

"Telephone for David!" Marcus roared.

He saw the annoyance on Grethel's face. "Can't it wait?"

"Man says it's urgent."

Grethel signaled the pilot to cut the engine. In the silence that followed, Ross pulled off his helmet. "What's going on?"

"Phone for you," Marcus explained. "Man called Yardley says he has to speak to you urgently."

"Yardley? Oh shit!" Ross jumped from the doorway and jogged toward the clubhouse, the bulky chute and its straps restraining his movement. He pushed past a couple of others, calling apologies. It was difficult to maneuver with all that equipment.

He snatched up the receiver. "Yes, sir. Ross here."

"Get back as quick as you can," Yardley ordered. "There's been an explosion on N Street. Looks like they've got Clive."

Ross felt his stomach lurch. "Where? Where did it happen?"

"In the elevator of his apartment. The emergency services are trying to cut him free, but it doesn't look good. There're no sounds coming from the car."

"I'm on my way."

Ross hung up, hands fumbling at the webbing straps to get the parachutes off him.

Grethel walked in. "What's going on, Dave?" He saw Ross's face. "Christ, what's up? You look like you've seen a ghost."

Ross was almost incoherent. "Got to go . . . friend of mine . . . bad accident . . ." His fingers ripped at the webbing.

"Okay, okay, leave that stuff alone. Let me get it off." Grethel unbuckled him expertly. The reserve came away, and the chute dropped to the ground behind him.

Ross took off, running to the storeroom for his jacket with his keys, then to the parking lot. The rear wheels of his car spun in the dirt before it rocketed off, narrowly missing the gate.

There was silence as they watched him go, then someone said quietly, "Jesus Christ!"

Grethel looked around. "Well," he said. "Poor old Dave." He picked the main chute up by its straps. "And here we are, cloud ceiling three and a half thousand, Cessna ready, chute packed, and no takers. Sophie hasn't shown up yet, has she?"

"No."

Grethel's eyes settled on Sue. "How about you, young lady? You going to win Dave his dollar?"

"Ah, no thanks, Pete. Anyway, that chute's packed for a free fall."

"No sweat. I can change it to a static line in two minutes."

There was a barrage of good-natured teasing and advice. Sue blushed and hesitated. Maybe if she just went and did it now, without thinking about it in advance, it wouldn't be so bad. That was the worst part, the anticipation.

Grethel saw her thoughtful expression.

"Come on, Sue," he urged. "Give it a go."

She grinned suddenly. "Okay," she agreed. "But make it fast before I change my mind."

Grethel whooped with glee while the others applauded and whistled. "Right, you're on!" he cried. "Go get ready while I do the static release. You'll be down before you know it."

In the storeroom, searching through the rack of old jumpsuits, Sue again felt the fear, the special sense of aloneness and unreality she'd known before. She found the faded red jumpsuit she'd used the first time and pulled it on over her jeans. Then she looked for boots that fit.

Grethel got the static line from the cupboard and, true to his word, was ready when she emerged from the store-room. Two minutes later, Sue stood on the porch, with the main chute and the reserve strapped and hooked on, with Grethel, firm and confident in front of her, going through the procedure for exiting and the correct stable position. She found it difficult to concentrate. Her mouth was dry. She just wanted to get it over.

They walked out to the Cessna.

Sue sat in the doorway, watching the ground pass slowly beneath her as they taxied and turned.

The pilot made his final checks and pushed the throttle forward. The plane began its takeoff run.

Police had cordoned off the front of Clive Lyle's apartment building, and two fire engines stood by. A crowd of spectators gathered behind barriers, watching idly. Television vans were drawn up, to relay coverage of the rescue work, although the building had been evacuated the reporters were not yet allowed in.

In a car two blocks away, Brian Stewart sat beside General Lyndon Yardley.

Stewart was pale and rubbed automatically at his beard with a hand that shook slightly. He chained-smoked cigarettes. Yardley's face was granite, impassive.

"We were fixing breakfast," Stewart explained. "There wasn't any milk in the refrigerator, so Clive said he'd get some from the delicatessen." He glanced swiftly at Yardley. "I stayed over with him," he said.

"Yes," Yardley said. "I know."

"Clive got dressed and I was frying sausages. He said, 'I won't be long,' and then he went out. A minute later, maybe two, there was this bang. The building shook—you know, literally trembled. I thought maybe a plane had crashed nearby. I looked out the window, but there wasn't anything to see. Then a while later, I heard people shouting and running. I went outside. At first everyone thought the cables in the elevator had snapped and it had gone crashing to the bottom of the shaft." He inhaled deeply on the cigarette. "I knew, I just knew Clive was in there. I ran down to the basement with them, and we levered the elevator doors open, but there was nothing. The shaft was full of smoke and all sorts of shit: dust, paper."

Yardley's driver opened the door and handed over paper cups of hot coffee. Stewart took one. "Thanks," he said gratefully. He drank and smoked some more.

"We ran up the stairs," he continued, "I guess there were half a dozen of us, and we found the car stuck between the third and fourth floors. There was no sound, no one calling. I yelled 'Clive! Clive!' Nothing. Just silence."

Yardley nodded. "What time did you get to the apartment last night, Mr. Stewart?"

"Around 7:30."

"Did you notice anything unusual? Anyone who might have been suspicious?"

"No."

"Did anyone come to the door while you were there?"

"No. No one."

"How about telephone calls?"

"There was one. A friend of Clive's, David Ross. He phoned to ask Clive over."

"Nothing else?"

"No." Stewart finished the coffee. "What are Clive's chances, sir?"

Yardley didn't reply. After a pause, he said, "I'm going back there to see how they're getting along. You want to come, Mr. Stewart? You feeling strong enough?"

"Yes. I'd like to."

Yardley showed his identification to get them past the police cordon, and they climbed to the fourth floor where the rescue effort was centered. The area around the elevator was occupied by half a dozen men. Everyone else stood well back.

The doors had been forced open, and an oxyacetylene torch was cutting through metal. The dazzling blue-white flame ate implacably into the car's roof.

There was a smell Stewart didn't recognize, but which gripped at his stomach. Yardley knew what it was though: blood.

Pete Grethel leaned over to see the position of the DZ. The cloud ceiling was just above them and the Cessna bumped and bucketed in turbulence. He spoke to the pilot, and as the plane banked around before beginning its run-in, Grethel put a reassuring hand on Sue's shoulder.

The Cessna droned through the sky at 3,000 feet, and banked again.

Grethel stared out, calculating the position of the DZ

against the direction and force of the wind, choosing the right moment to send her out.

"Get your feet out!" he shouted.

She pulled herself around, hampered by the chute, and the wind whipped hard at her legs. She struggled to get her left foot onto the step and keep it there.

Grethel tapped the pilot on the shoulder. The engine cut. "Get out!"

Her hands were slippery with perspiration. She lumbered up, snatched forward at the strut. She didn't feel she could hold on for long. Her fingers slid on the metal. She could feel her heart. The Cessna lurched in an air pocket. "GO!"

Sue held on, fingers gripping and slipping and gripping again. She thought she was going to be sick. She wanted to get back inside. She looked desperately at Grethel, trying to tell him this.

His face contorted, and he screamed, "GO! GO!"

Sue dropped.

The force of the blast took her breath away. The static release pulled clear.

She began to count: One thousand. She had fallen 32 feet. Two thousand. Her speed accelerated to 64 feet a second. Three thousand. She reached 96 feet a second. Four thousand. One hundred and twenty-eight feet a second. She kept her arms flung wide and her back arched in the starfish position.

She looked over her shoulder to see what had happened to her chute. The white sock streamed uselessly behind her. The wind whistled and buffeted in her ears. She reached her terminal speed the fastest a human body can fall, 126 miles an hour; 176 feet a second.

She lost stability, tumbling through the sky, over and over, curling instinctively into the fetal position while her hands fumbled for the ripcord of her emergency chute. She yanked it free.

The silken bundle flashed past her face and trailed behind in a second Roman Candle.

On the ground at the DZ, the waiting skydivers watched the plunging figure in numb, unmoving disbelief.

Sue didn't see what had happened to her reserve, knew only it had not opened.

She uncurled slowly from her tumbling fetal ball. Her arms stretched out, back arching, stable once again, face down toward the approaching earth.

She drew in a deep breath and began to wail. The noise ended with the dull sound of impact.

12

The rescue crew cut away enough of the elevator roof for a man to be lowered through. The two squatting on the roof turned on an emergency light and shone it into the car.

Yardley and Brian Stewart heard one of them say, "Oh Jesus Christ." in a voice so toneless everyone knew what he was looking at.

The man turned and gave the order, "Just bring bags. I dunno how many are in there—five, ten, who can say?"

Brian Stewart felt his cheeks becoming wet with tears although he wasn't aware of crying, only of being cold. Yardley neither moved nor reacted. He seemed alone, somewhere miles away.

The man put his legs over the edge of the hole and lowered himself into the car. An emergency light followed after him, to dangle over the side.

The stench of blood and death was strong in the corridor, but almost overwhelming inside. The man could see the jagged gasping metal below the elevator control board, where the explosive had been placed. He was deep in blood and slime and meat and bone. The first bag was passed to him and he filled it with the biggest pieces he could see immediately around. A finger with a ring on it.

A foot in a shoe. Half a foot without a shoe. He'd been in some filthy places in his life, but never anything like this charnel house. He tensed to stop himself vomiting over the whole disgusting mess, and threw in pieces, enough so he could stand and feel the elevator floor beneath his feet.

He passed up a bag, and a replacement came down.

David Ross ran along the fourth floor corridor, eyes bright with fear and anger. He saw Yardley and hardly recognized Brian Stewart crying silently.

"What's the news?" Ross was breathing hard, having raced up the stairs.

"Not good," Yardley said. "We're ninety percent sure Clive's in there, but we don't have a positive ID. There were others too. They're bringing them out now."

Ross walked to the elevator doors, showed his DIA card, and climbed onto the roof of the car next to one of the rescue squad. He peered through the hole at a scene lit by a single electric bulb and cried out an involuntary noise, because nothing in his life had prepared him for such slaughter.

"If you're here to help, then help," the man beside him said coldly. "If you're going to fall apart, go some place else."

Ross bit his lip so hard he could taste blood. "Sorry," he muttered.

A second bag was handed up. Ross took it and passed it to those on the landing. He steeled himself to look back in, staring around to see if anywhere in that gory heap was his friend.

The worst of the blast had been taken by those immediately in front of the control panel. They were literally pulverized, but the force decreased as it went through every obstacle. Further off there were whole arms and legs, with more being uncovered by the man filling the bag.

Ross hunted for anything that looked like Clive, or part of him, but how can you identify someone you love by a bloody limb, or a piece of meat, or a curdy gray mess of brain?

Ross's mind was clear now, emotion drained away. He looked down, imprinting the scene on his memory so he would never forget it, however long he lived. He watched unmoving until the next bag was ready. The vacuum in his brain began to refill with a very pure and intense hatred, the simplest, strongest emotion he had ever known. It tingled his fingers and made his body seem light.

He knew who'd done it: not precisely who, not the actual person, although he'd find that out if it took him the rest of his life.

It was the KGB. And Clive had been their target. The others were just unlucky, the random coordinates of their lives bringing them to that elevator in that building at that moment, where they were wasted. Ross understood the term for the first time in his life.

The rescuer in the car came across a body almost intact, and without thinking Ross let himself through the roof to help slide the man into the plastic sack and heft him up so others could pull him out. Hell, he wasn't even a man. Through the muck and caked blood on the face, Ross could see he was just a kid.

I'll find the people who did this to you, Ross promised silently in the harsh light. I'll find them, and I'll make them pay.

He turned to the farthest corner of the car. There was a jumble of bodies and limbs. Ross edged over to them, touching dead flesh without feeling the touch, still intent on the hunt for Lyle. Maybe Clive was already in a bag, in unrecognizable pieces. A pathologist would tell it was him from a couple of teeth, a severed finger that matched DIA prints.

Ross dragged another body into the center of the floor: in that confined space, only a little distance. There was so much blood and shit around it was hard to make out the features. Ross moved an arm draped over a corpse, then shifted position to help get the victim into a fresh bag.

And then Ross stopped—froze.

He turned back to touch the arm again, his face alert. He stared up at the other rescuer. "Get a medic!" Ross ordered. "We've got a live one!"

He found the hand, felt for the pulse. "Hurry!" he shouted.

He worked feverishly, panting, but still being careful not to harm the survivor, caught in a tangle of limbs. Ross became aware of the medic dropping down, a third man in the cramped space, kneeling beside him, feeling the pulse.

"Let's get him out," the medic said. A stretcher came through the roof.

Ross and the others untangled and shifted, until the man was free.

Bloody, covered with the vile, stinking rain of the explosion, but just recognizable under the scum and crust, and alive, miraculously alive.

The blood throbbed in Ross's head as he knelt beside the figure being strapped onto the stretcher until his mouth was an inch from the man's ear.

"It's okay, Clive," he whispered. "I'm here. It's all right."

The intensive care unit of the DIA hospital was one floor below the plastic surgery unit where Elaine Ross was lying, sipping a cup of coffee.

Ross and Yardley paced the corridor while Dr. Peter Barry and his team worked. They could see Lyle was on IV, but they had no word of his condition.

They walked in silence for several minutes. Finally Ross asked, "It was the KGB wasn't it?"

"If Clive was the target, yes."

"I'd like your permission to work on this case," Ross said.

Yardley looked at him speculatively. "Why, David?"

"Because any action against Clive is an action against me. Because I want to find who did it and kill them." Ross's voice lacked emotion, and its impact was greater because of this. Yardley gave a grunt.

"Let me think it over," he said. "Let's see what the experts come up with first."

It was an unsatisfactory reply, and Ross clenched his fists until the muscles cramped in his hands. He went to stand by a window and stare out into late Saturday Washington. Yardley continued to prowl.

Finally they heard footsteps coming along the corridor, and both went to meet Peter Barry.

"Let's hear it," Yardley said. "Layman's language, please."

"Clive's in shock," Dr. Barry said. "He lost a lot of blood from a shrapnel wound in his arm. He's still unconscious although the brain scan shows no apparent damage. No limbs broken. There're a lot of superficial wounds, and he's badly bruised. His blood pressure's way down." Barry shrugged. "He'll live, if he gets over the shock."

"Do you think he might not?" Ross asked.

"Hard to say. There doesn't seem to be a physical reason for him to be unconscious. It could be that the shock was so profound and deep that nothing we do will make it recede. If it's irreversible, he'll die."

"I see," Yardley said. "When will we know?"

"I can't tell you that, Lyndon. We'll just have to wait. Meanwhile, we're doing everything possible."

"Can I go in?" Ross asked.

"Sure. Don't try to wake him though. It won't do any good. His mind's shut off, and all we can do is hope it sorts itself out. He's young and fit. There's a chance."

Ross and Yardley went into the room. Clive's bed had been raised at the feet so his head was at a lower level. Dextrose and blood fed into his veins. He'd been cleaned up, but his face and arms were patterned with small cuts and emerging bruises.

Ross touched Lyle's forehead. It was cold and clammy and his breathing was rapid, shallow. The beeping of the cardiac monitor beside his bed was fast but weak. They watched for several minutes, then looked at each other and walked out.

"Be in my office at nine tomorrow morning," Yardley ordered. "I'll let you know the latest on the bomb and any other leads that've come in."

"Yes, sir, I'll do that."

"And David, if it was the KGB, and they were after Clive, they might have others on their list. So watch out." He cleared his throat. "You might find when you get home," he added, "that someone's been through your apartment. It was on my instructions. Bomb disposal people. Just a precaution."

"They didn't find anything?" Ross asked.

"No, all clear. But that doesn't mean you can relax your guard."

"No, sir," Ross said. "I won't. See you tomorrow, General."

Ross took the elevator to the basement garage and drove back to N Street. He had to detour around the police barricades and the crowd that was still outside Clive's building.

Ross let himself into his apartment. There were signs that a squad had been through—magazines and books shifted slightly, furniture a little out of alignment. Ross was glad: at least he knew there wasn't a bomb waiting for him.

Ross felt curiously alive and aware. Sensations and sights were registering strongly on his brain. And beneath was the feeling that had grown in him when he looked through the roof at the carnage. Revenge. He'd felt the need for it once before after the KGB had taken Rabinovich, but it had faded away. Lyle even had to remind him of it a couple of weeks later.

Ross doubted it would leave him now, not after what he'd seen.

He opened a can of beer and drank it without pause, slaking a thirst he'd hardly noticed; then he wanted something stronger. He had a bottle of Stolichnaya vodka, and he picked it up, torn between the desire to smash it against a wall and rid himself of everything Russian in his apartment, and the fact that his enemy was the KGB, the Party hierarchy, not the Soviet people. He poured half a tumbler, wishing it was chilled and drank it down. The clear liquor warmed his stomach but had no other effect.

Ross wandered through the apartment, Elaine's bedroom, his own, the guest suite, the living room, the kitchen, thinking and wondering what to do next. The walls seemed to close in on him. He knew he ought to have something to eat although he felt no hunger. He let himself out and walked not noticing where he was going. At one point he found himself outside Julie's penthouse and rang her bell but got no reply. Maybe she'd stayed at the club for a drinking session or gone to Andy's apartment.

Ross prowled the night streets, heedless of time.

It was around midnight when he got back to N Street. The crowd outside Lyle's building had dispersed although lights still burned in some windows and police cars were parked at the curb. Ross stopped, debating whether to go up and see if they'd found anything. After a moment, he moved on. Yardley would fill him in soon enough, and he'd only be in the way now. Let the experts decide how the bomb was assembled, where the assassin had stood to detonate it, whose fingerprints could be picked up. Then they would see. The KGB may have sent in a *mokrie dela* agent from outside. If so, Ross would have to discover that person's identity through the DIA's own sources and track him down—inside Russia if necessary.

Ross turned into his apartment building. The lobby was in darkness. He paused, alert, remembering Yardley's warning, then he went in.

The hair prickled on the back of Ross's neck.

There was someone there. He could see nothing, but instinct warned him of another presence, deep in the shadows. Ross crouched, moving silently sideways out of silhouette, his back to the wall, eyes and ears straining.

The light switch, on a sixty-second timer, was a few feet away. He inched toward it, scarcely breathing.

He heard a shuffling of feet nearby. He marked the position.

His hand touched the switch, his body became still, readying itself.

Ross tensed.

His fist slammed into the button, and as the light came on, he was already lunging through the air toward the source of the sound, leading with the side of his foot in a blow to smash into the solar plexus. It connected, and he heard the cry as he snapped his foot back for the next attack.

Pete Grethel curled on the floor, gasping and retching.

The tension drained from Ross's body. "Oh Jesus," he said.

He lifted Grethel under his arms and, half-carrying him, took him into the apartment.

Ross laid Grethel on the couch and went to get a wet

cloth. Grethel's face was ashen and his breathing ragged, but his eyes watched with loathing. He had been drinking heavily: Ross could smell it.

He undid Grethel's shirt and felt to see if anything was broken. He guessed he'd missed the floating ribs, and Pete was just badly winded. Ross got him a glass of water and waited for him to recover, disturbed by the accusing, hate-filled stare.

When finally Grethel could talk, he gasped, "Fucking . . . shit . . . what did you do? . . ."

Ross tried to put an arm around Grethel's shoulder, to apologize. "Pete, I'm sorry. I didn't know it was you," he protested, but Grethel shrugged him off.

"You killed her!" he accused. "You bastard, you killed her!"

Ross felt himself go cold, and he stood very still. Grethel struggled to sit. His breathing calmed. He drank the water, but his eyes never left Ross.

David took a chair nearby and waited.

Grethel launched into another stream of abuse, but Ross cut him short. "Start at the beginning," he ordered. "Do you want a drink?"

Grethel shook his head vehemently. "I don't want any of your liquor, mister," he said. Then he began, "Sue's dead. She put on your chute, your reserve." Ross's blood chilled. "We kidded her into making one more jump— Jesus, I kidded her into it. It was me! I dispatched her, poor scared kid. Hanging onto that fucking strut!" Ross's hands were damp and he felt his spine crawl. "Her main canopy didn't open," Grethel said. "Someone tied it closed with string. Fucking string! So she pulled her reserve and that didn't open either. More fucking string!" He seemed about to cry but pulled himself together with an effort. "The cops have been around at the clubhouse all day. They're gonna want to talk to you, Mr. Accountant." He got unsteadily to his feet. "I dunno what the hell mess your life is, but what right have you got to involve us in murdering shit like this? Tell me that! What right have you got to hang around with ordinary guys? You know what Sue looked like when we picked her out of the hole she made in that field? You want to know, Mr. Accountant? Well, I'll tell you. She didn't have a face, that's what. She was a stinking bag of fertilizer! Every bone crushed. Every one!" The anger went out of Grethel's voice. He finished drained. "Those chutes were yours, Dave, weren't they? Why in fuck's name wasn't it you? That sort of thing's your game, isn't it? Why involve us?" He went to the door. "Stay with your own crowd, whoever they are. Don't come fucking up decent people." Grethel drew up his body and looked squarely at Ross. "That's what I came to say," he concluded.

Ross sat, stricken and sick.

It was the KGB again, it had to be—almost simultaneous attacks on the two agents heading the Rabinovich operation.

These were things he couldn't say to Grethel, however much he wanted to; and at that moment, Ross wanted to confide in Pete, tell him what had happened and why, win back his friendship and approval.

But Grethel was right. He shouldn't involve others in DIA business. Even a casual association, like the skydivers, was a risk.

Ross felt emotionally drained. "Get out of here, Pete," he said flatly.

Grethel left without a word. A few minutes later, Ross locked his apartment and went to get his car.

Lyndon Yardley's house was a thirty-minute drive away. Ross had never been there, but he knew the address and found it without trouble. There was no name on the gate, only a number.

Ross knew from the moment he walked into the grounds that he was under electronic surveillance and a warning would sound inside the darkened house.

It was late, after one, but Ross didn't care, and he knew Yardley wouldn't either. He rang the bell and waited.

Through a speaker set into the side of the door, Yardley's voice said tinnily, "Come in, David."

A buzzer went off on the door, and Ross pushed it open. He was in a hallway, confronting a second door. The first closed solidly behind him. He looked into the lens of a closed-circuit television camera. After a moment, the internal door buzzed and Ross went in.

Yardley waited for him, a paisley-patterned silk dressing gown over his pajamas, and slippers on his feet.

"Come on in," the Director invited. He led Ross to a living room that was comfortable, but anonymous, as if the furnishings had been chosen by a government agency. There was nothing that gave a clue to Lyndon Yardley. "You want a drink?"

Ross nodded. "Yes please. Straight vodka, if you have it."

"A beer chaser?"

"That'd be fine."

Yardley got the drinks, and a whisky for himself.

"Sit down," he instructed. "What's on your mind?"

Ross told him what had happened at the club. He omitted what Grethel had said about him: Yardley would read that for himself the following day when he called for transcripts of monitoring from Ross's apartment.

Ross finished the story, and his beer. Yardley didn't offer him another. At last the Director said, "I'll bet a dime to a dollar the key to the sabotage is in that club—one of the members, someone you know."

Ross looked incredulous.

"It has to be, David. I'm not saying whoever it was

actually fooled around with the chutes: that might be a professional from outside. But the basic information about you had to come from someone you know there.'' Yardley studied his hands. ''I expect you'll want to keep tabs on that, too. I'll let you have all the official reports. Take a look at them, and see if maybe there's a role for you.''

''I'll do what I can, General,'' Ross promised.

''Take it carefully, David, step by step. I want to be fully informed of your progress at all times. And if it comes to the point that you're ready to act . . .'' he got up to show the meeting was at an end '' . . . you're not to do anything without my clearance. Do you understand?''

''Yes, sir.''

''Good enough. Now go get some sleep.''

''I will, thank you.'' Ross walked toward the front door. ''Any news on Clive?'' he asked.

Yardley shook his head. ''No change.''

Ross drove home through the almost deserted streets.

In the morning, he spent an hour at Lyle's bedside. The cardiac monitor was steadier, stronger, and his skin slightly less clammy, but he had remained unconscious.

Ross touched Lyle's face with the side of his hand and spoke to him softly, not trying to wake him, but hoping that a familiar voice might somehow penetrate his shocked sleep. Lyle didn't stir.

At last, Ross returned to the office they shared and made a list of the members of the skydiving club. He compared this with a photostat of the membership roll obtained by the police, and found that he didn't know the bulk of those who paid their annual dues. There was really just the hard core of fifteen skydivers, with ten or twelve groupies and a small, shifting population of beginners.

Ross ordered computer reports on the entire membership. They arrived late in the afternoon, and he organized the collected information onto a card index system. In one box, he kept the active membership, while the rest fitted into two other boxes.

The biggest file was the most surprising, at least initially, because it was for Sophie Johnson, the newest recruit. When Ross read through it, he could see why. Because of Sophie's political contacts and the occasional sensitivity of her job, she had been security vetted—not for a particularly high rating, but at least people had taken a look at her and found nothing suspicious. Ross felt that, in a way, they'd done his job for him.

Pete Grethel seemed to have led a blameless life, apart from a couple of parking offences and one speeding ticket which cost him $100.

Andy Marcus was a surprise, not because anyone had got him on a drug bust, but because he had once appeared in juvenile court for stealing and wrecking a car; and again, a year later, for knocking in someone's windshield with a tire iron.

Julie Klein's dossier told him nothing he didn't already know, and none of the others contained items of interest.

Ross drew up a chart which he pinned on the wall. It covered every one of the hard-core members of the club and the current hangers-on: names going down in a long list. The horizontal columns were divided into days, starting from the abortive snatch of Rabinovich. That date marked Ross's return to the skydivers, so any information on his jumping had to be obtained some time after that. The problem was, how to fill in the columns?

He telephoned Lucy who was working on her day off to ask if Yardley was free again. After a pause, he was told to come over.

The Director waved him toward the armchairs at the side of the large office, while he finished signing documents. "I won't be a moment, David," he said.

Yardley pushed a button on his desk and waited until Lucy had collected the paper, before joining his agent.

"What's on your mind?"

Ross explained about his card index system, and the chart he'd devised. "The problem's going to be filling it out," he said. "I guess the police will be working along the same lines, but there's no guarantee they'll cover all the blanks. I want to go ask questions myself."

Yardley thought about this. "I don't think it's a good idea," he said finally. Then seeing Ross's disappointment, he added, "Not yet, anyway. The best thing is to let the police do the legwork, see where the gaps lie, and then consider how to get them filled. Do you know who's heading the investigation, by the way?"

"Someone called Flynn. He's a lieutenant."

"Has he talked to you yet?"

"No, sir."

"I'm surprised to hear that. It doesn't sound too efficient. Well, let's wait and see." Yardley reflectively rubbed a fingernail with his thumb while he thought how to phrase his next remarks. "There's a reason for not getting too obviously close, David," he said, "and it's this: let's say the police don't crack the case, and you do. Suppose you amass enough evidence to satisfy me you've found the killer, or his accomplice, but it's not enough to sway a court of law, given the fact there'll be a lawyer who'll twist judicial process until it disappears up the prosecution's ass. Now, if the police knew you were hunting around, that would make it difficult for me to say: 'Okay, bring the guy in. We'll interrogate him under drugs and when we're through, we'll sanction him.' " He looked at Ross. "You see, the civilian authorities would be too close. There might be an investigation, and the arrows could point straight at you, at us. I'm not saying I wouldn't be able to block that, but we'd run the danger of raising questions." He scratched the top of his head thoughtfully. "You know how the CIA would love a chance like that. They'd secretly feed the flames and build up pressure for an inquiry. Our strength is that we work alone. We're low profile, and we don't leave piles of dirt lying around for people to fall over. But if anything goes wrong, our enemies'll jump on us."

"I see that," Ross conceded. "I guess the best thing for now is to watch and wait. If there are obvious holes, maybe I can try to fill them in at the end. That wouldn't trip over anyone else's feet."

"That sounds fine. But I repeat, keep me fully informed, David. In advance, please, if you're proposing to take any action."

"I will, General. Thank you."

"Have you seen Clive today?"

"Yeah. I looked in for an hour. He seemed better, but still unconscious. What news about the bomb?"

"The forensic people say there's trace evidence it was detonated by radio. I reckon we know where the assassin was waiting, too—the apartment directly opposite Clive's. There's one of these peepholes in the door. The police got a search warrant and broke in. They found a girl dead in bed. The autopsy says she had a heart attack around the time of the explosion. Seems she'd had a visitor."

"Fingerprints tell us anything?" Ross asked.

"Nothing yet. But she was full of some guy's semen, so obviously she'd had a busy night."

"A rape."

"They say not. Might have been a boyfriend. Might just have been a heart attack too, but I don't believe that for a moment. It's too much of a coincidence. I've asked the coroner's office to see if they can turn up higher than usual level of potassium, or traces of prussic acid in her body. They're also going to look for a pinprick."

"If we find the boyfriend," Ross agreed "we've probably got the assassin. Unless he broke in later while she was alone and asleep. But that's a bit hairy for this sort of operation."

"If we'd been doing it, we'd have got in early and stayed overnight," Yardley said. "The KGB are good, and I'll bet that's what they did. The girl's from New York. She hadn't been to Washington before and didn't have any close friends here. So maybe the KGB guy introduced himself to her somehow and got invited to the apartment that way."

"Shit," Ross said. "Now try to find him."

"He's probably back in Moscow." There was a glimmer of a smile on the Director's face. "Wherever he is, he's in for a little surprise."

"What's that?"

"The autopsy says the girl had venereal disease. It's in the early stages, so she probably hadn't noticed it particularly. But there's a good chance she infected him."

"That'll be the first of his worries," Ross said. "Let's see if we can add a few more."

There was a knock on the door, and Lucy came in. "Excuse me, General, but there's a Lieutenant Flynn on the phone, asking to speak to David."

"About time too," Yardley said. "Okay, David, make an appointment to see him. Give him full cooperation on anything to do with the skydivers. Anything to do with the Agency is our business, of course, not his. If you hit any gray areas, check with me before answering questions. If he tries to lean on you, let me know right away."

"Yes, sir." Ross stood to leave. "What happens about the neutron files, General? You want to put someone else onto them?"

"Your research? No, I don't think so. You're just going to have to work harder, that's all. If I remember correctly,

it was you—wasn't it?—who said that anyone coming in
fresh would have to start from the beginning. So keep at it.
Your skydivers investigation shouldn't take more than an
hour or two a day. I mean, you're just milking other
people's reports, aren't you? Maybe later you'll need more
time, but for now, I guess you can ride both horses."
Yardley cleared his throat. "Of course," he added, "If
Clive dies, I'll assign someone new to you. Think you can
handle that?"

"Yes, General."

"Off you go then."

Ross spoke to Lieutenant Flynn and arranged for him to
come to the DIA building at four that afternoon. Flynn
seemed to be taking things at a more leisurely pace than
Ross would have.

Ross returned to his office. It was nearly lunchtime, and
although he could put in some work on one of the neutron
files, he knew he wouldn't be able to concentrate. Not
today. Instead, he went over to the DIA hospital building
again and took the elevator to Lyle's floor.

Peter Barry was in the room, completing some checks.

"He's awake," Barry said.

"Fantastic! That's great news!"

Barry walked out of Lyle's room, motioning Ross to
follow. In the corridor he said quietly, "The trouble is, we
can't get any response from him. He's not talking. His
eyes are open, and he's looking around but that's all."

"Can I sit with him a while?"

"As long as you like."

"Thanks." Ross went in and pulled up a chair near the
head of the bed. The blood transfusion had been discon-
tinued but Lyle was still on an IV. Ross took Lyle's hand
and held it. The light brown eyes moved across, rested on
his face without recognition, and looked away again.

Ross began speaking softly. "Hi Clive—I'm right here—you're going to be all right, you hear?"

Ross scrutinized Lyle's pale, motionless face. Was anything getting through? There was no way of telling. It was worth trying anyway because nothing else was working.

So Ross spoke, calm and steady, about the DIA and themselves; good times they'd had together and friendship. He spoke for almost thirty minutes—it seemed interminable—before getting around to the events of the last few hours. "You remember we were talking about revenge, Clive? Well, actually you were talking about it. I didn't think it was such a hot idea. But I want to tell you, you were right. I haven't killed anyone before, but I've been trained for it. I know how to do it." It seemed for an instant that Lyle stirred.

And then he answered, so softly Ross almost missed it. "What took you so long, Dave? I waited. I thought you'd never come."

Emotion rose in Ross's chest, threatening to choke him. He squeezed Lyle's hand and put his face against it. He could feel a slight answering pressure. Ross knew his cheeks were wet with relief. "Oh shit, Clive," he whispered, "you had me so scared."

Ross drew away and saw Lyle's eyes on him. There was hurt in them, but acceptance too.

"How am I?" Lyle asked.

"You're fine," Ross said encouragingly.

Lyle shook his head. "Bullshit. Tell me the truth, Dave. What did I lose? What did they amputate?"

"Nothing, Clive," Ross said. "You've got everything. Arms, legs, fingers, toes." Lyle looked doubtful. "I swear it, on my honor. Everything: balls, cock, they're okay. You're bruised and you're cut. They had to give you some blood, but that's all."

Lyle began to cry noiselessly, and Ross bent forward to

hold him. "It's okay, Clive. It's okay," he murmured. "Everything's all right."

Lyle's voice came low, appalled. "It was terrible, so terrible."

"I know."

"There were people all over me . . . bits . . . just meat . . . and blood, . . . and you didn't come . . . oh Jesus . . ."

Ross patted and rubbed Lyle's back, soothing him as he wept and trembled, and spoke to him reassuringly about how he was going to be fine, and about those other things too: the job they still had to do, a bigger, more important job than ever. Track down the KGB and make them pay.

Lyle went compulsively over and over the scene in the elevator, almost choking on the words, and as he did so, Ross became aware of others in the room, close but not intruding, listening as Lyle's mind released some of the terrible debris that had weighed it down and brought him near death.

Gradually he quieted and fell into exhausted sleep. Ross laid his head gently on the pillows and looked around.

Peter Barry and two nurses stood at the end of the bed. "That was well done, David," Barry said. "Let him rest now—he'll feel better when he wakes."

Ross moved away, emotionally drained himself. It had been a harrowing experience.

The doctor fell into step in the corridor. "I was afraid," Barry confessed, "that his mind would suppress everything that happened in that elevator. He'd have been like a volcano, and we wouldn't have known when he'd blow. I guess I'd have advised Yardley to take him off active operations. But now we've got a good chance of getting him back to normal."

"You think so? He seemed pretty badly shaken."

"Oh, he is," Barry said. "But he's young and strong. There's a lot his mind has seen and come to terms with already. And he's done a lot too, as you know. So it shouldn't be too hard. You can help him, David. Talk to him, tell him what you're doing, include him in the planning if possible.''

"I'll do what I can, doctor," Ross promised.

"Thanks. I know you will."

Barry shook Ross's hand warmly at the elevator, and watched until the doors had closed and the young agent had gone.

Ross went to the DIA cafeteria and ordered a late lunch. Once he started eating, he realized how hungry he was. It seemed weeks since he'd left to do his first free fall, instead of just over twenty-four hours. It was mid-afternoon Sunday: hard to believe.

Ross checked the time and found that Lt. Flynn was due. He walked to his office to await the call from security, and the telephone began ringing before he'd got his key in the lock. Flynn was on time.

Ross removed the skydivers' chart from his wall and locked it in a drawer. Then he went to the elevator to meet the lieutenant.

On the way back, he bought them a couple of plastic cups of coffee from the machine. No fresh ground beans served by efficient secretaries on this floor.

He gestured to Lyle's chair, the only spare seat. There wasn't room for any more furniture, and they almost never had visitors anyway.

Flynn presented his ID and glanced around the anonymous, sparsely decorated office.

"Nice place you've got here," he observed.

"If you say so," Ross replied. "What's on your mind, Lieutenant?"

"This parachute accident yesterday." He looked at Ross shrewdly. "You know about it, of course."

"Yeah. I wouldn't call it an accident, though. I'd say it was murder."

Flynn grunted and reached into his pocket for a notebook.

He was in his mid-forties, Ross guessed, and at around two hundred pounds, too heavy for his height. He had a face that looked as if it had knocked around more than most, but for all that, it had a dry, humorous aspect. His skin was lined and there was a thin white scar that started at the side of his neck, just at the jawbone, and got lost somewhere under his chin. Ross couldn't tell how far the cut extended. It had probably been made by a knife.

"Why do you think it was murder, Mr. Ross?" Flynn asked.

"Those were my chutes," Ross replied. "They'd been packed for my first free fall. Hell, I was in the plane, ready to go, when I got called back. If it hadn't been for that, it'd have been me they scraped off the ground."

"Why exactly were you called away?"

Ross explained about Yardley and told Flynn what had happened to Clive Lyle. The lieutenant tried unsuccessfully to hide his surprise. He knew about the N Street explosion, but no one had suggested they might be connected.

"Who do you think it was, Mr. Ross?"

David shrugged. "Try the KGB," he offered. "I'd guess it was one of their operations."

"Do you mind telling me why, or is that a dumb question?"

Ross considered this. It wasn't dumb, but it was a gray area and he needed clearance. "I can't tell you specifically why, Lieutenant, except that Major Lyle and I were working on a particular project. Incidentally, we'd appreciate it if you kept the DIA out of your reports as far as possible, and particularly out of any briefings you might give the media."

"We've already been leaned on about that," Flynn said. It was clear he didn't like it and considered it interference with a routine police function.

"I'm sorry." Ross did genuinely sympathize. "It's always bad to feel some other guys are pulling strings to stop you doing your usual job. But in this case, there really are good reasons for it, believe me."

"I don't suppose it'll make much difference to the final outcome," Flynn admitted. "Just as long as we're satisfied you were the target, and it's not some psycho having a crack at the club without caring who got killed."

"I see what you mean," Ross said. "No, because of what happened to Major Lyle, I'd say it was a calculated attempt to take us both out at the same time. It's too much of a coincidence to be anything else."

"Maybe. Got any thoughts on specifically who was responsible for the parachute job?"

Ross shook his head. "I've been through the list of current members, and I just can't believe it was one of them." He explained Yardley's theory that a skydiver might have been pumped for information by a third party. "You get a couple of these guys together, and they'll talk shop for hours," Ross said. "I guess they're as bad as policemen."

"Believe me," Flynn said earnestly, "no one's as bad as policemen."

"Well, you know what I mean."

"Except for one thing." Flynn leaned back in the chair and regarded Ross unblinkingly. "It doesn't work. We were thinking about it when we were working on the psycho scenario. Let me demonstrate it to you." Flynn was obviously further ahead than Ross imagined. "Suppose you're our unknown skydiver, and I'm from the KGB. Imagine it's—say—a week ago. You don't know who the hell I am really, except I'm pretty knowledgeable about parachuting, and I tell you a couple of stories about what I've done, and what other guys have done, and you're feeling relaxed with me. Okay? So now I ask you, 'Hey Dave, you got many students at your club? Hell, we're having a bitch of a time getting anyone new at ours.' What do you say to that?''

"I guess I'd say, uh, well, we're having a pretty average time," Ross replied self-consciously.

"Oh? How many have you got?"

"Two."

"Oh yeah? Who are they?''

"There's a guy called David Ross, and a woman called Sophie Johnson.''

"David Ross, huh? That name rings a bell. What does he do?''

Ross grinned. "He's an accountant.''

"No kidding?'' Flynn didn't smile back. "How many jumps has he done?''

"Five. His first free fall's coming up Saturday.''

"Hey, great. Does he have his own chute yet?''

"Oh no. The students use club equipment. Maybe he'll buy his own later when he's got more experience.''

"You got a lot of equipment at your club?''

"Actually, no. There's only the one main chute. The students share it.''

"So this girl—what's her name? Sophie Johnson—she wears the same chute as David?'' Flynn asked.

"That's right.''

"Is she also jumping next Saturday?''

"Yeah. She's doing her second static line.''

"Great. Who goes first? Sophie or David?''

Ross hesitated. "I don't know who, aside from Pete Grethel, would know that. Oh, and maybe Sophie. Pete would have packed the chute at the end of last Sunday's jumping. I wasn't there, but that's what usually happens.

Sophie would probably have been watching him because she's new and pretty keen. The others would have been inside drinking beer although I guess it's possible one of them saw Grethel.''

"How would they know the next jump was yours and not hers?''

"Pete would have fixed the chute with a ripcord, instead of a static release.''

"Okay," Flynn said agreeably, "let's say someone noticed the ripcord. It doesn't matter. So now the KGB agent asks you, "Where do you keep your equipment, Dave?''

"In the storeroom.''

"Do you lock it up?''

"Yeah. Sure we do. It's about the only thing of value in the whole place." Ross began to see what Flynn meant. The conversation was sounding strange. Skydivers are interested in jumping, not clubhouse security. Talk like that was the sort of thing a man would remember later.

Flynn sipped his coffee and grimaced. Hot, it tasted pretty bad; lukewarm it was disgusting. "What about the airfield itself?" he persisted. "That must be pretty well guarded.''

"I guess so.''

"Do you have security guards, dogs, that sort of thing?''

"Yeah, I guess.''

"When does the students' chute get packed, Dave? What's the routine? Do you do it just before a jump?''

"Well, usually it's packed at the end of the afternoon and stored away. That takes care of the first customer the next jumping day. Other than that . . .'' He stopped and shrugged. "Okay," he conceded, "you've proved your point. It's not easy to learn the things you need to know just by talking to someone. But there are other ways they could have done it.''

"Such as?''

"Gas someone when he's asleep. Pete Grethel would be ideal because he's the instructor so he knows everything. Then give him an injection—Pentovar's a good one—and if you ask him what he thought about when he jerked off at Christmas five years ago, he'll tell you."

Flynn raised his eyebrows. "Is that so?" he murmured. "You can really do that?"

"Sure. No sweat."

"Well, that raises a lot of new possibilities. And you say Grethel wouldn't know anything about it? Not even next morning when he woke up?"

"He wouldn't remember enough to make any difference," Ross affirmed.

"What sort of world do you operate in, Mr. Ross?"

"A hard world, Lieutenant. You wouldn't believe it."

"I guess not." He thought for a moment. "If you're right, there's no point spending too much time on the drugs angle, because we'd never find out, would we?"

"No."

"Which brings me back to the original hypothesis. Either your KGB man spoke to one of the skydivers, in unusual depth about routines and security, or he spent time at the club. You get many hangers-on there?"

"Some. Mostly women. You know, girl friends. And groupies. They're there to get laid."

Flynn looked at him shrewdly. "You laying any of them, Mr. Ross?" he asked. "You don't mind me asking you this, do you?"

Ross felt his face redden. He returned the lieutenant's gaze. "Actually, I am," he said. "But she's a skydiver. A woman named Julie Klein."

"I met her. A nice looker. You're married, aren't you?"

"Yes."

"To an older woman," Flynn observed.

He'd obviously done his homework before getting around

to Ross. David didn't much like the line of questioning, but he felt his respect for the police officer increase.

"Yes, my wife is older."

"Anyone else sleeping with Miss Klein?"

"Don't fuck around with me, Lieutenant," Ross said. "You know this already."

"I'd like to hear it from you," Flynn replied.

"She's also sleeping with Andy Marcus."

"Anyone else?"

"Probably, but not from the skydivers, as far as I know."

"How does Marcus feel about you and Miss Klein?" Flynn asked.

David smiled at him, remembering the three of them together. "That's not a problem, Lieutenant," he said. "Believe me, there's no jealousy. Andy and I are happy to share Julie, and Julie's happy to share us."

"Is she now? Is she happy sharing you, Mr. Ross? I'm not talking about Marcus now. I'm talking about your wife."

David drew a sharp breath. He hadn't considered that possibility—Julie trying to kill him because he'd gone back to Elaine. But no, it was absurd, and he said so. "And don't forget the attempt on Clive's life," he added. "This is a KGB thing, not a jealous woman's anger."

"No? What if she was the one who spoke to the KGB man and gave him the information he needed?"

Ross shook his head. "It's hard to believe," he said. "We're just not that serious."

"Okay, let's leave it for the moment." Flynn checked his notebook. "We think we know when it was done, by the way," he observed.

"When what was done?"

"Fixing the parachutes. There's an airfield security report that the dogs became disturbed around two A.M. last

Thursday. A guard checked the hangar and the clubhouse. They were both locked, and he couldn't see anything through the windows. Apparently the dogs were going mad. It looks like our guy must have been in there at the time.''

"Any fingerprints in the club?"

Flynn laughed. "Is the Pope a Catholic?" he asked. "There are a million, Mr. Ross. It'll take us weeks to sort them out. We've been concentrating on fingerprinting the three chutes that were sabotaged."

"Three?" Flynn was full of surprises.

"Yup. The two Sue Collins was wearing—main canopy and reserve—and another reserve in the storeroom cupboard. You know how they stack them at the side there? Anyone drawing equipment is going to pick up one of the two top reserves, and the killer wasn't taking any chance on them selecting one that worked."

"Whose prints were on the second reserve?"

"Grethel's. You understand, there aren't many places on a parachute pack that'll pick up prints; just the metal bits—ripcords, buckles, that sort of thing."

"So, a dead end."

"Unless Grethel's our guy," Flynn suggested.

Ross shook his head. "That can't be," he said. "First, Pete wouldn't bother sabotaging three chutes. He chooses them, so two would be enough. Second, when I didn't jump, he certainly wouldn't kid Sue around until she agreed to go up. He'd go into the storeroom, pop the chutes and untie the string, so Sophie Johnson could use them when she turned up. He'd live to fight another day."

"Yeah, I guess that sounds right." Flynn closed his notebook. "Well, Mr. Ross, thanks for your time. I'll probably want to talk to you later."

"Any time, Lieutenant."

The men rose, and Ross escorted Flynn back to the elevator, locking his office door behind them.

"If you get any bright ideas, Mr. Ross, I'd be glad of a call." He paused. "Tell me, if the KGB is involved in this, why the hell aren't I tripping over the CIA all the time?"

Ross's expression did not change. "We thought it best not to alert Langley," he said.

"Surely this is their territory?"

"It's our territory, Lieutenant. It was an operation against our guys, not theirs, and we've elected to let the police handle it. We'd appreciate it if you kept it that way."

Flynn was familiar with interdepartmental rivalry. It was the story of his life. "As bad as that, huh?"

Ross presssed the elevator call button. "As bad as that," he agreed.

Flynn put out his hand, and Ross shook it warmly. "A pleasure talking to you, Lieutenant. See you again."

"You surely will, Mr. Ross," Flynn said.

As soon as he had gone, Ross took the stairs to Yardley's floor to fill him in on the conversation. Flynn was obviously a clever and a thorough investigator who considered all the angles. Ross thought most of the blanks on his wall chart would be filled from the daily police reports Yardley was getting.

Then he went by the hospital, but Clive was still asleep. He watched for several minutes, wondering if he'd lapsed back into unconsciousness, but his color was good and the clamminess had gone from his skin. Lyle's breathing was even and deep. The cardiac monitor had been disconnected.

Ross picked up his car and drove into the Sunday evening traffic. The night stretched ahead of him, with nothing in prospect but his empty apartment. He thought he ought to call on Brian Stewart to let him know Clive was going to be okay, but there was no reply when he knocked at the door. He scrawled a note on a piece of paper and pushed it through Stewart's mailbox on the way out.

Outside, Ross sat unmoving behind the wheel of his Chevy. He wasn't tired, and it was too close to lunch for him to be hungry. He thought about Pete Grethel's visit and what he'd said. Grethel's accusations had left deep wounds.

Maybe the others regarded him with contempt now, too. Andy Marcus. And Julie—what about her? Ross might be a leper to them all.

Half an hour passed. He saw Brian Stewart returning home and taking the note out of the lobby mailbox. Ross debated following him in to give him a fuller account, but still he did not move.

It was getting dark.

He wondered about the skydivers' club, what they'd done that day. Had anyone turned up? Had anyone jumped? Were they all out there now, getting drunk, laughing too loudly, exorcising ghosts?

He started the engine and pulled out slowly, heading for Julie's apartment. There was only one way to find out which doors were slamming in his face, and that was by knocking on them. Then he wouldn't have to agonize. He could learn to live with the truth. And anyway, although he'd been warned off his own active investigation at this point, Yardley hadn't ordered him to stay away from any of his friends. Maybe he'd learn something from their conversation.

Ross rang the bell and stood back, preparing himself for the rejection. After a moment the door opened.

Julie stared at him as if he was a stranger: no way of knowing how she felt. Ross waited passively, arms by his side. Then she gave a cry and ran to him. He felt his breath coming out in a long, relieved sigh as he buried his face in her hair.

Inside, she spoke compulsively, reliving the events of Saturday. She had gone to the DZ with a crowd of others to cheer Sue's landing and her courage. Ross found himself listening to the details with a clear, detached mind. He was interested only in facts which might lead him to the killer, and he prompted her into remembering who was at the DZ, and who stayed at the club; whether anyone refused to go along and watch Sue's jump and what happened after that.

All the people Ross knew were accounted for. There were a handful of late arrivals that day, among them Sophie Johnson.

"Poor Sophie," Julie said. "You should have seen her face when she heard about Sue. She went so white, I thought she'd pass out."

"I don't blame her," Ross sympathized. "It might easily have been her."

"She didn't stick around. I don't think we'll see her again." Julie fixed them drinks, continuing her story from the bar. "We had the police there for the rest of the day," she said. "They gave Pete a hard time because he'd packed the chutes. Pete already knew how it happened. As soon as the Cessna landed, he drove like a maniac for the DZ, although he realized she had to be dead. But he thought it was his fault. Then he saw how the canopies had been tied closed with string. Pete never uses string to sort the rigging lines, although some guys do. It look a lot of time to convince the police about that. Now they think it was murder." Julie glanced at Ross, almost timid. "They think someone was trying to kill you, Dave."

"I know."

"But who? Why?" Her voice was anguished.

"I don't know. What do the guys at the club say?"

She returned with the drinks, and Ross took his gratefully.

"They don't know what to think," she said. "Pete took

it very hard, and after the police left he had a lot to drink and began shouting that it was your fault. We tried to quiet him down but it was as if he'd gone mad. Then he grabbed a six-pack and drove off by himself.''

Ross was glad the other skydivers didn't share Grethel's view of him.

"Julie," Ross asked seriously. "Do you remember if anyone outside the club's been asking questions about me? Another skydiver, maybe, from out of town?"

She shook her head. "No," she said, "not to me."

"Has anyone else mentioned something like that happening?"

She thought hard. "No. Dave, what's going on?"

"I wish I knew," he said. Then, remembering one of Flynn's lines of inquiry, he added, "Of course it might not have been aimed at me. It could just have been a psycho who didn't care who got killed."

"Oh God! Do you think so? That's almost worse!"

"It's possible," Ross shrugged. "You didn't go back this morning?"

"I was going to," Julie explained, "but I thought it would be such a bad scene I stayed away. It's just as well, because a couple of cops came around to talk to me. Mostly about you."

"I had one of them come to see me, too."

"What did you say?"

"That I didn't know who was responsible."

"What did you tell them about me?"

"They wanted to know if we were sleeping together. I said we were."

"That's what they asked me. They also wanted to know about Andy and about your wife."

Ross sighed. "It's such a mess, isn't it?"

"I didn't understand what they were after, Dave. What were they trying to prove?"

"I don't think they were trying to prove anything in particular," he said. "They were just covering possibilities." He didn't feel inclined to tell her that she had been—and perhaps still was—one of the suspects. Although not as far as he was concerned.

Slowly Ross began to unwind, but through that night, even when they were in bed, he was aware that something had changed, that he was keeping an emotional distance not only from Julie but from everyone. Grethel was right: he was a threat to them all. If the KGB had another crack at him now, Julie would be in danger. And while civilian casualties in a war were inevitable, that didn't mitigate the basic unfairness of this situation. She didn't even know she was taking a risk being with him, and he couldn't tell her; so he was using her selfishly, and he wasn't able to stop doing it. Not for the moment, anyway. He retreated within himself, building a protective shell, watching, waiting. Listening. Thinking of revenge.

The following morning, Ross called at the hospital and found Lyle awake but depressed. The horrors of the blast were heavy on his mind, and Ross spent thirty minutes talking to him about Flynn and the police investigation, trying to capture his interest. Lyle seemed hardly to be listening.

Later, Ross dropped in on Yardley to pick up the latest batch of police reports, which he studied, filling in the first blanks on his wall chart. Flynn and his team had interviewed all the currently active skydivers although not yet in great depth.

After lunch, he went back to the neutron files, wading again through NSA intercepts and reports from agents within the Soviet Union.

He felt frustration building inside him.

Ross ended the day with another visit to Lyle, whose

depression had become so deep it was almost impossible to coax a coherent sentence from him.

By the time Ross drove out of the DIA garage, he was profoundly relieved the day was over. He headed for his apartment to pick up some clothes and then to the penthouse where Julie waited.

Lyle's recovery was slower than Ross expected. The depression stayed with him for two days before he shook it, but afterward he kept to himself in his hospital room: reading, listening to music, and not showing much interest in the hunt for either of the KGB killers —assuming they were different men—or in Ross's research in the neutron files. His mood was remote.

When Ross asked Barry about this, the doctor said, "Give him time, David. He'll get over it."

One floor up in the hospital, Elaine continued her recovery. The first stitches had been taken out and she was in pain, despite the medication she was given. They were weaning her off strong drugs, which meant she had to grit her teeth and wait for flesh and skin to heal. She had restless nights too because the sleeping pills now being prescribed were mild.

Elaine bore it stoically, feeling that in the end it would be worth the discomfort. Her face was still swollen, and every morning her legs felt as wobbly as a newborn foal's. But each day brought her nearer home.

She looked forward to the moment she'd return to her husband and see his reaction.

Yardley handed over the typewritten sheet. "Have a look at that, David," he said.

Ross settled back in the armchair and began reading.

At last, a DIA report from inside Russia, the first response to their neutron queries.

As usual, the source had been deleted in this retyped version, but Ross could tell from the information it contained that the mole was well placed within the KGB itself.

It told them that Rabinovich's project at the Dubna Atomic Center had been code-named Scimitar, and was concerned with the development of an eight-inch shell, carrying a one-kiloton neutron warhead—almost a twin to the American W-79 artillery shell. There were some technical details about the Scimitar project which meant little to Ross, and the final section was devoted to Rabinovich himself.

Yardley could see the point Ross had reached, and said, "This last bit'll interest you, David."

It summarized the trap the KGB had set for them in Central Park: a vindication of Ross's action in aborting the kidnap. David tried to keep himself from grinning, but the corners of his mouth twitched. He resolutely did not look at the Director.

Then his triumph faded.

The report ended by saying Rabinovich would remain in New York for the duration of this round of negotiations, but that when he returned to Moscow, he would be arrested and tried for crimes against the State. It was not known whether this meant imprisonment in a labor camp or death.

"Poor little guy," Ross said. "I'll bet if he knew that, he'd make a run for it."

"Rabinovich is just going to have to take what's coming to him," Yardley said. "No point worrying about that."

But Ross couldn't shake the memory of the frightened scientist, gambling for his life in the CIA safe house; and then the sight of him on his return to New York—almost emaciated, with eyes so blank they blocked any sense of what was going on in his mind and signaled only that he'd suffered terribly. You poor bastard, Ross thought. You haven't seen anything yet.

He returned the report. "The only important thing from our point of view is Rabinovich's involvement in the Scimitar project," Ross said.

"Maybe that's what he wanted to tell us about when he tried to defect."

"Well, it wouldn't have been enough to abort the talks."

"No." Yardley replaced the report in a folder and put it to one side. He regarded his agent shrewdly. "How are you getting along, David?" he asked.

Ross shrugged. "Not much progress. I don't even know if it's worth carrying on with the files. What do you think, General? If Scimitar was the only thing Rabinovich had, it doesn't tell us anything new. We might as well pack it up."

The Director was doubtful. "It's premature for that, David. We've only got this one report. I don't think we can assume that's all there is. Don't forget," he pointed out, "the Soviets were prepared to abandon the SALT talks if we didn't give Rabinovich back. Surely they wouldn't do that because he'd tell us they were building neutron artillery shells. It doesn't make sense. I mean, if the negotiations succeeded, the whole enhanced radiation system would be banned anyway. It couldn't matter less if we knew about Scimitar or not."

"I see what you mean, General. I guess there should be more to it than that. I'll keep looking."

Yardley rose in dismissal. As Ross walked toward the door, he asked, "What news of your wife, David?"

Ross hadn't thought much about Elaine since her departure almost a week earlier. So many things had happened.

He replied, "Uh, she's out of town, doing some work for the FBI, sir. I'm not sure exactly where."

"When's she due back?"

Ross looked slightly embarrassed. "To tell you the truth, I don't know," he confessed. "She wasn't very specific. She said a week to ten days, so I guess it'll be soon."

"Well, give her my regards when you see her. She's keeping well, I hope?" Yardley knew exactly how Elaine was. He received regular progress reports from Peter Barry and had even sent flowers to her hospital ward.

"Yes, General. Very well."

"And you'll be looking in on Clive again today?"

"I will sir. But he seems to be making slow progress."

"So I hear. Well, keep at it."

Yardley watched his agent leave, thinking what a pity it was he had to remind Ross of the existence of his wife.

Lyle's bed was rumpled but empty. Six days had passed since the elevator bomb. Ross went to the ward's reception area.

"Where's he gone?"

"For a walk," a nurse replied. "He didn't say where."

"How was he?"

"The same."

Ross went in search of Lyle, trying their office, the cafeteria, walking along corridors Clive might have taken, and ending up in the gymnasium building. The gym itself was empty, but from the raquetball courts below came the sounds of hard play. Ross looked into the small spectators' gallery.

Lyle was leaning against the wall, watching, uninterested, as two agents slammed the hard rubber ball around, moving fast, reacting instantly.

Ross went to stand beside him. "Hi!"

Lyle hardly moved his head. Only his eyes flickered idly to focus on his friend. "Oh, hi!"

"What you been doing?"

"Not much." It seemed an effort for Lyle to talk.

Ross put an affectionate arm on his shoulder. "How're you feeling?"

"Fine. First rate."

"It's good to see you up and about at last. You want to go to a movie tonight?"

"I guess not."

"How about the theater?" Ross suggested, trying to interest him in something. "There's supposed to be a great play on at the National. I bet we could swing a couple of seats if we asked Lucy to go in to bat for us."

"I don't really feel like it."

"How about going out for a drink? Might do you a bit of good."

Lyle shook his head listlessly and continued staring into the court. The players were sweating as they moved to meet the ball ricocheting off the walls so fast it took concentration to follow, but Lyle's gaze was unfocused.

"You want to get laid, Clive? Would that help?"

Lyle didn't bother replying. Ross stared at him in frustration. He wasn't even trying. If he carried on like this, Yardley would take him off active duty and it would be a hard road getting back.

Ross put his big hand on the back of Lyle's neck and twisted his head so it turned toward him. Lyle neither resisted nor complained. His expression was passive. Ross felt frustration giving way to anger. He felt the need to shout, to do something to gain Clive's attention, to hit.

"Let's go," Ross said shortly.

He pushed Lyle toward the empty gym and through to the locker room. "Strip," he ordered. "It's time for a workout."

"Oh hell, I don't feel like that, Dave. Really."

"Strip, you bastard, or I'll do it for you," Ross said

grimly. He went to the lockers and pulled out a couple of karate uniforms. He threw one at Lyle. "Get this on."

They changed in silence, Ross ready for action a good couple of minutes before Lyle had donned the traditional white trousers and jacket, tied with the black belt designating his level of competence.

"Listen," Lyle said. "I'm not in the mood for this,"

"Come on!" Ross said. He put a hand behind Lyle's back and gave him a shove, so hard he almost stumbled.

Ross was ready for Lyle to swing around and strike at him with foot, or fist, but there was no reaction.

Lyle waited in the center of the gym, trying to snap himself out of the reverie that held him in its deadening grip.

Ross took up position facing him, knowing he must be the one to cross the line of confrontation. "Come on, you miserable sonofabitch!" he snarled. "Move, you pathetic fucker!"

He landed a punch on Lyle's nose, and a stream of red immediately began flowing. Lyle shook his head to clear it, licked his lips, tasted the blood—and remembered the elevator, the blast. It seemed he was trying to escape from a trance, but all his movements were too slow, too late.

Ross began to shout, to revile him for cowardice, for unmanliness, and he punched and slapped, hoping desperately to beat some sense into Lyle. Clive tried to respond, and actually landed a punch that jerked Ross's head sideways, but it was a miserable effort for a man who had once been an instructor at Fairfax.

The fight didn't last long. To Lyle, it seemed to go on for hours: to Ross, forever. It was no contest, only the pointless baiting of a man who quite simply lacked the will to defend himself. When Ross finally lost the heart to go on punishing, he stopped and stared abjectly at Clive whose face was puffy and bloodied, and who watched mutely.

"Oh shit, Clive," Ross whispered. "What am I going to do about you?"

Lyle turned and walked slowly back to the locker room, stripped as if it required all his mental and physical effort just for that simple task, and stood under the shower for a few minutes. Ross watched him towel himself slowly dry, dress, and leave the gym without a word.

Ross felt deeply ashamed.

Ten minutes later, he went back to the DIA hospital to talk, to say he was sorry, but Lyle was back in bed, his eyes closed, apparently asleep. Ross was sure he was feigning, so he put his hand gently on Lyle's cheek and made his quiet apologies as if Lyle was listening. There was no response, and after a minute, he left.

The rest of the day seemed interminable. It was impossible to concentrate on the neutron files or pay much attention to isolating the questions that had to be answered on his wall chart. Ross badly wanted to go out and get drunk, but he didn't want to do it by himself, nor did he want Julie with him. He wanted another man there, another agent: and in his DIA life, there was only Lyle. He knew others slightly and could count none of them as friends. They had their own working partnerships, their own personal links forged through operations, literally with blood, and strangers could not easily intrude.

Maybe he should find Andy Marcus and go out on the town with him. They had something in common at least.

But Ross wanted a man he could talk to about his job and his problems, not a civilian who might become an unfortunate casualty of a secret, undeclared war. It occurred to Ross that he now had fewer friends than at any time in his adult life.

He didn't go to Julie's that night. He went home, locked

himself in his apartment and drank enough iced vodka and beer to dull his pain, and when that was finished, he went onto straight bourbon before falling into bed, fully clothed, for a fitful, dry-mouthed, bad-dreamed sleep.

In the morning, Ross thought he was dying. He gulped water and took four aspirins to check a throbbing headache. His muscles felt sluggish and his liver sent out urgent messages, warning against alcohol at any point in the future.

Ross arrived at work, still in bad shape. Usually he had Saturdays off and he might have stayed in bed waiting quietly to die, but Yardley had him on a hard schedule.

He had difficulty focusing on a note left on his desk. When he did, he recognized Lyle's writing. It said simply: "Gym—ten o'clock."

Ross checked his watch blearily. It was 9:30. What the hell was Clive up to?

He bought a couple of cups of coffee from the machine in the corridor, but they simply increased his nausea, and he walked sluggishly to the gymnasium.

Lyle was waiting. Not the Lyle of yesterday, with the slumped shoulders and the uncaring eyes, but the agent who had trained him: the biggest shit he'd ever met, hard and unforgiving. A transformation, complete and unexpected.

Lyle was practicing focused strikes on a makiwara, a vinyl bag mounted on rubber cables that absorbed the shock of his blows. His fist shot out. His speed was a little slower than usual, but more than enough to do damage, particularly against a hung-over opponent.

David stood in the doorway, staring wordlessly. Then he groaned.

Lyle paused in his workout. "Go get changed, David," he ordered. "You and I have a couple of things to settle."

Five minutes later, he beat Ross up without difficulty.

At the end of the session, Ross's lip was split and his cheek grazed. His ribs ached on his left side and the biceps of his right arm felt numb. But at least his hangover had gone.

Then Lyle showered changed, and checked out of the hospital. He joined Ross in their office.

"So," he said. "What have you been doing while I was away?"

13

Lyle worked with fierce concentration, going through every word of the police reports and computer printouts, comparing them against Ross's card index and wall chart, insuring that every fact was familiar to him, every entry correct. Lyle's cold single-mindedness was as surprising to Ross as anything he'd ever seen in this complex, sometimes cruel man. Revenge burned in him with a heat so intense that Ross felt his own sense of vengeance inadequate.

Ross realized that, during the days Clive was in hospital, he had merely been jogging along the track of the KGB agents. His work was thorough and good: Lyle had no complaints about it, but it lacked the killer edge. That, Clive provided.

He questioned Ross closely on his association with the skydivers, going over how he'd come to join, what people had said to him, what they'd done, who'd suggested a particular course of action, how Grethel had packed his chutes, who'd been watching. Ross racked his brains to remember every detail and nuance of conversations. Lyle demanded details about himself and Julie Klein; about Andy Marcus. It was as if he had a microscope, and was minutely examining every particle of Ross's recent life.

Lyle spent a considerable time on Marcus and the cocaine incident. What mention of drugs had there been earlier? Who'd said what? Had Ross taken coke a second time? What had he said to Andy when he'd refused? Had Ross said something, even as a joke, to make Marcus feel he risked a bust?

When Lyle had finished, he left Ross in the office and went to see Yardley.

The Director scrutinized Lyle carefully as he stood in front of his desk. "Good to have you back, Clive," he said.

"It's good to be back, sir."

"Are you okay? Would you like a couple of weeks' leave? I'd be glad to let you have the time."

Lyle shook his head emphatically. "No thanks, General. There's too much to do. And I'm feeling great. Back to normal. But there was something I wanted to ask you."

"What is it?"

"You remember you showed me that transcript of tapes from Julie Klein's apartment, the night David took coke?"

Noncommittal: "yes."

"I'd like to see all available tapes from the apartment up to date, and anything else that includes her and Andy Marcus."

Yardley inspected his fingernails. "May I ask why?"

Lyle explained: "First, I'm looking for simple motives, nothing to do with the KGB. There are two possibilities. One is that Julie Klein, who's a pretty selfish piece of work in my view, tried to get David away from his wife and when she failed decided to teach him a lesson. The second is that Andy Marcus thought David might tip the FBI off about the drugs and wanted to get him out of the way. Maybe Marcus is deeper into the whole scene than we think."

Yardley considered the propositions for a moment before he rang for Lucy.

When she'd gone, Yardley said, "You're not to take the transcripts out of this office, Clive. Read them here. Spend all the time you want. And you're not to tell David they exist; at least, not without my specific permission. Is that understood?"

"Yes, sir."

Lyle went over to the chairs at the side of the office and when Lucy returned with the dossiers, read them carefully, in sequence.

Two hours passed, during which Lyle sipped occassional cups of coffee, and Yardley sat at his huge desk, continuing to work as if he was alone, fielding a series of telephone calls from the Pentagon.

As Lyle read, he realized Ross had told him everything of significance. It became increasingly difficult to sustain either of his theories.

At last he closed the files and sighed.

Yardley looked across. "No luck?"

"No, sir. There's no evidence of anything unusual on the tapes."

"So?"

"So I guess we can forget the simple solution and go for the KGB. I just wanted to be sure in my mind."

Yardley smiled. "I understand. Is there anything else you need?"

"Not at the moment, sir." He got up and crossed to the desk, returning the folder. "Although I guess we might soon get to the point where we need to start our own investigation."

"Any specifics? As I told David, I don't want you tramping over the official inquiry. It might cause trouble later."

"No, General, nothing I want to put to you right away.

I'll need a few days.'' He paused. "I take it we've got some leverage in the police department?''

"Some.''

"Well, do you think you could light a fire under their backsides? I'd like detailed reports on all the skydivers and groupies by Monday. We need to know who they talked to about David and this other student, Sophie Johnson. Also their alibis for the night we think the chutes were sabotaged.''

"I'll see what I can do,'' Yardley said

"Thank you, sir.''

Lyle went back to their office to find David immersed in the neutron files.

"Where've you been?'' Ross asked.

"Doing some thinking,'' Lyle replied. "Here, give me one of those.''

They worked in silence for the rest of the afternoon. At five, Ross checked his watch and yawned. "Let's call it a day, Clive,'' he suggested.

Lyle didn't move. "Forget it,'' he said. "We've messed around long enough. The speed we're going, it'll take another six months to get through the files, and that's not good enough. We're gonna work until we can't concentrate any more. Okay?''

"Okay, okay,'' Ross said. He thought he could keep going for another two or three hours until he became too tired to be of any use, and he'd still be in time for dinner with Julie. She'd planned spending the day at the club, and it would be interesting to hear what she'd picked up.

They worked on, making occasional notes but finding nothing that looked like a crucial piece of the puzzle.

Just before eight, Lyle closed his file and pushed it to one side. He sat back, hands behind his head, and stared at the ceiling. Several minutes passed.

Ross continued reading. He wasn't going to be the one to call a halt.

At last Lyle said, "Let me ask you something, David."

"Sure, shoot."

"You know how the NSA works. Jesus, you've spent years with those computers. Now, of the stuff we're going through at the moment, how much will be on computer records?"

"Most of it. All the intercepts will be. Everything the NSA picks up from inside the Soviet Union and the Eastern Bloc. The guts of a lot of agents' reports also get put onto disc. Tapes, too. But if you asked the NSA to give you what they have on Russia's neutron plans, the computers'll just spew out the stuff we've got now. It wouldn't help us."

"I wonder," Lyle said. "I've just got a feeling we're going about this the wrong way. Or at least that we ought to be using the computers to look at details, at the same time as we plow through this garbage."

Ross was interested. "In principle, I'm sure you're right, but in practice, how are you going to do it? What are we going to feed into the computer? What are we going to ask for?"

"I've been thinking about the report from Moscow on Rabinovich, and this project he was working on at Dubna," Lyle said.

"Scimitar?"

"That's the one. It rang a bell in my head, and I couldn't think why. Then, sitting here now, it came to me. Do you remember the code name for the first Soviet neutron missile?"

"You mean the equivalent of our Lance? It was Cutlass."

"Yup. That's what it was. Cutlass for the missile, Scimitar for the shell. Cutlass . . . Scimitar . . . see the pattern?"

"Code names on the same theme. You think other parts of their program will follow those lines?"

Lyle shrugged. "Maybe. It isn't very smart from a security point of view, but then the military aren't always very smart."

"If we give the computers related code words," Ross suggested, "they'd be able to pull out references in the intercepts. It might save some time. It's certainly worth a try. Is there a Roget's anywhere?"

"In the library, I guess. You want me to look?"

"I'll do it," Ross said.

He was back in ten minutes and scanned the index while Lyle got out a pad to note down words.

"Scimitar . . . sharp edge . . ." Ross murmured, turning to the page and skimming upward. "Okay, here we go: cutlass, hanger, broadsword, sword, falchion . . ."

"What the hell's a 'falchion'?" Lyle asked himself, writing quickly.

" 'Tomahawk, adze, hatchet, cleaver, chopper, pangar, parang, creese, kris, kuri, dah, dao, machete, draw-knife, plane, scalpel, secateurs, clippers, shears, aesculap. . . .' " He looked up. "I guess that's enough for a start."

"They don't sound very Russian to me."

"No. Well, that's enough to be getting on with. It won't be everything, so let's pin the list on the wall where we can look at it and add whatever else we think of. I'll come in tomorrow morning and put it into computer language." He caught Lyle's eye. "Not tonight, Clive, because I'm tired now. I can't guarantee getting it right. And if it isn't exactly right, we're wasting our time. The computers won't understand."

Lyle sighed. "Okay," he agreed. "It's 8:30. That's not too bad." He locked the bits of paper in the filing cabinet. "I take it you're going to be with Miss Klein tonight, so there's no point my asking you over for a drink and a meal?''

"Yes to both."

"Take care," Lyle said. "I'll see you tomorrow at nine. Think you can make it?"

"If you can, I can."

"That's the spirit," Lyle encouraged. "Follow my example and you won't go wrong."

Lyle was already at work by the time Ross got in. The list of Scimitar, Cutlass, Hanger, Sword, and all the others— even Falchion—was on the wall, and Clive had brought in a thermos of coffee so they wouldn't have to drink the muck from the machine. Ross also noticed a couple of bakery boxes on top of the filing cabinet, presumably their lunch. They could keep working while they ate. When Lyle put his mind to it, he drove himself and others relentlessly.

"Morning, Clive," Ross said cheerfully. "Cracked the problem yet?"

"Won't be long. Help yourself to coffee and get started. How's Julie?"

"Oh, she's fine. She says the club's pretty much back to normal. Most of them went to Sue's funeral last Wednesday, although she had to pick that up from one of the girl friends. No one else was saying a word, as if Sue never existed. She's just been written off—boom! Gone, finished. No mention of her. Or me, come to think of it. Sophie Johnson's staying away, but that's no surprise. Julie says there's a new student who just walked in, and Pete Grethel's putting him through ground training. They're fixing up an old chute, so he can make his first jump next Saturday." Ross poured coffee into a plastic mug. "You want one of these?" he asked Lyle.

"Yes, please."

"I'll lay you any money you like," Ross said, "that when he does, they'll put him through the initiation ceremony—drinking out of that fucking skull." Ross mimicked Grethel's lazy drawl. " 'Now this here's one of our founder members and club mascot, Sam. Sam holds the club record for the longest delayed first free fall . . .' Jesus. And I'll lay you odds no one lets on what happened to Sue. The only thing that'll be different is the guys are going to get very, very drunk."

"That's survival," Lyle said. "It's the same in the military."

Ross grunted, took his coffee to his desk and set to work. He spent an hour drafting the computer instructions in such a way that they wouldn't trigger reams of printouts on Soviet agriculture and so he'd be able to add to the list of key words without problems. He became completely absorbed, enjoying being back in the field in which he'd originally specialized.

When he was through, he asked. "Is Yardley in today? I'd better clear this with him."

"I already have," Lyle said. "The NSA is expecting you."

"Christ," Ross said, "you don't waste time, do you?"

"No."

"You want to come with me, Clive?" he asked and regretted his words immediately. Of course Lyle didn't want to; there was no point in duplicating work. Ross raised his hands in surrender. "Okay, I'm sorry," he said. "I'll be back as soon as I can."

The National Security Agency is the biggest government installation in the Washington area. Government manuals describe it as "established pursuant to Presidential directive in 1952." They say it "performs highly specialized technical and coordinating functions relating to the national security."

In fact, the ultrasecret establishment is even more of a world of its own than the DIA. Although theoretically part of the Department of Defense, it is not subject to military rule, which makes it free from the pressures of interservice rivalry.

The NSA covers eighty-two acres in Fort Meade, Maryland, and one of its few public boasts is to house America's longest unobstructed corridor, extending 980 feet.

Within this extraordinary empire, bigger than the CIA and costing considerably more, is the Office of Production, known as PROD, where electronic espionage is practiced in its purest form and billions of dollars' worth of decoding machines and computers are in daily operation.

It was to PROD that David Ross was heading—his old stamping ground from the days before the DIA. He had his papers checked at the perimeter security post but, as Lyle said, they were expecting him.

In one of the air-conditioned computer rooms, Ross shook hands with men he knew well and explained what it was he wanted.

The team on duty inspected his draft computer instructions with eyes that began critical, ready to find fault, but soon became respectful. Ross obviously knew what he was doing.

He watched as the codes were programmed into a group of Univacs, and joined the men in a cup of coffee while the first printouts emerged.

Before he left, Ross arranged to phone through additional keywords from time to time.

He was back in Washington in time for sandwiches with Clive Lyle. They divided the printouts between them and read carefully as they ate. Much duplicated what they'd already found in the neutron files, but there were also references to intercepts they wouldn't reach for weeks at their current rate of progress.

Ross and Lyle pored over the new information. The most interesting dealt with field tests of Scimitar—interesting, but not what they were looking for. In the CIA safe house, when Lyle asked Rabinovich if his information was good enough to abort the negotiations, he replied: "That is the news I bring. Something to anyway stop the talks."

But there was nothing here that would affect the official American view to the slightest degree.

Ross dropped the printouts on the desk and cursed. "A waste of time," he said. "Maybe they're not using knife code names any more . . .?"

"Could be. But maybe we haven't come up with the right word."

They stared at the list on the wall. Lyle took a pen and added one more: "Scythe."

"How about names of other tools, Clive?" Ross suggested. "Chisel . . ."

"Okay. No harm in trying."

Ross phoned the additions to the PROD office, and he and Lyle returned to their scrutiny of the files.

Whether Yardley had lit a fire under the backsides of the Police Department, or whether Lt. Flynn and his team had, in any case, been completing in-depth interviews with everyone currently connected with the skydivers, the latest and fattest batch of reports was delivered by early Monday afternoon, and Ross and Lyle took turns reading them aloud, while the other made notations on the wall chart.

Gradually the spaces filled up, particularly the night of Wednesday into Thursday. More than half the skydivers had been accounted for, in the sense that they were in bed with someone who vouched for their presence. This was by no means conclusive—a couple could have been working together on the operation against Ross, or one partner might be covering for the other—but the agents agreed that in the absence of alternative pointers, this became an increasingly long shot. Among the alibis was Julie Klein's: she'd slept with Andy Marcus.

Pete Grethel was foremost among those who had been alone.

None of the interviews produced any recollections of conversations with outsiders about students, and in particular David Ross.

When they'd filled in as much as they could, the agents sat back, staring at the chart, looking for a pattern, a gap, even a question that meant anything. It remained as elusive a puzzle as the one they faced with Rabinovich.

They drank coffee and pondered, discussing individual skydivers, and Ross's personal assessments of them. All possibilities led to the same blank wall.

"I don't even know what to suggest," Ross admitted finally. "I reckon Flynn's done a good job so far, but where does he go from here? And where do we go?"

"I don't know," Lyle said. "I wish to hell I did."

"What's the progress on your own case, Clive?" Ross asked. "Have the cops got anywhere? Maybe there's a tie-in."

"There isn't," Lyle said. "We know the bomb was detonated by a radio signal. We know the KGB bastard was in that girl's apartment, because the autopsy turned up a higher than normal potassium level, and after we'd made them look three times, they found the pinprick on her arm. But other than that, no one saw him come, no one saw him go. We know a bit about him now. He's fair, because the police picked up a few blond hairs on the pillow that didn't belong to the girl and some reddish-brown pubic hairs that weren't hers either. We know from the semen that his blood group's A Positive, along with a lot of the rest of the world. He came in wearing a black suit made of wool— they found fibers. He screwed her on the living room couch and again in bed. They got stains to prove both those. And he may have picked up syphilis. Now tell me who to look for.''

"It's like trying to come to grips with a phantom," Ross said, "except, which of the skydivers is blond, with A Positive blood?''

"It doesn't matter who," Lyle pointed out, "because we've accounted for all of them that Saturday, and my guy was blowing up the elevator at around 8:10. Even assuming he went straight out of there to the club, he couldn't have made it before nine. There're only four blond members, not including yourself, and they were all at the airfield by 8:30. Don't think I didn't consider that possibility.''

"Not very helpful then.''

"It was a good idea," Lyle acknowledged. "It might have meant something.''

They worked through the files until eight, when both were prepared to admit their concentration was going.

When they parted, Clive went back to his apartment, and Ross headed off to meet Julie Klein.

The last stitches came out in the morning. Timothy Peal removed the thin blue gut so delicately, Elaine felt scarcely a twinge. When he was finished, he scrutinized her, his deep-set dark eyes intent on every detail.

At last he sat back, smoothed a finger over his temple and tried to repress a smile. "Well, well," he said. "I guess that's one of my better efforts. How do you like it?''

Elaine already knew. She'd stared at her reflection a dozen times a day as the swelling subsided and a more youthful face looked back. She bit her lip and tried not to cry. "I think," she said, "it's . . . beyond belief. I never imagined I'd look anything like this. I've lost, what? Ten years? Dr. Peal, I can't thank you enough.''

The surgeon waved a hand dismissively. "Nothing to it, really. But I'm glad you're pleased. You'd go through it again, then?"

"Oh, would I! I feel I've discovered the fountain of youth."

"Well, if you want a repeat some day, come back to me. We often get better results the second time around. And, meanwhile, try to keep your present weight."

When he'd gone, Elaine dressed and packed her small suitcase. She put on her usual minimum amount of make-up, smiling at herself in the mirror. The four white lumps on her neck from the anesthesia needles had almost disappeared. What she needed now was to get her hair done, buy a new dress, and go home to wait for David. And watch his face.

My God, she thought, he won't believe it.

She spent a happy few hours in Washington, as confident now as she'd ever been, trying on clothes: nothing too young, but nothing matronly, either. A new look for a new woman.

She ordered a bottle of Dom Perignon and a Napoleon cognac to be delivered to Timothy Peal with a note of renewed thanks, and she went home.

The apartment looked almost as she'd left it. Perhaps David was away again. That would be awful.

She checked the laundry basket and the refrigerator, her guide to her husband's movements, and found the one full and the other empty, except for a carton of sour milk. Then she went shopping.

She thought she'd buy something simple for dinner as there was no way of telling when he'd be home, and she chose prime steaks. By the time she'd finished her arms were full.

She packed everything away and sat in the living room, reading, listening to music, waiting for his return.

The hours passed, and her sense of euphoria dissipated, to be replaced by disappointment. The big entrance she'd planned—what had happened to it? Where was David?

Shorty after eight, she called the DIA and asked for his office extension. She heard the telephone ringing, unanswered. Perhaps Clive Lyle would know. She hung up and dialed his apartment, but Lyle wasn't home either.

It could be they were both out of town on an assignment. Elaine fought her feelings. She went back to her book, forcing herself to concentrate but finding the words blurring. She put a Brahms concerto on the turntable and mixed a martini.

Time passed as slowly as she'd ever known until finally she could bear it no longer and did what she'd promised herself never to do: she telephoned Lyndon Yardley.

He, surely, would be able to say if David would be coming home and, after all, these were special circumstances. Anyway, she could thank him again for the beautiful roses, even though she'd already sent a note of appreciation.

The Director answered curtly, "Yes?" which made her instantly nervous.

"I'm so very sorry to disturb you, General," she said. "It's Elaine Ross."

There was a pause before Yardley replied: "Mrs. Ross, how nice to speak to you. I've heard good reports of your progress." His voice had become warmer, and this gave her courage.

"Oh, yes," she said, "it's a wonderful job. I can't tell you how grateful I am. And for the roses, too . . ."

"I'm glad you liked them."

Elaine cleared her throat. "The other reason I phoned, General, was David. Uh, I hesitate to ask, but I'm home now and he's not. I wondered if you could give me any indication whether I should expect him tonight."

Yardley didn't miss a beat. "Indeed you should," he said cheerfully. "David's been rather occupied recently. I've been keeping him busy, and I'm sorry to say I didn't realize you'd be out so soon. I'll call him right away and tell him the good news. But it may be—oh, an hour or two before he walks in."

"Oh, please, I don't want to interrupt anything important," Elaine said.

"Mrs. Ross, as far as I'm concerned, you're more important than what David is doing at this moment and I mean that most sincerely."

"I'm very grateful, General," she said. "Thank you again, a thousand times."

Elaine felt considerably better when she hung up. She had time for another martini and a soak in the bath. Her debut had not been canceled after all: merely postponed.

Julie and Ross groaned simultaneously in frustration when her telephone began ringing. They lay quietly in each other's arms, waiting for the noise to stop. It had been a near thing, and Ross's breathing was heavy. He smothered his face in Julie's glossy hair and nibbled the lobe of her ear.

The phone rang on.

Finally Ross said savagely: "Jesus, they're not going to give up, are they? I'd better go see who it is."

He pulled gently out of her and padded into the living room.

"Yeah?"

"David, it's Clive."

"Oh Jesus, Clive! You really pick your moments," Ross complained.

"Tough luck," Lyle said. "I want you at my place as soon as you can make it. And I mean soon."

"Huh? What's up?"

"Two things: the first is something I want you to hear, because if we move on it, we're going to move quickly."

"Yeah? Well, okay."

"And have a shower before you leave, Dave. The second thing is your wife's beck, and she's wondering where the hell you are."

Ross stood naked in the penthouse and sighed. Then he moved fast.

Lyle checked the television monitor in the hall cupboard and saw Ross waiting outside. He opened the door.

"Hi!"

"Hi!" Ross followed Lyle through to the living room.

"You want a drink?"

"Yeah. Got a beer?"

"Sure." Lyle pulled a couple of cans from the refrigerator and snapped them open. "Sorry about busting into your sex life, but it was important. Yardley phoned to say Elaine was asking where you were. He said I was to reunite the two of you as soon as possible." Lyle filled the glasses. "Actually, that was only the gist of what he said. His precise words were . . ."

"Thank you, Clive. I guess I can do without the General's precise words."

Lyle handed him his drink, then touched the back of Ross's neck. "Your hair's still wet," he commented. "I'll give you a dryer before you go. You'd better not show up looking like you've just stepped out of a shower."

Lyle took a seat nearby. "Now the reason for pulling you in here." He took a drink of beer. "I've been thinking about your chart," he said, "and the card index, and all that stuff. None of it's got us nearer finding who sabotaged the chutes, and it occurred to me we were approaching it the wrong way.

"This is how I see it—tell me if I'm wrong. The KGB

could only have had two weeks' notice you were jumping, again, because that's how long it was between the Rabinovich operation and your first free fall. Correct?''

"Sure."

"But even if they'd had your number earlier than that, it couldn't have been that much earlier—a few weeks at most, from the time you decided to join the skydivers. So if they were going to get one of their agents into place so he could assess security, find who packed the chutes and all the rest, that would be the first possible date. You agree?''

"Yeah, that's right."

"Okay. Now there are two ways the KGB could have acted. The first was to have someone talking to one of the skydivers about you—which would be easy enough, except no one remembers anyone doing that—and then going on to ask about security and packing procedures, which would be more difficult. And no one remembers that either."

"Unless they used drugs," Ross observed.

"Unless they used drugs," Lyle agreed. "But we'd never find out if they had, so let's concentrate on things we can actually get a grip on."

"What's the second way?"

"The second way's the most obvious. They infiltrated someone into the club after you joined. That way it'd be easy to learn which chutes were used, who packed them, where they were kept, and when you were going to jump.

"Yeah, but who could that be? We've been through everyone, and they look clean."

"We've been through it the wrong way. We've been looking at it negatively. Now, who's new at the club? —taking everyone into account, skydivers, girlfriends, groupies, the pilot."

"Well, me, Sue Collins, and Sophie Johnson."

"Forget Sue: she's dead, and she predated you by a week."

"Me and Sophie Johnson."

"Exactly. And we'll rule you out too."

"Ah, come on, Clive. Sophie's a beginner! She made her first jump the week before Sue crunched. She doesn't even know how to pack a chute."

"Says who?"

"Says she. She used to watch Pete Grethel doing it and say how she'd never trust herself with anything like that. I was there. I heard her."

"How was she at ground training?" Lyle asked.

Ross thought for a second. "Pretty good, actually. She took a while to get the idea of the rolls, but once she did, there was no problem. Pete said she was a natural."

"What about her first jump?"

"I'm told it went fine. Everyone was pleased."

"So maybe she was faking being a beginner."

"Oh, bullshit," Ross scoffed. "Sophie did okay, but so did I. And I was a beginner."

"Okay. But let's imagine you're an expert parachutist and Yardley sends you to Moscow to kill some poor bastard skydiver. Are you telling me you wouldn't be able to go through basic training without letting on you knew what you were doing?"

"No, sure I could. But we've got no proof Sophie did. And don't forget, she's been security cleared. She's personal assistant to a Congressman, for Christ's sake."

"I know we've got no proof," Lyle argued reasonably. "What I'm saying is, Sophie's the only person who fits the new scenario. So I think we should concentrate on her and look for proof. Anyway, just because a pretty minor security check's been made on her doesn't mean she's clean. Think of all the people working for the government who've been given a higher rating than Sophie Johnson—

guys who've taken the polygraph test even—and turned out later to be drawing a salary from the Soviets. Now it seems to me there're two possibilities with Sophie. First, she really is a beginner but she told the KGB what they wanted to know, and they sent an expert in to fix the canopies; and second, she's the expert, and she did it herself.''

"And how are we going to prove these, Clive?"

"We run a new security check on her—in depth, back to her childhood in Kansas City, and see what comes out of the woodwork. And, if she is a parachutist, she must have done some jumping in the United States over the last few years. It's the sort of thing people keep up, isn't it? I don't think she'd have done it in Washington: skydivers are a pretty tight community. So you and I go back in her past, to San Francisco. She lived there for years. We ask the skydiving clubs. We show her photograph around. We see if anybody recognizes her." Lyle finished his beer. "How about it?"

"It can't do any harm. I think we're barking up the wrong tree, though."

"Can you find a better tree?"

"No," Ross admitted. "I can't."

"Then we agree?"

"I suppose so."

"Thanks for the enthusiasm. We'll see Yardley first thing tomorrow. Come to the office with your bags packed. If he gives the go-ahead, we'll take a lunchtime flight to San Francisco. Which means," Lyle added, "you've only got a few hours with Elaine. I suggest you get your hair dry and go see if you can make her forget what a shit she's married."

Ross left Lyle's apartment five minutes later and drove the short distance to his own block, feeling guilty and shabby, made worse by the knowledge that Julie Klein was

not at all pleased with him running out on her like that.
She might even start her telephone calls again.

There was a soft light in the living room, and Elaine
smiled at him with genuine pleasure as he walked in. She
got up from the armchair.

Ross stopped short and stared. "My God," he said,
puzzled, "what's happened to you? You look . . . Christ,
you look . . . fantastic!" He put his arms around her and
kissed her. "What have you been doing?"

"It's a new hairstyle," Elaine said. "And a new dress,
too."

He took her hand and led her to the sofa. "I can't get
over this. You look amazing."

"I'm glad you like it. How about a drink? Have you
eaten?"

"Yes, but I could put away a martini, I guess."

"So could I." She went to mix their drinks.

"How was the FBI?" Ross called after her.

"They were fine, no trouble. They just needed reassuring, so I reassured them."

"It took long enough," he commented.

"Did you miss me?"

Ross smiled. "Sure," he said. "Hey, listen, I've got
some bad news. I'm going away tomorrow."

"Oh no!"

"Only for a few days, to San Francisco. Clive and I
ought to be back before the weekend."

Elaine hid her disappointment. "We really have to work
it so we coincide in this apartment," she said. "Still, we
do have tonight, so we ought to be grateful for that."

Ross was glad he'd had the shower.

Sometime during the night he woke and felt Elaine's body
warm next to him. She was breathing easy and deep. He
stared into the darkness, pondering. It was good to have

her back. They'd made love that night better than ever before: for him anyway. He'd felt a strange possessiveness, and a tenderness too, as if he might be losing her.

Ross's eyes tried to penetrate the blackness.

Something was going on, and he couldn't put his finger on it. The first time she went to the West Coast, she came back changed: more assured and confident. Something had happened out there. Something . . . or maybe someone.

This time, the difference was dramatic. She was younger, as if she'd had a long, relaxing holiday. Without him.

With whom then? Ross wondered if the FBI really had called her back or if that was an excuse because she'd found another guy in San Francisco or LA. He remembered the improvement in their sex life dated from her first return.

Ross chewed his lip. Stupid of him not to have realized it earlier. Elaine was being fucked by some California stud (an FBI man? a beach bum? his mind tried to visualize the competition) and it had changed her life.

How long would it be before she found another excuse to fly out? Maybe permanently?

His heart felt heavy. It didn't help to remember that he'd been sleeping with Julie Klein, and that before her there was a secretary at the Embassy in Moscow when he was on his first DIA assignment, and before her Lyle and he had had a night with a couple of beautiful hookers because Ross was in the middle of a crisis, thinking he was impotent, and Clive had taken him out on the town to prove it wasn't true. But those women were all different! They were just fucks! They didn't mean anything. And he knew that Elaine didn't just fuck. She made love, and she cared about the man she went to bed with. And that hurt.

Ross suddenly wanted her very badly. He moved close, feeling her warmth, stroking her body so she stirred. He penetrated her even before she woke, with a yearning, and desperation, and sense of impending loss. But at that moment, she was in his bed, and she was his, no one else's, and he pushed and plunged, increasingly savage and uncaring. Her arm gripped his back, nails digging into the muscles. She cried out, loud—he thought at first in pain but it didn't stop him—until he came in a combination of fury and love.

When his movements, the last spasmodic jerks, subsided, he heard her whispering delightedly in his ear, "David . . . my darling . . . my darling." He relaxed in relief and exhaustion. As he fell asleep, Ross thought: beat that, you bastard.

Sitting in the first-class section of the 747, they started with a list of subscribers to skydivers' magazines, piles of printouts of names and addresses, underlining those in San Francisco and copying them into notebooks. It wasn't necessary to get every individual—just a fair selection among whom to start inquiries and discover someone in charge of a club in the area. They just had to hit the right person and the whole skydiving scene would be open to them.

Ross and Lyle broke for lunch but worked on during the movie, and by the time the aircraft touched down at San Francisco and they'd checked into the Mark Hopkins on Mason Street, they were ready to begin.

Ross leafed through the telephone directory, fitting numbers to names, while Lyle made the calls. Because of the time change, it was still mid-afternoon, and the first names drew blanks. A woman answered the third call but was suspicious of Clive's motives and hung up on him.

The fourth connected them with a man who'd stopped skydiving two years earlier, but he told them about his old club, and the name of the person in charge.

Ross looked up the listing for Buster Chant, except of

course there wasn't any "Buster" in the book, so Lyle worked his way through the "Chants" until he found a woman who told him Buster was at work and gave a number.

Lyle made the call, and a slow-speaking, deep-voiced man agreed to meet for a drink and a talk on his way home.

In the bar, the men exchanged courtesies and sized each other up. Ross mentioned he was learning to skydive in Washington, and Buster Chant relaxed immediately. He knew Grethel from a competition a year earlier and had heard of Andy Marcus.

When their drinks came, Ross got down to business. He handed Chant a visiting card showing him to be a representative of a firm of Washington lawyers. "We've been instructed by a legal firm in Kansas City to find a woman named Sophie Johnson," Ross explained. "She's been left a substantial legacy, but no one there seems to have kept in touch. They thought she'd moved to Washington, but we haven't been able to locate her—maybe because she's married and we don't know her new name. The possibility we're exploring now is that someone in San Francisco might have an address. We know she used to skydive here, so that's why we called you—to see if the name rang a bell."

"Sophie Johnson," Buster Chant said slowly. "No, I can't say it does. How long ago was she in these parts?"

"Two years," Ross replied. "But she lived here for nine before that."

"Well," Chant said, "I've been with the club longer than that, and I don't recall the name. I can have a look at the records if you like, but I'm pretty sure it won't be there."

Ross opened his briefcase and extracted a copy of the

photograph she'd submitted with a passport application in 1980. It was a good likeness.

"This is her," he said. "Our only lead so far. It was among her aunt's possessions."

Chant studied it briefly and handed it back. "No," he said. "Sorry."

"I wonder, Buster, if you'd help us with a list of clubs in the San Francisco area—and maybe the names of the guys running them?" Lyle asked. "I guess we're going to have to go to every one till we strike it lucky."

"Sure, no problem. Have you got a piece of paper?"

Ross pulled a notebook from his case, and Buster Chant took several minutes compiling the list.

"I reckon that's it," he said at last. "If I think of any more, maybe I can give you a call at the hotel."

Lyle rose. "Well, if you'll excuse me, I'll go get started on this. No need for you to hurry, Dave," he told Ross. "Relax and enjoy your drink."

While the conversation turned back to skydiving, Lyle returned to his room and the telephone directory. He'd almost finished when Ross knocked at his door.

"Sorry I took so long," he apologized. "Chant wasn't that easy to get rid of."

"That's okay." Lyle filled him in on the progress so far. Their first appointment was at nine in the morning, and four others had been arranged later in the day. This left a few clubs uncovered, but he hadn't been able to contact all the names on the list.

The following morning, Lyle and Ross presented themselves at a sporting goods store and went through their routine with a tall young man who was probably too young to remember Sophie Johnson if she'd been around his club longer than four years back. He also agreed to consult the records, such as they were, but he wasn't hopeful.

The second appointment, at eleven, was in the offices of

an insurance company. A mousy secretary showed them into the glass-fronted cubicle where Stan Corbett was on the phone.

He waved them toward chairs in front of his desk and when he'd finished his call, shook hands and apologized for keeping them waiting. Corbett was a big, cheerful man, almost bald.

"I seem to spend half my life on the phone," he explained happily. "It drives me crazy. Luckily, I skydive during some of the other half, so I keep away from the funny farm. Now how can I help you, gentlemen?"

Ross began to explain and was hardly into his story when Corbett said impatiently: "Sure, sure, I know Sophie. She used to jump with us. Went to Washington to work for her Congressman."

As quickly and as easily as that, they'd struck oil. Ross felt a wave of shock and indignation which he fought to disguise. Lyle's eyes shone.

"I wonder if I could just show you a photograph, to make sure we're talking about the same woman," Ross said. He handed over the color print.

"Yeah, yeah, that's Sophie."

"Have you any idea how to reach her?" Lyle asked, playing their story through to the end.

Corbett shook his head. "I guess if you checked with the politicos in town, they'd be able to tell you. I can't rightly recall the Congressman's name. I don't pay a lot of attention to that sort of thing—unless the guy's into insurance or skydiving!" He laughed. "And they never are. But I remember Sophie saying she was a Republican, so why not start with them."

"Thanks, Mr. Corbett," Lyle said warmly. "You've been a great help."

"Hell, glad to be of use. Is she going to get a lot of dough?"

"It'll be a big payoff," Lyle promised, rising to leave.

But Ross said, "I do a bit of skydiving myself, Mr. Corbett. How long was Sophie at your club?"

"Years," Corbett told him. "Five or six."

"So she wasn't a beginner?"

"She'd chew your balls off if you called her a beginner," he said. "She was good and I do mean good. Hell, she won an all-California accuracy competition against a lot of top people. If she'd set her mind to it, she could have represented the United States." He got up and crossed to a bookshelf crammed with magazines. Corbett explained, "I bring my hobby to work because I handle insurance for most of the skydivers in this area" His index finger moved along the row, occasionally pulling out an issue, then moving on. Finally he extracted half a dozen copies and began flipping through them on his desk top, murmuring: "It's in one of these, if I'm not mistaken."

Ross and Lyle watched fascinated.

"Oh sure, here she is!" Corbett said at last. "Sophie Johnson, winner of the two-day event."

She smiled triumphantly at them from the page, holding aloft a silver cup. There was no doubt it was her.

"Was she any good at packing chutes?" Ross asked. "I'm just a beginner—haven't done a free fall yet, and I thought maybe I could get her to do mine."

Lyle glanced at him, amused.

"Don't worry about it, Mr. Ross," Corbett said. "It looks hard but it isn't really." He smiled broadly. "But hell, you're a nice looking guy and Sophie always had an eye for the men. So I guess if you asked, she'd fix you up. In more ways than one." He winked obscenely.

"Is she a safe packer?" Ross persisted.

"The best! I taught her myself."

"I wonder," Ross asked, "if I could borrow this magazine? Maybe I can show it to her, remind her of old times. Break the ice.''

"I'll bet she's got a dozen, but sure, be my guest. Mail it back when you're through."

"I will," Ross promised. He extended his hand. "Mr. Corbett, you've been a great help. Thank you."

"My pleasure, gentlemen," he beamed. "And any time you want insurance, Mr. Ross, I'll be glad to put you in touch with someone in our Washington office who doesn't faint when a skydiver asks for a couple of hundred thousand dollars worth of life cover."

"I will," David said. "Thanks again."

In the elevator, the agents stared unblinkingly at each other.

Ross felt they'd reached a threshold. He was aware of a liquid sensation in his gut, almost a tingling.

"Well, Clive, I guess that's it," he said.

Lyle nodded. "It sure is."

They caught the evening plane home.

It was Yardley's habit in matters like these to keep his agents at attention in front of his desk. It reinforced in their minds the fact that they were under discipline and that what followed was neither casually decided, nor lacked authority.

Lyle knew the form, and when they entered he came to attention two paces from the huge mahogany expanse. Ross, who had been about to pull up a chair, took his cue from Clive and braced.

Yardley regarded them gravely. Behind his head, the American flag hung limp from a bronze pole. No papers were in evidence.

Lyle fixed his eyes on a point over and behind the Director's head.

"Yes, Major Lyle?" Yardley invited.

"Sir, our inquiries in San Francisco show that Sophie Johnson is a skydiver with several years' experience. We spoke to a man called Stan Corbett, who's in charge of the club she jumped with. He identified her immediately by name, and then from her passport photograph. Further, he produced a skydiving magazine from six years ago, which carries a picture of her winning a prize in a state competition." Lyle handed it over, open to the page.

Yardley studied it and checked the date.

"Mr. Ross," Yardley asked, "what was your understanding about Miss Johnson's parachuting career?"

"Sir, when she joined the club she said she was a rank beginner. She went through ground training and then made what she said was her first jump. She also said, in my hearing, that she'd never be able to learn how to fold a parachute, although Mr. Corbett confirms she's an expert packer. He taught her himself."

Yardley pushed the magazine to one side and inspected his fingernails. The men waited.

"Major Lyle," he said, "give me a reasonable explanation for Miss Johnson's pretense. Could it have been, for example, that she felt herself out of training and thought it better to start from the beginning again?"

"In my view, sir, no."

"What about you, Mr. Ross?"

"I think it's unlikely," Ross agreed. "There was no reason she couldn't come right out and tell the truth. I guess she was acting a part."

"What do we know," Yardly inquired, "of Miss Johnson's movements on the night of Wednesday/Thursday, immediately before the killing of Miss Collins?"

"She told the police she was alone at home," Lyle replied.

"So she had no alibi?"

"No, sir."

"And what do we know of her movements on the Saturday in question?"

"She wasn't at the club when I was there, sir," Ross said. "She arrived later after Sue Collins had jumped."

"How did she react to the news of Miss Collins's death?"

"Julie Klein told me she almost fainted," Ross said. "She left the clubhouse soon afterward and hasn't been back."

"I see." Yardley laid his palms flat on the polished wood of his desk. "Miss Johnson works for a Congressman, of course, and security check was run on her. What did it say?"

"It gave her a clean bill of health, sir," Lyle reported, "but it wasn't for a high classification and didn't go into any particular depth."

"Very well." The Director stared first at Lyle, then at Ross. "Do either of you have anything further to say?"

"No, sir," replied Lyle.

"No, sir," said Ross.

"Do either of you entertain any doubts of Miss Johnson's guilt in this matter? Any reservation at all?"

They did not.

Yardley nodded. "Thank you. You may go," he said.

Lyle about-faced, Ross following, and they left the office. In the corridor, Ross touched Lyle's arm.

"What the hell does that mean?" he asked. "What happens now?"

"It means we pay a visit to Sophie Johnson," Lyle said. "What the hell do you think? You want an engraved invitation?"

Ross felt his knees turning to jelly.

She walked briskly along the sidewalk, heels clicking on the pavement, one hand underneath a paper bag full of groceries that she knew would burst if she neglected it for a moment. She hummed softly as she moved out of the way of an old lady and nodded good-humoredly when a man stood aside for her. It was Sophie Johnson's first good day since the Saturday she failed to kill David Ross.

Trevor Prince, her KGB contact, had listened grimly to her explanation that afternoon when they met in Mount Vernon Square and found an almost empty bar where they could talk. At least, where she could talk, because Prince's cold silence spurred her into increasingly detailed justifications, while his light blue eyes watched, expressionless. Sophie was in serious trouble. Her first *mokrie dela* assignment had been a fiasco, and she didn't even know how it had gone wrong: just that Ross was at the club, ready to jump, and had been called away. She felt she had to persuade Prince she'd done everything humanly possible, but how do you convince the KGB that you suffered from plain bad luck?

Sophie drank dry martinis. Trevor Prince ordered a scotch, and it sat untouched on the table in front of him while she called for refills and her voice took on a tinge of hysteria. Once, she reached across to touch the faintly pitted, dry skin of his face for reassurance, but drew back when she saw the warning in his eyes.

As she launched into her fourth run-through of events, Prince cut her short. "Tomorrow night," he said softly, "be in your apartment. I'll see you there."

He paid the bill and walked out, leaving her nursing her martini, palms like ice, as if death might be reaching to touch her. She would know next day. Should she run? Where? If she did, she'd never be able to stop, and both sides, Americans and Soviets, would be her enemies. She wondered if she should call a CIA man she knew slightly and confess to him; but there was no guarantee she wouldn't spend the rest of her life in jail.

She walked the streets for hours and, in the end, did nothing. When Sunday night came, she was waiting for Trevor Prince and whatever verdict had been handed down from Moscow, with all the resignation she could summon.

Prince stayed in her apartment no longer than five minutes. He accused her of incompetence and said she should have foreseen the possibility that someone else might use the parachute. She should have been there to make sure nothing stood in the way of Ross's jump, that no one called him back. She was warned, a first and final warning, that such negligence would not be tolerated again. Then he walked up to her and with his fingers touched her body, gently at first, locating major nerve centers, and suddenly squeezing until she writhed and fought to hold back her screams. He left without another word.

She wept herself to sleep that night in fright, and relief, and remembered pain.

The days stretched out, punctuated by interviews with the police and fear they would discover her guilt, fear too that Prince would come back. Her nights were filled with troubled dreams which, when she woke sweating in the darkness, instantly retreated, elusive and cunning, and lurked unexamined in the shadows, waiting for her to slip again into exhausted sleep.

But finally it all passed. The police had not been to see her for days, and last night her rest was calm and unbroken.

The phantoms were at peace. In the morning, she felt reborn, and now, when she got home, she planned phoning Pete Grethel. She needed someone, and she wanted him.

She turned into her building and smiled brightly at the doorman. "Evening, George. How are things?"

"Fine, Miss Johnson. Did you have a good day?"

"Yeah, for a change." She pressed the elevator button and rode up the twelve floors.

Outside her apartment she paused, transferring the bag of groceries to one arm and fumbling for her key. She stepped inside and closed the door behind her.

As she did, two men appeared in the small hallway, their faces hidden behind gas masks.

Sophie froze, eyes wide with shock. She took an involuntary step backward, bumping into the door. There was terror in her voice. "What the . . ."

A canister held by one of the men hissed at her. She barely repressed a cry, and turned to grapple with the latch, holding her breath, while her package dropped to the floor. A hand slammed down over hers, hard and painful, crushing her fingers against the metal lock. She fought and wriggled, making desperate grunting noises, trying to strike at him. Her lungs were bursting. She couldn't help herself: she had to have air. She gave a small gasp, taking in the minimum amount possible, but that was too much.

She felt her strength drain from her. Now her breath came in unrestricted pants.

The hissing of the gas stopped. She stared defeated at the obscene black mask, at the man's eyes impassive behind the goggles, the snout of the air filter making him seem like an insect observed through a microscope; and she wondered, as her legs crumpled, if this at last was the elusive horror that had tormented her sleep.

Lyle lifted her under the arms and pulled her into the living room. Ross helped get her onto the sofa before unscrewing the plastic top from a small injection ampule, and sliding the needle efficiently into a vein in Sophie Johnson's right hand.

The ampule stayed in place, leechlike. The drug dripped into her bloodstream.

Lyle opened the windows to let the gas disperse. While it did, he moved the dropped package from the hallway into the kitchen. After a few minutes, he peeled off his mask

and breathed deeply. When he was satisfied, he said:
"Okay, David. I guess we're ready."

Ross removed his mask and placed it, with Lyle's, in a
small case.

Ross took a cassette recorder and positioned it near
Sophie. He pushed two buttons. "Okay," he said, "the
tape's rolling."

Lyle shook the woman's shoulders. "Wake up!" he
ordered. "Wake up! Can you hear me?"

And she replied, "Yes."

"What's your name?" Lyle asked.

"Sophie Johnson."

"Is that your real name?"

"No," she said as the drug unlocked the deepest secrets
of her mind. "My name is Nadya Chebrikov."

"Where were you born, Nadya?"

"Leningrad."

She told them, unemotionally and in detail, what she
knew about Trevor Prince—her only KGB link in America—
about her instructions to kill David Ross, and how she had
gone about it. She detailed her activities in Washington;
where she had planted bugs and when, which documents
she had been asked to get by Prince, and which she had
been able to provide.

The tape ran out, and Ross turned it over. Later, the
ampule became exhausted, and he jabbed a second needle
into her other hand.

They changed tapes.

By ten o'clock, Sophie had been answering questions
for four hours and there was nothing more for them to
learn.

"You happy, David?" Lyle asked.

"Yeah, I guess so."

Lyle switched off the recorder. "Let's pack up," he

said. They put everything back into the case, except the one Pentovar ampule, still dripping into her vein.

Ross felt nervous and uncertain. They were reaching territory he had never trodden before, and as the critical moment approached he wanted to distance himself from what was to happen.

"Listen," Ross said, "I need to go to the john. Is that okay?"

"Sure. Leave your gloves on, though."

"You go ahead, huh?"

"No," Lyle said. "I'll wait for you to get back."

Ross's heart sank. He went to the toilet and emptied his bladder, taking his time. Then he stood bleakly in the tiny room, wondering if he was going to throw up.

He flushed the bowl and returned to the living room.

There was the strangest sense of unreality. In a way, he didn't even feel he was there, as if this was a dream and soon he would wake. His head was light, and that liquid feeling in his gut, pulsing, almost sexual, was back, very strong. He found to his disquiet that he was getting an erection.

Sophie lay silently on the sofa. Lyle sat in a chair, watching him.

Ross cleared his throat. "Listen, Clive," he said, "I don't think I want to be a party to this."

Lyle's voice was neutral. "Why not, Dave? Don't you think she's guilty?"

"Oh sure, she's guilty as hell. But—Jesus, shouldn't we call the FBI? We've got her confession, so why don't we let her rot in prison for the rest of her life? That's a pretty terrible punishment."

"You think those tapes are acceptable as evidence?" Lyle asked. "Well let me tell you they aren't. She'd be out of jail in twenty-four hours, and the law wouldn't be able to touch her. And you know it."

Ross punched his fist into the gloved palm of his hand. "Clive, I can't do it! Not to a woman! It isn't right! I know she's guilty, but it just isn't right!"

There was a silence. "Dave, come on over here," Lyle said.

"Huh?"

"Yeah, come here, next to me."

Ross approached reluctantly.

"I've got something you ought to see," Lyle said. He reached into his shirt pocket and pulled out a brown envelope. "I want you take a look at these."

"What are they?"

"Photographs."

Lyle rose and put an arm around Ross's shoulders, their bodies brushing. "Go on," he urged. "They won't bite."

Ross took the envelope reluctantly and pulled out a series of color photographs.

Sue Collins, after impact.

He felt his stomach churn. He wanted to move away, but Lyle was holding him tight.

She had hit the ground in the starfish position, and her arms were out, her face down. Blood congealed around the edges of her body.

In the next picture, they had turned her over. There was no face left. Ross saw what looked like yellowish-gray curds, the exposed white of bone, bloody meat: nothing at all of the plain, friendly, willing girl who every week brought them pizzas and hamburgers, made sandwiches, and asked friendship.

Ross tried to push the photographs into Lyle's hand, but Clive whispered urgently, "There's more, Dave. You've got to see them all!"

Ross's fingers moved numbly, flipping over to the next.

It was the autopsy. Sue was naked, so they could see the extent of the damage. Her stomach had split open and her bowels, gray sausages curling around and back on themselves, spilled onto the table. There seemed to be no shape to her limbs, as if she was a partly deflated balloon; but then as Pete Grethel said the night she died, every bone in her body had been smashed. On the big toe of her right foot, someone had tied a Label.

There was a buzzing in Ross's ears. He was in the middle of a nightmare, only vaguely aware of Lyle's touch and his voice, soft, confidential, giving a commentary. "Those are her brains, over there, see them, Dave? I guess that red ball where her mouth ought to be is one of her eyes . . . I can't see the other, can you? . . . Shit, it messes them up when they crunch at that speed . . ."

Ross thrust the photographs away, and this time Lyle took them, and released him, letting him stand alone and stricken.

Lyle spoke normally again. "You're a funny guy, Dave," he said. "Rabinovich gets taken from us, and you want revenge. But a couple of hours later, you go cold on the idea. Sue Collins dies instead of you and, Jesus, do you ever want revenge! But a week goes by, two, and you cool off. Some KGB bastard tries to kill me, and instead he blows up a handful of innocent folks. Do you know, they couldn't identify three of those people? Not at all. One guy they could because they found five teeth. Five fucking teeth! That's all they had to bury and be able to say: Yeah, well these teeth surely belong to Mr. Roland Brooks, because we've got pictures of them on his dental chart. Otherwise, they just shoveled a couple of spadefuls of meat into each box. You were in that elevator, Dave, you saw it, you know what it was like. And Jesus Christ, were you ever burning for revenge then! Oh shit, the fire was in you! You were gonna track that sonofabitch KGB man to the ends of the earth! Yeah, and maybe you would have too. But let me ask you, Dave, if you caught him, what would you do? Let him off with a warning? Call the cops?"

Ross listened, his emotions wrenching in different directions.

"Dave," Lyle explained, "the cops don't operate in our world. You say you're a DIA agent, and I tell you, Dave, you're a fine theoretical agent. You've got a lot of personal courage, and you've got a great mind." Lyle's voice became contemptuous. "But that isn't enough! You want to stay with us, you've got to become a soldier! We're fighting a war! And that means, when revenge burns in you, it burns with a heat so white the only way of stopping it is to find whoever's responsible and kill!"

He pointed at Sophie Johnson, lying relaxed as the last drops of the drug dripped into her bloodstream. Ross could see the muscles bulging in Lyle's neck.

"You say she's a woman," Lyle said savagely. "I don't see a woman there. I see the KGB! She tried to kill you, Ross! And instead she murdered some innocent fat kid! Hey, I didn't tell you, did I? The autopsy showed one thing in Sue Collins's body that wasn't broken. You want to know what that was? Shall I tell you, Ross? Her fucking hymen! She kept her virginity to the end. Now isn't that good news?"

"That isn't true, Clive."

Lyle laughed at Ross. "Oh yes," he said scornfully, "it's true all right. But what d'you care? You weren't trying to get into her pants, were you? No one was. The rest of you were screwing away, but not Sue. She wanted to, though. I'll bet that's why she hung around the club. I'll lay you a million bucks that's why she went up that Saturday, because she wanted to make herself more acceptable to the rest of you! But now it's okay. You've found the KGB agent who killed her, and you're content. You're ready to walk off and forget about it."

Ross shook his head slowly. "No," he said.

"Well, then," Lyle offered, "you'll call the cops, and when some sharp lawyer springs her first thing tomorrow morning and she gets away free, like a good citizen you'll say 'Shit, isn't that a disgrace. I must write my Congressman.'"

"No," Ross whispered, his face the color of chalk.

"Then," Lyle said, "what in the name of all that's holy are you going to do about it, you pathetic, cowardly fucker?"

Ross bit his lip. His fists clenched tight. "Tell me what to do," he whispered.

There was a pause. "How high are we?" Lyle asked.

Ross's heart lurched, but he replied, voice steady: "Twelve stories."

"Go out onto the balcony, Dave, and look down. Tell me what you see."

Ross moved as in a dream.

The night air was cool: the lights of Washington shone all around. He came back into the living room.

"There's a straight drop," he said.

"Anyone in the street?"

"Some. Five or six, I guess."

"Well, we don't want anyone else to get hurt, do we?"

"No." His erection bulged in his pants. If Lyle noticed, he said nothing.

"Okay, take the needle out and put it in the case." He watched as Ross did so. "Now," Lyle said, "we wait for her to wake up."

"Can't we do it when she's unconscious?" Ross asked hesitantly.

Lyle shook his head. "We want her to know what's happening," he said. "Just like Sue Collins.

"But we don't want her to struggle too much, and we

don't want her making a noise: at least, not till she drops. So we immobilize her.''

"How?''

"Karate,'' Lyle said. "Hit at her elbows. I'll hold her up while you do it.''

Ross could hardly believe it was happening. Lyle pulled Sophie Johnson to her feet so Ross could smash his clenched fist into her elbow joints to paralyze her arms temporarily. He punched experimentally.

"Oh, shit!'' Lyle said in disgust. "Harder than that, for Christ's sake!''

Ross's fist powered in. Sophie groaned. He moved around and smashed into the other joint.

"Okay, that's fine.'' Lyle pulled a handkerchief from his pocket, rolled it into a ball and fed it into her mouth. Then he began to slap her. "Wake up, you bitch!'' he snarled. Lyle's eyes had become almost yellow and his face was savage.

Sophie Johnson opened her eyes, blinking, looking blankly around before remembrance flooded in, and they saw pure fear. She tried to move her arms, but they flapped like broken wings.

"You tell her, Dave,'' Lyle ordered.

Ross drew himself up and looked squarely at her. "You are an agent of the KGB,'' he said slowly. "You are guilty of crimes against the United State of America, and you are guilty of murdering Sue Collins. We know what your orders were, Sophie. We know about Trevor Prince.''

She watched, mesmerized.

"And now,'' Ross continued, "we're going to kill you in the same way you killed Sue. We're going to drop you over the balcony into the street. It's twelve stories, Sophie, straight down. I don't think you'll have reached terminal speed by the time you hit the sidewalk, but I guess it'll be fast enough.''

She made a desperate gagging noise and tried to run, but Lyle blocked her. Her useless arms twitched convulsively.

Ross said to Lyle. "Let's do it." He felt calm now.

They half pushed, half carried Sophie to the balcony. She was trying to scream through the gag. Lyle took her arms, Ross her kicking legs, and they hoisted her up so she balanced on the edge.

Lyle looked down to make sure the sidewalk was clear below. He nodded at Ross, jerked the handkerchief free, and a shriek erupted from her throat.

They pushed. Sophie dropped from sight, her screams growing fainter and ending abruptly.

"Let's get out of here," Lyle said.

They collected their case and let themselves out of the apartment. The corridor was empty. They took off their cotton gloves and pushed them into their pockets and waited for the elevator.

Lyle put an arm across Ross's shoulders. "Well," he said, "you've finally lost your cherry. Congratulations. You're one of us."

Ross felt he'd been turned to stone.

"The next one'll be easier," Lyle promised.

14

Back at attention in front of Yardley's desk, after midnight. Lucy long gone, of course. Signs of fatigue in the Director's face, but his eyes watchful.

He steepled his fingers, as if in prayer. "Yes, Major Lyle?"

"Sir, the mission has been successfully completed." Lyle stepped forward, placed the cassette tapes in the center of Yardley's desk, and returned to position.

Yardley stared at the small plastic reels but made no attempt to pick them up. They lay on the polished mahogany like rare exhibits, dangerous to touch.

He looked at David Ross, tall and straight, eyes focused on infinity, the muscles in his face tight and unmoving. A barrier had been crossed that night. Now they would see how he coped.

Yardley glanced at Clive Lyle, similarly erect and immobile, but his eyes clearer and confident. Ross would need Lyle now. If the men drew closer, the blooding will have been successful. If not, the Agency could face trouble. The important thing was that he should be given little time to brood. Action was a great healer.

"Mr. Ross," he asked, "have you anything to say?"

"No, sir." His voice was neutral.

"Gentlemen," Yardley said, "I congratulate you both. You've done a good job. I take it there's information on these tapes that needs to be acted upon?"

"Yes, sir," Lyle confirmed. "Another KGB agent has been named. A man called Trevor Prince. He has an apartment in Washington."

"Excellent," Yardley approved. "Mr. Ross, are you prepared to pay a call on this Trevor Prince?"

"Tonight, sir?"

"No, not tonight. It will require certain preparations. Tomorrow perhaps."

There was a silence. Yardley pressed. "Well, Mr. Ross?"

"Yes, sir."

"I'm glad to hear it," the Director said. "Now I suggest you both go home and get some sleep. I'll want you in the office at nine."

He watched them leave and, when they'd gone, picked up the tapes and inspected them. He pulled a cassette recorder from a desk drawer and settled down to listen.

By afternoon, they would be transcribed and the information edited so that it appeared to be an agent's report originating from inside the Soviet Union. It would then pass into the DIA archives, and the original tapes would be destroyed: an insurance policy against the possibility that some day the Agency might be dragged into the political arena; or worse, into civilian legal processes where the fact of their secret war was not acknowledged.

Outside, Ross's Chevy followed Lyle's MGB toward N Street, but when Clive turned into his underground garage, Ross didn't continue on to his own apartment, but found a space nearby. Elaine was at home, but she wasn't expecting him and, in any case, home wasn't what he wanted. Ross sat motionless behind the wheel for a few minutes, collecting his thoughts, feeling a strange emptiness.

Lyle had used him. He'd known from the beginning he would balk at a cold-blooded killing, and he'd gone to Sophie's apartment with those photographs, to goad him across that last terrible hurdle.

Lyle had made him a murderer, and tomorrow night he'd be asked to kill again.

The next one will be easier.

Ross wondered if it would.

He got out, picked up his brief case, and took the stairs to Clive's apartment. The elevator car had not yet been replaced.

Ross rang the bell. Lyle opened the door and stood aside for him to enter.

"I want to stay over tonight, Clive," Ross said. "Do you mind?"

Lyle shook his head. "Whenever you like."

The death of Sophie Johnson rated a paragraph in the *Washington Post* because of her political connections. It was also on the early television news. There were no signs of a struggle, or forcible entry, and it was thought she had committed suicide, although police investigations were continuing.

Trevor Prince's apartment was under DIA surveillance before Lyle and Ross reported for duty, and there was an unusual tension in Yardley's office as they met to discuss the contents of the tapes.

Prince's name had been run through the computers, but there was nothing of interest on the printout, except that he ran his own small import-export company and was unmarried.

His apartment was on the third floor, so the agents knew they would have to use another method of sanction.

They did not talk of this with Yardley, however. They spoke merely of surveillance, interrogation, and Prince's background. His execution rode beneath the surface of their day like a killer shark, a constantly moving shadow.

Ross was learning the unspoken language of the Agency, of things implicit, of subjects alluded to. In the early planning stages they talked bluntly of sanctioning, yet as the time approached everyone slipped into a kind of code. Only the men directly concerned discussed among themselves methods and proposals and drew the equipment they needed on their own authority.

When they'd finished in Yardley's office, Lyle gave Ross a refresher course of the Fairfax lectures on human blood circulation: where in the body air should be injected so it reached the heart first, causing death, and where it would travel immediately to the brain, causing irreversible neural damage and probably death. It was clear from this that Ross alone would kill that night while Lyle watched, and the knowledge made him only slightly sickened. Lyle was right: it did get easier.

They decided to use basically the same method of ambush against Prince that they had with Sophie Johnson although it wouldn't be as easy this second time. Prince was a *mokrie dela* agent and therefore every bit their equal. Sophie had been an amateur by comparison.

"We'll need to get him deeper in to his apartment before we gas him," Lyle said. "The hallway's no good—he'll bust right out of there in a second, and we'll have to fight him, which means there'll be noise and the place'll be a mess. Also there'll be marks on his body."

"So what do we do?"

"We get a guy on a radio to give us a couple of minutes warning he's on his way," Lyle said. "We fill the living room with gas, so it's waiting for him when he walks in. He won't notice it until it hits the back of his throat." Lyle grinned wryly. "As we both know, when you taste it, it's too late."

"That sounds okay," Ross agreed.

The surveillance crew reported that Prince had left his apartment at 9:30. Yardley's orders were that he was not to be followed in case he noticed something unusual and began taking extra precautions or made a run for it.

By three that afternoon, Ross and Lyle were in place, gas masks around their necks, canisters ready. They searched the bedrooms, their cotton-gloved hands leaving no traces, keeping everything neat and in place. They found nothing suspicious, although a thorough inspection of every book, magazine and newspaper, and a microscopic examination of the entire apartment would probably turn up adequate evidence. For the DIA anyway.

Then they settled down to wait.

The hours dragged on.

Night fell. They left the lights off in the apartment. Every fifteen minutes, they made a brief check call on their button microphones to ensure communications were unbroken with the team in the street.

By nine o'clock, when Trevor Prince had still not arrived, Ross began feeling jumpy. He longed to talk, to move about but, apart from the necessary radio calls and vital instructions, the rule was silence. They sat in the darkness of the living room, waiting.

Ten o'clock came. Eleven. Midnight. Ross was fighting to keep awake now. Constant tension, lacking action, was exhausting, and their ambush had been in place nine hours.

Just before one, the radio earpieces crackled: "Abort! Abort!"

Lyle was on his feet in an instant. Perhaps Prince was coming in with a party of people. They might have less than a minute to get clear.

"Pack up!" Lyle ordered. "Let's get out of here."

Their eyes used to the darkness, each seized a gas canister and dropped it into the open attaché case. They hurried through the hallway and out into the corridor, closing the front door behind them.

They walked swiftly for the stairs, feet echoing in the building, and reached the street without seeing anyone. A couple of blocks away was their car, and they headed for the DIA.

Yardley was waiting. They could tell from his face the news was bad. He looked disappointed and tired.

"Sit down," he said. "I'm sorry it's been a long and useless night for you. When Prince didn't show, we checked the airport. I'm afraid the bird has flown."

"When?" Lyle asked.

"Lunchtime. He took the Concorde to London, and I assume we'll find he changed planes for Moscow or somewhere in the Eastern Bloc."

Lyle rubbed his hands over his eyes. "How the hell did he know?" he wondered aloud.

"I suppose the news about Sophie Johnson tipped off the KGB," the Director said. "I guess they didn't buy the suicide theory and pulled Prince out right away. As you can see, they didn't waste time." He shrugged. "Still, maybe he'll be back. They might reconsider the situation in a couple of weeks when everything's calmed down. If we lie low, they might decide they overreacted. We'll have our chance then." He studied his fingernails. "Uh, there isn't anything in the apartment to let them know you were there?"

Lyle shook his head. "It's just as he left it."

Yardley said: "Then that's it. You might as well go home, both of you. Thanks for your efforts."

As they rode down to the garage, Lyle asked: "You want to stay over at my place again, Dave?"

"I guess not," Ross said, "thanks all the same. I reckon I'll go home."

"Okay." They headed for their cars.

Ross tried to analyze, as he drove through the almost empty streets, his emotions at the end of this long day. If it had been yesterday, and they'd aborted the killing of Sophie Johnson, he'd have been relieved, grateful. Why now did he feel angry? Why did he feel cheated?

He was across the barrier, totally into the DIA's world, and the landscape looked different, barren. He searched for the old points of reference, the codes and morals he had brought with him into manhood, but they had gone.

And he was going home to his wife, to the familiar warmth of her body, yet knowing something there had changed, too. More new territory, uncharted and personally threatening.

Shit, he was tired.

Elaine woke at the sound of Ross moving around the apartment. "David, is that you?"

Who the hell do you think it is? "Yes."

There was a pause while she found her dressing gown and came out to greet him. Ross couldn't get over how much better she was looking. The sight stung him, and he retreated further behind emotional defenses.

"I'm so glad you're back," Elaine said, stretching up to kiss his cheek. "When did you get in?"

"The day before yesterday," Ross said.

She looked puzzled. "Oh, why didn't you come home last night?"

"I was busy."

She could hear the remoteness in his tone. Something had happened, and he was forbidden to share it with her or with anyone outside the closed ranks of the DIA. Her heart went out to him. When all was said and done it was a lonely burden for one man, and she had the wit not to press him. So she said, "Is there anything I can get you? Coffee? A drink? Something to eat?"

"No thanks," Ross said. "I guess I'll have a shower and come to bed."

She noticed he said "come to bed," not "go to bed," and she was glad. There was some comfort she could give him.

But her husband was a stranger when he climbed in beside her and pulled her toward him without preliminaries, his face cold and determined, strong hands gripping her shoulders, her hips; violence, almost hatred in what he did.

When Ross was finished, he rolled off and turned out the light.

After several minutes of lying stunned in the darkness, Elaine began to weep silently: for herself, sore and stinging, and for David, for the terrible unknowns that had made him this way.

In the morning, Ross awoke, still a stranger, a dangerous light in his eyes that simultaneously warned and challenged.

Elaine felt increasingly nervous. She forced herself to be calm and fixed his breakfast, allowing him the silence he seemed to require. When he left for work she was profoundly relieved.

Lyle, too, noticed the suppressed violence as soon as Ross walked in and guessed it was a reaction to the aborted Prince operation. David had been emotionally geared up to kill, and now he felt let down. That happened sometimes. Lyle thought he knew how to handle it. After an hour of paperwork, he said: "Come on, Dave, let's go to the gym."

They changed into karate uniforms and began their training workout, Ross pushing himself with a grimness even intense exertion couldn't dispel. Lyle could see the hatred in his face, which sometimes, when David thought he wasn't watching, was directed at him. He knew there was going to be trouble and waited to see what form it would take.

They'd almost finished when Ross turned and said, in a voice low and contemptuous, "Lyle, you're a cocksucking little fairy shit, and I'm gonna kill you."

"Why don't you try, Dave?" Lyle countered.

The next instant, Lyle was fighting for his life against a ferocious Shorin-ryu attack, in which a blitz frontal assault from moderate or long range is delivered with total commitment, contravening the basic philosophy of this Okinawan martial art that its practitioners should never be aggressors—no first attack: but ideally, no second attack either, because there should be no need for it in this "one-punch kill" style.

Lyle, however, knew Shorin-ryu as well as Ross did, its techniques and dangers, and he stopped Ross's first strike with a focused block so hard he heard his oppponent grunt in pain. Ross followed with a series of rapid attacks. Advanced kareteka can generate power in a single punch or kick equivalent to 1,500 pounds, traveling at more than forty feet a second, with the maximum force concentrated on the moment of impact. One blow hitting home would end the fight.

Lyle blocked and countered rapidly, knowing that to stop Ross he was going to have to hurt him: this was no training session.

Despite the speed of the strike, blocks, counter-strike, Lyle kept his muscles and tendons loose for instant response, tensing only at the moment of focus, his stance shallower than the normal shotokan, improving his mobility.

In a flash, he saw his chance, and as he stopped a right-hand punch by Ross with a hard focused left block, his own right arm swung across his trunk and smashed forward and outward, into Ross's ribs. Ross's body arched sideways, simultaneously pulled by Lyle's left hand, while Clive's right arched around for a ridgehand to the groin.

It was over. Ross collapsed on the floor of the gym, the fight gone from him, hands between his legs, face contorted. He grunted with pain.

Lyle watched impassively. In a few minutes, he'd take him to the hospital for a checkup. There was the possibility of broken ribs, and his testicles might have been damaged, although Lyle had aimed slightly off center.

Then Ross began to throw up, heaving and groaning.

Lyle cursed. He ran to the changing rooms and used the telephone to call Peter Barry. He explained briefly what had happened and Barry said that Ross shouldn't be moved. He would come immediately.

Lyle got some towels and filled a glass with water.

Wordlessly, he cleaned up the floor, and held Ross's head so he could drink.

Barry arrived in the gym five minutes later, and knelt beside Ross. Lyle helped him remove the karate pants, and the doctor gently touched and prodded, while air hissed from between Ross's clenched teeth.

"Well," Barry said at last, "it doesn't look as if anything's ruptured, David, for which you can be mighty thankful. I guess you could do with an ice bag for twenty minutes or so, and I'll give you something for the pain."

"You ought to check the ribs on his right side," Lyle suggested.

Barry looked at him disapprovingly. "Let's get him over to the hospital and have him X-rayed. What the hell were you two playing at?"

"You know how it is with sparring—a little misjudgment and someone gets hurt."

"Two little misjudgments, Clive," Barry pointed out. "You'd better be more careful next time."

They helped Ross to his feet, got his pants back on, and took him the long, slow, sore walk to the hospital building.

Lyle stayed with him as he lay on a couch, an ice pack underneath and around his balls. Ross's face was no longer tensed in pain as the ice and the tablets Barry had given him took effect, and he stared at the ceiling. Neither man spoke; there'd be time for that later.

The X-ray showed two cracked ribs. Ross had escaped very lightly, and he knew it. He was still limping when he and Lyle returned to their office, but the violence which had simmered inside him and then suddenly erupted, had gone, leaving sadness and a sense of loss.

Lyle got coffee from the machine in the corridor, and sat down at his desk. "You want to talk?" he asked.

"I'm sorry, Clive," Ross said, "for what I did and for what I said. Thanks for not hurting me too badly. I guess I deserved it."

"Yeah, you did. What was it all about?"

Ross told him. There was the reaction to the killing of Sophie Johnson, and the aborting of the Prince mission. Forces had been unleashed in him that he found hard to control. And there was Elaine, the change that had come about in her; the possibility that she had taken a lover.

Lyle listened in silence. At the end, he asked, "What'll you do if you find she has?"

Ross shook his head. "I don't know. I could beat him up, I guess, but that wouldn't help much. I mean, it wouldn't wipe out what she'd done. I might still lose her, and I don't want to do that."

Lyle drank his coffee. "What do you think she'll do if she discovers your fucking Julie Klein?"

"I don't know that either," Ross said. "I hope she doesn't find out, and I hope she doesn't leave me. Jesus, Clive, I know it's a double standard, but it is different. I don't love Julie. I sleep with her sometimes, that's all. I don't want to marry her or anything like that—hell, it's the last thing I want. But Elaine's not casual like that. If she's screwing some guy, it's because he means something to her. It's serious. It's threatening.''

"Well," Lyle said, "I guess the only thing to do is to ask her. Maybe she'll tell you. Are you sure you want to know the truth?''

"Yes!" Ross groaned. "No! An, hell, I just don't know.'' Finally he said, "I suppose I do. I'm behaving pretty badly toward her right now. We'd better clear it up. I'll speak to her tonight.''

"If I can help," Lyle said, "give me a call.''

"Thanks, Clive. I appreciate it. And again, I'm sorry about this morning. I didn't mean it.''

"Forget it. How're you feeling?''

"Not too bad, considering.'' He threw the plastic cup into the bin at the side of the office. "What are we going to do today?''

"The neutron files, what else?'' Lyle said. "Have you thought of any more keywords for the computers?''

They turned their attention to the list pinned on the wall. Scimitar, Cutlass, Hanger, Scythe, and stared at it.

"Try Hammer and Sickle," Ross suggested.

"That's not bad. Okay.'' Lyle added them. "Anything else?''

"How about Weapon. We haven't got that.''

"No.''

"I can't think of any more. Let me phone those through.''

Within a few minutes the NSA had taken down the new keywords to add to the program in the Univac computers, and an hour later Ross received a telephone call from one of the PROD technicians to say that the word Sickle had triggered a printout.

Ross drove to Fort Meade to collect it. His balls were

only slightly tender now, but his ribs hurt if he moved suddenly.

The printout was an intercept picked up two weeks earlier, part of an exchange between Soviet pilots on a mission and an airbase in Afghanistan. It was brief, and Ross read it through, grimacing. Afghanistan, for Christ's sake!

He brought it back for Lyle to have a look at.

There was no indication what aircraft the men had been flying, although it could have been either MiG-21s or SU-17s.

"Red flight, this is Victor base. How do you read? Over."

"Victor base, this is Red leader. I read you five. Over."

"Victor base, this is Red two, I read you five. Over."

"Victor base, this is Red three, I read you five. Over."

"Red flight, Sickle is timed for 1230 hours. I repeat, Sickle at 1230 hours. Over."

"Red leader, understood. Over."

"Red two, understood. Over."

"Red three, understood. Over."

"Red flight, return now. Victor base, out."

Lyle shrugged. "It could mean anything. I guess Sickle was an operation against the Afghan rebels. From what I read in the papers, it sounds like the Russians are bombing the shit out of them."

"Do you think we should show this to Yardley?" Ross asked.

"Might as well. Cover our backs."

The Director read the printout and returned it. "Why don't you take a look at the reports from Afghanistan and Pakistan?" he suggested. "See what you can discover about Sickle. If your computer operation's going to mean anything, you'd better follow the results through to the end."

He was right as usual. "Listen, Dave, do you want to take on this Afghan research? It'll give you a break," Lyle offered on their way back to the office.

Ross, who felt he could do with a change, asked hopefully, "Are you sure you don't mind, Clive?"

"No, go ahead."

"Thanks a lot."

After lunch, Ross returned to the NSA to see if they could pinpoint the position of the Soviet aircraft at the time of the intercept.

Victor Base was in the northeast of Afghanistan, in Badakhshan Province, a hundred miles from the Soviet border; and the computers, measuring comparative signal strengths and directions of the intercept as received by three positions in the area—one of them on the roof of the American Embassy in the Afghan capital, Kabul—suggested the jets were over, or near, the northern part of the gigantic mountain wall known as the Hindu Kush, the Hindu killer. Specifically, they were probably approaching the Khwaja Muhammad Range.

Back at the DIA, Ross ordered from the Registry intelligence reports of actions in Badakhshan Province over the last three weeks. They issued him a fat file, going back a year.

The CIA station chief, based in Kabul, mentioned hearing reports of fighting in Badakhshan in almost every dispatch, but offered few incontrovertible facts. God knew how he received his information anyway, sitting in the Afghan capital with the Soviets in control around him, and regime informers everywhere. But word somehow passed down, from the Islamic rebels, through sympathizers, villagers, messengers. It was impossible to say whether the original news had been written—a piece of scrap paper in intricate Pashto script making the long, difficult journey to Kabul—or whether it had been passed verbally, undergoing changes as each new person received and relayed it, until finally it reached the CIA in mutilated form. Occasionally there were precise dates of bombing raids, skirmishes, battles. More often, the actions had taken place "over several days during the last two weeks."

There was one reference to a poison gas attack, killing dozens of civilians in Badakhshan in a period that might have coincided with the Sickle intercept, and when he leafed further back in the file, he found reference to mycotoxins—biochemical warfare agents—supposedly being used to poison deep wells and kill the *mujahideen,* the Islamic rebels.

There was no information about the Badakhshan incident from the U.S. Consul in Peshawar, the ancient city in Pakistan's Northwest Frontier Province that housed the headquarters of almost a dozen rival *mujahideen* groups and which, because of its proximity to Afghanistan, was an excellent listening post.

If Sickle had been a poison gas attack, it was hard luck on the *mujahideen* and whoever else was in the area but none of Ross's business.

Ross lost interest halfway through the afternoon, his mind focused instead on Elaine and what he would say to her that night. He sighed deeply and immediately winced, his cracked ribs sending a stab of pain through his chest. He kept forgetting he had to be careful. At least his balls had stopped hurting although he wasn't sure if this was because of the tablets. He'd find out later when the effects wore off.

He stopped by Lyle's apartment on the way home, ostensibly for a beer, but really to prepare himself to face his wife. When he'd finished, he rose and grinned sheepishly. "Wish me luck, Clive," he said.

Ross let himself into his apartment, tense with the prospect of what he might soon find out—presuming Elaine told him the truth, which was by no means certain. He wondered whether, if she asked him straight out about Julie, he would instinctively lie. He thought he probably would, and that gave him no comfort at all.

Elaine came out of the kitchen and stood watching him, almost warily. "Hello," she said. "How was your day?"

"Clive beat me up in the gym and cracked a couple of ribs, and he bashed my balls about a bit, but otherwise it was okay." Ross tried to smile.

Her hand went to her mouth. "You're all right?"

"Sure. No real damage done. It was my own fault, anyway."

They stood in silence, the physical gap between them only a few feet, the emotional one stretching for miles.

Finally Ross said: "I'd like to talk to you, seriously."

"Would you like a drink first?" Elaine asked.

"I guess so. Beer please."

She got one from the refrigerator, and mixed herself a martini, aware of her rapidly beating heart. She didn't know what was coming but felt instinctively it wasn't good news.

Elaine handed him the beer and sat on the sofa facing him.

Ross cleared his throat. "First," he said "I want to apologize for last night. I behaved badly, and I think I hurt you." He met her eye. "I can't tell you all the reasons I was like that, only the one that concerns you."

He presented his case concisely and in sequence: Elaine's first visit to the West Coast and the change that had come over her, the sudden difference to their sex life.

She listened quietly, not understanding what he was getting at.

Then, Ross said, there was her sudden second departure, ostensibly at the request of the FBI, and her return looking as if she'd been on a holiday.

"You weren't on FBI business, were you?"

"No," Elaine agreed.

"Please tell me the truth now," Ross continued. "It's important that I know. Important for both of us. Are you sleeping with someone else?"

Elaine looked at him stunned. Finally, she began to laugh, softly at first, then full-throated.

Ross, hurt, protested: "It's not funny, Elaine."

"Oh, but it is," she said, trying to compose herself. "Is that what you thought? That I'd been having an affair?"

"That's exactly what I do think," Ross said angrily.

"David, it's simply not true!"

"Then where did you go?"

"I didn't go anywhere," she said. "I stayed in Washington. I was a few hundred yards away from you most of the time." She sat beside him and took his unresponsive hand. "David," she said, "look at me. Do you like the way I am?"

"Sure. You look great."

"Well, we can thank the DIA for that, and specifically Timothy Peal. I went to have a face lift."

Ross stared, disbelieving. He put out his hands and examined her. She tilted her chin so he could inspect her neck, but there was no longer anything to be seen there. "You might be able to find the scars of a couple of stitches in my hair line," she said, "but anyway, if you think I'm telling a lie, you can always ask Lyndon Yardley. He sent me a beautiful bouquet of roses."

Ross was speechless, feeling he might choke. "Why didn't you tell me?"

"I wanted it to be a surprise. Part of the reason was I didn't want you to worry because I knew you were busy, but I guess mainly I hoped you'd just think how nice your wife was looking, without knowing it took a plastic surgeon to get her that way. Vanity, I'm afraid."

Ross drew her close, being careful of his ribs. He felt foolish, and boorish, and unkind. He remembered how he'd been with her the previous night, and he flushed with shame. "I'm sorry," he whispered.

"That's all right," she said. "I was afraid of losing you. The world's full of women who want you: young women, pretty. I couldn't compete with them. I still can't, but at least I don't look like the wicked witch of the west."

"You never did," Ross said. "You were always pretty, and gracious and charming, and intelligent, and all the things I ever liked." He drew away and smiled at her. "I love you," he said.

"I love you," she answered, and he kissed her with great gentleness, an enormous burden lifting from his shoulders, his heart full.

Ross decided in that moment that he would tell Julie it was off between them, permanently.

"David!" She leaned against the doorframe, smiling mockingly. "Are you going to be staying, or shall I keep my vibrator handy to finish myself when you suddenly take off."

"I'm only here for a few minutes, Julie. Can I come in?"

She stood aside. "Sure."

Ross walked into the beautifully furnished living room and sat down: not on the sofa, but on one of the armchairs.

"You want a drink?" she asked.

"No thanks."

"Are you sure? I'm having one."

"No, really."

He watched as she mixed herself a cocktail. She really was a most beautiful woman. A superb figure, an assured way of moving, skin so soft a man could spend a lifetime feeling it slide against his body and never grow tired, hair that shone. Ross felt a lump in his throat and thought he might change his mind and have that drink. Maybe even stay for one quick final session in bed? After all, last time didn't really count, because of Lyle's call.

She came and sat across from him, looking mischievous and speculative. "Don't bother saying you're sorry about running out," she said. "I've already forgiven you. I know you're not an accountant, and I guess you're something to do with the CIA, but you don't have to confirm that unless you want to. So save your breath."

"Okay," he said, "no explanations." He hunted for words. The speech he'd rehearsed on the way over vanished from his memory and he stared at her mutely. Then he thought: Jesus, I've got to get off this carousel. If I don't do it now, I won't ever.

An image of Elaine came to his mind and gave him strength.

"Actually," Ross said, "I came to say goodbye."

"Oh, shit, Dave! Are you off somewhere?"

He shook his head. "No, I'm staying in Washington." She stared at him. "It's been fantastic with you, but . . ."

She looked as if he'd struck her across the face. "It's been fantastic, but goodbye," she said dully.

The last thing Ross had expected happened. Julie Klein had started to cry.

"Hey, hey," Ross said desperately, moving to her, pulling a handkerchief from his pocket. "Here, use this."

She took it and dabbed her eyes, but the tears kept coming.

"Come on, Julie," Ross protested. "You knew from the start there wasn't any long-term mileage in our relationship."

"Yes," she said, in a small, shaky voice, "but that was at the beginning when I didn't care." She looked at him. "Dave, I think I'm falling in love with you."

"Please don't," he said. "I've got all the love I can handle at the moment."

She was still crying when he left.

As the days passed, Ross began to settle into the new emotional territory into which Lyle had goaded him. Changes took place within himself that he noticed and accepted without question. One was that he cared not at all for other people, except as far as they affected his work or helped him toward a goal, either professional or private. There were two exceptions to this. The first was Elaine, about whom he was now fiercely protective. She represented home and normality, a base he could touch to remind himself of the ordinary world, somewhere to relax in the illusion of peace and security. The other exception was the DIA: those who worked in the brotherhood of his strange new world, but particularly Lyle, with whom his bonds became of steel.

Ross also noticed a new assurance growing within himself, something beyond confidence. An arrogance. He had killed, with official protection, and he could do it again: not selfishly or wantonly, but coldly, efficiently, an action on behalf of the United States. He felt he had immunity from the ordinary processes of law and civilized life, and it made him special.

With this came an almost contradictory wariness. He was a hunter all right, but hunted too; and so he watched, and questioned, judged motives in the simplest everyday actions, looked for things unusual or out of place, became acutely aware of what was happening in his peripheral vision.

Lyle observed Ross's progress with pride, but kept quiet. Yardley also was pleased and said nothing, although he put through a salary increase to indicate to Ross he had satisfactorily passed a test.

Nothing more came from the computers concerning Cutlass, Scimitar, or Sickle. Ross and Lyle added a few new keywords, without result. In New York, the SALT talks continued their snail's progress. Rabinovich remained part of the Soviet team unaware that when next a halt was called and the negotiators returned to Moscow, he would again be plunged into a nightmare, and this time there would be no reprieve.

Every couple of days, Ross checked the Registry to see if anything fresh had come in from Badakhshan Province to explain the Sickle intercept.

The reports from the U. S. Consul in Peshawar contained nothing that threw a particular light on that one incident until suddenly, as Ross was looking through the latest dispatches on Thursday afternoon, there it was: a detailed account of the poison gas attack.

The Consul in Peshawar had been visited by groups of *mujahideen* with news of the incident, and the date coincided with the Sickle intercept. Later the Consul himself interviewed five refugees from the area who gave firsthand accounts.

Ross took the file to their office to show Lyle.

The attack had taken place shortly after noon prayers. The Russians had been launching artillery strikes and bombing raids on mountainous rebel hideouts for several days, and this one began later than usual. None of the witnesses had actually seen the poison gassing, but they had gone to the area later that day and observed the effects. Fifty or sixty *mujahideen*—estimates varied—had died immediately, some with terrible burns on their skin, others without marks, and a score of women and children had also fallen.

Many others who had been touched by the gas were found lying on the ground, ill and vomiting. Those who were able to speak said there had been an explosion in the sky, a blinding light that flung the white gas over everything, and people began dropping.

"That's odd, isn't it?" Lyle asked. "Have you ever heard of a gas being dispersed like that?"

"No," Ross said, "but God knows what scientists dream up in their laboratories these days."

"Yeah, I know what you mean," Lyle said. "I wonder where we can find out. Wasn't there a lot about gas being used in Kampuchea?"

"The papers were full of it a while ago," Ross said. "Laos as well. But I thought that was supposed to have come down as yellow rain."

"You want to get the files?" Lyle suggested. "Let's see if we can sort it out before we go to Yardley. He's sure to ask questions."

The Registry's records on Chemical Warfare, known also as CW, covered more space than they did even on the Soviet development of neutron weapons. Ross scanned the shelves, groaning, and finally selected the two most recent.

One contained the results of United States tests of leaf and stem samples from Kampuchea that showed levels of three potent mycotoxins up to twenty times greater than anything that might happen naturally. These produced bizarre effects in men: severe itching, or tingling of the skin, accompanied by small hard blisters, choking, vomiting massive amounts of blood, shock, and death.

Another report from Laos spoke of an airplane flying over the village of Va Houng, dispersing yellow gas that fell like rain and smelled like burning peppers. The village chickens dropped first, followed by the rest of the animals and eighty-three people, who took two or three painful days to die, during which they had intense diarrhea, vomiting, headaches, impaired vision, swollen throats, and painful breathing.

"Nice stuff," Ross said, "but different from the

Badakhshan attack. Nothing out of Peshawar about yellow rain. Also the Afghans seem to have died quicker.''

"A new improved version?" Lyle suggested. "I don't think it helps us particularly, but let's take it to the Director.''

To their surprise, Yardley showed keen interest in their research, listening with attention to Ross's explanation and shooting a series of questions at him. Ross didn't know the answers to most of them.

Yardley then called in a DIA expert on chemical warfare: a tall, thin man with spectacles and a crew cut who appeared perfectly calm and in control, but whose fingernails were bitten to the quick. "This is Captain Craig," Yardley said, performing perfunctory introductions. "Mr. Ross and Major Lyle."

Craig was shown the report from the Consul in Peshawar and glanced briefly at it. "Yes," he said. "I saw it when it came in."

"And what do you make of it, Captain Craig?" Yardley inquired, his voice remote. It was clear the CW expert was not one of his favorite people; but he had to be good, or he wouldn't be with the Agency.

"I don't know, General," Craig admitted. "The Afghans say it's poison gas, but they say a lot of things that aren't true. It's easy to misinterpret something like this, particularly if you're a tribesman. It doesn't make sense to me. It's got everyone stumped, actually, and we won't have any answers until we get more information and maybe samples of leaves from the area."

"Make a guess," Ross invited.

Craig picked up the report. "Okay," he said, "first we have a blinding light in the sky. That's the important bit—a blinding light. So whatever it was had to be delivered in an artillery shell or a missile that explodes in an airburst and spreads it over a wide area. This makes sense for about twenty seconds, until you realize that the heat of the explosion they describe might chemically change, or burn up, whatever poison the Soviets are using." He looked around to see if everyone understood. "Unless, of course, it's this heat that completes the production cycle, maybe because in its final form the CW agent's too dangerous to have around."

"Do you believe that?" Yardley asked.

"No, sir," Captain Craig replied. "Of course, anything's possible, but I just can't imagine what chemical could need that sort of final-burn processing. And, anyway, there's stuff available now that is so potent that a capful is enough to wipe out everyone on earth. Is it going to be something more scary than that?"

"So what's going on in Afghanistan?" the Director persisted.

"Well, let's have a look at the Soviet CW arsenal and eliminate what it isn't," Craig said. "We know they've got a lot of nerve gas called Soman, sometimes called Agent GD. It causes violent convulsions and quick death."

"Like the people in Badakhshan," Lyle pointed out.

"Up to a point."

"Can't they deliver Soman from a shell or a missile?" Ross wanted to know.

"Oh, sure," Craig said. "Missiles, or things like BM-21 rockets, no problem. Soman, or maybe one of the G- or V-type nerve gases; even something like HCN which is so toxic you just have to get a minute quantity on your skin and you're dead in a few minutes. But you see, none of the missile systems explode with a blinding light and the intense heat that's implicit. The same with artillery shells packed with chemical agents. It seems to me there're significant differences between these things and what we find in this latest report." He turned to Yardley. "May I smoke?" he asked.

"Go ahead," the Director said disapprovingly and pushed an onyx ashtray toward the scientist.

Craig lit up and inhaled deeply. "And it isn't a mycotoxin either because those symptoms are very different."

"All right," Yardley said, "then what the hell is it?"

Captain Craig looked profoundly unhappy and uncomfortable. "I repeat, General," he said, "I don't know. But speculating, just speculating, mind you, I'd be surprised to find it was a chemical warfare agent at all."

"Why?" Ross asked. "The Peshawar report says the explosion flung white gas over everything, doesn't it?"

"Yes, it does," Craig agreed. "But that might have been as illusion. I mean, usually they talk about rain. Yellow rain fell. In this case, it should have been "white rain fell," but instead we get gas being flung in an instant over everything. And that's unlikely, too. It could be they simply imagined white gas had come from the blinding white light because there wasn't any other explanation they could comprehend. To them, it wasn't a conventional bomb, so it had to be poison gas. And then there were the results: people dead on the ground without a mark. Others dying, also without a mark."

"So, Captain Craig," Yardley said, his patience at an end, "please be so kind as to tell us what you think—what you speculate—might have happened."

Craig stared at the table for a moment and sighed.

"You're going to laugh at me because this is so far out," he said, "but if I had to guess, I'd say it was an enhanced radiation device."

"A what?"

Craig looked defiant. "A neutron bomb."

There was a pin-drop silence in the Director's office. No one laughed. Ross and Lyle exchanged incredulous glances.

Finally Yardley murmured almost to himself: "Cutlass,

Scimitar, Sickle: A neutron missile, a neutron shell, a neutron attack. Well, what do you know?"

"It isn't confirmed!" Craig broke in, suddenly agitated, in case a wild goose chase brought the responsibility down on his neck. "It's just a guess!"

Yardley regarded him with a suddenly friendly eye. "We understand that, Captain Craig," he said. "Are you familiar with the neutron warhead?"

"Not in detail, sir. It's out of my field. Of course, I've read about its effects, which is why I think that's what the Russians might have used in Badakhshan. I repeat, might have used."

Yardley nodded. "You've been most helpful, Captain Craig. You may go now."

Craig rose at once, relief on his face.

"Yes, sir. Thank you."

When he'd gone, Yardley stared at his agents and said: "Well! How about that!"

"It's an interesting theory," Ross admitted.

"Except," Lyle pointed out, "the Soviets would be crazy to use a neutron bomb just at the time they're negotiating an international ban. Hell, remember all the propaganda they've pushed out about it—'the ultimate capitalist weapon, destroying people but leaving property intact,' the 'cancer bomb?' Why would they risk being caught with their hands in the cookie jar? Especially now?"

"Maybe they thought Badakhshan was remote enough for them to get away with it," Ross said. "It's hard to prove they've used a neutron weapon. The radiation blast occurs in a millionth of a second, and after that the area's pretty clean. I mean, men can go in a few hours later and the radioactivity's mostly dispersed."

"I think," Yardley decided, "we need to know more about Badakhshan Province and why the Russians might take a risk there. I suggest both of you concentrate on that problem and report to me as soon as you can.''

The agents went to the Registry for more and fuller files. It was late afternoon by this time, but neither of them noticed. They were totally absorbed in their task.

After weeks of useless research, a glimmer of light had unexpectedly appeared.

''That is the news I bring,'' Rabinovich, architect of the Scimitar project, had told them. ''Something to anyway stop the talks.''

Perhaps this was it: information that the Soviet Union was either employing, or intending to employ, neutron warheads in the grim and bloody struggle against Islamic guerrillas across their southern border.

As Ross and Lyle studied the records, what became apparent was the strategic importance of the remote northern area of Afghanistan, and the possible effect *mujahideen* successes might have on the Moslem communities in Russia's southern Republics—areas subdued by the Kremlin after long and bitter fighting decades earlier.

However, discontent still rumbled among the Moslems of Turkemenia, Uzbekistan, and Tadzhikistan, who had gone to great lengths to avoid learning Russian. So much so that as late as 1978, the USSR Council of Ministers felt it necessary to issue a decree on improving the study and teaching of their language.

With the USSR's Moslem birth rate three or four times that recorded for other Soviet groups, the potential problem Moscow faced was growing. There was evidence that just inside the Soviet borders, pockets of Islamic dissident factions were watching to see what lessons they could learn from the *mujahideen*'s confrontation.

And the Afghan rebels were being successful, at least to the point of holding the countryside and confining the Soviets to a handful of major towns and cities from which they ventured forth only in armed convoys, in tanks, or by air.

From a strategic point of view, too, there could hardly be a more vital area for the Russians than northern Afghanistan. Apart from the natural gas deposits, piped across the border into the Soviet Union, the only road from the frontier to the capital, Kabul, passed through rebel-dominated territory, particularly when it snaked down into the Hindu Kush mountains, entered the vulnerable Salang Pass, and came close to the *mujahideen* stronghold of the Panjshir Valley.

A journey along this narrow road was a tense game of roulette. Even heavily armed convoys had been ambushed. One vehicle would be blown up in the front, another disabled at the rear, and everyone trapped in between became a target for tribesmen hidden among rocks, whose fighting prowess was legendary, and whose treatment of the captured enemy in their *jihad*, their Holy War— particularly infidel Russians—could be so barbaric even the KGB was shocked. There were instances of prisoners being skinned alive.

Yet it was along this one road, in a country without a railway, that the Soviets brought men and supplies. Frequent attempts to flush the *mujahideen* from their mountain strongholds met with little success. Fierce battles had been fought. Sometimes the Russians, ignoring heavy casualties, pushed their way into the Panjshir Valley. But when they did, the *mujahideen* simply withdrew further into the mountains and waited until the enemy had left; as leave they must, because they lacked the manpower and the huge logistical support necessary to hold remote territory, temporarily conquered. In this, there were grim echoes of the American experience in Vietnam.

Recently, *mujahideen* attacks had escalated from sporadic, annoying ambushes of Soviet convoys, to major actions in which Russian casualties were reportedly heavy. The rebels boasted of capturing large quantities of arms and ammunition.

And on top of that there were reports of *mujahideen* raids, mounted from Badakhshan Province, actually across the border into the Soviet Union itself, bringing the war under the very noses of their own secretly resentful Moslem population: an intolerable situation for Moscow.

One other aspect also had to be considered. Almost immediately after the Soviet invasion in December 1979, construction of barracks, camps, airfields, and hospitals had begun. Some projects had already been completed, and the initial Russian force of 80,000 soldiers and airmen had been beefed up. Now other facilities were almost ready, and the invasion army could easily be doubled in size.

Yet if it was, how could Moscow assure regular supplies of gasoline, food, clothing, equipment, and men on rotation, when their only access road remained insecure? They could airlift everything they needed but that was an expensive and inconvenient option.

It was after ten before Ross and Lyle had put together what they felt was a fair picture of the situation in northern Afghanistan: the problems confronting the Soviet leadership and their possible solutions.

The more they studied the options, the more useful a neutron device seemed—provided it could be kept secret.

And where better to use it than the remote north of a country in which the few existing roads were either mined or unsafe, and where communications were carried on foot, on the backs of mules, or on caravans of camels? The world's newest nuclear weapon could be exploded in the far reaches of a country that in some respects was still in the Middle Ages. When word of the attack did filter through to the West, what would the tribesmen say of it?

What would the *mujahideen* report? "The Russians have used poison gas." And of this, there would be no proof.

Lyle looked quizzically at Ross, sitting thoughtful behind his desk. "What about it, David? Was Sickle a neutron bomb?"

"I guess it's possible," Ross said. "But how do we prove it?"

"God knows. Let's go see Yardley. Maybe he'll have an idea."

Ross looked at his watch. "Won't he have gone home?" he asked.

Lyle laughed. "You're kidding," he said. "Don't you know he lives here?"

"Sometimes it seems like it," Ross agreed, rising to his feet and stretching his big frame.

"Come on, let's get it over with. I'm hungry and I want to get out of here."

Lyle was right. Yardley was behind his desk, working on a batch of documents. Lucy had returned to her husband and her cats.

The Director prepared to close the file when he heard Lyle's knock on the door, and he called "Enter!" He watched his men coming in and motioned them across to the chairs at the side.

When he'd locked the file in his drawer, he joined them. "Well, what have you learned?" he asked.

Ross outlined the situation: the threat to the one-lane supply route to Kabul; the possibility of a further Soviet troop increase; the escalating fighting in the mountainous area that the Russians had failed to curb with conventional tactics; the possible repercussions of Islamic victories among Soviet Moslems in the border Republics; and finally, the very remoteness of the area, which made detection difficult.

Yardley listened carefully. "What is there left," he asked, "after a neutron attack?"

Ross shrugged. "Not much," he said. "A scorched area at ground zero. A heap of dead people, and a lot more who'll die in a few days, or weeks, or years."

"How're your ribs, David?" the Director asked.

"Oh, they're fine, sir. Back to normal."

"And your, uh, your testicles?"

"In working order. No problems."

"So you consider yourself fit for an operation, do you?"

"Yes, sir, I think so."

Yardley scratched the top of his head. "Tomorrow morning," he said "I want you both to see Peter Barry for full medicals. Then I want Clive to give you a workout in the gym, David, just to make sure." He frowned. "I notice you've not been back there since the, uh, accident."

"I wanted to give my ribs time to heal," Ross explained.

"Fair enough. But a proper workout tomorrow morning, please. If you're passed fit by Peter Barry and Major Lyle, you'll both leave Washington by an evening flight for London." He paused and regarded them seriously. "The point is this: if the Russians have actually used a neutron weapon in Afghanistan, it destroys all the propaganda they've been blasting out for years. It'll cause such a scare in the White House that the President won't be in any mood to talk about a ban. Hell, we've only tried it out on pigs. The Russians have actually used it on people. I'm prepared to bet public opinion will swing very quickly to our side, and there won't be a thing Moscow can do to stop it. Your job," he said, glancing from one to the other, "will be to bring back the proof."

"We go into Afghanistan, then?" Lyle asked.

"That's right."

"And what then, General? How do we prove they've exploded a neutron bomb?"

"You bring back three things, Clive. Three categories of things. First, leaf and stem samples from the area so we can see if some CW agent was used. Second, samples of the soil around ground zero. Analysis should tell us the type of device used. Third, you bring back people.''

"What, eyewitnesses?" Lyle asked.

"Selected eyewitnesses." He turned to Ross. "David, remind me about the effects on people of a neutron explosion.''

"Well, sir, that's hard to say. It depends on two things. One is the size of the bomb, and the other is the height at which it detonates.'' Ross leaned forward. "Let's say it was one of Rabinovich's one-kiloton Scimitar shells and it exploded 500 feet above ground. Now anyone within a radius of 2,500 feet of ground zero is going to get a neutron dosage of about 8,000 rads. That means they pretty well collapse within five minutes and die up to two days later. But let's say the same one-kiloton bomb explodes at 3,000 feet. Then the immediately lethal 8,000 rad dosage affects an area less than half the size—maybe only a radius of 1,000 feet.''

"But as you point out," Yardley observed, "everyone in that vicinity dies in a couple of days, so that's no good to us. What about further out?''

"Well, the radiation diminishes. Give it an extra 500 feet, and people might absorb 3,000 rads.''

"Which means?''

"Death in five or six days.''

"Okay, and beyond that?''

"As I understand it, over 4,000 feet, the dosage'll be about 650 rads, diminishing the further away you get.''

"How about those people?''

"They'll be sick a couple of hours after exposure, but they'll recover. At least, they'll feel better. Actually, most of them will die within six to twelve weeks.''

Yardley sighed and relaxed. "That's what we want," he said. "Find a selection of people who were in this 650 rad

belt at the time of the explosion and bring them to me."
Ross and Lyle looked startled. "I want them in America,"
he explained. "I want them examined and treated by the
best doctors in the country. I want them seen by the
International Red Cross. I want them interviewed. And
then I want them to die. On television." He smiled.

15

Peshawar is the capital of Pakistan's Northwest Frontier Province. Its heart is the old city, where the streets are crowded and noisy, clogged with cars, bicycles, cycle rickshaws, and people. Tribesmen with colorful turbans wrapped and twisted around their heads drink tea and gossip. Women, identically dressed head to toe in black, their faces veiled, trail children who, when they dart away or get lost, unerringly find their way back, locating exactly the right shapeless mass in an alleyway of female clones.

Into the old city came Lyle and Ross, guided by an aide of the U.S. Consul's, to shop for the Pathan dress in which they would cross into Afghanistan: clothing suited to the climate and conditions of at least five or six weeks' hard walking, and which would disguise them from the air, although anyone seeing them up close would know they were foreign. Their features, Ross's in particular, were too obviously Western. But in Peshawar, *farangis*—Europeans —in transparent disguises were almost commonplace. The agents were treading a path well-worn by foreign journalists who crossed the frontier with the rebels, usually only for a few days, occasionally for months, to observe and report on the fighting.

The aide was a young Bostonian named Steve Cook, a lanky, laconic man who was both a good listener and a fluent linguist. He spoke Urdu and Pashto, the main languages of the area, and also a smattering of Persian.

They found a place selling hats and caps, more stall than a shop, a kind of garage big enough for a medium-sized car, in which rough wooden shelves were piled with tribal headgear.

Cook rummaged through a pile of thick woven woollen hats, colored in brown, beige, or cream. They were like loose berets with long sides rolled up to form the rim.

Ross and Lyle tried on a selection. "They're pretty scratchy," Lyle complained.

"You'll get used to it," Cook said and began bargaining in Urdu with the storekeeper, finally beating down his price by almost half.

"You've got your own boots, of course," Cook said as they wandered further into the bazaar, ignoring greetings and entreaties from owners of curio stalls. The men confirmed they had. "Good, just so long as they're properly broken in and really comfortable." He glanced at them. "Actually, however good they are, you're probably going to have trouble with your feet, so take a few pairs of decent thick socks. It's a long walk."

In a clothing shop, they looked at the traditional *salwar* chemise—baggy pajama trousers and a loose shirt that flowed down past the waist. The *salwar* chemise came in individual boxes, marked according to size and color, and the shirts had labels proclaiming them to be "Wash-'n'-Wear, Trevira 65%, cotton 35%." Modern industry had caught up with tradition.

The agents tried on the clothes, rejecting the salesman's attempts to interest them in sky-blue and other bright colors, going instead for the dun or khaki that would be useful for camouflage.

The last important item of Pathan gear—and Ross and Lyle would only later realize how important it was—was the blanket carried over the shoulder, called a *sadr*. In winter a *sadr* would be of the warmest wool a man could afford, but this was late spring and Cook advised them to choose something in light cotton, also in a camouflage color.

When they'd done this, he took them to a stall where army surplus rucksacks and water bottles were on sale.

"I guess that'll do you," Cook said, when they'd made their purchases. "Tom Glenn's got the rest of the supplies you'll need back at the Consulate."

He drove them out of the old city and toward the army cantonment, where the sheet metal gates at the Consulate entrance were guarded by Pakistani sentinels.

The Consulate itself was immediately to the right of the driveway, up a flight of stairs. To the left, behind hedges and bushes, was a large, well-kept garden and the Consul's residence.

Tom Glenn greeted them at the front door, and invited them upstairs to his study: a room of bookshelves, paintings, and comfortable chairs. The men ordered drinks from a Pakistani bearer and talked generally until these were served and they were alone with the door closed.

Glenn lit a cigarette and regarded the agents with a calm, shrewd stare, behind which was the smallest hint of private amusement. "I've made a contact for you," he said. "As I told you this morning, there are half a dozen groups who'll be glad to take you across the border. Unless you've got any objection, I've settled on the Jamiaat-i-Islami. They're pretty good, and they're the people actually in charge in the Panjshir Valley area and right into Badakhshan, so you shouldn't have too many problems with *mujahideen* rivalries. How does that sound?"

"Sounds fine," Lyle said. "When can we cross the border?"

"You can arrange that tonight," the Consul said. "They know there's a time factor, but when exactly you leave is for you to negotiate." He paused and sipped his drink. "For the sake of simplicity, I've told them you're looking for evidence of chemical warfare. Is that okay? They understand poison gas, and they're eager to help."

"That sounds sensible," Ross said. "Are they willing for us to take people back with us?"

Tom Glenn allowed himself a smile. "They're delighted," he said. "My guess is you'll have about four healthy Afghans for every victim, especially if any of them are women."

"There won't be a problem about numbers, I don't suppose. I don't think our people are in the mood to quibble."

"Fine. Now the other thing is the stuff you need to carry in with you. I'm sure Steve advised you to take the minimum possible amount. Your pack gets heavier every mile, as I'm sure you know. So I'm mainly offering medical supplies." The Consul produced two plastic carrier bags. "I'm afraid these weigh eight pounds each," he apologized. "Feel free to throw out things you don't want. I've selected this stuff on the basis of what Steve and I would choose if we were crossing the border, which thank God we never will." He began emptying one of the bags on the table. "Here we go: one can of insect repellent spray. One tube of antiseptic, anti-itch cream for insects who aren't repelled." He looked up. "You might feel inclined to leave these behind, but let me warn you, you're going to be bitten rotten. And when you are, do not scratch, however much you want to. Once you start, it's just about impossible to stop and you'll be covered with sores in a couple of days. That can be pretty damn demoralizing." He held up another tube. "This is an antibiotic cream for cuts, burst blisters, that sort of thing. And this," he said, exhibiting another, "is for body lice. Before you leave Peshawar, have a long hot bath and run it all over you. The chances are you aren't going to wash properly for several weeks, so it'll give you some protection. If you do swim in a river, put more of it on when you dry off."

"You make Afghanistan sound real nice," Lyle said.

"Oh, it is," Tom Glenn said. "You'll have a great time." He removed a couple of small bottles from the plastic bag. "These are very important," he told them. "Water purification tablets. Drop two in your water bottles a couple of minutes before you drink. There's stuff in their rivers and wells that'd make the Mayo Clinic rewrite its textbooks." He returned to the contents of the plastic bag. "A couple boxes of Band-Aids," he announced, holding them up. "You're sure to have trouble with your feet. Everyone does. A bottle of vitamin pills to supplement your diet. They'll feed you as best they can, but what it is depends on what's available. Glucose tablets for energy." Out came a handful of bottles. "A lot of this stuff here isn't necessarily for you, but you'll find the Afghans look on you as doctors and come along asking for treatment. So here are a hundred aspirins, antibiotic eyedrops, a bottle of broad-spectrum antibiotics and some pretty powerful pain-killers." He delved into the packet. "Also Ace bandages and a few rolls of gauze bandages. Now the serious stuff." He produced a sealed plastic kit. "In here's morphine. Keep it for dire emergencies, preferably for yourselves. If you get wounded, it might take days or weeks to get you back into Pakistan, although if you lose a limb, say, and you can't get to a hospital soon, I guess you'll be finished anyway. And finally," he dug into the bag and held up a plastic bottle and a couple of rolls of toilet paper, "Lomatil tablets for diarrhea. Take two at the first sign of trouble and another dose four hours later. The toilet paper is optional. You can do as the Afghans do, and use your left hand, but most Westerners prefer at least this basic comfort.''

"Don't ever forget the basic law of good manners here," Steve Cook added. "You eat food with your right hand only. The *mujahideen* will think you're even more disgusting and ill-bred than they already do if they see you using your left. As it is they'll avoid eating from the same dishes as you. Actually they only put up with you for three reasons: you're against the Russians, you're in Afghanistan to help their *jihad*, and because of their code of hospitality. While you're under their protection, they'll guard you with their lives, even if they hate you. Of course,'' he added, blowing a lungful of smoke toward the ceiling, "once you say goodbye and walk away, there's nothing in the code to stop them coming after you and killing you.''

"Thanks a lot," Lyle said. Cook raised his beer glass in salute.

"I guess that's about all," the Consul said. "Anything you need to know? Anything we can help you on?"

"I don't think so," Lyle said. "Just point us in the direction of the guys who'll take us to Badakhshan.''

"We'll have a bite to eat first," Glenn said. "They're expecting you at half past nine." He paused. "Uh, there is a question I'd like to ask if you don't mind. What happens if the Russians catch you?"

"We try to bluff our way out," Lyle said. "We've got accreditation from the Voice of America." He smiled slightly. "Although they don't know it yet. They'll be told if and when the need arises. We'll have small cassette recorders. Our surnames are going to be different too. The Russians might just question us for a few weeks and then expel us. They've done that before with captured journalists.''

The Consul wasn't convinced. "Well, let's hope it doesn't come to that."

Dark figures closed around them in the narrow street, shadows of men and rifles.

Steve Cook spoke in rapid Pashto and was answered in a voluble flow. The figures parted, and they entered a cement corridor, bare except for revolutionary posters glued to the walls. Ahead were more armed men, then a courtyard in which an electric light burned. They were escorted to a room with a plain wooden desk, four old upright chairs, and more posters showing black and white portraits of young men with, beneath them, elaborate Pashto or Urdu script. There were no other furnishings.

The man behind the desk rose gravely to greet them, and Cook made the introductions in English.

"Engineer Mahmud," he said, "these are the men who want to go to Badakhshan. Mr. David and Mr. Clive."

They shook hands, and he motioned them to sit.

Mahmud looked like a painting of Jesus from a child's book of Bible stories. He had long black hair, a thick beard and fine features. His eyes were a serene tawny green.

"Mahmud is a brave commander of the Jamiaat *mujahideen*," Cook explained. "He has killed many Russians."

Mahmud nodded slightly in acknowledgment while he watched the two new Americans.

"He speaks English, and he'll take you to Badakhshan to get evidence of the poison gas. Then he'll bring you out."

Ross returned Mahmud's look squarely. "There may be people who have breathed the gas," he said, "and who need to see American doctors. These people might feel well now, but soon they will become sick and die. That's how this gas works sometimes."

"I understand," Mahmud said. "I will take you to see."

"We have to get to Badakhshan as quickly as we can, Mahmud," Lyle said. "How soon can we do it?"

"That will depend on how fast you walk, Mr. Clive."

"We'll do our best," Lyle said. "When do we leave?"

Mahmud made a fatalistic gesture with his hands. "In the morning, *insha Allah,*" he said.

The agents glanced at each other. They hadn't expected it to be that soon, but there was no reason to delay.

"That's excellent," Ross said. "What time?"

"You must come here at six."

The Americans stood up to go. "Thank you, Mahmud," Ross said. "We'll see you then."

"Insha Allah," the Afghan said.

They walked past the armed men at the entrance, into the dark street and along to Cook's car.

"What's with this Mr. David and Mr. Clive stuff?" Lyle asked.

"That's the way it is here," Cook said. "They use given names rather than surnames. I like it, actually."

"Well, everything seems okay. Mahmud looks like a good man."

"He is," Cook affirmed. "He's reliable, he's a fighter rather than a talker, and he'll look after you as well as anyone can."

As they headed for Cook's house where they were staying, their host added, "There's one other piece of advice I'd like to give you, and it's this. When you're in Afghanistan, keep close to Mahmud or whoever he deputizes to look after you. Don't go wandering off by yourselves, not even a block. You might think you look American, but to an Afghan you could easily be Russian. If you're alone, you could find stones being thrown at you, or you might get a bullet in the back. It's not worth the risk.''

They saw Cook's point. The trek to Badakhshan was starting to seem like a minefield: not only of potential danger from the Russians and the physical endurance necessary, but cultural barriers, general language difficulties, tribal rivalries, and the possibility of mistaken identity.

Although it was growing late and Ross and Lyle had to make an early start, they spent an hour with Cook jotting down useful phrases which might smooth their way. The first was the ritual greeting, *"Salām-o-alaikum"*—"Peace be upon you"—and the proper response: *"Aluikum-o-salām."* Among the others were sentiments with which their guides would be in complete agreement: *"Afghanistan zindabad!"*— "Long live Afghanistan!" and even more important: *"Russe murdabad!"*—"Death to the Russians!"

The men slept lightly, their rucksacks packed. They awoke before five, bathed, rubbed anti-lice cream over their bodies, and donned their Pathan disguises. When they were ready, they looked sheepishly at each other. Had any DIA agent ever gone into enemy territory in costumes so transparent, so amateurish? Ross had worried about whether to dye his hair black, to make himself look less obviously Western, but Cook said it wasn't necessary.

"Look," he pointed out, "there've been dozens of fair-haired journalists going across the border with no problems. If the Russians spot you, it'll probably be from the air and you'll look like everyone else. If it comes to the stage where they get a close view from the ground, the game's up anyway, and if they see you're a Westerner, they'll probably ask questions first, and shoot afterward."

The men checked their equipment a final time. In the pockets of their *salwar* chemises, they carried the Voice of America IDs and American passports, identifying them as

David Masefield and Clive Carmichael. Each man had a money belt, containing both Pakistani rupees and old Afghan currency. They had been warned—another piece of priceless inside information—that the Afghan money they used had to be old issue, printed before the communist revolution. The new currency notes were not acceptable outside Russian-controlled areas and in fact could be considered evidence of Soviet sympathies.

Cook drove them through the waking streets to the Jamiaat building where they were to meet Mahmud.

He left them at the entrance, having had a jovial exchange in Urdu with a few gunmen on duty with whom he shook hands.

"Good luck," Cook said. "We'll have a plane standing by in five weeks although I would guess the earliest you'll be out is seven or eight. If we don't hear from you in ten weeks, we'll start worrying."

"You do that," Lyle said. The agents followed the gunmen through the courtyard where four *mujahideen* were standing barefoot on mats facing Mecca, saying prayers. They went into the bleak office.

It was empty. They put down their packs and pulled up chairs.

There was no sense of urgency in the movements of men in the corridor or the courtyard, no feeling that preparations were under way to take two Americans into Afghanistan, nor indeed was there a sign that anyone was proposing to go across the frontier at all. Lyle caught Ross's eye and glanced heavenward.

At 6:40, Mahmud's calm countenance looked in at them from the doorway.

"Salām-o-alaikum," he greeted them courteously, not reacting at all to their supposed disguises.

"Alaikum-o-salām," Ross replied formally.

"What's the holdup?" Lyle asked, cutting through the niceties.

"If you are ready, let us go," Mahmud suggested. Ross and Lyle slung their knapsacks over their shoulders and followed him out into the narrow street. They walked to the end of the block where there was a main road, and Mahmud stopped, watching the traffic.

"What are we waiting for?" Lyle wanted to know.

"We must take a scooter rickshaw to the bus station," Mahmud said.

Scooter rickshaw? Bus station? The agents exchanged glances.

"Where are we taking a bus to?" Lyle wondered aloud. "Kabul?"

"Parachinar. It is near the White Mountain. When we cross that tomorrow, we will be in Afghanistan."

They stood at the curb of a busy Peshawar street, the unflustered *mujahed* commander and the two men from the Defense Intelligence Agency with their brand-new tribal gear and their army knapsacks. Ross, who wasn't widely experienced, knew he was conspicuous, but felt resigned. No one seemed to be paying them much attention anyway, not even the scooter rickshaws which, when they passed, were already hired.

But Lyle's heart was in his boots. He had been on covert operations before that required disguises, but nothing remotely approached the amateurishness of this mission. Yet what could he do? Things had passed out of their hands. Mahmud was their guide, chosen for them—presumably out of dozens—by senior and experienced United States diplomats, and now they were stuck with him.

They had to believe he was the best available, and that he would take them deep into Soviet-occupied territory in the safest, most efficient manner possible. And get them out again. Lyle knew he should be feeling angry, but instead he was numb.

If Yardley could see us now, he thought, scanning the traffic for an empty scooter rickshaw, he'd have a heart attack.

Then he thought: Shit, if the CIA could see us now, they'd roll on the ground laughing.

The prospect made him go cold.

At last, Mahmud flagged down an empty scooter rickshaw and gave the driver instructions. The scooter swerved into the traffic and threaded its way through cars waiting at a light until it was ahead of them all. The agents sat in grim silence.

It stopped abruptly at the entrance to an open square of ground. Beyond were the buses, each an intricate work of local art, with every available inch of bodywork decorated. On the side of one a tiger sprang, jaws agape and fangs gleaming. Surrounding the beast were lotus blossoms and foliage. Another featured detailed pastoral scenes, complete with a waterfall, and farther off was a bus boasting a huge painting of mountains and deer. Every vehicle was surmounted by intricate fretworks of shiny tin, and parts of their windows were covered with colored cellophane in yellow, red and blue, making them look like the stained glass of some zany mobile revivalist chapel.

And then there were policemen, uniformed, loitering in small groups. There was no way they could have missed noticing Lyle and Ross, but they left them alone. Cook had been right. The agents were on a well-trodden journalistic route and the Pakistani authorities, at least in Peshawar, were turning a blind eye. Lyle felt himself relax slightly.

"The bus is leaving," Mahmud announced. "It's time to go."

They followed him, weaving through the crowds toward

one of the most elaborately decorated vehicles. As they approached, they could see it was not only full, but that a swarm of men were trying to force their way on.

Mahmud addressed the intending travelers in his calm but authoritative voice, and miraculously the crowd gave way. Orders were shouted inside. Lyle and Ross saw men and women coming off the bus, showing no signs of annoyance.

Mahmud motioned the agents aboard. Every eye turned to stare as they made their way through the garish interior to three newly vacant seats.

The Americans put their packs on the floor by their feet and squeezed in. It was an uncomfortable fit even for Lyle, but Ross, a taller and bigger man, found himself with his knees pressing hard against the back of the seat in front, and almost no room to move. Mahmud took a place farther forward in the bus.

The aisle began refilling with those temporarily displaced until it seemed impossible for another person to squeeze aboard.

The inside of the bus was, if anything, gaudier than its exterior. The sides and ceiling were covered with shiny tin, beaten into the shapes of flowers and decorated with verses from the Koran in sweeping stylized script, studded with gold and silver glitter. The interior lights were red and yellow, and just beside the driver hung a battery of colored bulbs, that flashed whenever he hit the brakes. This action also triggered a musical device, and the first bars of Lara's Theme chimed monotonously.

The bus rumbled slowly out of the station and into the morning traffic, heading for the road that would take them through closed tribal areas to the Afghan frontier.

After an hour, Mahmud pushed his way down toward them.

"Soon we will reach many roadblocks," he said, "and

the police will come and search. If they speak to you, do not answer. Act as if you do not understand.''

Out of the window, the country was dry and arid, rising to hills of brown sand and rock, dotted with thorn scrub and occasional herds of goats. The sun was getting high. Heat radiated from the floor, through the soles of their shoes. Around them, people shifted uncomfortably. Everyone began to sweat. It must have been worse for the women, black-garbed in what looked like linen tents trailing to the ground, their faces covered with black veils.

The bus vibrated with the straining engine and bumped over the uneven road. Ross bunched his *sadr*, the brown cotton sheet slung over his shoulder, into a ball against the trembling window, rested his head on it and tried to sleep.

The miles rolled by.

Some . . . where . . . my . . . love . . . there . . . will . . . be . . . songs . . . to . . . sing . . .

The bus shuddered to a halt. The engine was switched off, and there was complete silence. They were at their first roadblock.

Two policemen came to speak to the driver and glance at the luggage piled onto the roof rack. Ross and Lyle avoided looking in their direction.

A minute later, the engine coughed back into life, and they were waved through.

Ross concentrated on trying to sleep. His legs were tingling and although he flexed his muscles to restore the blood flow, it was a losing battle.

Lyle sat relaxed, his mind alternating between alertness for potential roadblocks and freewheeling over what confronted them still further ahead. What would they find when they got to Badakhshan? How would they choose the survivors? He and Ross had to calculate precisely where people had been at the time of the explosion—presuming it was a neutron blast—and from that try to guess their chances. Yardley wouldn't thank them for bringing back a dozen guys who had three years, or five, or fifteen to live. He wanted people who'd last that number of weeks after reaching the States; otherwise their publicity value would drop almost to zero. And what was the guarantee he and Ross would be able to find Afghans fitting this macabre bill? Particularly since the best examples would be dead long before they reached the spot.

Some . . . where . . . my . . . love . . . there . . . will . . . be . . .

A barrier up ahead. Three armed policemen standing by the side. Lyle saw Ross's eyes flicker open, register the roadblock, and close again. He might as well pretend to be asleep.

Lyle sat quietly, apparently indifferent.

The policemen climbed onto the roof and inspected the luggage. Now that the bus was no longer moving, and it was almost midday, the temperature inside mounted steadily. Lyle felt beads of perspiration dribbling down his forehead. He wiped them off with his *sadr*. A few minutes later he became aware, without looking around, that at least one policeman had boarded the bus and was making his way forward.

Lyle felt a rough push at his shoulder, and he turned. The policeman standing over him gave an order in a language Lyle didn't understand and pointed to the rucksacks at his and Ross's feet. David continued to feign sleep.

Lyle pulled out his pack and opened it. The policeman sorted through the medicines, the cassette recorder, toilet rolls—contents which were obviously Western. Ross's pack was the same.

The policeman jabbered aggressively, but remembering Mahmud's advice, Lyle stared back dumbly and shrugged. The policeman gave an exclamation of disgust, followed by a gesture of dismissal and moved further along. Lyle closed the packs and stowed them on the floor.

A few minutes later, they were moving again. As they pulled back onto the road, Ross, his eyes still closed, said: "That was a close one."

The day stretched on, a succession of roadblocks in unchangingly barren countryside. At one nameless town, they bought cold Cokes and fruit for lunch. A few passengers disembarked, others boarded. The number of travelers remained constant.

Occasionally, Mahmud turned to look at them, but he didn't speak beyond offering cold drinks during short stops.

In the late afternoon, the bus began to climb. The rugged, stony landscape gave way to paddy fields and golden wheat, ripe for harvest.

It was seven in the evening, and the sun was going down before they drove into the town of Parachinar: a collection of shacks serving as shops, with some mud-walled buildings. In the distance, they could see the four tall minarets of a mosque.

Mahmud got up, nodding to them to move. Lyle pulled out his pack. "I guess this is it," he said.

"Shit!" Ross exclaimed through clenched teeth. "My legs are asleep." With difficulty he extricated himself from the cramped seat and into a half-crouch. He was too tall to stand upright. They pushed out with the disembarking crowd, Mahmud a few feet behind.

As soon as he touched ground, Ross stretched and gave a groan of relief. "Jesus, that's better," he muttered.

Then Mahmud was beside them. "We must go quickly," he urged. "If they see you here, they will send you back."

He went swiftly across the road toward a corrugated iron gate, the agents close behind him, and entered a dirt-floored courtyard. At one side stood charpoys, the common bed of the subcontinental peasant, a rugged wooden frame on four conical legs, with jute strings plaited to form a platform on which a person could lie.

One side of the courtyard was a rock and mud wall, but the others were brown mud-walled rooms, with staircases leading to flat roofs upon which people could also sleep.

Mahmud was greeted by three men whom he embraced affectionately, touching cheeks on one side, then the other. "These are *mujahideen*," Mahmud explained to the agents. "They will come with us into Afghanistan."

"*Salām-o-alaikum*," Ross said politely, and received the ritual response.

Mahmud pointed to the charpoys a few yards away. "You will sleep there," he said. "This is our hotel for the night. Here we are safe."

Ross and Lyle stretched out on the jute strings, looking at the darkening sky. After the heat and discomfort of the eleven-hour bus ride, the rough beds seemed almost luxurious.

In the soft light of sunset, turbanned men laid rugs and began praying aloud, totally unselfconscious, first standing, then kneeling, then prostrating themselves, then standing again, hands clasped across their chests and voices raised to God.

In the gloom of a corner, someone scraped at a large blackened pot.

After dark, the agents were brought a pot of green tea and a bowl of coarse sugar which was heaped into chipped cups before the light brew was poured in. The tea was very sweet, but fragrant and delicious.

Mujahideen sat around the courtyard, talking quietly.

Neither Ross nor Lyle could understand the apparent total lack of weapons. When Mahmud came over with their dinner—a tin plate with hard-boiled eggs and bread wrapped in a filthy cloth—they asked him about it.

He produced a pistol from his belt. "This was kept for

me here," he said. "We don't carry weapons on the buses because the police take them if they find them. We will get whatever we need at the *mujahideen* center tomorrow." He shrugged. "Perhaps a Kalashnikov, perhaps an American G-2 or G-3."

It didn't seem to matter either way.

Mahmud went to join the other Afghans on mats a distance away, eating their evening meal, while a small boy passed among them distributing ovals of unleavened bread and pouring glasses of water.

That night, Ross found it difficult to rest. Flies kept settling on his face. He lay staring at the star-filled sky, and watched the full moon rise slowly over the wall.

There was a constant coming and going in the courtyard, men talking earnestly in low voices. On a nearby charpoy, someone shouted "Allah!" in his sleep.

A baby in an adjoining room began to cry, its howls continuing unabated for what seemed like hours. Finally its mother brought the infant to the window in an attempt to distract its attention by showing it the bright moon and succeeded only in pointing the source of the screams directly at the sleeping men. Everyone woke, even Lyle who seemed to have had no trouble dropping off earlier. The woman retreated. At last the child's cries became muffled and finally stopped.

There was comparative quiet, during which Ross fell into a light sleep.

Mahmud woke them at 3:45 A.M. There was no question of dressing because they slept in their *salwar* chemises, and had no other clothing. It was only a matter of pulling on boots, hitching packs, slinging *sadrs* over their shoulders, and they were ready to go.

Dark shapes of *mujahideen* moved into the street, walking for several minutes, veering down into alleyways, until finally they reached a tractor onto which was hitched a blue trailer. By the light of a torch, they could see it was decorated with childlike paintings of flowers and fierce tigers. Everyone climbed aboard.

The tractor engine roared into life, and they rumbled through the town, following a long road past the mosque and up into terraced fields of wheat, lurching and bumping over farm tracks, for more than an hour until the tractor could go no further and they were at the foot of the White Mountain.

The *mujahideen* squatted by the side of an icy river, undid the cords of their baggy cotton trousers and performed the ritual Islamic ablutions.

Lyle, watching from a distance, advised quietly: "Never drink downstream of these guys, David."

When they were finished, the sun was rising, and it was time for morning prayers. The *mujahideen* gathered, barefoot on their *sadrs,* with Mahmud at the front chanting the litany.

"*Al-lah ak-bar!*"—"God is great!" His voice was high and unhurried, caressing the words so each syllable emerged pure and distinct.

Ross sat on a rock, watching the scarlet ball of the sun quickly grow too bright for his eyes, and found himself needing to pray: not for divine guidance to lead them to irradiated Afghans who would die for Yardley and the world's television audience—although the Lord surely knew there was a purpose in that grim search—but simply: Dear God, show me what to do. Give me the strength and courage to do it. Keep Clive safe. Keep me safe too.

It was the prayer of a child, but there didn't seem anything else worth saying.

When the *mujahideen* had finished, they gathered up their *sadrs* and followed a rocky path beside the river, with the mountain rising high above them. Soon the path ran out and they crossed to the other side of the gushing water, jumping from rock to rock. Farther on they had to cross back, wading through the current. The water was fast-flowing and bitingly cold: nothing more than newly melted ice, and the stones over which it raced were loose and slippery.

Although the agents' trousers were soaked, the exertion of the climb generated enough body heat to keep them warm, and they splashed through after the *mujahideen*.

The climb became steeper, the path rocky and narrow. They were noticeably nearer the snow line, and the first refugee traffic of the day came toward them: women and children laden with bundles of blankets and pots and pans; barefoot men with steel cases strapped to their backs, on their way to safety.

The *mujahideen* paused for a rest.

"How're you feeling, David?" Lyle asked, taking a seat on a rock next to him.

"Okay. It seems pretty easy so far."

Twenty minutes later, they reached the first snow, from where they could see refugee groups sliding down the thick white expanse from the top of the mountain, baggage and all, shouting and laughing at the exhilaration of the ride and the speed with which they were shifting themselves and their belongings a thousand feet down a precipitous slope.

But if Ross had thought the climb easy in the initial stages, he changed his mind as the amount of oxygen in the high air diminished and his body became exhausted.

He found he had to stop for rests at increasingly short intervals, and Lyle was no better. The line of *mujahideen* was now strung out over a good quarter mile, and some had fallen behind the agents.

Within seconds of pulling himself off a rock and trudging up the path, Ross's heart was pounding hard and fast, forcing him to stop every two hundred yards. In the final stages of the climb, with the summit tantalizingly close, this was reduced to a pitiful hundred yards. Lyle stuck with him, slumping with oxygen starvation when he did, and gasping in lungfuls of thin air.

Most of the *mujahideen* were already at the top, recovering and waiting for the others.

At last Ross and Lyle made it to the summit of the White Mountain, 11,000 feet up, and fell into the snow, chests heaving.

Mahmud gave them a few minutes to get their breath before coming over and pointing to the west. "There is Afghanistan," he said.

The men turned and stared down the other side of the White Mountain, past the snow line and into a rocky gorge. At the base were trees and fields and, beyond them, stretching into the distance, the rocky brown of semi-desert.

High overhead an eagle floated on currents of air, wings motionless. Then, edging into the silence, came the distant sound of a jet fighter-bomber cruising a parallel course. A warning of dangers to come.

"Welcome to my country," Mahmud said.

"Thanks," Ross said. "I hope we can do you some good."

"Insha Allah," Mahmud replied.

"At least it's downhill all the way from here," Lyle observed.

"That is only for a while," Mahmud said. "Then we reach the truly high mountains of the Hindu Kush."

"Higher than this one?" Lyle asked.

Mahmud smiled. "This is a child." He pointed to the dark gliding shape of the eagle. "In Afghanistan, we have mountains so high, not even birds can fly over them. In the seasons of the year that they try to pass, they must land near the tops of the mountains and walk across."

Lyle laughed. "You're kidding me," he accused, but Mahmud shook his head.

"I do not lie," he insisted. "Hunters wait at these places to shoot the birds."

Ross sucked a fistful of clean, white snow, scraped from underneath a grayish crust. "Mahmud's right," he said. "The Hindu Kush reaches around 19,000 feet, and that high, the air's too thin to fly. Migrating flocks would have to land and leg it across the top. I guess it makes them pretty easy targets for anyone who feels like making the climb."

Lyle lay back in the snow, watching the eagle. "What a place," he marveled.

"Now we must go," Mahmud said. He signaled to the others, and the *mujahideen* collected their packs and *sadrs*.

It was not yet midday when they crossed the frontier.

The descent was, in its own way, as difficult as the climb. The slope was covered with loose pebbles that gave way without warning. Several men fell heavily until the group reached the thick snow, where they unfolded their *sadrs,* and using them like toboggans, slid deeper into Afghanistan, shouting and laughing.

The only problems with the cotton sheets were that they were impossible to steer, and rocks, jutting slightly out of the snow, could be painful when hit. But Ross, Lyle, and the *mujahideen* played like kids, their *salwar* chemises soaked with melted ice. Almost incidentally, they dropped down hundreds of feet.

Where the snow line ended, the Agam River began: pure, near-freezing water. The agents filled their bottles and followed the others down the slope, passing refugees hunched under the weight of their belongings during the final gruelling climb.

The path the *mujahideen* followed hugged the edge of the rocky gorge. As Ross knew, thinking about what they were doing would be a serious error. He kept close, not looking down the sheer drops, or up at the steep climbs, or to check what, if anything, anchored flimsy bridges. His eyes stayed on the feet of the man directly in front—usually Lyle—walking without question where he trod, with single-minded blinkered determination.

As the afternoon wore on, the number of refugees they passed increased. The women were almost all veiled, and turned modestly away when they saw the *mujahideen* and the Americans. Everyone else exchanged ritual greetings.

Grandfathers carried small children on their backs. Younger men were bent under loads as heavy as that strapped onto any donkey: mostly rolled-up blankets surrounding a sack of wheat to provide food for the family until they reached the refugee camps and registered for aid.

Mahmud called a halt at a lookout post 150 feet above the river, and Ross, when he sank onto the ground, back against a rock, felt as exhausted as he ever had in his life. He bitterly regretted the fight he'd picked with Lyle that caused him to stay off training while his ribs mended. He'd lost that peak physical edge, and it was hard winning it back.

They'd been going now for almost twelve hours, and there was no sign of the *mujahideen* center at which they were supposed to spend the night.

It seemed no more than two minutes before Mahmud motioned them to their feet again and they continued along the narrow path cut into the side of the precipice.

Below Ross, the drops varied between 150 and 300 feet, and he knew a single clumsy move would send him tumbling unstoppably onto jagged rocks. He thought briefly of Sophie Johnson. Lyle was ahead, and Ross forced himself to keep up. Further in front, walking effortlessly, were the *mujahideen*

Ross gulped water as he walked and refilled his bottle whenever they crossed the river, not bothering with the purification tablets Tom Glenn had provided. The melted snow, at this point, was surely as fresh and clean as it was possible to get, and he felt he'd need his tablets later. He found his water bottle was lasting him only half an hour, and there was still the semi-desert to come. He wondered how he would ration himself then, and he hoped he could trust his body to adjust to whatever was necessary.

Mahmud dropped back to speak to the agents. "It's three more hours to the *mujahideen* center at Torabora," he said. "I do not think we'll reach there tonight." He pointed at the sky. Clouds were gathering, and it seemed it would soon rain. "I have friends near here. We will stay with them."

Ross agreed with relief.

Further down the path, they came across a man carrying two chickens. "Mahmud!" Clive called. "You think we can buy one of these from this guy? I wouldn't mind chicken for dinner." In an aside to Ross he said: "God knows what we're going to eat from now on."

The bearded leader spoke quietly to the farmer, agreeing on a price. Lyle took the cash from his money belt and handed it over. The farmer pulled out a knife and pierced holes in the chicken's wings, breaking the bones while it squawked in panic. He bound its leg and handed the bird to Mahmud who carried it away, spots of blood dripping onto his shirt.

Mahmud may have thought his friend's house was nearby, but to Ross, the remaining journey seemed endless. He willed his body on and forced his mind to remain alert for the pitfalls of the treacherous path.

The first drops of rain began to fall.

Finally they reached a collection of rough, mud-walled buildings around which were irrigated, fertile fields of wheat. Trees of ripening figs and mulberries shaded the hard sand compound of the dwellings.

Mahmud went to a doorway, and within seconds was surrounded by turbanned men who embraced him with warmth and affection. Ross and Lyle watched from rocks a short distance away, sheltered by trees.

Mahmud returned to them. "You must wait here until the guest room is ready," he instructed. "It will be only a few minutes."

Half an hour later, they were ushered in, and the guest room turned out to be a mud-walled, mud-floored building, completely open at one side. Perhaps it had been a stall for animals, but now it was cleared and a rug thrown on the ground.

Everyone removed their shoes and sat down. The Americans lay back against their packs, exhausted. Ross was glad to see that Lyle was in only slightly better condition than himself.

That night, by the light of a kerosene lantern, they ate the chicken they had bought, served with *nān*, the dry, unleavened ovals of bread that form the staple diet of the Afghan. There was also a substance neither Ross nor Lyle could identify, but which tasted like thick, sweet tapioca.

The agents were given their own bowls, with the *mujahideen* eating communally a few feet away. As Steve Cook had predicted, Islamic believers took brotherhood with infidels only so far.

As soon as the meal was over, blankets were brought in. The drizzle that had been going on for two hours turned into a violent electrical storm. Thunder rumbled through the gorge, and sheet lightning illuminated the furthest recesses of the shed.

The men accepted the blankets politely, but when their host had moved away, Ross asked quietly: "Do you want to use these things, Clive? They're probably full of lice and bedbugs.''

"You know," Lyle said, "I don't think I care. We've got the cream on us, and it's going to be mighty cold tonight.''

The others were pulling the blankets over themselves without reservation, and Ross's combination of tiredness and growing chill persuaded him to take his chances. Yet for the second night, he slept brokenly, this time attacked by unseen insects. Itches started gently and became tantalizing, insistent, challenging him to scratch. Ross lay still, trying to relax, comforting himself with the thought that if lice and bedbug bites were all he took out of Afghanistan, he'd be lucky. And Yardley's victims, of course.

At last, he dropped off to sleep.

The low voices of the *mujahideen* pulled him back into consciousness in the early hours, and he became aware of flies buzzing around his head and landing on his face.

The kerosene lantern cast a faint glow over a turbanned group, Mahmud among them, talking earnestly. Ross rolled over to look at Lyle who was still asleep. He checked his watch and found it was four.

Outside, the rain had stopped, and there was blackness.

Ross felt the stiffness of his muscles and the nagging, stinging bites covering his stomach and legs. He reached out to touch Lyle's shoulder.

Clive was awake in a moment, half sitting up, registering the scene. Neither man spoke. Ross saw Lyle's hand go to his stomach to scratch, then pull back. The bugs had got them both.

Two Afghanis arrived carrying trays, and the lantern was moved to the center of the room. Mahmud noticed the Americans were awake and greeted them with the ghost of a smile. A grubby cloth was spread over the rug on the floor, and the *nān* distributed. Sweet green tea was served in glasses. Flies crawled over everything.

Afterward, Ross and Lyle went into the yard beneath the fruit trees to stretch, walk around a little, and get their muscles working again. They wrapped their *sadrs* around their shoulders for warmth. From inside the shed came the chant of the morning prayer, a man's voice calling ritually to God.

"Al-lah ak-bar!"

Silence.

"Al-lah ak-bar!"

"You been bitten?" Lyle asked finally.

"Yeah."

"That's the last time I use one of their fucking blankets," Lyle said.

"I guess it'll be the last time you need one, maybe until we get into the high mountains again. We ought to be in semi-desert in a day or two, and God knows what the temperature will be then."

When it was light enough to see the track, the *mujahideen* moved out, quickly and quietly. There were poppy fields now, and they could see the pods striated with thin cuts, from which the black opium sap had oozed for collection by the farmers.

As the gorge swung around and more cultivation lay before them, Mahmud stopped and pointed. Lying near the track was the three-foot-high tail fin of a Soviet bomb, ripped off and flung away in the explosion: their first evidence that this scene of rugged splendor was a battle ground between the tribesmen and Moscow.

Then Mahmud pointed across the Agam River, where protruding from the opposite bank was the gray metal of an unexploded bomb, impacted in the earth.

"The Russians came five days ago," Mahmud explained.

"What're you going to do with that, Mahmud?" Lyle asked. "It looks pretty dangerous left where it is."

"We will saw the casing in half and take out the explosive," he said. "We use it for making our own bombs."

"Christ! I wouldn't do that?" Lyle said. "It's suicide."

"It's not a *mujahed* who does the work," Mahmud replied. "We bring one of the prisoners from the center. We sit on this side of the river with rifles so he cannot run away, and we watch him do it."

Lyle and Ross exchanged incredulous glances.

"Russian prisoners?" Clive asked.

"Sometimes we have Russians, but not now. The prisoners are collaborators or spies. We know the names of those who help the government, and when we catch them we bring them here to answer for their crimes."

They continued in silence.

In the middle of a field of opium poppies, two craters, six feet in diameter, had been blasted into the earth, while further on, another unexploded bomb was almost buried among clover. They skirted it, close enough to read the Russian markings spray-painted below the gray metal fins. Forty yards on was another—this time half-exploded. The fin had been blown off, but otherwise the casing was intact, and inside was waxy, orange-colored explosive.

"It doesn't say a lot for Soviet quality control, does it?" Lyle said. "There seem to be a hell of a lot of duds coming out of one raid."

"There are more nearer the center," Mahmud confirmed.

"How many people were killed in this raid?" Ross asked.

"No one," the rebel leader said. "Three were hurt, but not badly. The Russians tried to attack the *mujahideen* center, but almost all their bombs and the rockets from the helicopters fell in the fields. They could not succeed."

"What happens when the Russian planes come?" Lyle wanted to know. "What do you do?"

"We have places on the top of the mountains," Mahmud said, "and we fire at them from there."

"Do you ever hit any?" Lyle tried not to grin.

"Sometimes," Mahmud said. "The helicopters have armor plating underneath, but if they come into the valley to fire rockets, then the *mujahideen* on the top are able to shoot down on them and *insha Allah,* kill the pilot. That is why they do not like to fly too low here."

As they approached the Torabora rebel center, the agents saw more evidence of the Soviet attack, and if the failure rate of the bombs themselves was something to marvel at, so was the lack of accuracy. The raid was aimed at a selection of mud-walled buildings clinging to the sides of a ravine and the bombadiers had managed to miss just about every time.

Lyle ran a practiced eye over the ravine, wondering why this was so. It wasn't a particularly difficult run-in for a MiG. A pilot could approach over the adjoining valley, make a tight turn at the mouth of the Agam River, and have maybe fifteen or twenty seconds to zero onto the target before pressing the bomb release.

Perhaps the attack had been mounted not by Russians, but by Afghan pilots, the remnants of a demoralized force, reduced by ideological purges and desertions, although U.S. intelligence maintained that most were carried out by the Soviets themselves. If this was true, it meant the pilots were either badly trained or very nervous. Lyle wondered if the Russians had been so psyched by stories of Afghan brutality and the fear of what might happen if they fell into *mujahideen* hands, that they simply got rid of their bomb loads as quickly as possible and headed for the safety of their base.

Lyle could see their point. Who the hell wanted his cock

cut off by some tribesman who thought he was doing it for God, and to spend his last hours screaming as his skin was peeled away from his body, and he died of shock and loss of blood?

Mahmud, ahead, turned and caught Lyle's eye. Lyle smiled amiably at him. "*Afghanistan zindabad!*" he said.

There was a shout of delighted laughter from the other rebels. "*Afghanistan zindabad!*" they yelled back.

The men walked three hours before reaching Torabora. The buildings had mud walls so thick and hard they were like reinforced concrete. One of the Soviet bombs had scored a direct hit on the main building, smashing through the mud ceiling and exploding in a room, but apart from the hole in the roof, it had caused no damage. Even the wooden charpoy in the room was intact, and there were no other furnishings, no curtains or tables, chairs or clothes, to be blown to bits or burst into flame.

The agents found themselves surrounded by a dozen curious Afghans, armed with a widely divergent selection of weapons. Some carried old Lee-Enfield rifles; others had captured Soviet Kalashnikovs with bayonets fixed and ammunition pouches around their waists. There were a couple of pistols and some old American M-1s.

"*Afghanistan zindabad!*" seemed to have gone down well earlier, so Ross repeated it to break the ice, and won a response almost at the level of children. He and Lyle were hugged and patted on the back, while the *mujahideen* laughed and chattered among themselves.

A huge white mulberry tree grew just outside the center, and two men climbed it to hang on the branches and knock the juicy, sweet fruit into *sadrs* stretched out beneath: yet another use for this supremely functional garment. In two days, Ross had used his for sleeping, for warmth, for wiping sweat from his face, for tobogganing, as a table-cloth, and now, to collect pounds of mulberries of a variety he had never seen before, but which tasted as if they were dipped in honey.

Mahmud went into the center while Ross and Lyle sat under the tree and ate, and the *mujahideen* tried to prompt them to say *"Afghanistan zindabad!"* once again. When the agents tired of that game, Ross tried *"Russe murdabad!"* and the rebels crowed with delight.

Mahmud returned after a few minutes.

"Are we going?" Lyle asked, reaching for his pack.

The Afghan commander shook his head. "No," he said. "We must stay here today."

Lyle groaned. "Ah, come on, Mahmud. You know we've got to get to Badakhshan quickly, otherwise we won't be able to take these people to America. They'll all be dead."

Mahmud was unmoved. "We can make up the time later," he said. "Today, all the commanders from the area are coming to Torabora, and we must have a meeting. We will leave at dawn tomorrow."

Ross and Lyle exchanged exasperated glances: except that as far as David was concerned, his disappointment was feigned. The prospect of a day's recovery before the next session of hard walking—perhaps unbroken for weeks—was a marvelous one, even if he was determined not to let Lyle know that.

"Insha Allah, we will find the people you want," Mahmud said. "We will walk more every day, and we will get there in time."

There didn't seem to be an alternative. Ross settled back and ate a mulberry.

"There are things for you to see here," Mahmud observed. "We have a prison on the hill." He indicated farther up, another mud-walled building. "There are men there who have spied for the Russians."

Mahmud called to a group of Afghans a distance away,

and one of the men detached himself and came over. "This is Mohammed Iqbal," he said. "He will stay with you and show you those things you want to see."

"Does he speak English?" Lyle asked.

"I managed to get by at Harvard," Mohammed Iqbal replied.

The agents stared at him in surprise. "Now what the hell," Lyle asked, "is a Harvard man doing at Torabora with an AK-47?"

Mohammed Iqbal laughed. "First I am a Moslem," he said. "Second, an Afghan, third a *mujahed,* and fourth a Harvard man."

Lyle shook his hand warmly. "You wouldn't say that if you'd gone to Yale. Hell, I never thought I'd hear another American accent this trip. When were you there?"

"Until '78 when the Russians invaded my country. Then I came to Pakistan and joined the Jamiaat-i-Islami. Since then, I've been doing what I can to help our *jihad.* Mahmud tells me you're going to Badakhshan."

"That's right," Lyle said. "We're with the Voice of America, and we're trying to get evidence that the Russians used poison gas there."

"There's no doubt," Mohammed Iqbal said. "A lot of people have died."

"Yes, but how do we prove it?" Ross asked. "We want to see what we can find in Badakhshan and maybe bring out some of the victims."

"That would be good," Iqbal agreed. "I hope you make it." He paused. "Mahmud says you want to see the prison."

Ross and Lyle looked at each other. "Might as well," Lyle said. "Doesn't seem to be much else going on today."

Iqbal led them up a rough dirt path that wound beside a stream and toward a mud building fronted by a veranda. He walked with easy assurance and seemed as acclimatized as any of the *mujahideen*. He wore the same filthy clothes, the *salwar* chemise, the tough black sandals in which his feet had become as hard as the leather itself, and a turban of twisted skeins of wool faded into a yellowish sand color. But while Mahmud was serene and Biblical, with calm green eyes, Mohammed Iqbal had a hint of cruelty about him. Behind a friendly façade, he was watchful. Mahmud may have made his peace with Allah, but Iqbal had a long way to go.

Still, the agents were glad to have found him. Conversation with Mahmud tended to be rudimentary, and it was good to have someone around who was at least familiar with Western concepts and interests. Maybe even jokes. And they ought to be able to learn about other *mujahideen*, too, and what problems they might face during the long walk to Badakhshan.

A group of armed rebels sat guard on the veranda of the mud house, and, in Pashto, Iqbal ordered them to produce the prisoners.

After a few moments, from a gloomy room shuffled an old man and two boys, hardly more than teenagers, wearing leg irons. The old man avoided everyone's eyes, his shoulders hunching nervously. One of the boys stared defiantly into the distance, while the younger looked directly at the Americans, smiling as if to pretend he wasn't really with the prisoners, trying to show friendship, to win favor and hide fear.

"This man and his sons were supporting the Russians." Iqbal said: "They worked as spies in Jalalabad. Also when the communists were handing out land, they accepted it. We sent a group of *mujahideen* to their house five days ago to arrest them and bring them here."

The younger son locked his gaze on Ross, appealing silently for confirmation that it was all a mistake, a joke even, urging that he do something to save them.

"What's going to happen to these people, Iqbal?" Ross asked.

"There's a judge," Mohammed Iqbal replied, "an Islamic judge, a mullah. He'll come here and question them. Inquiries will be made around their house in Jalalabad. If they're guilty, they will be punished."

"How?" Ross persisted.

Iqbal shrugged. "Of course it depends on their crimes. How much help have they given the Russians? How much spying have they done? Perhaps they'll be jailed for two or three years if it isn't serious. If it is, they'll die."

From out of the gloom straggled a long line of other prisoners, shuffling uncertainly into the light. They stood against the wall.

Mohammed Iqbal walked along, prodding this man, ignoring that, reciting names and offenses. "This is Zal Khan," he said, pointing at a frightened young man.

"How old is he?" Lyle asked.

"Eighteen," Iqbal said. "He's been here a month."

"What's he charged with?"

Iqbal asked the others, and the guards began to laugh. Even some prisoners giggled.

"It's not political," Mohammed Iqbal admitted at last. "He's been doing things not in accordance with the Islamic code." He cleared his throat. "He was found having sexual relations with another man."

"You don't say," Lyle said.

Iqbal moved down the line. Toward the end, he stopped and with a flip of his hand, ordered a prisoner to step forward.

"This," he said, "is Mada Khan. He was in the communist militia. The government gives money to them and rifles to kill the *mujahideen*. We captured him in the town of Bachir twenty-five days ago. He's very dangerous, but now his case has been completed."

"What does that mean?" Ross asked, feeling he knew the answer.

"It means," Iqbal said, "that we've got work for him this morning. You saw that unexploded bomb up the ravine?"

Ross nodded.

"Mada Khan's going to get out the explosive for us. Do you want to come and watch?"

Ross glanced uncertainly at Lyle. "What d'you think, Clive?"

Clive, conscious that Ross's blooding with Sophie Johnson could probably do with some reinforcement, said: "Sure, why not? Nothing else going on today."

Ross turned to Iqbal. "Does he know what's going to happen?"

A grin wavered on the Afghan's lips. "Not yet," he said. "I'll tell him now."

Mohammed Iqbal spoke briefly to the prisoner, who if he understood what was in store, gave no hint. Mada Khan couldn't have been older than twenty-three, and he held himself with dignity.

The others were hustled back into the darkness of the building, while Mada Khan was given a hacksaw. Then, with an armed escort of *mujahideen* and the two Americans taking up the rear, he followed the path to the rebel center, before veering off back to the ravine.

They walked for thirty minutes until, across the Agam River, they saw the partially buried gray metal of the bomb.

Iqbal, Ross, Lyle, and another armed rebel settled onto a rock commanding an unobstructed view, and watched two *mujahideen* escort Mada Khan across the river, wading sometimes thigh deep through the icy current.

When they got to the bomb, the *mujahideen* explained in detail what Mada Khan had to do. The distance was two

great for Ross to see if there was any change in the
prisoner's expression. He wondered briefly if Mada Khan
would try to run, particularly when the guards were in
midstream, returning to the safety of the southern bank.
But he realized it would be hopeless. The scramble up
hundreds of rocky feet to the top of the ravine made him
an easy target, and in hostile *mujahideen* territory, he had
no chance.

They watched him begin sawing at the metal casing a
few inches above the point where the bomb protruded from
the earth.

Ross became aware of Mohammed Iqbal's eyes on him.
"Perhaps you're wondering about the Geneva Convention,
David," Iqbal said. "Well, it doesn't apply in Afghani-
stan, either for us or for the Russians."

The sound of the river obliterated the scraping of the
hacksaw as it grooved and heated the metal around the
explosive. The *mujahideen* waited, relaxed and were only
academically interested in the grim drama being played out
less than 200 yards away. If the bomb did detonate—and it
seemed to the agents the chances were good—they'd be
safe from anything other than an unlucky shrapnel wound.

Iqbal went on, "But the thing about Afghanistan that
you should know if you want to understand us is that we're
not without mercy. In certain circumstances, Mada Khan,
as well as other traitors, and yes, even the Russians, could
call on any Afghan for help if they knew something about
our customs."

He tried to get Ross's attention, but the big American
only glanced briefly at him before his gaze was drawn
irresistibly back to Mada Khan's gamble with death.

"There's an unwritten code here called *pukhtunwali*,"
Iqbal explained. "Every Afghan man and woman is bound
by honor to respect and abide by it, or he'll disgrace
himself and his family."

Across the river, Mada Khan's right arm sawed rhythmically, while his left wrapped around the Soviet bomb to steady himself.

"Pukhtunwali," Iqbal continued, "requires every Afghan to defend his motherland, but it has another element as well, which is called *ninawati*. When I tell you about *ninawati*, you might think it's a contradictory code, because it means every Afghan must grant asylum to a fugitive, no matter who he is." Mohammed Iqbal leaned back on the rock, his Kalashnikov by his side, and he watched Mada Khan almost dreamily. "It's well described in an ancient legend," he said. "About a thousand years after the birth of Jesus, peace be upon him, the Sultan Mahmud of Ghazni, a feared ruler, went hunting. He saw in the distance a particularly handsome deer, and he spurred his horse after it. The Sultan fired an arrow, and hit the deer. Although wounded and losing blood, the animal took shelter in a *ghizhdi*—an Afghan tent—and the Sultan tried to run in after it. Inside the *ghizhdi* was a poor shepherd in tattered clothes who barred the Sultan's way and refused to let him take the deer. The Sultan was angry and threatened to kill the shepherd, but the man stood his ground. 'This animal,' he said, 'has taken refuge under my roof, and I must defend it, even against one as noble as you. You may take my best sheep instead if you wish, but you cannot harm the deer as long as it's in my tent.' "

Across the river, Mada Khan kept sawing at the casing. Ross felt that time had stopped, but he asked automatically, "What does all that mean, Iqbal?"

"It means, that if Mada Khan had sought refuge in the house of any Afghan, even the family of a man he'd just murdered, they'd have to defend him, with their own lives, if necessary. He had come *ninawati* to their house, and they'd have no option. It's the same for any Russian.

If only they knew it, they could go to any Afghan tent, or house and claim asylum. There is none who would refuse."

Now he had the attention of both Lyle and Ross.

"You're joking," Lyle said.

"That's the custom," Iqbal said. "It's been like that for centuries, and the Russian invasion doesn't change the codes of our nation. We've had many invaders, starting with Cyrus the Great of Persia and going through Alexander, Tamerlane, Babur, and the British. Do we have to throw over our way of life because of some infidels who will, *insha Allah*, be driven off as the others have been?"

"Don't the Russians know about *ninawati?*" Ross asked. "Mada Khan surely does since he's an Afghan."

"Ah yes, but we didn't give him the chance. We took him by surprise. And I doubt if the Russians are interested in discovering our customs. If they knew anything about us at all, they'd never have come here."

"I guess that's true," Ross said. "Most Western analysts say they didn't realize what they were letting themselves in for."

"Perhaps," Iqbal said. "But the Soviets work on long time spans. Ten years is nothing to them, or twenty, or thirty. They're not like the Americans. We look to you for help, but already your enthusiasm's draining away." He shrugged. "You've got other, newer wars, other interests. Other administrations."

The men stared thoughtfully at the solitary activity on the opposite bank. It was taking Mada Khan a long time to saw through the casing, although obviously he was going slowly, not allowing the friction to build up too much heat; praying, no doubt, that no spark would detonate the explosive.

"What's this big meeting today, Iqbal?" Lyle asked, but the Afghan seemed not to understand the question. Lyle explained, "Mahmud told us the *mujahideen* commanders from all over this area are coming to Torabora for a pow-wow.''

"Some are coming," Iqbal said, "that's true. There'll be a reunion, and a discussion of battles and Russians killed. But no more than that."

"So why's Mahmud staying around for it?" Lyle persisted.

"There's something else you should know about the Afghan people," Mohammed Iqbal said. "We believe in superstition and astrology. Even educated Afghans do to some degree, just as in the West. If a black cat crosses your path, isn't it considered bad luck? Do you walk under ladders? If you spill salt, don't you throw it over your left shoulder?"

"Well, I don't," Lyle said, "but a lot do."

"It's the same here," Iqbal replied, "and particularly with the uneducated. Mahmud's very religious, and he believes in signs. This morning, before dawn, he opened the Holy Koran and read the first line that came to his gaze. Then with a mullah he interpreted it, and it was decided that this wasn't an auspicious day for travel. It happens to coincide with the arrival of other leaders, so the matter was solved."

"I don't understand," Ross said, taking his eyes from the opposite bank for a moment. "Mahmud's not uneducated. Maybe he didn't go to Harvard, but he's an engineer."

Iqbal looked at Ross. "Engineer Mahmud is a *mujahideen* commander. Some say there are none braver than he. He's twenty-five, and he's been fighting for nearly four years." He paused. "'Engineer' is a courtesy title. He left Kabul University in his first semester to fight against the Russians."

"And his family?"

"They're farmers, simple peasants."

"Are you saying that every day we're going to depend

on the Koran to decide whether we move or not?'' Ross asked.

"No," Iqbal said, "I don't think it'll happen again, not once you're properly under way. From tomorrow, Mahmud will trust in Allah and not look for more signs."

"I'm glad to hear it."

On the far side of the Agam River, Mada Khan stopped and stood back, surveying his work. Ross thought it extraordinary that he'd got so far without being blown to pieces. He wondered what would happen if he actually succeeded in his task and retrieved the explosive for the *mujahideen*. Would they take pity on him? Or would they give him another bomb to saw into, and then another, until one day his luck ran out and he disintegrated in a shower of bloody fragments?

Mada Khan began working again. He had to be right up against the explosive, ready to break through with a heated blade: the most dangerous part of an insane operation.

Ross held his breath, his body tensed for the bang.

Then Mada Khan stopped again, inspected his work critically, and took the tail fins firmly in his hands. They watched him twist.

Incredibly, the fins moved.

He'd done it: sawed through the casing; and now he was easing it off.

The *mujahideen* murmured appreciatively among themselves. "That's good"; Mohammed Iqbal said."We'll probably use it for a land mine."

Inch by inch, the casing twisted and lifted. The metal was heavy and even from that distance, the men could see the prisoner straining under the weight. At last it came free, and the explosive was exposed. Mada Khan pulled and prised at the waxy substance, taking off chunks and stacking them into a sack by his side. It took perhaps another twenty minutes for this to be completed and, at times, the prisoner's arm disappeared inside the bomb casing, scooping out explosive actually around the faulty detonator.

Now that it was comparatively safe, two *mujahideen* slung their Kalashnikovs over their shoulders and headed for the river bank, wading across to bring Mada Khan back.

Ross felt the air expelling slowly from his lungs, but Lyle sat quiet, realizing instinctively that in this primitive society, where vindictiveness was more a part of daily life than the strange code of *ninuwati,* and where forgiveness was foreign to the nature of the people, the show was not over.

Mada Khan held the heavy bag of explosive over his head as he forded the icy river. They all went to join him and his armed escort, and the Americans could see the toll that had been taken. The prisoner's face was wet with strain and fear. The look in his eyes was different too, calmness gone, and only the remnants of dignity left. He seemed haunted and scared, in control of himself by the thinnest, most vulnerable thread of manhood.

But the *mujahideen* were in good spirits, talking and laughing, although none offered a word of praise for Mada Khan's success. They followed the path back toward the center.

Near the white mulberry tree, the sack of explosive was handed over to other rebels, who clustered around to inspect it with interest and no sign of apprehension. It could have been a commodity as innocent as sand.

Mada Khan stood a short distance away, watching with dread.

Suddenly Mohammed Iqbal snapped a command, and the *mujahideen* turned abruptly toward the prisoner. They motioned sharply with their Kalashnikovs for him to move on up the path.

"Come on," Lyle said. "We may as well see the second half."

They climbed the ravine, almost to the top, before moving through the rocks and bushes to the left. One *mujahed* led the way, with Mada Khan directly behind, and after him, the rest of the armed band and the Americans.

They could hear the prisoner murmuring softly, almost to himself: "Allah! Allah!"

They walked for almost an hour, around a hill, through a smaller gorge, to a place remote from the paths used by refugees and far from settlements.

There was nothing special about the spot they chose to kill Mada Khan. It was a piece of open ground, rocky, with a few wildflowers in yellow and mauve, and it commanded no majestic view. All one could say for it was that it was private and difficult to find.

The *mujahideen* cocked their Kalashnikovs and the slamming home of the bolts sounded both loud and final.

Mada Khan jabbered a plea to Mohammed Iqbal, and although the agents could not understand the reply, the contempt in Iqbal's tone was unmistakable.

There was no order to fire: nothing formal, or quasi-official, merely an explosion of noise lasting no more than two seconds, but ringing in the ears while it echoed through the mountains.

Mada Khan was knocked back, arms flung wide. He fell and lay bleeding on the earth. His fingers moved, trying to clutch the air.

Ross watched, curiously dispassionate now, a spectator rather than a participant.

The others turned to walk off, but he stayed, unable to leave.

It disturbed him first, then it outraged him, that Mada Khan was being left alive. He knew from the Fairfax lectures that it was difficult to kill a man quickly by gunfire. A single bullet could easily miss the heart and other vital organs, and even several bullets might leave a target able to crawl, maybe able to retaliate. Death could come slowly. The only sure way was the *coup de grâce*, the bullet in the brain. Yet these people were walking away, leaving Mada Khan in pain on the ground, with one of his legs pulled up and a hand moving slowly and instinctively across to a chest wound, perhaps to ease the hurt, or staunch the blood.

Ross stood rooted to the spot, staring at the dying man. The others were already several yards away, not bothering to look back, and Lyle was going with them.

"Mohammed Iqbal!" Ross shouted.

His voice echoed back at him.

He was aware of everyone stopping, then returning. Lyle reached Ross first, followed by Iqbal.

"This man's still alive," Ross said, his voice expressionless.

Iqbal shrugged, and Ross wanted to hit him. "He'll be dead soon," the Afghan said. "It's of no consequence."

Mada Khan half-turned onto his side, and they could see a trickle of blood coming from his mouth.

Ross thrust out his hand. "Give me a rifle!" he commanded.

He heard Lyle warn softly: "David, lay off."

But Iqbal rattled out a few words of Pashto, and Ross felt the metal against his hand. His fingers closed over it. He was familiar with the AK-47. It had been part of the Fairfax course, and he scarcely glanced down as he cocked it. His gaze was on the man in pain. He walked the few feet separating them and touched the muzzle to Mada Khan's temple. The man stared at him, mutely pleading.

The explosion echoed in the hills.

Ross stood back and watched, but there was no further movement. He turned, his face a mask, and threw the rifle to one of the rebels.

He could see Lyle wasn't pleased, but he didn't care. There were a lot of things he had to put up with in Afghanistan, a lot he could do nothing about, but in this one instance, he had the opportunity to show a modicum of mercy.

The group retraced the path to the Torabora center, with Ross something of a hero. As far as the *mujahideen* were concerned, his action hadn't been one of charity, but a demonstration of hatred for the Russians and their spies—as if their visitor couldn't resist the chance of putting his own bullet into the condemned man. They smiled and spoke to him in a tongue he didn't know, but with an approval which needed no translation. Only Iqbal seemed uncertain and slightly withdrawn.

Lyle fell into step with Ross. "Look, Dave," he said. "I know you did that for all the right humanitarian reasons, and if I didn't work for the DIA, I'd respect you for it. But let me ask you this: why are you in Afghanistan?"

Ross frowned. "What do you mean? You know why we're here."

"What's your cover story?"

"I'm a VOA correspondent."

"Is that so?" Lyle sounded surprised. "And I guess they teach VOA guys to handle an AK-47 the same time they show them what button to press on the tape recorder?" Then without raising his voice, he became angry. "Use your head! You're supposed to be here as a journalist, and a journalist is a noncombatant. He's a professional watcher, he's not a doer. He's a voyeur. He's a fucking leech! He's the eyes and ears of democracy, and if he doesn't like what he sees and hears, he's the guy who walks away and throws up in a corner. But he does not, repeat does not, pick up a rifle and finish off an execution."

They walked in silence for several minutes while Ross thought about that.

Clive was right, of course. He should have let Mada

Khan die in his own time and too bad if it hurt. But he'd reacted instinctively, and his instinct had been wrong. Wrong again.

"Sorry, Clive. That was stupid," Ross said at last.

"I guess it doesn't matter much," Lyle said. "It would in other circumstances, but not in this hopeless shithole. These guys wouldn't know journalistic ethics from a hole in the ground."

But Mohammed Iqbal, a former alumnus of Harvard, trod carefully through the hills, deep in thought. Shortly before they reached Torabora, he slowed down to wait for Ross and Lyle.

"I think you've just become a *mujahed*, David," Iqbal congratulated him. "Where did you learn to use a Kalash like that?"

"All rifles are pretty much the same," Ross said. "I used to go shooting with my dad."

"Oh, yes?"

Lyle, anxious to divert the course of the conversation, asked, "What'd Mada Khan say just before your men opened fire, Iqbal? Was he asking for mercy?"

Iqbal shook his head. "No. He wanted time to pray."

"Why did you refuse?"

"Of course I refused," Iqbal said. "By fighting against the *jihad*, he damned himself. That's why we took him far from the center. He died without the rites of Islam and, in our belief, his soul will be in torment for eternity."

They turned onto the path leading to the prison, behind whose walls others probably awaited a similar fate, and further down the slope, toward the buildings of Torabora itself.

It was mid-afternoon and late for lunch, but a cloth was spread out for them under the mulberry tree, and a plate of *nān* appeared, followed by a bowl of yoghurt and another of potatoes, swimming in a greasy, reddish gravy. And of course, there was green tea. Ross ate hungrily.

In the afternoon, the Americans walked down to the bank of the Agam River and sat idly on rocks, bathing their feet and watching the torrent.

If the rebel commanders from the districts around Torabora had arrived for their meeting, there was no sign the agents could detect. Occasionally in the distance, they heard an aircraft—a helicopter or a jet—but never close enough to see. On the opposite bank, a *mujahed* lay beneath a tree, a rifle near at hand.

At sunset, when the men returned to the center, most Afghans were at prayer, but afterward Mahmud brought a number of turbanned men to greet and embrace them— obviously the visiting commanders.

With darkness, everyone moved into one large room of the center. The Americans were given a charpoy a short distance from where the others hunkered down comfortably or lay on rugs. There was much talk and laughter, particularly as Ross's exploits were recounted, but little sign that this was anything other than a reunion.

After they had eaten, Mohammed Iqbal came over to the charpoy.

"You'll sleep in the clinic tonight," he told them. "It's up on the roof. There are two beds there, and you'll be more comfortable. Tomorrow at dawn, you leave for Badakhshan, and *insha Allah*, I'll be coming with you."

Ross, whose enthusiasm for Iqbal had diminished since the events of the day, said neutrally, "That sounds fine." But Lyle seemed pleased.

Iqbal led them up a mud staircase on the outside of the building, onto the flat roof, where a one-roomed clinic had been constructed. Like everything else, it was made of hard mud. In the lamplight, boxes of medicines—antibiotics, analgesics, vitamins—glowed dully.

"As you can see, the clinic's empty at the moment," he said.

"What sort of things do you treat here?" Lyle asked.

"Everything," Iqbal said. "We've got a doctor. He even performs operations."

"In this place?" Ross sounded stunned. It was as filthy as the rest.

"Sure," Iqbal said. "If someone's injured by a bomb, the doctor helps him. He sews people up, removes bullets. He's got local anesthetics, of course, but he can also give a general."

Iqbal set the lamp down on a rough table and leaned against the doorway, watching the agents spread their *sadrs* on the hard rope of the charpoys. "Actually," Iqbal went on, "the most difficult operation he performed here was only two days ago. A *mujahed* had been caught in a bomb blast, and had a chest wound. Bits of his lungs were coming out. You could see them."

"Where's he now?" Lyle asked. "Six feet under?"

"Now he's okay," Iqbal replied. "He's in a safe place, away from here."

"Good luck to him."

"There's a Persian proverb," Iqbal said. "Unless God does it, what can a doctor do?"

"Yeah, verily," Lyle murmured. "Well, goodnight. See you in the morning."

Mohammed Iqbal took the lantern, leaving the small clinic in darkness.

Ross and Lyle removed their Pathan hats, propped their packs behind their heads for pillows, their *sadrs* underneath and around them for what minimal extra warmth was needed.

Iqbal climbed down the steps to the ground.

Instead of entering the main building where the others were settling to sleep, he moved off toward the mulberry tree.

Another Afghan sat beneath it, an unmoving shadow.

He was one of the visitors who had arrived that afternoon from Jalalabad, four days' walk away: a place where a big Soviet base had been constructed, but where the streets after dark were no-man's-land; or if they were anyone's, then they were the *mujahideen*'s.

Iqbal squatted next to the visitor, talking quietly about inconsequential things, while his eyes flicked and watched the darkness.

He knew where the sentries were placed: he knew the closest spots a spy could lie without being noticed.

There was no one near.

Gul Hafiz waited patiently, answering Iqbal's formal inquiries and observations with courtesy, until at last Iqbal was ready. "There is a message you must take back," he murmured. "The Americans are leaving for Badakhshan tomorrow to look for evidence of poison gas. Their names are David Masefield and Clive Carmichael. They are supposed to be journalists for the Voice of America, but you must say that I saw one of these men handle a rifle, and he worked it like a soldier. Say I am going with them, and I will report again when we get to the Panjshir Valley. Do you understand?"

Gul Hafiz stroked his beard as if in thought. "I will tell them," he said. "Mr. Clive and Mr. David."

The men rose and walked without another word into the mud building to spread their *sadrs* on the hard floor. In the morning, Gul Hafiz would return to Jalalabad and Mohammed Iqbal would begin the long walk to Badakhshan.

Not all the Russian spies in the Afghan *jihad* had been accounted for and were burning in hell. Some were trusted *mujahideen* who had proved themselves publicly many times.

In the clinic on the roof, Ross and Lyle slept deep and dreamlessly.

16

It felt as if they'd walked forever in the ravine leading from the summit of the White Mountain, but the narrow mud cliff path led to a final crossing of the Agam River and suddenly they were out. The clear mountain water turned muddy and became sluggish.

The fields gave way to semi-desert. Cultivation ceased, and ahead lay steep sandy hills. The temperature rose steadily until it was well above 100 degrees. Ross had to drink. Every time he took a gulp from his bottle, he held the warm liquid in his mouth for as long as possible, but even as he did, his tongue craved more.

After an hour, they reached a stream. Ross's thirst was fierce, but he paused dismayed at the edge.

The water was unmistakably yellow, as if dyed by man (the Russians perhaps, poisoning the supply?), or else it had picked up trace minerals from the rocks and soil over which it passed. Whatever the reason, it looked terrible.

The Americans stared uncertainly at each other. Both their water bottles were empty.

"What do you think?" Lyle asked.

Ross looked again at the sluggish water, and then downstream at the *mujahideen*, who always had a thousand stories to tell about how the Soviets were poisoning and destroying, but who were drinking without qualm.

Ross shrugged and knelt by the edge.

Whatever the stream's color, the water tasted fine and, even better, it seemed they would have a longer stop here because the Afghans were undoing the cords of their baggy *salwar* trousers for the ritual ablutions before prayers.

Ross and Lyle took the opportunity of the break not only to relax on a rock, but to find the Lomatil tablets and swallow a couple each in an attempt to counteract, in advance, any aftereffects of drinking unpurified water.

Through the day, almost imperceptibly, the hills became greener.

At one stage, Mohammed Iqbal waited for the Americans to catch up before pointing out gouges in the earth and grass, the heavy track marks of Soviet tanks.

"There was a battle here," he said. "The Russians attacked in tanks and with helicopters. I guess some spy told them where the *mujahideen* would be." He looked blandly at them. "A lot of Russians died, maybe a hundred. They had to ferry them out in choppers."

Ross felt there was an unreality about this war, as though the battles were either long over or far away. If it hadn't been for the helicopters his sense of remoteness, of being in a totally unpeopled wilderness, would have been complete. They had seen no other people, not even a refugee, for hours, and they shaded themselves as best they could with their *sadrs* from a sun that heated the air to at least 115 degrees. Ross looked back at the fringes of the horizon, to the green of trees and grass rising up the frontier mountains, and at their summits, the snow. He sank into a reverie in which marching was automatic, and his senses, other than registering thirst, were dulled.

Lyle, although more experienced, was feeling the same,

and even the *mujahideen* had lost the edge of their concentration.

Two hundred yards ahead, a man's foot was suddenly blown off, and the agents hardly noticed. They were aware only of a cluster of *mujahideen* and thought the Afghans had found something interesting. They were in no particular hurry to find out what it was. It was only later, reconstructing the events, that they recalled hearing a puny sound; at that distance it was hardly more than a pop, and when the man fell, he made no noise, at least none that carried. It was as if he had stumbled.

When they reached the group, they pushed forward to see what the excitement was.

Mahmud knelt beside the *mujahed*, tying a cord around his calf to stanch the pumping blood. The injured man watched passively, apparently in no pain. His foot hung by tendons and a strip of flesh and skin.

Mahmud pulled out a dagger and cut, severing it decisively. The man gasped and cried out.

Ross and Lyle had both been trained in battlefield first aid, and there were things in their knapsacks to help the injured rebel and ease his pain which, at this moment, was dulled by adrenalin but which would soon have him in agony.

Ross took charge and ordered, "Clear these men away, Mahmud. We need room."

Mahmud gave the instructions and the other *mujahideen*, except for Mohammed Iqbal, moved out. It was a general assumption that all Westerners were qualified to cope with medical emergencies. Iqbal was the only Afghan in the group who knew better, and he was interested to see how professionally the Americans dealt with this crisis.

As he unbuckled his pack, Ross asked, "What caused it, Mahmud?"

The commander shrugged philosophically. "He stepped

on a mine. The Russians have dropped them all over the country. Some are like packs of cigarettes, or watches. Some are compasses. Others are children's toys, or birds.''

Around them the *mujahideen* were spreading out carefully to see if they could find any other booby traps.

Ross wet a strip of gauze to clean the edges of the wound. He smeared antibiotic cream over a pad and bound the stump, first with gauze, then elastic bandage. He was reaching into his pack for the sealed box of morphine when Lyle touched his shoulder.

"Let's talk," he said simply.

Ross frowned, not understanding what his comrade wanted, but Lyle was already walking away. When they were out of earshot of the others, Lyle asked, "You weren't going to give him morphine were you?"

"Yeah, of course," Ross replied.

"How much have you got?"

"Enough for a couple of days."

"Same with me. How long will it take that guy to get back to Torabora where they've got their own drugs?"

"Late tonight, if they push it," Ross said.

"So why waste our stuff on him?" Lyle asked.

"Shit, Clive, he's going to be screaming in about five minutes! I don't know why he isn't already."

"But we won't be around to hear it, will we? And he'll only have to hang on until tonight."

There was a long silence while Ross thought. Finally he said, "You can be a bastard, you know!"

"That has been mentioned before," Lyle agreed. "The point is this: between us we've four days' supply of morphine. Now let's suppose you step on one of these Russian surprises up in Badakhshan, or suppose I do. It's a long way home, and we're going to need every bit of help we can get."

Behind them, the *mujahed* was beginning to moan.

Ross turned abruptly and went back. He rummaged inside his pack for a bottle of painkillers and gave the man six, a hefty dose. "He needs to be taken to Torabora as quickly as possible," Ross told Mahmud. "Then he must go to Pakistan to a hospital."

Mahmud nodded. "We will get a donkey," he said. "There's a village an hour's walk away."

"That sounds fine." Ross looked squarely into the Afghan commander's eyes. "I've done all I can for him," he said, "so let's get moving. The sooner he reaches a hospital, the better."

Mahmud called an order and the *mujahideen* gathered around. He told one of them to stay with the injured man, while the others resumed their trek without a word to their maimed comrade, who was now unable to suppress his pain.

Ross found Iqbal falling into step beside him. "It's lucky we've got you along, David," the Afghan said. "That was a good battlefield dressing."

"That's not what a doctor'll say when he sees it," Ross said sourly.

"I was impressed. Where did you learn that stuff?"

"Weren't you ever a Boy Scout?" Ross asked, not wanting to continue the conversation. "They give badges for First Aid."

"The Boy Scouts weren't very big in Kabul," Iqbal said. "You're full of surprises, David. Were you in the army?"

"No, never."

"You should have been. You'd have fitted in well."

They walked on, towards poppy fields already harvested, and acres of wheat, ripe for cutting.

"I listen to the Voice of America a lot," Iqbal said, "but I've never heard you on it. Now if you were Fred

Brown, I'd know who you were. I guess Fred's a friend of yours?"

Ross grunted. "We've met."

"Have you done a lot for VOA?"

"Yeah," Ross said, "but deskwork and broadcasts for other regions. South America, Africa. This is our first tour in Asia."

"Your big break?" Iqbal chuckled, but when Ross looked at him he saw his eyes were watchful.

"It'll be a big break if we can prove the Russians are using poison gas," Ross said. "Otherwise it's going to be a pain in the ass."

"You don't like our country?" Ross could tell Iqbal was mocking, his voice pretending hurt.

"Sure, it's great. I'd like to see it in a little more comfort, I guess, without the Russians flying around looking for things to shoot up, and guys getting their feet blown off."

"Wouldn't we all?"

The sun was going down when they came to a village of high-walled houses set beside irrigation canals. The group headed into the gloomy, cool alleys and straight for the mosque, where Mahmud summoned the elders. Within minutes, donkeys were saddled and a party was on its way to pick up the injured *mujahed* and his companion.

When this had been done, the Afghans gathered for evening prayers, while Ross and Lyle sat on a low, white-painted wall, watching the ceremony and listening to the leisurely, timeless chants.

Children clustered talking and giggling around the Americans but scattered when the men had finished praying and came out into the courtyard. Some elders shouted angrily after them for making such noise.

Iqbal touched Ross's arm and led him and Lyle deep into the darkened alleys. Ahead, half in shadow, were male figures, watching suspiciously. Ross remembered Steve Cook's warning about being mistaken for a Soviet and tried to stay close to Iqbal, who was walking fast.

Around one corner, there was a group of men, almost blocking the way. Iqbal threaded his way through easily and disappeared, but Ross and Lyle were forced to slow down, and suddenly found their path being blocked. They tensed, ready to fight.

Out of the gloom, a man asked one word: *"Russe?"* They could hear the threat in his voice.

Ross replied, emphatic and loud: "No! *Russe murdabad!"* He pointed to himself and Lyle. "Americans! *Americano!"*

Iqbal, who finally realized the two were no longer with him, came back looking for them. He appeared on the outskirts of the shadowy, belligerent mob like a relieving force of cavalry and spoke to them in Pashto. The change from implacable hostility to relaxed laughter was instantaneous.

"Come on, it's not much farther," Iqbal urged.

He brought them finally into a high-walled courtyard. At one side, cows grazed placidly in troughs. Charpoys were placed in a line at the other.

Ross and Lyle were given their own beds, with mattresses for extra comfort, if one ignored lice and bedbugs; and they lay on their sides, relaxed and watching.

In the failing light and the inadequate glow of a solitary lantern, it seemed they had been taken to a film set, which gradually filled with wondrous characters. The colors were muted, dulled by the light. In front of the cows, turbanned heads, bearded, ancient, weathered faces, were reflected in the glow of the single lamp. An Afghan with one good eye, the other opaque, watched the Americans unblinkingly, as an anthropologist might study a rare species. Bandoliers of bullets glinted.

Had anything changed here, apart from the weaponry, in a hundred years, or five hundred?

Above, the deep blue sky faded into black and stars appeared.

A small boy brought water, pouring it from a teapot into a decorated tin beaker, and offering it to the agents in turn. They drank, and found it cold and refreshing, although a few minutes later, Lyle produced another dose of Lomatil.

The food at dinner was much the same as they'd been offered on the way down the mountains, except this time it included a dish of plain yoghurt, which both men agreed was the best they'd ever tasted.

It finally slaked Ross's thirst, and that night he slept as well as he ever had.

While the Americans were heading north toward the town of Sarobi—a route that skirted the capital, Kabul, and allowed them to swing northwest toward the Panjshir Valley—those *mujahideen* commanders who had attended the Torabora reunion were returning with their men to their own sectors.

One of these units, among whose members was Gul Hafiz, walked northeast from the Agam River gorge, through the same bleak semi-desert, toward the city of Jalalabad.

Every settlement they passed, however poor, offered shelter and the best food it had. Many villages, however, were deserted: the fields overgrown with weeds, the people gone to refugee camps in Pakistan. The *mujahideen* passed by without comment. There were still fruit trees to provide nourishment, although the closer Gul Hafiz's column got to Jalalabad, the fewer mulberries were available. The season for them had almost finished in that area, and the grapes, which hung, swelling slowly, were too hard to eat.

Gul Hafiz was in his late forties, older than most of the other *mujahideen*. He was devout, praying five times daily, and keeping every religious ceremony observed by the

majority Sunni Moslems of Afghanistan, particularly the
fast during the month of Ramadan, even though there were
religious dispensations permitting those who had to travel
to eat between sunrise and sunset. A few *mujahideen* took
advantage of the dispensation, but never Gul Hafiz. He
was, after all, a Hadji, one of those fortunate and wealthy
enough to have made the pilgrimage to Mecca, and he
showed this in the traditional way by dying his beard with
henna, turning it orange. There were other Islamic customs
about which Gul Hafiz was known to be strict, including
almsgiving and *zakat*, the donation of two and a half
percent of net income to the poor. Since leaving his business as a merchant in Kabul and joining the *jihad*, the
amount at his disposal was very small, but he gave what
he could.

The public image of Gul Hafiz was irreproachable.

Privately, he was wealthier than ever. His capital, sup-
plemented by the Russians in gold coins or ornaments, was
hidden against some future, more propitious time.

Gul Hafiz was part of a small informer network, which
included Mohammed Iqbal, from whom he was now relay-
ing a message. The other members were Saiful Jamal, who
ran a tea house in Jalalabad, and a friendly, courteous
Russian he knew as Sharaf and had met only once at a
nervous midnight rendezvous inside the heavily guarded
Soviet camp on the outskirts of the city.

Sharaf was himself a Moslem, born in Tadzhikistan, and
he made it clear to Gul Hafiz that upholding the faith in
Afghanistan was a top Soviet priority. That settled, they
spoke about money.

Now Gul Hafiz was living out his dual life, without the
mujahideen being at all suspicious, and with his private
wealth increasing satisfactorily.

If a traitor or a Russian spy was captured—and usually
they were simple people who had foolishly joined one of

the communist parties or the militia—Gul Hafiz was happy to take part in the executions or the tortures; and when it came to an attack or an ambush against the Soviets, he fought as hard as any true *mujahed*. As Sharaf had pointed out, there was no other possible course of action if he was to remain above suspicion. However, Saiful Jamal occasionally tipped him off about an impending Soviet action that could put him in special danger, so providing him with the opportunity of falling ill, volunteering for other duty, or making certain he was out of harm's way.

Every month, gold coins, rings, and ornaments were weighed carefully on scales by Saiful Jamal—the amount depending on the information provided, but agreed on after considerable haggling. Gul Hafiz hid them in a place known to none but himself.

If the Russians eventually won, he would be rich and well-placed in the new administration. Yet if the *mujahideen* drove the Soviets out, he could return to his business as a merchant and prosper as an admired, notable fighter in the *jihad*.

Gul Hafiz's journey to Jalalabad took him through the semi-desert until, nearer the city, the land became flatter and easier to walk. For a few miles, the *mujahideen* even followed a dirt road, the first they had come across, but it soon became a track, and then disappeared completely.

Farther on, Gul Hafiz and his group climbed the sides of a ravine and passed the burned-out shell of a school—buildings destroyed by the rebels themselves after they had been occupied by the Afghan communists in an attempt to control the villages below.

Even this close to Jalalabad, the rebels made no effort to conceal themselves or their weapons. Most had bayonets fixed to their Kalashnikovs, more for reasons of manhood than for likely use.

At one village, they learned that another band of

mujahideen had left a day earlier to sabotage the Jalalabad electricity supply—blow up pylons to plunge the city into blackness, and then harass the Russians and the Afghan engineers who tried to repair it. On a good day, the *mujahideen* could kill two or three repairmen and perhaps disable a tank.

And Jalalabad without electricity was *mujahideen* territory, even though the Soviet and Afghan armies were equipped with infrared sights enabling them to see in the dark.

A few hours later, the group came within sight of the city, and the Jalalabad–Kabul highway, the "black road," so-called because of its macadam surface. In the distance, they could hear firing, the staccato bursts of automatic rifle fire, and the booming reply of Soviet artillery.

They waded waist-deep through the river, just within sight of the ten-span bridge on which, as usual, two Soviet tanks were stationed, and made their way to the village of Chaharbagh Safar, on the outskirts of the city.

High overhead, a two-engined Russian transport plane spiraled sharply down toward the guarded airfield, not daring to risk a low, normal approach.

The voice of the muezzin called the faithful to prayer at the mosque as the sun set, and Gul Hafiz joined the men. The mosque was brick-built, with onion domes, but because of the extreme heat prayers were said in the open courtyard.

Night came, and the *mujahideen* dispersed to the homes of friends or to their families. A few returned across the river to a rebel encampment that was nothing more than a collection of charpoys under the trees.

Gul Hafiz walked alone, occasionally stopping to greet and talk to a friend but, as night closed in, setting a fast pace along a dirt road toward Jalalabad.

After a mile he was in a street, turning into another,

alone in an apparently deserted city. In the distance, dogs barked furiously as if sensing his approach.

He stopped at a door, knocked cautiously, and waited, pressing his body against the wood, keeping his silhouette hard against the edge of the building in case someone should see him.

He knocked again, this time more insistent.

From inside he could hear shuffling and a voice calling cautiously, ''Who is it?''

''Gul Hafiz.''

After a second there was the scraping of several bolts— Saiful Jamal was not a man to take chances—and the briefest glow of a lamp lit the street while he slipped inside.

The bolts scraped shut, and Saiful Jamal rose to stare at his visitor. His face wreathed into a smile. He held out his arms and the men embraced, shaking hands, kissing faces and beards.

Saiful Jamal lifted the lantern and led Gul Hafiz up wooden stairs to the room where rugs and cushions were scattered. A small charcoal fire burned on a metal plate in the center, and on it was a pot of tea.

''You are well, my brother?'' Saiful Jamal asked.

''Thank you.''

''That is good. May you live long.''

''And you, my brother.''

Saiful Jamal poured cups for them both, a strong brew, already mixed with milk and sugar. They drank, exchanging courtesies and small talk.

Toward the end of an hour, they were ready to get to business. Gul Hafiz recounted the details of the *mujahideen* meeting at Torabora and the strange *farangis* from America who were going to Badakhshan to look for evidence of poison gas. Their names, he said, were Mr. David and Mr. Clive, supposedly reporters for the Voice of America, although Mohammed Iqbal did not believe their story. Mr. David had used a rifle to finish off a man shot for spying, and there had been much talk of this among the *mujahideen*. The *farangi* handled a Kalashnikov as if he was a soldier himself. And Allah knew, there were *farangis* who could not tell a Kalashnikov from a Lee-Enfield. Saiful Jamal nodded agreement.

"Mohammed Iqbal, may his place remain green forever, said he would walk with these Americans and make another report when they reached the Panjshir," Gul Hafiz concluded.

"And that is all?" Saiful Jamal inquired delicately.

"That is all," Gus Hafiz confirmed.

The matter of payment took a further twenty minutes' discussion and inspection of the gold, followed by extremely accurate weighing, and when another cup of thick-tasting tea had been enjoyed, Saiful Jamal let his guest out the front door, and closed it quickly, sliding home the bolts.

Then he used a rear exit, just as heavily bolted, into an alleyway. The night was filled with gunfire as *mujahideen* attacked some police station, or perhaps ambushed a Soviet vehicle, and their war cries—*"Allah akbar!"*—floated through the air while the city dogs went insane with barking.

It was difficult to hear if anyone was approaching, but Saiful Jamal saw no one in the black streets which led to the edge of the Soviet camp.

He squatted in pitch darkness beside his customary tree and waited a few moments. Then, taking a box of matches from his pocket, he struck one, and held it steady in front of him until it had burned almost to the end and he could feel the heat on his fingertips. He lit a second match and did the same.

He waited. Sometimes the Soviet sentries did not notice

the first signal, and it was necessary to repeat it three or four times.

But now, he saw a match flare two hundred yards away.

He rose and began moving toward the spot.

This was the worst moment: this lonely stretch of no-man's-land. What if the *mujahideen* had learned of the rendezvous secrets and had killed the Russians? What if the dark figures about to surround him were Afghan?

The grass bent under his tread, crackling dryly.

He reached the trees and bushes, became aware of the silhouettes. Hands grabbed him from behind, swung him around so someone could shine a flashlight in his face. He blinked in the glare.

"Sharaf," Saiful Jamal said passively. That was the password.

One of the Russians grunted. Then he was pushed forward toward the camp. He threw his *sadr* over his head, covering his face so only his eyes could be seen—a precaution against recognition. Who knew where the *mujahideen* had their own spies?

The Russians exchanged other passwords with guards on the gate and Saiful Jamal was permitted through into a suddenly ordered, seemingly secure Soviet world: an island, isolated in a hostile sea. Beside him, boots crunched over gravel on the pathways. Saiful Jamal was conscious of how quietly he walked in comparison.

In the distance rifle fire cracked, and they could hear dull explosions. The dogs of Jalalabad barked and howled in useless frenzy. Above, a slow, dreamy firework display of tracer rounds continued, while to the west, magnesium parachute flares fiercely illuminated an area.

He was taken into a building and left alone. He knew that at least one armed Soviet soldier would be on guard by the closed door, and that there was nothing in the interior of the slightest interest.

The room was sparse. Thick curtains covered the window. There were three plain wooden upright chairs and a table without drawers. The only light was a bulb, covered with a cheap shade. It hung from the ceiling, pulsing rhythmically with the current from the camp generator.

Saiful Jamal stood patiently. There were still many hours before dawn.

Outside the door, he heard a noise and he cleared his throat. Sharaf never kept him waiting long.

17

The journey of a courier message from the Russian base at Jalalabad to Moscow can take less than eighteen hours if all goes well. It seldom does.

Sharaf, being a conscientious worker and a Moslem—so therefore feeling constantly on trial—completed his dispatch on Saiful Jamal in time for the first morning flight to Kabul.

Later, as he was laboring over mundane documentation, he paused to watch the Antonov at the end of the runway, engines roaring until he could almost see the plane bucking with the strain. The Antonov was off the ground quickly, and a hundred feet up it banked, climbing in a spiral directly over the airfield until it was beyond the reach of *mujahideen* fire. Then it set a course for the Afghan capital.

Sharaf's message was delivered to the KGB headquarters in Kabul and duly signed for. It was placed in a tray on the desk of a young major whose hatred for Afghanistan and its people bordered on the pathological. Later, other dispatches were recieved, signed for, and piled on top of Sharaf's contribution.

That morning, it was the major's turn on the roster to

represent the KGB at the funerals of Russian soldiers. In the early years, the Soviet dead were loaded into coffins and flown home for burial. But the losses had increased to a point where this was not practical, and a special cemetery had been demarcated on the outskirts of the city.

The major knew none of those killed, and few of the details, beyond the fact that they had been ambushed in the Salang Pass, north of the capital, and some had been mutilated. Whether this was done before or after death, no one said, and the major did not ask.

He stood in the graveyard, erect and stern in the heat, perspiration dribbling down his face, and waited for the ceremony to end.

When he returned to his office, the pile of papers in his in-tray had risen to the point where it looked about to teeter and scatter over the thinly carpeted floor.

The major did not read Sharaf's message that day, because he didn't reach it; nor indeed the next, owing to a clerical error that resulted in the incoming batch being placed on top of, rather than underneath, the previous day's documents.

It was only on the third day that he learned about Mr. David and Mr. Clive, and he read Sharaf's report three times, biting his lip in frustration. The illegal presence of foreign journalists in Afghanistan was routine, and no executive action was usually taken on it. But this time there was the warning that at least one of the men might be military and therefore perhaps worthy of capture to show the world just how deeply involved Washington was with the so-called spontaneous rebellion.

Secondly, they were heading for Badakhshan.

The major knew something had happened in Badakhshan—not the details, because Sickle was restricted to a limited number of people. But there'd been an operation that hadn't involved troops. Indeed, hundreds of men had suddenly been cleared out of a nearby area. After that, there was an information blackout.

With this evidence, the major deduced that Chemical Warfare agents had been used against the rebels, and he trusted they'd died in agony. But certainly the Americans had to be kept away from the area.

Then his eyes fell on the date of the Jalalabad report and his heart became heavy. How could this have been on his desk for two complete days without him seeing it? How he hated Afghanistan!

He immediately drafted a memorandum to the Colonel, implying that the Sharaf report had only just reached him, and concentrating on the possible implications.

The Colonel knew about Operation Sickle, and what he read from Sharaf and the Major displeased him greatly. He made a quick calculation. If the Americans had left Torabora seven days earlier, they would be at, or past, the town of Sarobi. From there to Charikar, near the mouth of the Salang Pass, was probably another week; and it would be outside Charikar that Mohammed Iqbal would make his next report.

The Colonel drafted an urgent message to Moscow.

It was this, air-couriered to the Soviet capital, that finally brought the three most important men in the KGB's First Chief Directorate—the section responsible for foreign operations—together in the large conference room.

The time elapsed since Ross and Lyle had left Torabora was nine days.

The portrait of Feliks Dzerzhinsky gazed with fixed reproach on those seated at the rectangular table.

At the top, Igor Vladimirovich Gorsky sat ramrod straight, his bright blue eyes alert despite his advancing years. He was aware that others had their sights on his position as head of the First Chief Directorate, but he did not intend stepping down for some years. And he need not, providing things went well—better than they had recently, at least. Gorsky was in a determined mood.

On his right, Anatoli Dmitrevich Sanko, who ran Department V, and whose agents had failed to kill either Lyle or Ross, was deep in thought. It was impossible to tell whether he was concerned for himself or not. With his family connections, probably not. There would have to be a putsch in the Politburo before his position was threatened.

On Gorsky's left, Yuri Andreyevich Zhikin's fingers were trembling as he lit a second cigarette. The first, only half smoked, had been stubbed repeatedly into an ashtray, but was still smoldering. His thoughts were filled with the recent occasions on which he had publicly expressed himself, at this very table, in favor of foreign operations that then failed miserably.

It was different with the others. Even when they were wrong, they were not alone. But Zhikin, of the Dezinformatsiya Department, had no powerful patrons in the Politburo or the Central Committee. Merely a lot of KGB officers who owed him favors and moral obligations: those easiest things of all to overlook when a man's stature is crumbling in official eyes.

Zhikin's rank as Colonel had been hard-won through consistent success in campaigns in the West. He could cite long lists of clandestine operations that had influenced the decisions of Western governments in a way favorable to the Soviet Union. At the pinnacle of these stood the UN talks on banning neutron weapons. And it was this pinnacle, teetering atop his whole career pyramid, that seemed to be on the point of collapse.

Here he was in the conference room, with Dzerzhinsky's eyes glaring from the portrait, about to make decisions that, if wrong, would obliterate every previous success. Zhikin felt his nerve cracking.

He knew with sick certainty that no matter which of the three suggested the final course of action at this meeting, his own predicament would remain the same. And even the fact that the Politburo itself would then have to approve the decision didn't help either.

If the time came to apportion blame, it would fall on the weakest person in the room: himself.

Zhikin knew how vindictive the KGB could be when it turned on its own, seeking a scapegoat, and his record of achievements over the years were mere pieces of paper, easily destroyed.

What mattered was now: this room, this moment. He inhaled lungfuls of smoke and wished General Gorsky would begin. Zhikin was always worst at waiting.

At last Gorsky said, "We've all seen the reports from Afghanistan?" The silence was consent. "We all know the details of Operation Sickle?"

Zhikin's cigarette ash narrowly missed the tray. "Yes, comrade General," he said. Then defiantly, in a sudden switch of mood, "May I say that I think I ought to have been consulted about this operation? To drop a neutron bomb at the very time the SALT talks are progressing, without even preparing other options, was foolhardy, at the very least."

"Nevertheless, it is done, comrade," Sanko replied dryly. "Our task now is to minimize the dangers."

Gorsky added, in an angry lecturing tone, "There are many things, comrade Zhikin, of which you are unaware, particularly about Afghanistan. At that time, there were reasons for Sickle. And surely, it couldn't have come as such a surprise to you? You knew Rabinovich was aware neutron shells and missiles were being prepared for use. That was, after all, the purpose of his defection. He was going to tell the Americans."

"There is, comrade General," Zhikin replied stiffly, "a

world of difference between a decision in principle and one in practice. Had I been aware of Operation Sickle, I should have argued strongly against it; and if I was over-ruled for military reasons, I would have prepared a number of defensive positions."

"Your objections are noted, comrade Zhikin," Sanko said. "Now perhaps we can get on."

Zhikin sighed and stubbed out his second cigarette. "What do we know about these Americans, David and Clive?" he asked. "Where do we estimate they've got to?"

Sanko unrolled a map of Afghanistan. "If they're fit men they should have passed Sarobi, here"—he pointed with a stubby forefinger—"two or three days ago. So we can expect them around the town of Charikar, here, in another two or three days. We have a man at Charikar ready to make contact with the Afghan who is traveling with them. Perhaps we'll find out more then."

"Mr. David and Mr. Clive. Are they Ross and Lyle?" Gorsky asked. "That surely is the crucial question."

"It's possible," Zhikin said. "But it might be coincidence."

"Well, what measures have been taken to discover their identities?" Gorsky demanded.

"Inquiries are being made with the Voice of America in Washington," Sanko replied. "We have someone there. It should be possible to find out if any of their people are in Afghanistan. Until we have surnames, we can't do more than that. Surveillance has also been ordered on the apartments of Lyle and Ross in Washington, but so far we have nothing." Sanko stared throughtfully at the ceiling for a moment, and then he said: "But as far as I'm concerned, it makes no difference whether these men are DIA agents or reporters."

Zhikin lit another cigarette. His hand had become steadier. "Why?" he asked bluntly.

"Because," Sanko explained, "once they get to the area of the blast, they'll be able to prove we detonated a neutron bomb. They need only take back samples of rock. Any scientific investigation will show what happened. Leaves and twigs from the surrounding trees will give further proof. By now, the vegetation will have withered and died. Western scientists will be able to say why." Sanko shrugged. "In any case, other neutron devices will be necessary in the future. You've read the intelligence reports, Yuri. You know how important it is for us to secure the road to Kabul."

"There will be more neutron explosions in Afghanistan?" Zhikin asked, hardly able to believe his ears.

"If necessary for security," Sanko said. "The whole area has to be cleared of bandits." He gave one of his rare smiles. "As we have said in the past, the one thing this bomb does do efficiently is kill people. Invisible death, almost. That's why we prefer it to chemical weapons, and it's more suitable to the terrain in the area."

"Invisible, yes—until the Americans find the evidence," Zhikin pointed out. "If they do, the negotiations will end, and the larger point, the reason we wanted the neutron ban in the first place, will have been lost because of this stupid, useless country to our south!" Zhikin's vehemence surprised the others. It was almost as rare as one of Sanko's smiles, and it underlined the high stakes he was playing for, both personally and internationally.

Gorsky stared at him with barely suppressed indignation. "Perhaps I should recapitulate our position," he said coldly. "We dropped the neutron bomb in Badakhshan for good military reasons and because we thought it was sufficiently remote to be safe for us. We intend dropping others in the same area for the same reasons although I take it this plan would be abandoned or postponed if thought wise to do so?''

Gorsky looked at Sanko for confirmation, and received a nod.

''Second,'' he said, ''we have two Americans on their way to Badakhshan. They could be Lyle and Ross causing trouble again, but they might be who they claim: reporters for the capitalist radio. But whoever they are, if they reach their destination and know what to look for, they can easily find evidence to prove what we've done. So they must be killed. They cannot be permitted to endanger the talks.''

Again he looked to Sanko for approval, and again there was an almost imperceptible movement of the balding head.

''And third, we're left with the problem of our road communications to Kabul. We will shortly be invited by the Afghan government to send further troops, and I'm able to say we will look favorably on this invitation. So we must do something about Badakhshan and particularly the Salang Pass. The question is, what?''

The men sat around the table, toying silently with different possibilities.

''If we've got an agent with them, why don't we order him to kill them himself?'' Gorsky asked.

''Who can trust an Afghan?'' Zhikin replied morosely.

Sanko nodded agreement.

''Well, couldn't he lure them into an ambush, and let us do the job?'' Gorsky suggested, annoyed.

''We've tried ambushing Lyle and Ross before,'' Sanko said with a flicker of self-deprecating humor. ''It's not easy. But in this case, how do we get our men into position? It's Afghanistan, General. And even if we did, what if they killed only one of the Americans? The other could still finish the job.''

The silence extended for several minutes. This time there had to be a guarantee the men would die. And who could promise that? Certainly Sanko, who headed the *mokrie dela* section where this sort of problem was routinely decided, was not doing anything except stare fixedly at the wall.

Zhikin sighed audibly, reminding himself: Whoever's plan it is, they're going to blame me if it goes wrong. So it might as well be my plan.

"Comrades," Zhikin began, "let me tell you some things about Afghanistan." He looked at them with the ghost of a smile. "I'm not trying to lecture you on the military situation, or the geography, but about the people themselves. I ask you to excuse this explanation, but what I say will have a bearing on what I later suggest.

"As we all know, the Afghan bandits, although misguided and paid by the Americans, are brave fighters. They face death without flinching. This has been so for hundreds of years. Yet in their culture, there are contradictions, fears of the unknown, superstitions. Among uneducated people—and here we are talking also about the bandits—there is great concern about what they call "the evil eye." When a baby is born, for example, it will not be left alone in a room for many weeks, or taken out of the house at night. If it's brought out during the day, a veil is put over its face for fear of the evil eye. Sometimes boys are given girls' names for the first forty days to conceal their sex from malevolent spirits.

"In Afghanistan, they call these supernatural beings jinns, shishak, and other things. It's believed they haunt graveyards, river banks, ruined houses. These spirits are much dreaded."

Gorsky and Sanko listened with attention. It hadn't occurred to them Zhikin would know so much about the minutiae of Afghan life. Sanko particularly was intrigued to hear how it could relate to a plan whose ramifications extended to saving the UN negotiations. Zhikin had his faults, but wasting time wasn't one of them.

However, Zhikin blew a cloud of smoke at the ceiling, and seemed to change the subject. "We have our own agent with the Americans. For simplicity's sake, let's assume they're Ross and Lyle. As we agree, it doesn't matter whether they are or not: we can't take the chance. Our agent," he consulted his sheets of paper, "Mohammed Iqbal, will make contact in two or three days near the town of Charikar.

"Now this is my suggestion. We give him a radio transmitter, small enough for him to conceal, that will let us track the Americans through the Panjshir Valley." Zhikin studied the map on the table for a few seconds, and then he pointed. "Here is Ruka," he said. "From the reports I have now been shown, I see we've suffered at the hands of bandits who live or are supplied from there. The town is in the hands of the enemy. So we wait until Ross and Lyle reach Ruka, and at an appropriate moment, we attack."

"How?" General Gorsky inquired sarcastically. "Don't you know how difficult it is to fight our way into the Panjshir, how many lives it takes, how many days?"

Zhikin gazed from one to the other. "We don't invade," he said simply. "You want another neutron bomb? Then have one. Drop it right there. Kill Ross and Lyle with radiation, unless they're near ground zero, in which case they'll be incinerated."

Zhikin saw Gorsky glance quickly at Sanko for his reaction, but as usual there was nothing to be read on the man's lined face.

So Gorsky said with forced joviality, "This is a surprising solution from you, Andreyevich." He had intended the patronymic to be playful, but it came out patronizing, as if the head of the First Chief Directorate thought the plan a bad one. "A few minutes ago, the idea of neutron explosions did not please you at all."

Zhikin, his courage totally in his hands now, faced the General. "I should certainly have opposed the dropping of the first bomb . . ."

"It was an artillery shell," Gorsky said irrelevantly. "The Scimitar project."

" . . . Whatever it was, I would have been against it." Zhikin caught Sanko's eye. "But that, we are agreed, is history, and there's no point wishing things were different. I am asked—we are asked—to consider what happens now. It comes down to this simple point: Ross and Lyle are about to tell the world what we did, and therefore they must be eliminated. The neutron weapon is the most efficient way of doing this."

Sanko, who had been staring strangely at the chief of the Disinformation Department, at his nicotine-stained fingers, his not quite clean nails, hair that certainly required washing, and probably several other things, too, suddenly asked, "But why were you telling us earlier about the jinns, Yuri?"

His use of Zhikin's first name made Gorsky wonder uncomfortably if his initial reaction ought to have been more positive.

Zhikin explained. "After the second explosion, we instruct our agents in Afghanistan to spread the rumor that Badakhshan and the Panjshir have become the homes of evil spirits, and it's unsafe for anyone to remain there, even *mujahideen*. They must continue the fight elsewhere."

Gorsky couldn't help himself. This time, he looked frankly incredulous.

But Sanko was still taking Zhikin seriously. "Why will they believe that?" he asked with interest.

"Because the rumors will say that those who inhabit these evil places will become possessed, and their children after them." Zhikin scratched the side of his head and smiled wryly. "And of course in a way that's true. People caught in a wide area around the blasts will go on dying for years. But don't forget the most important aspect of all. Fast neutron radiation alters the reproductive cycle."

Sanko thought for a second, taking this in. "How very perceptive you are, Yuri. If I remember correctly, every man within a two kilometer radius of the explosion will suffer gonad damage. At least within a two kilometer radius, it could be much wider. Those who get a low enough dosage to survive for several years will nevertheless find they are impotent. Others may be able to father children, but the genetic structure of their sperm will have changed." Sanko looked at Zhikin as the implication unfolded, and their eyes held. "The babies will be deformed. Pregnant women, perhaps they will abort. But perhaps they will produce monsters. Whichever way we look at it, if we explode neutron warheads around the Panjshir and Badakhshan, we could have the whole area cleared in nine months to a year, just by the cycle of birth and death." There was an edge to his voice, almost of wonderment, and it made Zhikin nervous again.

"With respect, comrade Sanko," he said, "I wasn't suggesting saturating the area with neutron bombs. We've had one in Badakhshan, and I think one other should be detonated near the mouth of the Panjshir. That will take care of Ross and Lyle. After that, let rumors and monster babies and impotent husbands—and their wives—spread the story. It would be a madman who took any foreigner there after that. Anyway, with the area cleared, it ought to be easier for us to set up observation posts and keep a check on infiltration.

"I also think," Zhikin added, "that we should speed up the progress of the disarmament talks and get the ban on neutron weapons signed quickly. Of course, if for some reason we are found out later, we can explain that the weapons were used before the signing of the treaty. They were therefore permissible at that time, and the unfortunate side effects make it even more desirable that they should never be used again.''

Sanko nodded slowly. ''Well, comrade General?'' he asked. ''What do you think of our friend's plan?''

Gorsky, taking his cue, replied heartily, ''It's a master stroke! I congratulate you, Yuri. Naturally, I must put it to the Politburo for their approval. This will be done today. But I'm sure they will applaud the plan, as I do. Unreservedly.''

''And so do I,'' Sanko said, offering another of his rare smiles.

Zhikin felt a warm charge of pleasure. If it worked, his position in the KGB power structure would improve immeasurably.

Of course, if it didn't . . .

But Zhikin shrugged off the idea.

Who can escape the effects of a neutron bomb? Not men behind the armor of tanks. Not those living in houses or hiding in bomb shelters.

Not David Ross. Not Clive Lyle.

18

The men's feet had blistered, as they'd been warned they would, no matter how well broken in their boots were. Ross and Lyle eventually lanced the worst blisters, rubbed them with antibiotic cream and put bandages over the mess, which was painful but better than walking on swelling reservoirs of body fluid trapped between skin and flesh.

The war remained far away.

Every midday, and each night, their column stopped at some house, some village, and was made welcome. The best of whatever the people had to eat was theirs, and it was almost unvarying. *Nān*, of course; potatoes in some oily gravy; pilau—spiced rice—and very occasionally a tough, gristly piece of meat. The agents bought chickens when they could and swallowed the vitamin tablets Tom Glenn had provided.

One notable evening in an otherwise monotonous, physically taxing existence, they reached a landmark: Sarobi, and an encampment about a mile from the town where, in honor of Mahmud, a sheep was slaughtered. They ate it roasted, with dishes of eggplant mixed with yoghurt and pilau. Neither man could remember anything from any restaurant in the States or Europe to compare with this magnificent gastronomic experience. It was a feeling of pleasure almost more basic than sex.

The next morning, they turned northwest for Charikar.

Given the fact that they were being mauled by mosquitoes and bugs in the night, dehydrated by searing temperatures during the day, and losing weight, they were still in fair physical shape. Their bodies were leaner, but they were harder too, and with the blisters healing, they found it easier to keep the fast pace set by Mahmud.

In spite of the danger of mines, they set off in the predawn blackness, stopping for prayers at sunrise and at four other times during the day. Often they walked until ten at night when, stiff and exhausted, they'd reach a collection of charpoys under trees that, in the day time, provided shade and camouflage.

The agents got no more than five hours rest before the cycle began again. Mahmud was keeping his promise to get them to Badakhshan as fast as he could, and they took pride in the fact that they'd never once caused the column to slow or come to an unscheduled halt.

Mohammed Iqbal spent increasing amounts of time with them during rest periods, asking about the Voice of America, and who they knew there. He tried particularly to get close to Ross, talking about rifles, wanting to know where he'd gone hunting in the States, and details of his career.

There was something about the Harvard-educated Afghan neither of the agents liked, but he was one of their few linguistic lifelines, and they would need both him and Mahmud when they got to Badakhshan—a goal that was finally in sight. When they were on their way back, with Yardley's slowly dying men and women, they'd be in a stronger position to tell Iqbal to shove off.

Meanwhile Ross tried to be as friendly as the basic courtesies demanded. When he had to, he made up stories about himself and the VOA, but mostly he lay exhausted on a charpoy, or under a tree, and groaned, "Not now, Iqbal, for God's sake."

Still, as the days went on, Mohammed Iqbal did learn some things he felt would interest his Russian friends.

The land changed. They climbed foothills, which became mountains—the start of the Hindu Kush. As the men climbed, so the temperatures moderated into the high nineties, then the more bearable eighties. The air became clear, cool, and still.

And one day, in the middle of the afternoon, they could see in the distance the low, uninspiring buildings of Charikar and the minarets of the mosque, and they realized that soon they would reach the narrow mouth of the Panjshir Valley.

Seventy miles up that, at the end of a potholed dirt road edged by the mountains of the lower Hindu Kush, they would encounter their next great obstacle—the track that rose high until it opened into a pass and brought them finally to Badakhshan, where their real work would begin.

Mahmud halted the trek at a *mujahideen* camp three miles from Charikar, so he could consult local commanders about the location and activities of the Russians, a process that would take many hours. Messengers had to be sent out. Men had to come from the town. Others would be brought from bases nearer the Panjshir. Meanwhile, the Americans could rest, and Mohammed Iqbal was free to take a few hours off and walk into Charikar.

The camp was almost identical to every other one Ross and Lyle had stayed at, in that it consisted of charpoys under the trees and a selection of weapons. There were two main differences. The first was that they were virtually in the shadow of an ancient mud and stone fort, looking as though it had been built by the Crusaders, and the second was that in this area the grapes were finally ripe. A *mujahed* cut them each a bunch, and the agents lay on charpoys in a nomadic, medieval world, with its seemingly far off, unreal war, eating the fruit that Afghans say with justice is the best in the world.

Mahmud was hunkering down on a filthy rug, deep in conversation with a group of men, listening calmly while they pointed and gesticulated, their voices raised sometimes with scorn, sometimes anger.

Mohammed Iqbal set off for Charikar, accompanied by a handful of other *mujahideen*. They left their Kalashnikovs behind, propped against charpoys.

The town's main street was lined with tiny stalls, tea houses, and stands where food was cooked and piled in heaps, abuzz with flies.

It wasn't difficult for Iqbal to get away from the others. They wanted to sit in a tea house, drink tea, and listen to local gossip, while he needed razor blades, batteries for a flashlight, and, of course, to complete his other business.

Iqbal made his purchases and wandered along the streets until he found the door he sought. He knocked, and after a moment a young boy opened. Seeing who it was, the boy stood aside.

The visitor was shown into a room in which cheaply made modern sofas were set facing each other, with a low wooden table between. There were no other furnishings.

Iqbal waited for three or four minutes until the door swung open and there, arms outstretched in welcome and a beam of delight on his chubby face, was Meermai Khan.

"May you not feel tired, you are most welcome!" he exclaimed.

Meermai kissed and embraced Iqbal, then clapped his hands and called an order to his servants.

All the formalities were observed: the inquiries after the health of families and friends, the serving of green tea, the general discussions of life. As usual, Meermai Khan's wife and daughters stayed out of sight. They would make a brief appearance a moment or two before he left, to greet him modestly.

If either man felt impatient for the business that pressed on both their minds, they did not show it. But at last Meermai rose, saying, "Come, my brother, let us walk in the garden. It is cooler there, and we can sit by the trees."

At the rear of Meermai Khan's house, shielded by high walls, was a veritable oasis, with grass, green trees, and shaded pools of water. There were flowers and birdsong.

He led his guest to a point far from the house, where a carpet was spread beneath a plane tree. They slipped off their sandals and sat, apparently admiring the cool beauty in this hidden private place.

Then Iqbal began. "I have found out more about the two Americans. You know of them, of course?"

Meermai nodded.

Iqbal recounted what he had learned; the battlefield dressing Ross had used on the wounded *mujahed*, the stories he had coaxed out about their backgrounds. He concluded that he found no reason to alter his view that the men were not journalists.

"Under their bowls, there are little bowls," Meermai said, quoting an old Persian proverb: the equivalent of smelling a rat.

"We have made good time since Torabora," Iqbal said, "and although these two, like all *farangis*, have had trouble with their feet, they have never complained, and they have not fallen behind. That is not easily done." He stared into the pond, in which grew a lily of the purest pink. "Tomorrow we leave for Panjshir."

Iqbal waited. If there were instructions for him, this was the moment he would receive them.

Meermai rose, Iqbal following after him, and together they strolled through the walled garden, pausing to pluck some grapes, or a fig. Meermai murmured in explanation, "Walls have rats, and rats have ears."

Iqbal glanced quickly around but there was no one else to be seen, and even a man on the other side of the high mud enclosure would have had trouble picking up their voices. His friend seemed overcautious.

Meermai reached for a fig, but when his hand came down to pass it to his guest, it contained, with the fruit, a small brown box. How this had suddenly appeared was a mystery, an act of conjuring. The unexpected feel of the metal almost caused Iqbal to drop it. His arm jerked in a spasm.

"No, my brother, do not be alarmed," Meermai Khan said, closing Iqbal's fingers over it with his hands. "Just put the box in your pocket with the fig. Later you can eat the one and find a use for the other."

They walked on.

Meermai was becoming fat in middle age, and he moved with his legs slightly splayed. His face was without lines, and his eyes lacked guile. This quality of innocence, unmirrored within him, made him a man from whom others frequently sought advice.

Meermai Khan said conversationally, "The two Americans are to be killed in the Panjshir."

Iqbal felt the muscles of his stomach tighten. Not, he hoped, by himself. It would risk exposure to the other *mujahideen,* or at least cause him to lose honor. "How?" Iqbal asked, in a voice as neutral as he could make it.

"Our friends say that you need not concern yourself with the problem, my brother. They will take care of the Americans themselves."

"In the Panjshir?" Iqbal could not restrain his scorn.

"I will explain," Meermai said patiently. "When you reach the town of Ruka, you will stop for the night, will you not?"

"Yes."

"And Mahmud will not be in a hurry to leave because it is there that more information can be discovered about the Russians in Badakhshan."

"Yes, but the Americans will want to go on. We're getting near now, and they are anxious," Iqbal pointed out.

"Surely if you tell them there are strategic reasons for the halt, they will understand?"

"I suppose so."

"Good." Meermai considered the matter settled. "You tell the Americans there are victims of the poison gas a short distance north of Ruka, and you take them to see. If other *mujahideen* wish to go with you, it makes no difference. But be sure as soon as you enter the Panjshir that you switch on that brown box in your pocket. And do not switch it off. It is a radio transmitter and you will see there is a small aerial to pull out. By the box, our friends will track you as you walk north. They are sending a small commando group to ambush the Americans. These men will drop by parachute the night you sleep in Ruka. They will kill only the Americans, although naturally you and the other *mujahideen* will return their fire." He caught Iqbal's gaze and smiled. "Our friends expect their commandos to die," he explained, "because it is important for you to keep your honor. No Russian prisoner must be taken. If one is captured, you just become angry and shoot him all at once. This will avoid interrogation."

Meermai paused by the side of a willow, whose branches dipped to touch a still pond. "When the Americans are dead, take the transmitter box and throw it away. You must not keep it with you."

A bird in the tree above their heads took off with a sudden flutter of wings.

"Those are the instructions," Meermai Khan said. "Do you have any questions?"

"One," replied Iqbal. "These commandos—how can I be sure their first bullet will not be through my own heart?"

Meermai chuckled and patted his back. He put an arm over Iqbal's shoulder. "Be assured, my brother," he said. "There are only two commandos, and their strict orders are to aim first at the men who do not have rifles. That is how they will know the Americans. They will carry out their orders."

"But in the battle that follows," Iqbal persisted, "my chances of being killed or wounded are just as good as theirs."

"There is a path to the top of even the highest mountain," Meermai said, quoting with satisfaction another of his favorite proverbs. "In this case, the commandos will be issued with three rounds of live ammunition each. The rest will be blanks. So you are free to pursue them as bravely as you wish, and hunt them down, and see them die. Blood for blood."

Again they reached the carpet laid beneath the plane tree and sat while Iqbal considered the proposition.

He thought first he might simply throw the metal box away and tell Meermai later that he had turned it on and taken the Americans to the north of Ruka as instructed, but there had been no ambush. He could feel his friend's eyes watching shrewdly.

No, that would be even more of a risk.

Suppose, he thought, feeling the hard edges of the box against his thigh, suppose I refused. Could I do it?

He knew he could not.

No voluntary confession to Mahmud or the others would help. He had done too much already. They had friends who were *shaheeds*—martyrs—because Iqbal had given information to the Russians or sent a band of men to a certain place where a Soviet ambush had been laid.

Nor could he abandon the Russians, for they would not allow it. They might expose him to the *mujahideen* or just order his death. This was simply done. He would have become a danger to Meermai Khan, Gul Hafiz, and Saiful Jamal. If any of those men suspected he was having a change of heart, they would do the deed themselves, despite their years of friendship, because they knew what they faced if ever they were discovered.

Iqbal realized in that moment it was not only his political commitment or the money which insured he would do as he was ordered; it was that he no longer had a choice.

Iqbal heard Meermai cough politely. He nodded. "I will do it," he said. "It sounds a good plan."

"Will you have more tea?" Meermai asked, indicating that their business was at an end.

The entrance to the Panjshir Valley is through a narrow gorge in very mountainous country, a strip of land across which the Russians, in a vain attempt to curtail supplies to the rebels, built a six-foot-high wall.

Mahmud pointed it out as they approached in the early afternoon, an ugly construction, blown with holes in places by the *mujahideen* out of contempt rather than because it represented a real threat to the people beyond.

Ross and Lyle stopped and stood together. It wasn't the Berlin Wall, no miles of barbed wire and watch towers, but it was just as ugly. Man showing himself in his true colors against the grandeur of the Hindu Kush.

The line of guerrillas was strung out as usual, with the front men already near the wall, following a well-worn track, and on the lookout for mines and booby traps.

Suddenly, coming their way through a gap in the wall, emerged a laden mule, followed by another, until finally an entire caravan passed through the supposed blockade. Presumably Soviet reconnaissance planes were recording movements like this every day, and presumably, too, the Russians no longer felt it worth their while to do anything about it.

Mohammed Iqbal dropped behind.

For days, the hard metal of the transmitter had rubbed against his thigh. He had it still in the pocket of his baggy *salwar* trousers with a piece of rag stuffed in after it, and his long chemise shirt reaching down to cover the bulge.

It gave him an uncomfortable, vulnerable feeling. This was the first time he had carried any specific thing for the Russians, some item which, if discovered, would lead to his death. Before it had only been information, never written down. Now there was a brown box, with a switch and an aerial, and at this point, here at the mouth of the Valley, he had to turn it on.

He moved off the path and walked some distance, to squat behind a rock, holding his *sadr* around him like a screen as Afghan men customarily do when relieving themselves. No one paid any attention.

From his pocket, he gently pulled the rag and laid it at his feet, then extracted the transmitter and stared. It was the first time he had dared look at it since the afternoon Meermai Khan handed it to him with a ripe fig. It had gone straight into his pocket then, in a deft, scared movement, and remained to rub and bump against his thigh, a constant reminder.

It was small, slightly bigger than an ordinary match box, and painted a matte color, so that when he threw it away, it would be difficult to find. There was a switch fitting flush against one side.

Mohammed Iqbal pushed it up. It revealed a small, white spot, which presumably meant it was now on.

He glanced around, but all the others had crossed the wall and he was by himself.

He put the transmitter to his ear in case it made any noise, but it was completely silent.

On the top, he saw a small, silver circle, protruding slightly. He slipped his fingernail underneath and pried. Up came the aerial, surprisingly short, no more than an inch.

Mohammed Iqbal put the box back into his pocket and stood up, tying the cord of his trousers. He slung his *sadr* over his shoulder and walked toward the wall.

As he passed through, he could see the others, far ahead, walking along the potholed dirt road which ran the entire seventy-mile length of the Panjshir.

He particularly noticed the box in his pocket now: perhaps because the aerial was extended, but more probably because he'd touched it, and inspected it, and done as he was ordered.

Iqbal lengthened his stride to catch up.

The small transmitter, crystal-calibrated, silently sent out an electronic signal, a long beep, every thirty seconds.

To the Russians maintaining a listening watch on that frequency at a base many miles away, it sounded like the high note of a morse key. They noted the time it began, and called the camp commander.

Ten minutes later, four Mi-24 helicopter gunships, the most sophisticated in the Soviet air force, took off and headed for prearranged positions that, on a map of the Panjshir, roughly formed a square. They flew high.

Every thirty seconds, the high-frequency beep sounded through the headphones of the technicians on board, and the sensitive directional equipment homed in.

The Mi-24s maintained radio silence.

Then two MiGs appeared, flying high toward the valley, cruising lazily along a few miles of its length before climbing and coming around again. They made four passes before returning to base.

That night, the coordinates obtained by the helicopters were plotted on a map and were sufficiently accurate for the lines to intersect virtually precisely.

Next to the map was a set of high-definition prints from the MiG reconnaissance cameras, and the Russians checked off landmarks shown in the four photographs. They compared these against the map and the coordinate lines.

"I think," a Colonel said at last, "that the man with the transmitter is that one there." He pointed. "That one right at the back. You see the shape of his rifle? Look on all these photographs how the lines intersect near him."

The Colonel picked up a magnifying glass and inspected the other figures dotted along the road. It was impossible to make out the features of any of them, of course, but the Colonel tapped his finger on one. "Here," he said—and on another immediately behind—"Here."

The others stared closely.

"Those are the only men not armed," the Colonel observed. "They must be the Americans."

The Russian officers peered through the magnifying glass at the figures. One of them—Clive Lyle actually—had turned to watch the MiGs pass over, just in case they suddenly banked and came in on a strafing raid.

In the photograph, his face was a whitish blur.

It seemed to Ross and Lyle, walking along the dirt road toward Ruka, that they had passed into a different country.

They saw the first traffic in weeks—a battered old bus parked ahead, with the lead *mujahideen* gathered around talking to the driver: they hoped they might get a lift.

The *mujahideen* began shouting and waving at them to come, and the agents broke into a trot.

The bus had seen better days, and the chassis slumped

heavily over the suspension, but everyone seemed confident it would still work.

Ross and Lyle dropped onto hard seats that had once been upholstered and now retained the remnants of the leather and almost none of the padding.

Ross began to chuckle. "After all this way," he marveled, "we catch a bus!"

"Amazing, isn't it?" Lyle agreed. He glanced around at Mahmud and saw the rebel leader sitting at the back looking, for the first time in their acquaintance, exceptionally pleased with himself.

"This road goes right to the end of the valley doesn't it, Mahmud?" Lyle asked.

"Yes. When the Russians come, we put mines along it."

"Any mines now?"

Mahmud shook his head, smiling.

"Then how about us commandeering the bus to take us the rest of the way? And maybe coming back to get us later when we've found those sick people?"

"It is possible," Mahmud said.

Lyle whooped with glee, not only because it meant less of a walk, but it would shorten their journey by five or six days.

Mahmud craned out of the window, looking back. He could see Iqbal running to catch up, and with a mischievous gleam in his eye the commander said something in Pashto to the others which made them crack up.

Iqbal was out of breath when he climbed aboard and the driver started the engine. The bus, shuddering with the vibration, lumbered forward. Between the poor state of the road and the absence of a functioning suspension, the passengers found themselves being thrown around, knocking hard against the sides of seats, the edges of the windows and each other. But they were moving much faster than they could have walked, and no one was in any mood to complain.

Only Iqbal was sick with apprehension. He had suddenly realized the drawback to the bus. Many of the seats were stacked with sacks of produce collected from farmers in the area, so the men had to squeeze onto the remaining ones, and the only vacant place he could find was on the right of the bus, next to a *mujahed*. The transmitter was in his right-hand *salwar* pocket.

Iqbal knew that if he sat as the others were, pressed close in the confined space, the man next to him could not fail to feel the metal. He wouldn't just feel it; it would dig into him every time the bus lurched or rocked. He'd wonder what it was; request Mohammed Iqbal to take it out of his pocket and put it somewhere else; and then everyone would see what it was.

So Iqbal perched on the outer edge of the seat, almost in the aisle, and held on grimly, trying to pretend it wasn't a strain sitting like that.

The bus rocked and vibrated past acres of ripened wheat and a waterfall cascading down one side of the rugged mountain barrier protecting the Panjshir. Fields were terraced as high as the soil extended, and the men could see teams of bullocks carrying harvest, or pulling wooden plows to prepare the land for the next crop.

At last they came to the mud-walled houses, shops, and stalls of Ruka. The bus lurched to a halt. The driver switched off the engine and in the almost deafening silence turned to grin in toothless triumph at his passengers.

Ross pulled himself out of his seat, groaning. "Jesus, I'm not sure I wouldn't sooner have walked." He bumped his shin and found he was limping.

"Come on," Lyle encouraged, "you've got to be tougher than that if you want to be a *mujahed*."

"I don't want to be *mujahed*, thank you," Ross said. "I

want to get to Badakhshan as fast as I can, do what I have to do, and get the hell out of here to Washington.''

Mohammed Iqbal was standing near, probably listening, but he was a Harvard man and they didn't feel they had to censor their conversation for fear of offending him.

They waited for Mahmud on the ground outside the bus while the others dismounted and wandered off.

Mahmud climbed down, still pleased at having been able to offer the Americans a ride: their first real transport in Afghanistan, which had been provided by Afghans, in an Afghan stronghold. He smiled amiably at them, and then said simply, ''Come.''

They walked through the bazaar, past stalls selling eggs, beef, vegetables, and, incredibly, imported goods—flash-lights, candy, and even chewing gum.

''Hey, Mahmud, wait a minute will you?'' Ross called, his eyes lighting on the merchandise. ''There's a couple of things I need to get.''

Even though Iqbal was with them, Mahmud doubled back to help negotiate the purchases.

Ross handed gum around as they walked to the house that would be their quarters for the night. It was a court-yard with charpoys, but beyond the mud walls the setting sun glowed on a harsh mountain backdrop and gradually softened it into something of exceptional beauty.

Ross and Lyle decided it was time for a council of war. They called Mahmud over, and when he came, Iqbal followed.

''How soon can we organize that bus to take us to the end of the valley?'' Lyle asked.

''When do you want?'' Mahmud replied. ''Tomorrow, if the driver agrees.''

In rapid Pashto, Mohammed Iqbal spoke to the com-mander. ''Would it not be better to rest at Ruka for a day and discover what the *Russe* are doing in Badakhshan?''

he asked earnestly. "There may be action there we don't know about."

"Perhaps we can discover these things tonight," Mahmud answered.

"What's going on?" Lyle asked.

"I was saying I think we should check on Soviet movements in Badakhshan," Iqbal said. "It'd be stupid to come all this way and walk into a trap."

Lyle agreed. "But we can find that out pretty quickly, can't we? I mean, this valley's got its own bus service. News travels fast."

"It's better to be sure," Iqbal said. "We don't even know if they've dropped new mines around the top of the Pass or if Soviet columns have been sighted outside one of their bases. And," he said, warming to his own pitch, "we ought to be able to learn something here about the survivors of the gas. Maybe a few victims are right here in the valley."

"I guess that's possible," Ross agreed, "but we'd need to go into Badakhshan anyway. We have to get samples of earth and leaves and things. Also I want to know exactly— and I mean exactly—where people were standing when the thing went bang."

"Perhaps there are survivors here who can tell you that," Iqbal suggested.

"I don't want to be told," Ross said. "I want to be shown."

Mahmud intervened. "Let's see what we can find out about the Russians." Then, "You have money to pay for the bus? For the driver and the gasoline?"

"As long as it's not too steep," Lyle said.

Mahmud looked as if he didn't understand. Iqbal translated for him.

"It will be a fair price," Mahmud promised.

"The other thing we have to know, Mahmud, is how

long it's going to take us to walk from the top of the valley to the place of the attack," Lyle said. "I guess we'll need a couple of days there, and I want to be sure the bus'll be waiting for us when we come back through that pass. That'll save another seventy miles."

"I will ask," Mahmud said.

"Also, how about a caravan of donkeys and horses for the rest of the journey?" Lyle continued. "What're our chances of hiring some animals to take us all out. That'll shorten the time some more, and I guess a lot of these people are going to be pretty sick."

"The caravans don't follow our route," Mahmud said. "Some travel to Kabul, others to Parwan Province and to Bamiyan."

"But if we made it worth their while, would they take us to Torabora?" Lyle persisted. "Or better still, right across into Pakistan?"

Mahmud looked doubtful. "It could cost much money," he said finally.

"How much?"

The commander shrugged. "I will ask."

Mahmud excused himself to talk to a group of men who had come to greet him. It was clear from the way they kissed and embraced him that he was a local hero.

Iqbal went off by himself. He wandered around Ruka, greeting people automatically, talking when he had to, feeling all the time the metal box in his pocket, and wondering how to coax the Americans north of the town in the morning.

It was getting dark, and the bazaar stalls glowed in the soft light of lanterns.

Iqbal considered his problem. Somehow, the Americans had to be kept in Ruka tomorrow, so they could be taken on the excursion to the north. But if there was no way of doing this, then the important thing was to make sure the bus wasn't available, and that they'd have to leave on foot. He walked toward the dirt road.

The bus was parked nearby, and farther along he saw, with a sinking heart, that there were two trucks. Three possible means of transport for the Americans.

Iqbal headed over to the trucks and found them empty.

He went into a tea house. If you wanted to learn anything, a tea house was the place to go.

The valley men knew all about the poison gas. They told Iqbal stories of what had happened, how people had died. But no one had heard the Russians were back in the area. Everyone believed the Americans could go there, *insha Allah*, without risk.

"Perhaps the drivers of those trucks outside know the latest news from Badakhshan?" Mohammed Iqbal suggested innocently.

There was a general shaking of heads.

"They have not been to the north of the valley for many days," a man replied. "But later they can tell you. They leave before dawn to collect harvest there, and the next day they will come back."

At least the trucks would be gone early. "Alas, that will be too late for us," Iqbal said, "for we may also leave tomorrow."

He finished his tea and walked back to the courtyard where they were spending the night. The evening was cool and he wrapped his *sadr* around him.

Dinner was being served when he got back: separately to the Americans as usual. Iqbal went to the communal bowls set in the middle of a blanket to join the *mujahideen* and their hosts. They made space for him, and he was handed an oval of bread.

"What's the news?" Iqbal asked Mahmud.

"There is no trouble from the Russians in Badakhshan,"

the commander replied. "The bus will take us in the morning. We go at dawn."

Iqbal's mouth became so dry he could scarcely eat.

That meant they'd drive into the ambush, and the plan would be useless. If the Soviet commandos tried to attack a busload of *mujahideen* when they only had three live rounds each, the chances of them killing the Americans before they themselves were hunted down were very small. And the Russians would blame him for failing to carry out his orders.

He ate slowly, listening to the conversations with half an ear, glancing occasionally at the Americans, who sat in a companionable silence on a charpoy, now fairly proficient at eating with the fingers of their right hands.

Mohammed Iqbal was not yet beaten. There was a way of delaying them a few hours, perhaps enough to persuade them to walk with him a little north of Ruka.

In any case, it was his only chance.

He waited until after the others had settled to sleep. He lay on his charpoy under the stars, listening to the low noises the men made in the dark courtyard, watching to see if he could tell who was still awake.

The hours passed.

At last, Iqbal sat up and looked around. No one stirred. He rose. Still no one moved. He walked swiftly as if he was going to relieve himself. His feet were noiseless on the hard sand courtyard and it was only outside in the alley that he put on his sandals.

Ruka was in darkness. If there were men awake, there was no sign.

He went cautiously to the road.

The black shapes of the two trucks were clearly outlined by the combined brilliance of stars and a half-moon shining through the clean, high air. To his left was the bus.

The question was, would the driver be sleeping inside it, as many of them did?

Iqbal approached quietly, watching for movement, hearing no sound. At the back of the bus, he squatted on his haunches, his hand feeling the left tire. It was smooth: almost no tread left.

He pulled out his knife and thrust the blade deep into the rubber. Once in, it was hard to get out, and he had to wrench at it to pull it free. The hiss of escaping air sounded louder than he'd expected, and he darted away in case the driver was aboard and would be awakened by the noise.

He crouched in deep shadow between two market stalls nearby. From that distance he could hear nothing.

Iqbal moved to the far side of the bus.

He was almost in the middle of the road, and there was no shadow there. Anyone looking out would be able to see his silhouette clearly.

The transmitter pressed against his thigh as he groped for the handle of the compartment housing the spare tire and moved it gradually around, ready to stop at the slightest sound, the tiniest grating of the lock.

Then Iqbal pulled.

It was an old bus; it was a miracle it still ran at all, considering the rudimentary attention it received. One of its lacks was oil, and the hinges creaked hideously.

Iqbal froze.

The seconds passed slowly and stretched to a minute, but there was no sound from inside.

Iqbal tried again, and immediately the dry metal scraped and rasped.

He tensed, heart pounding, ready to roll under the bus, to hide, or perhaps run down the nearby alley before the driver could raise the alarm. He collected his thoughts, which were edging toward panic, and decided he must be bold, and he must be fast. If he could get the cover open quickly, and puncture the spare tire with one swift lunge, then no matter how much noise he made, he would have done the job and be away before the driver came stumbling down the steps of the bus, which in any case were on the other side.

He prepared himself mentally. The knife was in his right hand, the fingers of his left were wedged under the small crack he'd opened so far.

He drew a breath and wrenched up the cover.

The creak of metal was nowhere near as bad as it had been when he was moving cautiously. He felt for the tire, thrust in the blade and withdrew it, not really listening for other sounds, just finishing the job as fast as he could. He dropped the cover back, its hinges almost silent now, and turned the handle to secure it.

Iqbal raced into the deep shadows between the market stalls and squatted, the blood pounding so loud in his ears he thought it would be impossible for him to hear anyone coming.

But he coud see nothing, no movement.

He slipped farther back up the alleyway, keeping close to the buildings. A dog began to bark and he stepped up his pace.

When he reached the courtyard, he went straight to his own charpoy and covered himself with his *sadr*.

Gradually his heartbeat settled down. No one had awakened.

In the distance, the dog continued barking.

Mohammed Iqbal fell into a light sleep. Once before dawn, a dream that was tormenting him caused him to shout ''Allah!'' so loudly that he woke himself and sat up, ashamed and bewildered.

Around him, others stirred. Iqbal lay back and tried to relax.

At least the bus wasn't going anywhere that morning. It would take the driver until lunch to mend even one puncture. But what could you expect with worn tires?

So he would offer the Americans an alternative. A short walk to see some victims of the Badakhshan gas. A short and final walk up the valley's only road.

When dawn came, they heard the engines. The courtyard was awake in seconds, *mujahideen* reaching for their rifles and slipping on their sandals, thinking the Russians were coming in with an air strike.

But the engines remained distant. They listened, talked, complained, and finally laughed.

Ross and Lyle sat on the edges of their charpoys, willing themselves not to scratch any of the night's new bites, and wondering what was going on. Were they going to be caught in one of those three-week-long battles for the Panjshir they'd read about in the files?

"What's going on, Mahmud?" Lyle asked.

"Russian helicopters," he said.

The agents listened also and, after a while, it seemed the helicopters weren't going anywhere. The noise was constant. They appeared to be hovering.

"I guess there's action on the other side of the mountains," Lyle said. "It was like this yesterday afternoon, remember?"

The four Mi-24s took the same positions they'd been in during the previous day's test, and the directional equipment homed in on the courtyard where the Afghans were now spreading mats for morning prayer.

Ross and Lyle went out with their dwindling rolls of toilet paper to find a piece of vacant ground, tenting their *sadrs* around them and making sure they weren't facing Mecca when they squatted.

Moslems, especially those fighting a *jihad*, are not tolerant of perceived insults to their faith.

Whether the Russian helicopters had been there or not, everyone in the Panjshir would have awakened at dawn. Ablutions have to be performed, prayers said, breakfast eaten, and then the merchants open their stalls, the farmers work their fields, and the flocks of sheep and goats are tended by herders, usually small boys.

One of these shepherds was Mir Gholam, the third son among four children. The flock he was herding was at the southern end of Ruka, toward the Soviet wall, and he was taking them into a side valley near a waterfall where the grass was sweet. This was not a big area, and he could graze the sheep there for only one day every few weeks, until the grass grew again.

Mir Gholam was light-skinned, with green eyes and black hair. His features were fine and proud, and although he was only eight, he was used to work and to adult responsibilities. When he grew up, he planned to join the *mujahideen*.

He called greetings to a farmer harvesting a field of oats before driving his father's sheep clear of the crop and into the side valley, where not even the light morning breeze could be felt, but where the thundering of a mountain torrent would provide his music for the day.

The sheep tugged and pulled hungrily at grass and young leaves.

Mir Gholam reached into a bush to snap off a branch, intending to whittle it into an arrow while he kept his watch, and he didn't notice the green plastic lodged there. It appeared to be half a butterfly. There was a central body section, containing the explosive, with a small stubby piece jutting from it; while on the other side protruded a larger flat disc of plastic, like a wing.

Had Mir Gholam seen it, he would have known immediately what it was, because the Russians had dropped thousands from helicopters, and he himself had destroyed many by throwing stones at them, or shooting with his slingshot and watching them detonate.

This time, he saw only the flash within the bush, and the stinging shock blast on his hand. When he jerked his arm away with a cry of alarm, he looked at the wound, baffled.

His hand! He still felt it, and he knew it must be there, but blood gushed and pumped from the stump of his wrist.

Mir Gholam knew enough about injuries, had seen enough, to understand his first action had to be to stop the bleeding. With his teeth and his good hand, he tore a strip of cloth from his shirt, hurrying, agitated. A tingling sensation grew in his fingers, and there was a feeling of light-headedness, but no pain. If it didn't hurt, it couldn't be that bad, his wound.

He wound the dirty strip of rag around his stump, and again holding one end in his teeth, tied a knot and pulled as hard as he could. The spurting stopped, and became an ooze. He tied a second knot to secure it.

He pulled off the small waistcoat he wore over his chemise and wrapped it around the stump. It soaked with blood.

Mir Gholam knew he had to get help quickly, but first he wanted to find out what had happened. He peered cautiously into the bush, at the place he had seen the flash and felt the shock, but there was nothing there.

He looked down, and then saw it, the tip of the small index finger just touching the dust, the other fingers caught in twigs and leaves. Finally he understood.

Mir Gholam began to scream.

He ran, stumbling because his head was so light and his face was tingling.

Sheep scattered and began to run bleating out of the side valley as he lurched and shouted.

Mir Gholam stopped and sat on the ground. His hand was beginning to hurt now, and not just a little, but really aching and throbbing. Then he lay down because it made his head feel better.

The sheep, having started on a course leading them out, continued on their way, slowing to eat but gradually moving farther from the child whose cries became hysterical, but which were as nothing against the thundering of the waterfall.

Half the *mujahideen* were on the bus before someone noticed the rear tire was flat.

Lyle, who was about to climb aboard, said, "Oh, for Christ's sake! What a great start!"

None of the others seemed concerned. Things were as Allah willed, and if the tire was flat, what could a man do but have it changed?

Ahead of them, the trucks started up, engines spluttering as they warmed.

"Why don't we go in one of those?" Lyle asked Iqbal.

"It won't take long to change the tire, Clive," Iqbal assured him, "and anyway, they're not going as far as we want."

Lyle grunted and went to sit with Ross against the side of a mud building, *sadrs* wrapped around them, waiting for the warming rays of the sun to rise above the mountain barrier. Mohammed Iqbal came to join them.

"It's a pity you're not going to have time to talk to those gas victims," he said. "They might give us some idea what to expect in Badakhshan."

"Yeah." Ross sounded polite, rather than enthusiastic. "What are they doing here, anyway?"

"Living with friends a mile away," Iqbal said. "When

people started dying, they decided to clear out." He paused to watch the wheel being lifted from its bolts and the spare tire rolled around from the side hatch. He could see the rubber sag. It was completely flat. "I heard from some men in a tea house last night that these Badakhshan folk aren't feeling too good themselves."

"No?" He detected Ross's sudden interest. "What's wrong?"

"Oh, stomach cramps, that sort of thing," Iqbal said vaguely.

The driver noticed the condition of the spare tire and shook his head, grumbling as he kicked and pressed, to see just how flat it was. Other *mujahideen* crowded around, and a lot of free advice was offered in Pashto before someone went to get a hand pump.

Iqbal broke the news to the Americans. "It looks like the spare's flat, too."

Lyle groaned. "I knew this was too good to last," he said.

"They'll put in some air, then we'll be on our way," Iqbal said soothingly.

It was the sheep beginning to trample through the edges of his field of oats that alerted the farmer to the fact that Mir Gholam was not doing his job. He shouted angrily, thinking the child had gone to sleep or was dreaming around the waterfall.

When there was no response, the farmer ran out, herding the animals back into the narrow side valley, partly to get them away from his field, and partly so he could find the boy and cuff him around the ears.

And there was Mir Gholam, asleep on the ground! The farmer strode towards him, shouting, until he saw the strange, uncomfortable position in which the child was lying; and as he got closer still, he noticed the makeshift tourniquet and the bloodsoaked waistcoat around the stump of a wrist.

He knelt. Mir Gholam's face was white with shock and loss of blood, and he was moaning. The farmer stripped a fresh piece of cloth from the boy's torn shirt and applied a second tourniquet, then made a slightly better job of bandaging the stump with the waistcoat.

He picked Mir Gholam off the ground. The boy screamed with pain.

The farmer put him down and stood indecisively.

There were *farangis* in Ruka who would have medicines. The question was, should he carry Mir Gholam two miles into town, even though he was in pain? It would mean going slower, and perhaps missing the *farangis* if they were leaving this morning.

Or was it better to run himself, and bring them back here to the child?

The farmer decided to run. He set off at an even jog, hoping he would not be too late.

The Mi-24s maintained their positions, their pilots making slight course corrections because of the wind, or sudden updrafts of air.

The directional equipment on each of the helicopters flashed compass references onto screens, and the technicians radioed data to the ground.

The lines intersected in Ruka itself, first in one place, then in another, which was at, or near, the road, and was considered a good sign.

American listening posts, set up in the area by the NSA, eavesdropped on the communications between the helicopters and the ground, but it was only much later that they, and General Lyndon Yardley, were able to piece together what had happened, and realize that Ross and Lyle had been betrayed.

In any case, even if the NSA had known details of the agents' movements and had thought to tell Yardley, there was nothing anyone could have done.

In fact, at that time who the hell knew where Ross and Lyle were precisely? They could only surmise it would be somewhere around the Panjshir, but Afghanistan is a big place, and there was a lot of room for error.

The driver pumped and pumped, and when he grew tired, one of the *mujahideen* took over. Finally someone heard the faint hissing of escaping air, and it was then discovered that the bus had two punctures.

A lot of tension, bottled inside Clive Lyle over the last weeks, came out in a burst of uncontrolled anger and abuse, while Ross urged, "Cool it, Clive! It's okay man, it's okay. They'll fix the wheel, and we'll go in a little while."

Ross rose, pulling Lyle up. "Come on," he suggested, "no point in hanging around here calling them names. Let's go for a walk."

"Ah, great, Dave!" Lyle snarled. "let's see what's on at the movies."

"Why don't we walk up the road and see the gas victims? It's not far," Iqbal said.

"That sounds fine," Ross said enthusiastically. "How about it, Clive? We might hear something interesting."

"Yeah. Like how soon we can get back to the States."

"How long will it take to repair the tire?" Ross asked.

"Well, he's got two of them to fix," Iqbal said, "so I don't suppose he'll be ready until after lunch. But if he is, they can always pick us up along the road. No problem." He smiled.

"Okay. Hey Mahmud," Ross called, "Iqbal's going to take us to see some gas victims up the road. Is that okay?"

"Come back in two hours," Mahmud said.

The men headed north.

None of the *mujahideen* offered to go with them. If they hadn't understood the meaning of the things Clive Lyle had been saying about them, they certainly understood the tone. It was lucky for him he was their guest.

The farmer reached the buildings of Ruka at about the time Ross and Lyle were leaving the other end of town and the Mi-24s were reporting new coordinates from the transmitter in Iqbal's pocket.

The farmer ran to the *mujahideen* around the crippled bus and gasped out his story. No one had any doubt that the *farangis* must be called back.

Mahmud gave the order, and he, the farmer, and three rebels hurried along the street to what looked like a closed garage—the sort that usually turned out to be a shop but which, in this case, actually housed a captured Russian jeep.

The engine turned, sluggishly at first before it caught, and the driver reversed quickly into the road.

The next set of coordinates intersected at the northern boundary of Ruka.

Both the Soviet officers, clustered around the map in their operations room, and the artillery battery well shielded by distance and mountain from the target area, pinpointed the place.

Ross and Lyle heard the jeep behind them and turned in surprise.

"Well, I'll be . . ." Ross said, recognizing it as Soviet

and thinking for an insane moment the Russians had broken through.

"It's Mahmud," Iqbal said. His voice sounded strained and sullen.

The jeep pulled up beside them. "Come!" Mahmud ordered. "A boy has been hurt by a bomb. You must help." He explained what had happened.

Ross got in immediately, Lyle after him. But when Mohammed Iqbal began climbing in, Ross said, "Hold on, Iqbal. I guess you'd better stay behind. It's almost full house now and we've got to bring the kid in."

"I will come!" Iqbal insisted.

Lyle, his temper not properly repaired, said, "The hell you will, Iqbal! There's no room, you understand? Savvy? We'll see you back in town."

Iqbal tried to push his way in and Lyle turned angrily to Mahmud. "Will you please tell this joker to get off? There isn't room for him and the kid. Shit, don't they teach them anything at Harvard?"

Mahmud spoke briefly in Pashto, and Iqbal, furious, stalked away, returning to town.

The jeep turned, wheels spinning in the dust, and headed back through Ruka toward the side valley where Mir Gholam lay clinging to life.

The jeep was south of the town before the Mi-24s reported the new coordinates on Iqbal's transmitter.

The Colonel was baffled. "Perhaps they've forgotten something," he said. "Let us see."

The jeep could go only as far as the edge of the field of oats where Mir Gholam's sheep, who had wandered back, were greedily destroying some of the valuable crop.

Everyone climbed out and ran, following the farmer

who alternated between shouting and waving wildly at the animals, and leading the Americans to the injured boy.

They knelt by the child, turned him over on his back. He was conscious, but it would have been kinder if he hadn't been, because then he would not have suffered the surging agonies that now racked his body, making him alternately moan and scream.

Ross reached into his pack and felt at the bottom for the sealed plastic kit of morphine. He glanced at Lyle, his eyes bright with challenge. "You want to go talk about this, Clive?" he asked.

"No," Lyle said. "I guess I'll give you mine, too."

Ross turned back to the child. He half-filled a syringe and plunged it into a vein in Mir Gholam's arm. The morphine took effect quickly, and the boy fell silent.

Ross closed up the kit and looked around. At the end of the side valley was the waterfall, and one of the things they could do with was some passably clean water.

"Let's get him over there," he said, and he picked the boy up as gently as he could while Lyle carried both their packs. They made their way to the icy, fast-flowing stream.

There was a flat rock on which Mir Gholam used to lie watching the sky and his father's sheep and on which he was now laid while Ross and Lyle peeled off the bloody waistcoat and inspected the stump of his wrist, and the jagged edges of bone.

The Colonel waited twenty minutes, impatiently striding up and down the operations room while the coordinates came in, showing the lines intersecting back in the town itself.

Finally he ordered: "A message to Moscow. Top Priority."

An aide waited, pen poised to take it down. It was addressed to Sanko himself, who, well aware of the stage the operation had reached, had stayed overnight at Department V, the headquarters of *mokrie dela*.

Even though it was just dawn, he was in his office and replied immediately, "If no movement north in ten minutes, proceed as planned."

So it was that ten minutes after the receipt of Sanko's orders, when the coordinates remained unchanged because Mohammed Iqbal was in a furious temper in a tea house, hardly able to be civil to any of the others, instructions were radioed to the hovering Mi-24s, and picked up by the NSA.

"Blue flight: Falcon. Over."

And even as they answered, one after the other, the helicopter gunships were moving out of the area as fast as they could back to the safety of base.

In Ruka, everyone noticed the change in the sound of the engines, except Ross, Lyle and the *mujahideen* who were tending Mir Gholam and were aware only of the thundering water.

The Russians were going away.

The Afghans looked at each other and shrugged.

For safety's sake, the Colonel decided to target the artillery on a point north of Ruka, just in case during the twenty minutes between withdrawing the Mi-24s and firing the shell, the Americans began walking north again.

Not that it mattered. The sort of ranges they were dealing with really made no practical difference. The LL scale—military terminology for "latent lethality"—would kill the Americans just the same whether they were incinerated in the area immediately around ground zero or died a few days later. They were a long way from home, and nothing could help them.

*   *   *

Ross and Lyle worked together, having to shout above the noise of the water to hear one another. They fought to save Mir Gholam's life, even though the battle was as good as lost unless he was moved quickly to a hospital. And the nearest was in Kabul, under the control of the communists.

They'd stopped the flow of blood and made the boy swallow antibiotic tablets. They decided to give him some painkillers later, before the morphine wore off, so the hard stuff would last longer.

Mir Gholam was awake, and with quiet, trusting eyes, watched the Americans working on him. His arm no longer hurt, and he felt strangely peaceful.

The farmer, helped by Mahmud and a couple of *mujahideen*, went back to get the sheep out of the oats field once again, while Ross and Lyle completed the bandaging.

Fifteen miles away, an artillery battery received a radio order and fired a single shell.

No one on the ground saw it go, beyond the smoke of the initial explosion. It produced a concussion wave of sound, almost like a physical blow.

It arched invisibly up, over the Hindu Kush, and began its descent into the Panjshir.

The Scimitar warhead was programmed to detonate at 500 feet, so on the ground, the Afghans heard only the first second of the distinctive whistling noise of an incoming shell.

A neutron bomb is a nuclear weapon, although it differs both from the atomic bomb that destroyed Hiroshima and the thermonuclear H-bomb, in that it reverses the proportions of the disruptive energy released.

It does not rely on blast, or shock waves, although there are those too for a short distance around ground zero; but more than eighty percent of its energy is released as an intense pulse of lethal neutron radiation, known as "prompt radiation" because it occurs in less than one-millionth of a second.

Ross and Lyle could not hear the brief, deadly whistle of the falling shell: but the white light of the explosion lit up the day as if it had been night, and a second or two later, the sound roared in like an express train.

The agents stared open-mouthed at the sky, as if the world was ending, and then they saw, rising above the side valley, the distinctive mushroom cloud.

There wasn't the massive fireball of the conventional nuclear explosion, but it was big enough: and because they knew what it meant, they watched in awe and fear.

The spinning smoke ring swelled as it rose into the clear morning. At the other end of the side valley, Mahmud and the *mujahideen* stood watching, frozen like statues.

Ross turned abruptly and ran a short distance before falling to his knees and vomiting, chest heaving, stomach muscles straining. Lyle, suddenly nauseous himself, followed to help but before he reached David he knew he was also about to be sick.

For three or four minutes the men knelt at the icy, fast-flowing stream washing their faces, and drinking the pure cold water.

Lyle said something, but it was impossible to talk above the noise of the water, so Ross motioned him away.

When they reached the end of the side valley, they looked down toward Ruka. Nothing seemed to have changed. Ross stared again at the mushroom cloud, checking the direction it was floating now that its shape was breaking up. He licked his index finger and held it high. It cooled on the south side, meaning the light ground breeze was also blowing away from them.

"Well at least the wind's in our favor," Ross said.

"Whatever radioactive shit's floating around up there is going farther down the valley."

Lyle's voice was calm. "It was a neutron bomb, wasn't it?"

"I guess it was. One of Rabinovich's little surprises."

Lyle turned to face Ross. "You're more of an expert than I am. What does that mean for us?"

Before Ross could answer, Mahmud, the farmer, and the *mujahideen* who had been helping herd the sheep came over, and their expressions, although serious, were also calm. Death in a *jihad* was, after all, a one-way ticket to Paradise, although it was impossible to tell if any of them yet imagined they might personally be affected.

"That was Russian poison gas," Mahmud announced gravely. "Now you have seen it for yourselves."

"Yeah," Ross said. "I guess we have."

"We must go into Ruka," Mahmud said.

"No!" Ross said vehemently. "No, Mahmud, we have to wait here a few hours. It's still dangerous there. We can only go in the afternoon."

Mahmud considered this, then shrugged. "We will sit by the water and wait," he agreed.

The Americans watched the *mujahideen* herd the sheep into the side valley, and noticed how, one after another, the Afghans went a distance from the others and threw up: the first symptom of the invisible death.

"Come on, Clive," Ross said. "Let's go find a place to talk."

At the beginning of the side valley was a short climb to a large rock, and they made their way onto that.

"Jesus, I wouldn't mind a cigarette now," Ross said.

"Smoking shortens your life," Lyle reminded him.

Ross grinned without humor. "You don't say? Well, a bourbon then." He stared into the sky. The mushroom cloud had gone. He began almost apologetically. "Let me tell you what I know, and what I don't know. First, I don't know how big that nuke was. One kiloton? Ten kilotons? Second, I don't know how high they detonated it. I guess if we had an inclinometer and some graph paper we could make a pretty fair guess. But we don't." Their eyes met. "You see, Clive, gauging what neutron effects there are, and when they come, depends on knowing that basic stuff. Oh sure, we can estimate it, and we will as soon as the radioactivity's cleared enough for us to walk in. But we won't be certain."

"So we won't know when people will die?"

"No," Ross confirmed. "No more than we could have in Badakhshan, weeks after the event. At least, we've got a better chance to guess at it now, and a shorter distance to travel."

"So there's no way of knowing when someone like Iqbal's going to croak because we left him behind?"

"I'd guess within ten days," Ross said "if he isn't dead already."

"And we don't know when Mahmud and his merry men will die?"

"No."

"Or when we will."

It was a statement, not a question. Lyle knew as well as Ross that one of the first symptoms of fast neutron radiation was nausea, and they'd both experienced that.

"No, we don't know," Ross conceded.

"So," Lyle said, "what we have to do now is collect around us a bunch of people we think'll make it back to Pakistan and then to the States, and hope we'll be there ourselves to see it through."

"Yeah. I guess that's it."

"You think we'll get Purple Hearts posthumously, or before the fact?"

"Fuck off, Clive." Ross wasn't in the mood for jokes.

His mind was preoccupied with what they'd find when they reached Ruka later that day, and how they'd get their caravan of the dying on the trail for Pakistan. "Okay," Ross continued, "I've told you what I don't know, so now here's what I do know. We're going to find a lot of burns on people near ground zero. We haven't got the morphine to help them all, so I suggest we keep it for the kid."

"We're taking the kid with us?"

Ross looked surprised. "Of course," he said. "What do you think?"

"He's going to die," Lyle said.

"We're all going to die, Clive," Ross pointed out. "But what are we gonna do with the poor little bastard meanwhile? Leave him here and hope a Soviet field ambulance turns up? Christ!

"Anyway, look at it from Yardley's point of view. Imagine we bring him a fantastic looking little shepherd boy with big green eyes, whose hand's blown off by the Russians on the same morning they hit him with a neutron bomb. Just think what it'll be like as we watch the kid die on TV surrounded by new toys. Yardley'll be dictating terms to the President. Even I might get a Purple Heart, and I'm not even in the army."

Lyle stared at his partner. "I guess we have made you one of us, haven't we?" he said.

"God forgive you." But Ross was trying to smile. Then he continued. "So: the neutron effects. Okay, most of the people in this area are going to die slowly, but a lot have probably realized by now they're finished. The first series of symptoms are called 'prodromal,' which I guess is really a premonition phase. Nausea, vomiting, cramps, diarrhea, panic, helplessness. Those close to the blast who got really high doses of neutrons—say 8,000 rads—we'll find them listless, sweating, shocked; things like that. It probably means there's some cerebral bleeding."

"When do they die?"

"The high dose ones, sometime tomorrow, I suppose. Then as you move away from ground zero, we get into a murky area. Let's say the bomb zapped some guy 1,000 rads. Well, he might keep going for as long as five or ten days, but that's still no good to us, because it doesn't get him back to Washington for Yardley to put on show.

"What we're really looking for," Ross said, "are people who've taken around 200 rads. Between that and 1,000. Out of that bunch, which I hope includes us, we ought to have enough survivors to make it to Pakistan, take a plane and tell the world."

Lyle stared toward Ruka. "Well, look on the bright side," he said at last. "At least we don't have to walk to Badakhshan."

There was a thoughtful silence before Ross went on. "There's one other thing we've both got to watch out for," he said. "There's never been a proper study of what the neutron bomb actually does to people. It's all theory, based on what happened during tests on pigs. But we do know that at high levels of radiation, brain cells and nerves disintegrate."

"Yeah?"

"Which means it's impossible to predict how people are going to react in the future. We don't know what their behavioral patterns will be, or their feelings or their capabilities. We don't know if they'll respond to commands, or make valid judgments." He caught Lyle's eye. "That goes for Mahmud and," he added, "it goes for you and me, too."

Lyle was quiet for several moments, and then he groaned. "Oh Jesus, what a mess!"

"Yeah, but at least if we can get the circus into Pakistan, I guess it won't have been entirely useless. Anyway, cheer up. Haven't you ever thought about dying for your country?"

"Fuck! Certainly not!"

"Yeah, well," Ross said, "some are born great, and some have greatness thrust upon them. We've just had it thrust upon us, so let's lie quietly and think about things: man's place in the universe and suchlike. And when the radioactivity around Ruka's settled down, let's for God's sake collect our rocks and leaf samples quickly, and our survivors, and get the hell out of here."

Lyle lay back on the rock, feeling the warm sun on his face.

"Wouldn't it be funny," he said, "if the Russians dropped another of Rabinovich's bombs right now."

"Hilarious, Clive. Now shut up and let me think."

North of Ruka, at almost the precise point Ross and Lyle had boarded Mahmud's jeep and gone to tend Mir Gholam, there was devastation.

This was ground zero, and within a 550 foot radius, not a tree, bush, branch, bird, animal, insect or blade of grass remained. In places, the rocks and sand had melted and fused, absorbing radiation whose half-life was only a few hours.

Lyle and Mahmud stood on the edge of the totally destroyed sector while Ross paced across it, trying to determine from the scorched diameter the probable size and height of the airburst, although its designers—and here he thought again of Rabinovich—could have built special characteristics into this one.

The *mujahideen* who had been with them in the side valley had peeled off after they drove down the potholed road into the eerily quiet settlement. These men were going to the houses of people they knew—one of them to his own home—to learn the extent of the damage. Ruka might easily have been a ghost town and of course, as far as its present inhabitants were concerned, it soon would be.

At ground zero, Ross chose smallish rocks which weren't too heavy to carry and looked as though they'd been melted in a furnace. Further away, where trees still stood, he plucked twigs and yet further, samples of stems and leaves which were already beginning to wither and die.

All these Ross neatly labelled with the place, date and time of their collection, and his signature. For all he knew, neither he nor Lyle would survive the journey, and the best they could hope for would be that some *mujahed* had the wit to take these otherwise worthless packets into Pakistan and sell them to Tom Glenn or Steve Cook. It was a bit like throwing a corked bottle into the ocean with a note calling for help and hoping eventually it would wash up somewhere sensible.

When he had finished, Ross divided the samples between himself and Lyle, and then they went toward the town itself.

Ross paced out 1,500 feet from ground zero. It took him halfway into Ruka. Everyone in this radius, he thought, would have been bombarded with enough fast neutrons possibly to have radiation-induced skin burns, and enough damage to their central nervous systems to be dead in twenty-four hours. As for the rest of the village, clearly it came within the 1,500-plus rad belt, and effectively everyone else would be dead in a week or ten days.

They'd have to look for Yardley's survivors farther afield.

He told this to Mahmud.

The young commander's face registered neither shock nor despair, merely acceptance. He murmured fatalistically: "This world is a hell for true believers."

They walked off the dirt road and into the alleyways.

The bazaar stalls were closed. As they passed one mud-walled house, they could hear the sound of lamentation.

Mahmud stopped and knocked. After a minute, the door was opened by a young man, and Ross could tell from his gaunt, bloodless face and the way he stood holding his stomach as if it was cramping, that he was in the prodromal stage, the premonition of death.

When the man saw Mahmud, he invited him and the Americans in, and led them to the room from which the weeping came.

The body of an old man was laid out, flanked by women who pulled veils over their faces when they saw the strangers, but continued to slap themselves and tear at their hair, wailing in the customary manner.

Presumably the old man had died of heart failure soon after the explosion, and Ross wondered if anyone realized how lucky he was not to have to endure the nightmare days to come. Soon, who would there be left with the strength or the will to bury the dead?

Ross watched one of the women pouring water from a pitcher, pausing constantly to drink as she read Koranic verses over the corpse. Dehydration was another prodromal symptom.

They went into the street.

A man was slumped against the side of a house, drenched with sweat and holding his hands over his ears as if to block terrible sounds that only he could hear. The skin had peeled off his forehead and cheeks, exposing raw flesh.

Mahmud stopped at the door of another house and knocked. No one answered.

He knocked again. Finally he pushed it open and called out in Pashto.

Hearing nothing, they entered cautiously.

The family was lying in a room stinking of vomit and excrement. There were three adults, one an old woman, and four children; but none could rouse themselves even to look at the strangers.

Ross and Lyle tensed against the smell, trying to breathe as shallowly as possible.

Mahmud's face was becoming strained. Perhaps he hadn't really believed Ross earlier when he said the people of Ruka would all die, but the message was sinking in now.

Along another alley, they found a naked man: someone Mahmud knew well. He called sharply, embarrassed, but the man stared as if he did not know the commander, and continued on his way.

Mahmud said bewildered, "This gas, it has made people mad."

Ross tried to explain, "It's not gas, Mahmud. It's a new bomb that sends out rays, like the sun. Only they're bad rays. They go through the walls of houses, through tanks even, and kill the people inside."

But it didn't look as if Mahmud understood.

They searched for the *mujahideen* who had been with them in the side valley and when they found them, it was clear from their faces they had seen similar horrors.

The man whose family lived in Ruka spoke rapidly to Mahmud, a conversation that became increasingly anguished.

Mahmud turned to the Americans. "His two sons and his wife are sick and he thinks they will die if you do not help them. He asks you to give them medicine to make them well."

"There is no medicine, Mahmud," Ross said regretfully. "I wish to God there was."

The commander translated this and the Afghan jabbered back at him.

"He believes you have things in your pack that can save his family," Mahmud repeated.

Ross was shaking his head helplessly, when Lyle caught the wild, antagonistic glint in the *mujahed*'s eye. "Uh,

Mahmud," Lyle said, "actually there's something I've got which might do them a bit of good."

Mahmud turned and relayed this news, and Lyle found the Afghan's hand gripping his arm, pulling him along the alley, almost running towards the house where his family lay dying.

"Jesus Christ, Clive," Ross said in a low voice as they went, "what sort of line are you selling these guys?"

"Just trying to stay alive, Dave," Lyle said. "Just a while longer. Did you check that guy's face? He was going to kill if we didn't do something. It doesn't matter what."

The Americans were ushered into the *mujahed*'s house. The two boys were howling in a room with their mother, who although weeping herself, turned modestly from the strangers, hiding her raw face. Both boys also had radiation burns on their arms and faces.

The room smelled of vomit, but obviously an attempt had been made to clear it up.

Lyle opened his pack and was about to go to the woman when Ross reminded him, "Uh, Clive, do the kids first, huh? You're not supposed to go near the lady."

"Oh, yeah, sure." Lyle turned to the *mujahed*. "Bring water."

Mahmud translated and the man ran to fetch a glass and a beaker made of beaten tin.

Lyle sat the boys up gently and, despite their terrified screaming, managed to get them to swallow three painkillers each and one vitamin capsule. Ross was surprised at how well he handled the children, talking to them in a soothing, confident voice. Then he passed the same number of pills to the *mujahed* and indicated he should feed them to his wife. The man's face was a study in gratitude.

Out in the street, deeply breathing the sweet, fresh air, Lyle said decisively, "Okay, that's it! We've got to get this show on the road tomorrow morning at the latest.'' He called Mahmud. ''Now this is very important,'' he instructed. ''We must go right now to the north of Ruka and find people to take to America. Tomorrow morning at dawn, we leave.''

''There will be many here who must be buried,'' Mahmud said.

''Then that work will have to be done by someone else,'' Lyle said stubbornly. ''We can't hang around, Mahmud, because if we do, a whole lot more people will be dead. And then it'll be too late. So give some other *mujahideen* the responsibility—some people further up the valley where these death rays didn't reach.''

Mahmud thought a moment, saw the sense in Lyle's argument, and nodded. ''I will do it.''

''Great. And another thing: there's a limited number of people we can take to America. You're the commander, so you're going to have to be strong with them. Mr. David here will choose who is to come because he knows which ones the doctors may be able to help and which ones can tell the world how the *Russe* are torturing the Afghan people.''

They walked through the bazaar and found to their surprise that one stall had reopened. The imported flashlights, batteries, chewing gum and all the other items were neatly laid out, but the owner had his back to them.

Mahmud called a greeting, ''*Salām-o-alaikum*''—Peace be upon you—and when the man turned to see who spoke, he spat contemptuously in the gutter and began muttering to himself about Russians, growing increasingly loud and angry, as if they were the invaders. Finally he seized a handful of batteries and threw them with force and accuracy. The group scattered, becoming scared now, really getting spooked while the trader railed furiously against them, then began to laugh, high-pitched and mad as he put them to flight.

They stopped running when they reached the road and their jeep, where another sound caught their attention.

Mir Gholam's severed hand was again sending pulses of agony up his arm, and whenever he could summon the strength to scream, he did. Otherwise he whimpered, clenching his teeth in a haze of pain.

The group caught the beginning of a scream. Ross was unslinging his pack to get at the morphine even as they ran towards the Russian jeep where he lay.

When he'd given the small boy the second half of one of his precious phials, Ross suddenly felt a black mood of defeat and resignation threatening to overcome him.

What's this about? he asked himsself. We're all going to die anyway, every one of us.

And then he remembered what it was about. It flooded back to him with such intensity that it might have been a drug as powerful as morphine coursing through his bloodstream.

It was about those people blown to pieces in Clive Lyle's elevator, about Sue Collins, smashing into the ground, and about the families, burned, puking, hurting, going mad, dying right now, around him in Ruka. In the end, it was about revenge.

Whatever else they did, at whatever cost, they had to get back to Pakistan, to the States, with their people and their samples.

Ross said grimly, "Let's go."

They drove north, veering off the road and onto paths, or making their own tracks to small farm houses, checking precisely where people had been when Rabinovich's shell exploded. From this house, Ross chose two: the husband who'd been working in the fields farther out, and the son who'd stayed with his mother; from that hut, he decided it

wasn't worth taking anyone; from another shack, he selected a daughter who had been alone there at the time,
together with her father—but only because he insisted on
coming along to escort her. Ross suspected the father
would be dead before they reached Pakistan.

It grew dark, but still they drove, Mahmud knowing his
way in his beloved valley as if it was bright sunlight.

Ross decided that twenty was the maximum number
they could cope with and hope to feed at villages along the
way. Some would inevitably die, but he hoped most would
survive to provide the human publicity fodder to wreck the
neutron talks.

When they were finished, they drove back.

They parked the jeep in the garage, with Mir Gholam in
a drugged sleep inside, and Mahmud led them through the
alleyways to the courtyard where they'd spent the previous
night.

Ruka was in total darkness, but not in silence. All around
were pitiful sounds: weeping nearby as they passed a
house; sudden hysterical screaming in the distance, then
from behind them a series of anguished beseeching cries to
Allah; a stereophonic nightmare of terrible suffering.

At the edge of the courtyard Mahmud struck a match and
found a lantern. It cast a soft glow, enough to let them see
the shapes of men; some lying on the ground, others on
charpoys.

They went to each in turn. All had suffered intense
radiation burns, as if the skin had been flayed off them. A
few were obviously dead, and others seemed to be in
coma, from which, if they were lucky, they would never
emerge. Perhaps Mahmud still recognized the men, despite
their raw faces; but if he did he gave no sign.

At last he said abruptly, "We will go from here."

They walked back into the street, turning south toward
the end of the valley and the Russian wall, while the

sounds of dying grew more distant and were finally lost in the night.

And then, up ahead, off the road they saw it—an area of light, of campfires and lanterns. The men stopped, wondering if the Russians were already moving in.

Mahmud spoke to the other *mujahideen,* and suddenly there was a wave of relieved laughter.

"It's a caravan," the rebel commander announced. "It must have come this afternoon. We will talk with them."

They strode off, Lyle hurrying to catch up with Mahmud. "Listen," Clive said. "I don't care how much money they ask for because we can pick it up in Pakistan, but I want those donkeys and horses to take us out. All the way out, okay Mahmud? Will you fix that?"

"I will try," he replied. "I will see if I can get a good price."

Lyle clapped him on the back. "Thanks," he said. "We're going to need all the help we can get."

As they approached the camp, they were aware of dark shapes moving warily around them, as if to fight.

Mahmud, sensing a threat, slowed his pace and called out calmly, *"Salām-o-alaikum,"* and from several sides—including, the Americans noticed, behind them—came the cautious response, *"Alaikum-o-salām."*

Mahmud launched into a stream of language—Pashto, Urdu, who cared—but the explanation was obviously clear and concise. He turned several times to gesture to the town.

The tension eased and they walked deeper into the camp. Ross and Lyle were shown to a separate carpet on the ground, while Mahmud and the other *mujahideen* sat on a bigger covering and discussed their predicament with the leader of the caravan.

Green tea was brought, and the Americans drank it gratefully. By the time dinner was served, it seemed

Mahmud and the others had got down to some hard bargaining.

It was nearly midnight before Mahmud joined them. "They are not willing," he said, and the agents felt a surge of disappointment, until he continued, "But they say they will do it for two thousand American dollars."

Lyle was about to accept, but Ross made a small warning gesture while he considered the implications.

If they agreed to the first asking price, the caravan leader would be sorry he hadn't started higher, and they'd find themselves being hassled, having to fight every step of the way. He would gladly have promised ten times that money, but there were local circumstances to take into account.

Ross turned to Mahmud. "Thank them, and tell them the cost is too high. We will pay one thousand American dollars only."

He sat back, pretending indifference, but he noticed a gleam of humor in Mahmud's eye. The commander returned to the main gathering and reported the counter-offer. It was clear from his tone and the way he shrugged at the voluble response that he was bargaining seriously.

"I hope you know what you're doing, Dave," Lyle said.

"Leave it to me," Ross assured him.

At length, Mahmud returned. "They say that considering the distance, and the dangers involved in carrying people touched by the Russian gas, and because they must leave their regular trading route and lose much money, they will do it for not less than eighteen hundred American dollars."

Now Ross was sure of his ground. "Please tell them," he said, "and this is my final offer, that I will pay one thousand five hundred dollars when they get us across the border into Parachinar."

This time, Mahmud was gone only a few minutes. He came back to say, "They want a thousand now."

Ross looked inquiringly at the *mujahideen* commander. "What do you think?" he asked.

"I would give them half that," he said, "and the rest in Pakistan." He smiled. "They know they cannot cheat the *mujahideen* by taking your money and leaving you later, because we will bring them before an Islamic court to answer for their crimes. You are safe."

Ross, wishing it were true, fumbled with his money belt and handed over five hundred. "It looks like we've got ourselves a caravan," he said.

The men slept about four hours before the bustling around them, the talking and packing, dragged them from deep slumber. Ross had never imagined he could be as comfortable on a thin carpet laid on hard ground as he was in his own bed in Washington. Or Elaine's bed. Or Julie Klein's. How long ago and far away all that seemed.

They sat up and looked around. It was clear that the caravan, which included camels and herds of sheep and goats, was getting out of the Panjshir as quickly as it could.

When Mahmud saw that the Americans were awake, he came to greet them.

"Have any of the people we're taking arrived yet?" Ross asked and was relieved when Mahmud pointed to a group around a smoldering fire a short distance off.

"Great!" Ross said. "How many to come?"

"A few. Not many."

Then Lyle's voice, "How about Mir Gholam, Dave? Do you think he's still okay?"

Ross rubbed his eyes. "I guess he's screaming his head off by now," he said, "but I can't hear him, so I'm pretending he's not." He looked helplessly across at Lyle. "Shit, what else can I do, Clive? There's not enough morphine to take him all the way to Pakistan, so we're going to have to ration him.''

"How about antibiotic tablets and cream?''

"Some, for all the good they'll do,'' Ross said. "But I haven't got much left in the way of clean bandages.''

"No. Me neither.''

They stood watching the activity around them. Finally Lyle admitted, "This caravan isn't going to save us a hell of a lot of time, is it?''

"Not a lot,'' Ross agreed. "Maybe a day if we can get things really moving, but it's going to save energy, and I hope keep a couple of people alive a little longer.''

Just before dawn, when the Afghans were spreading their prayer mats, Ross and Lyle walked back toward the town.

From a long way off they could hear the sounds of Ruka dying, floating through the still air, as if they were approaching hell itself.

Before they reached the garage where the jeep was kept, they recognized amid the screams and cries, Mir Gholam's piteous sobbing. Ross began to run.

The morphine quietened the boy. Ross held him in his arms, patting his back, while the child's head lolled on his shoulder.

It was hopeless. They were at least ten days from Torabora, probably nearer fourteen. Add another two until they reached Peshawar and hospital treatment, and whichever way you worked it out, you had an eight-year-old amputee whose morphine, even rationed, would be finished before they were halfway, and whose stump somehow had to heal itself with the magic combination of a broad-spectrum antibiotic and a couple of tubes of cream that were good for infected blisters. If the boy had been a horse, Ross would have shot him right there and ended the misery; but because he was a human being, it was considered proper and civilized to allow him to suffer. He thought of Mada Khan, and how clearcut that decision had seemed.

"If this was my son," said Ross, almost to himself, "what would I do? What the hell chance has he got? When the morphine runs out, he's just going to have to scream. But Clive, if I gave him all of it now, every bit, yours and mine, he'd just never wake up. And he wouldn't feel a thing."

Lyle stayed silent in the gloom of the garage, while from outside came the ceaseless cacophony of extreme suffering. Their eyes met. "Or if I took a knife and cut his throat," Ross said holding the child tight against his chest, "he's already so drugged he wouldn't know what the hell was going on, and we'd even save our morphine." There was a long silence before Ross said quietly, "Ah, shit."

He turned back to the jeep and laid Mir Gholam gently in it. "I can't do it. I'm sorry, Clive."

"No sweat, Dave."

Then Ross's gaze focused on the vehicle. "Jesus Christ," he said in wonder. "We haven't been thinking at all, have we? Why don't we drive to Pakistan?"

"Can we?" Lyle asked.

"I don't see why not," Ross insisted. "Even if there aren't roads, it shouldn't worry this little baby too much."

"We wouldn't be able to carry twenty people, Dave," Lyle reminded him. "We'd have to leave most of them behind."

"Well," Ross said, suddenly excited, "maybe you and me could split up—draw straws, toss a coin. One of us takes the jeep with a couple of *mujahideen,* the kid and a few of Yardley's victims, while the other goes along with Mahmud and the caravan."

"There's got to be a catch to it," Lyle said. "If there wasn't, surely it'd have occurred to Mahmud, even if you and I hadn't been thinking straight for a while back there."

"Let's go ask."

They went to find the rebel commander and met him just outside town as he was on his way to get them.

Lyle was right, of course. Mahmud explained that the few roads were either mined by the *mujahideen,* or liable to Soviet roadblocks near military installations, but most important of all, there was a serious shortage of petrol. Mahmud took them back to the garage and turned on the ignition. The fuel gauge was just above empty. "We have no more," he said, "until the next caravan."

"What about the bus?" Ross asked.

"It uses diesel," Mahmud replied, "and it is not good off the roads."

"It's not much good on the roads," Lyle said.

There was a movement in the entrance, and the three men turned quickly.

In the doorway stood Mohammed Iqbal. *"Salām-o-alaikum,"* he said. His voice sounded normal.

Mahmud smiled with joy and went to embrace his *mujahed* brother: the first man he'd seen in Ruka who looked and sounded as he had before the Russian bomb went off.

"Iqbal, how're you doing?" Lyle asked. He and Ross moved closer looking carefully at him. There were no signs of radiation burns.

"I was sick yesterday," Mohammed Iqbal admitted, "but I'm fine this morning."

Ross looked away, knowing that prodromal symptoms can give way to a feeling of well-being, which masks damage to bone marrow. The truth was that Iqbal would probably die in a few days. He'd been too close.

"Where were you when it happened?" Ross asked.

"In the tea house down the road," Iqbal said. "And you?"

Ross pointed vaguely off into the valley. "A couple of miles along the road."

"Wasn't that lucky?" Iqbal said. Then after a silence: "What was it? Some sort of nuke? I saw the mushroom cloud."

"Yeah. A neutron bomb."

Gradually things began to fall into place in Iqbal's mind. It had been impossible to think clearly yesterday, but this morning everything was capable of a logical explanation. The transmitter he had been given to carry and had since thrown away—flung as far as his strength would take it into the rocks and grass near the road—and his instructions to make sure the Americans went north; at last he knew what they meant.

The Russians had used him as bait and, like bait, he was disposable.

"What's the plan?" Iqbal asked.

"We're pulling out now," Ross said. "We've got our victims and we're taking them to Pakistan and then to the States."

"So let's go."

It hadn't occurred to Iqbal that he might not be included in the evacuation, and now that it came to the crunch, neither Ross nor Lyle could find it in their hearts to turn him away a second time. He had gone to Harvard after all, and suppose by some miracle they did manage to get him as far as Washington—there were a couple of old Harvard men close to the President who wouldn't be too pleased to hear one of their number had been nuked.

Before they left, Ruka, Ross and Lyle returned to the courtyard where they'd slept that first night, and took from the bodies of dead *mujahideen* two Kalashnikovs, webbing equipment, and rifle bullets.

They had the feeling they might need them before this assignment was over. Maybe even against each other.

And so it was that when the caravan plodded out of the Panjshir Valley, through the hole blown in the Russian wall, and headed toward Charikar, they took with them the means of defense against those who might slip into madness and unpredictability—plus the person who caused the attack in the first place and who, despite the realization of his betrayal by Moscow, clung to the belief that because he had served them faithfully and had by a miracle survived, they would reward him well.

And he still had a card to play: the two Americans. Iqbal knew they were alive, even if the Russians did not. Iqbal knew where they could be found and where they were heading.

It would be a long, hard road back to Pakistan, and he was prepared to make it longer and harder; impossible, if he could.

And this time, he'd be watching his own back, guarding himself against his own side. Being aware when action was coming, and knowing to stay well clear.

19

They made slower time to Charikar than the agents had hoped but at least Yardley's victims were able to ride.

Mir Gholam was strapped to a board on top of a camel's pack, and Ross—sometimes riding, sometimes walking—listened abjectly to his cries of pain and delirium in the hours before his next ration of morphine.

When they camped overnight near Charikar, Iqbal slipped away into town, to the house of Meermai Khan, wondering grimly what the reaction would be. Had his friend sent him into a trap, knowing he was to be killed? It would be interesting to see his face when a ghost presented itself before him.

He reached the entrance and knocked, covering himself below the eyes with his *sadr*.

It was Meermai himself who opened the door, peering into the darkness at the shadowy figure, but clearly not fearful for his safety.

"Who are you?" he asked.

Iqbal stepped forward so the glow of the lantern could light both their faces before he pulled aside his *sadr*, watching for the response. But the other man's guileless eyes displayed only pleasure at his return. Meermai embraced and kissed him in the same affectionate way as always, making Iqbal uncertain, hesitant. Perhaps he hadn't known what the real plan was after all.

Iqbal brushed aside the formalities. "Can we talk?"

Meermai Khan immediately became grave. "Of course," he said. "Let us go into the garden."

They walked beneath the deep black shade of the trees, around ponds where stars were reflected in the still water and past bushes whose blossoms put out their scent only at night.

Iqbal noticed none of it as he told what had happened in Ruka, and about the bomb that killed nearly everyone there, except for himself.

Meermai hissed through his teeth. He stopped.

"The Americans?" he asked. "What happened to the Americans?"

Iqbal wished he could see his face again. "They are alive," he said neutrally.

Meermai hissed a second time. "Where?"

Iqbal shrugged. "Somewhere."

They walked in silence, while Meermai considered the situation and, consummate bargainer that he was, understood what Iqbal must be feeling, and how he should be handled.

At last, Meermai said sadly, "I blame myself, of course. It was I who gave you the instructions, not knowing I was putting my brother in peril." He lifted his head to the sky and cried in anguish, "Allah!" He didn't look to see what effect, if any, this demonstration was having on Mohammed Iqbal but continued to berate the Russians and blame himself. He thanked God many times for sparing Iqbal's life.

He let another silence fall before moving onto his next theme. "These friends of ours," Meermai Khan declared with a delicate emphasis that might have been anger or might have been scorn, "are greatly in your debt. They will surely pay handsomely for the work you have done and the dangers you encountered even though"—and here his voice became thoughtful—"even though the Americans are unfortunately still alive."

He let that point sink in, that the mission had not actually been accomplished.

Meermai sighed. "Sometimes I do not understand our friends. They can be brutal and unforgiving, even to those who fight valiantly for their cause."

And now he did look toward Mohammed Iqbal, underlining the hint, the implied threat.

He stopped in the darkest part of the garden, beneath the willow where the branches draped to the ground around them and on one side touched the still water.

Meermai asked quietly, "What will you do, my brother?"

"You were right when you said they owed me," Iqbal replied. "They do owe me, and I want payment."

"At the same time," Meermai said sighing again, "they will tell me that the mission was unfulfilled: the Americans are alive."

Now there was triumph in Iqbal's voice. "Ah yes, but I know where they are! I know everything!"

"And can you complete the mission?" Meermai's voice was cautious.

"I can!"

"By yourself?" Again the delicate emphasis of a supreme negotiator.

Iqbal paused and thought. "Perhaps not by myself," he conceded. "Not now that they are armed and there are still other *mujahideen* with them."

"So our friends will have to come to your aid, will they not?"

"But if they do," Iqbal argued, "will they come with

another neutron bomb? Will they kill me, their friend, as easily as they do their enemy?''

"No!" Meermai Khan's voice was low but emphatic. "I will speak with them myself. How many Afghans," he asked rhetorically, "would aid the Russians if it became known this was how they were treated? No! It was a serious error and it can never happen again. And they must pay you well for it," he concluded positively.

Iqbal found himself becoming restive in the blackness beneath the willow and he wanted to walk again. In the distance, he could see the glimmer of the lantern. He tried to move away, but Meermai's soft hand held on to his arm, urging him to stay.

The blackness was good. Meermai knew it made Iqbal uneasy, that it would concentrate his mind and end foolish talk.

"What do you propose?" he asked.

Iqbal tried to assemble his thoughts, and at last a plan began to form. "Let them attack three days from now," he said finally, anxious to be free. "On the second day, I will say I am sick. I will fall back."

"But what will they attack, my brother? Where?" Meermai's question was whispered, asking that a secret be shared between friends.

"A caravan," Iqbal said after another pause. "They are paying it to take them and some survivors into Pakistan."

If the slightest glint of light had penetrated the shelter of the willows in that silent garden, Iqbal would have seen, unmistakably, the gleam of victory in Meermai's eyes, and he would have known he had played his hand too early.

But there was only darkness, and Meermai's soft, insistent touch.

And still Meermai seemed to expect something more. "Where?" he breathed. "Where is it?"

Iqbal could no longer stand the blackness, the gently

squeezing touch of his forearm. He had to get out. "Three miles west of here," Iqbal said desperately, supplying the puzzle's final piece.

Meermai Khan gave a long sigh, and his hand released Iqbal.

"They will be pleased with this news," he murmured almost to himself. "Very pleased."

He ushered Iqbal from the darkness and along the path toward the lantern. "It is agreed then," he said, "an attack three days from now. I will tell them." A pause. "Will you take tea, my brother? Have you eaten?"

"No. I will go back. We leave at dawn."

"May Allah go with you," Meermai Khan said.

The huge, shaggy camels of the caravan glided superciliously over the ground followed by donkeys, horses, and the herds of sheep and goats. The nomads themselves mostly walked beside the animals that carried their possessions. When they made camp at night, they unloaded tents of wooden lattice work covered with a thick black woolen felt, which could be extended and quickly erected. Each tent sheltered an entire family.

Two days out of Charikar, what Ross had feared the thing he'd hoped to head off by bargaining at the beginning, suddenly happened.

The leader of the caravan issued fresh demands. He had now realized that the route they were taking, although the quickest, would soon offer insufficient pastures for the flocks on which their lives depended.

So that afternoon, while Mir Gholam howled with pain on the back of a camel that lay looking indifferent in the shade of a tree, there was a long, angry exchange between the *mujahideen* and the men of the caravan. First, double money was demanded and Ross refused. Then with all of them gathered around nomads on one side, Americans and *mujahideen* on the other, the caravan leader declared it was impossible for them to go on at all. They wanted their dollars now, and they were turning back.

Fingers moved down the webbing straps of the rifles ready to unsling them, and for a time, it seemed as if the angry words would turn into a battle.

Ross, realizing they were on the edge of disaster, proposed a compromise. "Let half the caravan go where it likes," he said. "Let the sheep and the goats be taken to pastures. We want only enough horses, donkeys and camels to get us to Pakistan. For that we will pay the agreed amount, and we will give them an extra two hundred dollars if we move faster." So it was that the day before the Russians were scheduled to make their second attack, and with Mohammed Iqbal feigning sickness, the caravan divided up.

As it did, Iqbal wondered uneasily if this would upset the Soviet plans, but he decided, rightly, that the MiGs that now flew twice daily over the area on photo reconnaissance, would show that although the flocks were being left behind, the Americans were still out in front, heading for Pakistan.

Iqbal's apparent sickness surprised neither Ross nor Lyle. They hadn't expected him to last more than a few days anyway, and they still had Mahmud.

They left him with the nomads and their flocks. When they were out of sight, Iqbal recovered sufficiently to head back to Charikar where, a week later in Meermai Khan's house, he actually did die, racked with fever and dehydration. Meermai, who had received handsome payment for Iqbal's information, watched him closely during the final painful days. He kept everyone else away in case Iqbal's wandering mind revealed dangerous information.

In Charikar later, they spoke well of Meermai's charity to the unfortunate *mujahed*, particularly because he had stayed at the side of a man touched by the Russian gas with no thought for his own safety and would not even allow his servants near.

When he heard the remarks, Meermai dismissed them with a wave of his plump hand.

"We all do as Allah commands," he said modestly.

At the time they split up, Ross's main preoccupation was the boy, for whom he felt increasing responsibility but for whom he could do no more.

The morphine was finished. Mir Gholam had also eaten every strong painkilling drug they possessed and was now reduced to aspirin, which made no discernible difference to his suffering.

Every touch on the child's crippled arm, however gentle, caused him to scream. His eyes were wild and it seemed to Ross, they had turned from the trusting eyes of a child to those of an old man.

The smaller caravan moved only slightly faster than the old one, and there was an unsettling sullenness about the nomads.

On that second evening out of Charikar, they pitched camp and as usual Ross supervised the unloading of the board on which Mir Gholam endured his unrelieved torture.

As a routine, Ross himself changed the bandages at night, boiling the old ones in a tin can over a fire, smearing the last of the antibiotic cream over a wound which would not heal. And now, with the dressings disintegrating through washing and overuse, and the boy weeping pathetically, almost beyond exhaustion, Ross made a new discovery.

He tried to feed Mir Gholam, coaxing him to eat spoonfuls of curd, a little *nān*, some fruit, but the boy refused. He was wasting away before his eyes.

Ross sat with him as darkness fell and the campfires

were lit, feeling as desperate as he had ever done in his life. He talked to the child in a language he couldn't understand but which Ross hoped would comfort by the gentleness of its tone.

Lyle left them alone at these moments and sat facing away, looking out over the increasingly barren landscape toward the distant mountains forming the frontier.

Later they tried to sleep, while Mir Gholam cried hoarsely on the edge of the camp. It was incredible to Ross that one small body could contain such a capacity for suffering. He lay and listened, powerless to help.

It was after midnight that Lyle heard Ross suddenly get up and go to the sobbing child. Lyle waited, sick at heart for David and for the boy; feeling, like the others, personally worn down by this public suffering, yet knowing instinctively that he could say nothing. Mir Gholam had grown to mean something special to Ross—a symbol almost. The son he'd never had maybe. A chance to save as well as to kill. Jesus, who knew?

An hour passed, then blessedly, the noise stopped.

He heard David coming back and saw from his silhouette against the night sky that he was carrying his pack.

Ross eased himself onto the ground beside Lyle, and such a stillness came over him it was as though he had fallen into a deep sleep, although Lyle knew he was awake.

The silence extended not only from Mir Gholam, but throughout the camp. It was almost uncanny.

Slowly it dawned on Lyle what had happened. He rolled onto his side, staring at the unmoving shadow next to him, and said one word very quietly.

"Measles?"

Ross didn't answer, but Lyle thought he saw a slight movement of his head.

Lyle reached out to touch his friend in compassion.

Then Ross's voice came, drained and barely audible: "We've got to bury him in the morning. Will you help me, Clive?"

"Sure I will."

Ross found it necessary to explain. "He had gangrene." Lyle could tell he was near weeping.

"Try to sleep, Dave," Lyle said. "There's a long way to go yet."

But they both lay awake, Ross's thoughts as tortured as Mir Gholam's body had been; Lyle thinking: Well, shit, that's something I've never done. I've never killed a kid.

In traditional Afghan funeral ceremonies, the body is washed and dressed in a winding sheet of cotton. Then it is placed on a bed and covered with clean sheets while prayers are said and people come to pay their respects.

Had he died at home in normal times, an eight-year-old like Mir Gholam would have been placed in a coffin covered with rich cloth and flowers.

But all they could do for him that morning at the edge of the semi-desert was lower him into a grave, dug north to south, and on Mahmud's instructions, leave a wedge-shaped pit at the bottom, so he *could* lie with his face pointing towards Mecca. Mahmud recited a verse from the Koran, and offered prayers for the departed soul.

Lyle stood close to Ross, almost touching, but David seemed calm and distant.

Around them, what was left of their caravan waited sullenly to depart.

They shovelled soil into the grave, and when this was done, they walked away.

Ross didn't look back.

There was no Russian attack that third day.

It had been decided at Politburo level in Moscow that

neutron weapons would not be used so close to a foreign border, because it might achieve precisely the object they wished to avoid.

They would therefore stage a conventional ambush— commandos, helicopter gunships, tanks: the weaponry with which the Russians usually confront the *mujahideen*. Reconnaissance photographs showed the caravan heading toward a series of barren hills, through which there was a small pass.

The caravan's steady rate of progress, if maintained, would bring the Americans into the pass on the afternoon of the fourth day.

The men selected for the assault were mostly from the southern states of the USSR, and therefore facially similar to many Afghan tribes. Because they would have to spend the hottest part of the day lying in wait on the high ground, they were to be dressed as *mujahideen*, and of course, they carried the same Kalashnikovs. Any passing Afghans catching sight of them would have no reason to be suspicious.

No one saw the parachutes coming down late on the third night, but those in the caravan who were still awake heard the transport aircraft passing high overhead.

The commandos landed, regrouped found their bearings. By the time dawn came, they had pitched small dun-colored tents on the hill tops overlooking the pass, giving some protection from the sun.

The temperature rose quickly and by ten o'clock had passed 100 degrees.

The photo reconnaissance MiGs flew more frequently over the caravan. Ross and Lyle had become used to one in the morning, and another in mid-afternoon, but the first jet passed fairly high shortly after they began to move, and every two hours there was another.

With hindsight, it's easy to identify events like these as obvious clues, but the agents had no reason to suspect they were being tracked. They were concerned with the simple business of keeping people moving, of watching the nomads whose tempers had not improved, and monitoring the health of Yardley's survivors. And of each other.

One of the survivors—the father who insisted on escorting his daughter, Nasreen, to America—had, as Ross suspected, been bombarded with fast neutrons well over the 1,000 rad dose and could not last the journey. He now lacked the energy or the will to sit on a donkey and had to be strapped on the same wooden platform they had used for Mir Gholam, atop a camel's pack.

When they stopped for lunch that fourth day, they found he had died.

While his daughter wept and lamented, the *mujahideen* took turns in digging the grave and saying prayers.

The next set of Soviet reconnaissance photographs received at the base in Jalalabad showed the caravan stopped for longer than usual, and a close examination revealed why.

The Russian officers could see the freshly dug grave with the body beside it.

"Do you think it's an American?" one of them asked.

The others laughed. Someone patted him on the back. It was a nice thought, but would make no difference to their operation. Moscow's instructions were that they had to bring back two foreign corpses and their packs, so there could be no doubt about identification.

The question now was how long the burial would take and what time the caravan would reach the ambush point. From the grave of its latest neutron victim, this was less than two hours.

In fact, the first camel entered the pass shortly after six in the evening, climbing steadily up through the stony, sandy ground, following the tracks of centuries, with the animals behind being urged on faster by the nomads who wanted to make camp before it grew dark.

Ross and Lyle were walking together. Nasreen was on a donkey, weeping for her father and praying for his soul. Mahmud stayed near her, calm and serene as always, signaling by his constant presence that he, the commander, would now be responsible for her safety and virtue and that she could rely on him as if he was her brother.

From the high ground the Russians watched the caravan come into the trap.

Some used binoculars to try to identify the Americans but no one could because all those below were now armed, and at that range, not enough detail could be made out on the faces of moving men.

Tanks and armored personnel carriers had already left Jalalabad and were heading swiftly for the area to give support in case the operation was incomplete by nightfall. With their infrared lights and special glasses, they would be able to see in the dark while the enemy remained blind.

This column of armor raised a great cloud of dust as it moved, and the noise of the engines could be heard a long distance away. But neither the cloud nor the sound had yet reached the point of the ambush.

The last stragglers climbed into view and the commandos waited for the order to attack.

Without warning, the valley exploded in deafening blasts of noise, flashes, spurts of dust, rearing, panic-stricken animals and shouting, falling men. Ross, who had never seen battle, froze for an instant before being struck by a great weight—Lyle smashing into him to push him down behind a rock out of the way of the bullets and the shrapnel from the grenades. They huddled close, trying to work out what the hell was going on.

They unslung their Kalashnikovs and cautiously peered

around, up into the high ground from where the attack was being launched, identifying points where riflemen lay.

"Stay here!" Lyle yelled, and then he was gone, doubled over, running for new cover, taking the chance that four or five seconds' sudden exposure would not be enough for the Russians to get a bead on him. As he flung himself down, the powdery earth nearby puffed with bullets.

Ross began operating automatically, taking his time and as few chances as were absolutely necessary, and now feeling curiously remote. He watched for muzzle flashes, the small puffs of smoke, and wriggled into position so he could zero in on that man, just that one. It was not for nothing he had scored high on the Fairfax range.

The Russians had begun taking their first casualties.

Mahmud and the few not cut down in the first savage seconds were spread on both sides of the pass, getting what shelter they could from overhanging ledges of earth and stone, and protection behind often inadequate rock.

Mahmud, true to his private vow to look after Nasreen, raced toward her immediately when the fighting began.

Her donkey reared, throwing her, and he half-carried, half-dragged the terrified girl to the nearest cover, while the pass echoed with the concussion of battle, cries, and stampeding animals.

The Afghans are good fighters, brave and knowledgeable. Weapons are their constant companions from childhood, and they know how to use them. Those who made it to cover realized they had to hold out for nightfall, when the Soviet advantage would be reduced and they could move more easily in territory they knew well.

The firing became sporadic, each side waiting for individual targets to present themselves, and in this the commandos, occupying the high ground, were undoubtedly the masters. As the sun set, the survivors of the caravan were trapped, pinned down, yet all the Russians needed to do was draw back from some hilltop position and move in safety to another that offered a different perspective, a better view of a potential target.

The attrition rate for the caravan was slow but steady. One by one, the nomads were picked off and their rifles fell silent. The few *mujahideen* who remained fared little better.

But the shadows were lengthening, and as the handful of survivors began to think they had lasted the course, there came the distant sound of the armored column approaching from Jalalabad.

Lyle realized immediately what the Soviet tactics would be: to seal off the pass at each end and continue the battle with the advantages of night sights and probably an air attack.

The engines of the tanks and APCs came closer, became very loud, and soon Lyle could see the silhouettes of gun turrets moving past the mouth of the pass.

When the tank engines were switched off, there was an uncanny silence. Night closed in.

Lyle crawled in the darkness to where Ross lay.

"You okay?" he asked.

"Yeah. What the fuck's happening now?"

"They've sealed us off with armor, front and rear. They'll have infrared night sights, so they can see us, though not as well as daytime. I guess this is just a break in the action. We might get air attacks any time now, so we've got to get out of here."

"Sure. But how?"

"We run and we crawl," Lyle whispered. "Listen, don't worry. It's not that easy to keep a good watch through a tank periscope with infrared, so we've got a chance. But we've also got to watch out in case the rifles at the top of the hill have night sights." He touched Ross's shoulder: "Let's go."

Lyle began to crawl from the cover of the rock. Then he crouched and ran to the slightly deeper black he knew would be another. He moved silently. Ross waited until Lyle was running, then tucked in behind. Occasionally they would coincide for a few seconds, frozen behind a boulder, but often the other man simply disappeared into the total blackness and Ross had to crouch and run, not knowing whether he was still following Lyle or whether he'd overtaken him. When his feet dislodged a stone, it seemed as it slid to make enough noise to alert every Russian in the area.

But then suddenly, there Lyle would be again, just ahead, stopping only long enough to identify his next objective, moving steadily toward the end of the pass and the mouths of the Soviet tanks.

Across on the other side, no more than twenty feet away, a stone knocked loudly against another as it fell. Ross and Lyle froze. Perhaps the Russians were coming down the hill using their infra-red scopes. Perhaps instead of escaping, they were moving into another trap.

They listened intently. After several seconds, they heard a small panting sob.

Lyle called as quietly as he could, "Nasreen?"

And Mahmud's voice came back, also low, not carrying much farther than their straining ears. "Yes."

"We've got to get out of here now," Lyle said.

And he was off again, running silently for the next piece of cover, Ross behind him; then crawling to check ahead, listening, eyes straining in the darkness. There were no further sounds from the other side of the pass and no way of telling whether Mahmud and the girl were also moving out.

The last piece of cover was a thorn bush. Lyle lay on his belly, staring ahead.

This was it: the end of the pass; and ahead were the

tanks, only dimly defined against the starry night, but as soon as the moon rose, their outlines would be clear.

Lyle knew that the infrared beams of at least some of the tanks would be directed at precisely the point they had now reached—because it was the last logical place for anyone on his side to hide before making a break—and that the machine gunners would be ready.

Lyle looked back and then upward. They could take a risk: try to climb halfway up the hill and make their way around the circumference, potentially in full view of everyone, before making their descent well away from the mouth of the pass. They could do that and pray the Russians were concentrating on the obvious, not on the reckless.

He drew back and whispered, "Follow me."

Ross obeyed automatically, back the way they'd come. Once out of sight of the tanks, they climbed the hill, it seemed almost up to the rifle positions, but gradually traversing toward the waiting armor.

In the distance, they heard the sound of helicopter engines, and neither doubted for a second where these were heading.

Lyle speeded up his pace to a point Ross thought made it inevitable they would be seen, and as he ran and scrambled, his body tensed for the machinegun fire he knew would cut him down.

The helicopters came nearer.

Ross and Lyle were down the hill now, crawling furiously, keeping as low as possible and heading for the space between two tanks—a gap of only six or seven feet. The first helicopters were almost overhead; the tanks only a matter of yards away. Lyle rose to a crouch and ran, Ross after him, charging past the black-tracked, threatening silhouettes; yet no one fired, no one saw, and they kept running, getting as much distance as they could until suddenly high above their heads, there was a series of cracks, and magnesium flares lit every inch for hundreds of yards.

They dropped as if felled by bullets. The light was so dazzling that within its radius it created a landscape without shadows, a place where every texture and imperfection could be seen.

Lyle began to move again, crawling for the nearest rocks. When they were both behind them, they threw their *sadrs* over their heads and watched the helicopters spiralling down into the valley.

Whatever it was they were firing exploded in a million lethal fragments, bright with flame and death.

Each helicopter loosed two rockets on every pass, and as the explosions reverberated through the night, climbed away to rejoin the spiral.

The flares faltered and began to go out.

Ross and Lyle scrambled to their feet and ran.

By the time the next flares went up, they were on the outer edges, in a twilight zone, and they continued running until they reached total darkness, and were able to turn and watch the attack, as if it was taking place in some distant floodlit football stadium.

They sat, catching their breath among the rocks and watching the show.

"I hope Mahmud made it out in time," Lyle said. "If he didn't, he's dead."

It seemed impossible that anyone still in the pass could survive. The helicopters were saturating the area, methodically hitting each section in turn.

The third set of flares cracked into life. Outside the ring of tanks there was no sign of movement.

They waited another ten minutes before Lyle stood up. "We may as well push on," he said. "It doesn't look like anyone else's coming out."

The men walked until dawn, following what they hoped was the general direction of Torabora, and wondering how they would fare without Mahmud or one of the *mujahideen* to vouch for them.

They found out shortly after sunrise, when in the distance, in the middle of the dry, sandy scrub, they saw mud buildings surrounded by green trees and fields—a place where there was a well, a small farm.

Ross led the way, and walked toward a group of Afghan men who stared with open hostility.

Ross smiled cordially. *"Salām-o-alaikum,"* he greeted them and got a mumbled response.

He pointed to himself and Lyle. "Americans," he said. *"Americano."* But the men still weren't smiling. Ross shook his head. "Not *Russe,"* he explained. *"Russe murdabad!"*

He tried to tell them they had been with *mujahideen* who'd been killed in a battle with the Russians, to indicate they wanted to get to Torabora quickly.

The Afghans stared.

Ross found himself wondering if they'd found the only village in the country that supported the Soviet invasion; and that was the moment he and Lyle felt the muzzles of rifles digging sharply into their backs. Men had crept up behind them.

The language was now international. They unslung their Kalashnikovs from their shoulders, slowly took off their packs and dropped them on the ground at their feet. Then they put up their hands.

Ross tried to protest again, Lyle joining in indignantly: Death to the Russians, they said, Long live Afghanistan, and the man in front of Ross suddenly spat straight into his face. Ross could feel the mucus, just below his eye, dribbling slowly down. His instinct was disgust, to wipe it

away, but he realized that if he moved a hand now, they
would kill him immediately.

The Afghan motioned with his head and they walked
along a path toward a shed, whose walls were of the thick,
hard-baked mud, and whose door, although wooden, was
stout. They were ordered inside and it slammed shut. They
could hear a lock click.

It was pitch black. They waited until their eyes adjusted
and they could at least see each other's outlines, before
moving cautiously sideways to the wall, then forward and
going all the way around the room. It seemed empty.

Finally they sat against the far wall, close enough so
their bodies touched: human contact in the darkness, friendship in a hostile place.

"I don't know about you," Lyle said, "but I'm pretty
well beat. I'm going to get some sleep."

"What do you think they'll do to us, Clive?" Ross
asked.

"I don't know, Dave, but I guess whatever side they're
on, we're on the other. In a place like this, that's not
good."

"Shit, what a trip this has been," Ross said. "We get
ourselves nuked and now maybe we don't even fly home
to tell them the good news, give them the proof." In the
darkness, he tried to grin.

"Get some sleep," Lyle advised.

The Russians went into the pass at dawn, collecting bodies
and rifles, and pieces of bodies, and bandoliers of ammunition. They also found some hand-woven carpets which
the nomads had been carrying to sell and which had miraculously survived, and took them away too.

They found no one alive.

The body bags were loaded aboard Mi-8 helicopters and

flown back to Jalalabad, with the packs and personal belongings for identification.

Some victims had been so badly mutilated that the doctors found themselves looking for examples of Western dentistry.

Helicopter gunships were also dispatched to the spot where, shortly before the ambush, the *mujahideen* had been photographed burying a man, and there they dug up the body of Nasreen's father. He too was taken to Jalalabad.

Ross found he could sleep. He had become fatalistic about the whole operation, and his own uncertain future, so when he spread his *sadr* and settled onto it, he fell quickly into a deep, dreamless slumber.

It was so deep, in fact, that when the shed door opened several hours later, Lyle had to shake him awake.

Men with rifles were silhouetted in the doorway.

The agents sat and waited. Ross remembered Mada Khan and found his palms beginning to sweat.

A figure detached itself from the group and came toward them. Ross felt hands on his biceps, pulling him to his feet, and then, unbelievably, he was being hugged and kissed in the traditional Afghan manner, and it was Mahmud's voice murmuring, "Forgive them, Mr. David, they saw you had rifles and thought you were *Russe*."

Ross stared at the figure in disbelief, stuttering: "Mahmud . . . what the? . . . how the hell did you get out?"

But Mahmud was busy hugging Lyle, apologizing to him too. Now he was half-turned and the light was on his face, they could see his shame and deep embarrassment; and beyond him, the same look on the faces of those who had arrested them earlier, and particularly the one who spat at Ross.

"Mahmud," Lyle said, "you're a miracle worker. Please tell these guys there're no hard feelings. It's all okay."

"None at all," Ross confirmed, and to show it, he went to the others and greeted them again formally, while Mahmud explained in Pashto and said the Americans were prepared to accept the hospitality of the house.

For the first time, Ross and Lyle were invited to eat with the others around the *dastarkhan*, the big sheet of cloth on which the bowls of communal food were laid, and dig in with the true believers.

It was the first decent meal they had had in several days, and both were very hungry. Their host urged them to eat more and more, and while they did, they heard from Mahmud how he and Nasreen had escaped from the ambush, using tactics similar to the Americans', but moving slower because of the girl, and escaping at more of a tangent.

"Where's Nasreen now?" Ross asked.

Mahmud indicated the main house. "With the women."

"And our packs?" Jesus, the rock samples and the leaves.

Mahmud smiled. "They are safe. You will have them when we have finished. Nothing has been taken."

It was late afternoon before they were ready, and Nasreen emerged from the house, veiled, so they could set off again, heading for the mountain range, which, if not safety, at least meant the completion of the mission.

Yardley's survivors had dwindled to four.

The portrait of Feliks Dzerzhinsky seemed to be glaring at Yuri Andreyevich Zhikin with special venom this warm Moscow morning, as Sanko read the latest report from Afghanistan in an unemotional voice. The head of *mokrie dela* operations was a difficult man to shake, even in adversity, but then, Zhikin reflected bitterly, that was easy to understand. After all, who was his father-in-law?

And who was going to take the blame for the mess?

Gorsky, the head of the KGB's First Chief Directorate fixed Zhikin with a steely, unwavering stare, approaching contempt.

Zhikin smoked, scattered ash, and thought miserably about his career, which had risen so steadily over many years and had now become so precarious.

When Sanko was finished, Gorsky asked coldly, "And what is your comment on that, comrade Zhikin?"

Zhikin coughed to clear his throat. "I don't know," he mumbled.

"What did you say?" Gorsky demanded. "I couldn't hear you."

Louder. "I don't know, comrade General."

There was no disguising the contempt now. "You . . . don't . . . know. You get us into this mess, and you don't know."

"Perhaps the Americans are dead," Zhikin suggested without hope. "They were in the area of the Ruka attack. They must have been affected. Because we haven't found their bodies, that doesn't necessarily mean they're alive. They could have fallen in the Panjshir, or on the road to Charikar. We only have the word of this one man, Mohammed Iqbal, that they were escaping."

"Do you believe they're dead, Yuri?" Sanko asked.

Zhikin filled his lungs with smoke. He sighed it out. There was no point lying. "No, I don't."

"Why not?"

"Because if Iqbal was telling a lie, he'd have asked for payment immediately. He did not. Also, the caravan was in the place he described, taking a route that was foolish. There couldn't be enough grazing for the flocks, as we saw later when it had to split up. The Americans, or at least one of them, must have been there then."

"But the military commanders in Jalalabad say the entire caravan was trapped in the pass," Sanko offered. "They give us their assurance no one escaped."

"Then where is the evidence?" Zhikin asked.

"So you agree," Sanko persisted, "that your plan has failed?"

"It will only have failed when the West is able to expose our neutron attacks," Zhikin said. "But yes, I agree. It didn't do what we . . ." he corrected himself, ". . . what I thought it would, and our international position is now in great danger."

Gorsky's pale blue eyes gleamed with triumph. The fool had condemned himself out of his own mouth! Something else to report to the Politburo later in the day.

"So what," Sanko continued, "would you suggest we do now?"

Zhikin felt his shoulders sag. It would be the last time he was ever asked that. "I suggest," he said sadly, "that we work on the assumption the Americans did escape from the pass and are continuing toward Pakistan. I suggest we search for them. Let us stop all refugee traffic going up through the Agam River gorge into Pakistan. We've dropped antipersonnel mines there before, so let's drop more of them, millions if you like, over every route. Let us strafe and bomb. And let us, please, get these UN talks concluded quickly."

"We are going as fast as we can, comrade Zhikin," Gorsky said primly. "Too much speed makes the Americans anxious."

"Meanwhile if you wish, my department will prepare plans to combat the hostile reaction we can expect from the West should Lyle and Ross reach their destination." Zhikin shrugged. "I regret, comrades, I can offer nothing more than that."

"It's not much," Gorsky observed icily.

Zhikin stubbed his cigarette into the ashtray. "No," he agreed. "It isn't."

The ferocity of the Soviet air attacks on the trails leading to Torabora and the White Mountain were without precedent in the years of savage but sporadic war. The Afghans had become used to an air raid every week or two, but not the constant assaults to which they were now subjected.

Helicopters scattered antipersonnel mines over wide areas. Some were plastic, like the one which blew off Mir Gholam's hand;' others were shaped like watches, pens, or packs of cigarettes.

Most were quickly found and destroyed by the people who watched them come down, but there would always be a few which, tucked invisibly into a bush or just off a path, would retain the power to maim or kill tomorrow, or ten years hence.

The bombing of buildings, of houses and barns, went on daily, but modern conventional weaponry is outclassed by the solidity of traditional Afghan dwellings and the fact that there's very little inside them that can burn. Whenever people heard the approaching helicopters or the scream of MiGs, they ran out to shelter some distance away under the trees.

The most damaging of the raids, the ones causing most injuries and deaths, were the antipersonnel strafing missions and the bombs that spread their destruction in shrapnel, or phosphorus, or napalm.

The refugee trails up the Agam River gorge were soon choked with fleeing families and with the wounded, everyone listening for the return of the planes, which now attacked indiscriminately. Most Afghans were forced off the usual paths and took longer, harder routes through the mountains beside the gorge, crossing back when they were well above the snow line and scrambling for the summit and the frontier.

Yardley's survivors made the best time they could, through days in which they seemed to be walking deeper into trouble.

At the first sound of aircraft engines, the four would scatter to seek hiding places in the shadows of rocks and trees and lie motionless until there was again silence.

Inevitably, their pace slowed. The mines, dropped everywhere, meant they could travel only in daylight, and then with caution—at the same time the air strikes were sent in.

But they did move nearer, they did manage to get at least one meal a day from some farm or village, and finally they reached the green, fertile belt at the base of the mountains.

The Agam River, brown and sluggish at this point, became clear and icy as they climbed toward Torabora, and the Americans drank with pleasure and relief.

Torabora itself had been heavily bombed and was now virtually deserted. Most of the *mujahideen* had gone farther up the mountains to live in caves or under the trees.

With the bombing, the detours, and the dangers from mines, it took several days to climb the White Mountain to the point where they could look down into Pakistan. But at least there still were the four of them, the only survivors.

Ross and Lyle were exhausted and dehydrated, aching at the end of the day, stunned by the concussion of the bombs, the sufferings they saw and had to pass by with not even an aspirin left to offer. But they felt no nausea, cramps, or listlessness: none of the signs that the neutron radiation was doing its destructive work. Not yet. Nasreen, too, seemed so far unaffected.

But they were no longer sure about Mahmud. One

morning, Ross noticed the commander's nose had begun to bleed, and although Mahmud smiled and made a gesture that it should be ignored, it wouldn't stop. After more than an hour, Ross insisted they rest.

An air strike had just ended, and there was a temporary lull. Mahmud lay back, his *sadr* soaked in the cold mountain water and draped over his nose, waiting for the blood to clot.

Later, when he ran suddenly off the trail they were following, Ross went after him and saw him vomiting.

Neither man said anything. Mahmud knew as well as anyone that his life was now on a time fuse, and no one could say when it would expire.

Across the border, sliding down the snow on their *sadrs*, deeper into Pakistan, their ears still listened for the noise of aircraft because they had already seen violations of the frontier by the Russians and heard the dull booms of attacks on that side.

Mahmud was going slower every hour. Lyle urged him on, forcing the pace, so they could at least get down to the valley, to the outskirts of Parachinar, before nightfall. The guards at the iron gates of the U.S. Consulate in Peshawar were at first reluctant to let them in because they looked so dirty and dishevelled until Ross lost his temper and abused them so loudly and rudely that there could be no doubt he, at least, was a *farangi*.

The gate was opened and, it being morning, they turned right and climbed the stairs to the Consulate itself.

Tom Glenn was in the reception area and failed to recognize either of his countrymen although he was always interested in talking to *mujahideen*—particularly now there was such a high level of fighting around Parachinar.

The agents had to admit, when they stared at themselves in a mirror later, that they did look different. Their faces were thinner, almost gaunt, and with the beards they'd grown, there were considerable changes.

In his office, with Mahmud and Nasreen sitting to one side, the Consul scrutinized the Americans. "How was it?" he asked.

"Well," Ross said, "we've got four survivors."

Tom Glenn raised a surprised eyebrow. "They're going to have a lot of room on the plane. There's a 707 waiting at the airport."

"That's fine. We can stretch out and sleep."

Glenn made a questioning gesture. "Where are they?"

Ross pointed to himself and the others. "One, two, three, four," he said neutrally. "Us. They detonated a neutron shell in the Panjshir while we were there. We're what's left."

He reached for his pack. "And in here, you'll find rocks and sand and leaves and things from around ground zero for the scientists to look at." He dropped his pack at the side of the Consul's desk and took Lyle's and put it on top.

Tom Glenn sat back in his chair, staring from one to the other. "Dear God," he said. "Is there anything you need right away?"

Lyle grinned. "There sure is. A bath, Tom. Maybe two or three in a row. And clean clothes. And cans of cold Coke, at least a dozen each."

"Easily done," the Consul said. "How about you, Mahmud?"

The *mujahideen* leader smiled wanly. "I need nothing," he said.

Ross said, "Mahmud's not been too well lately, Tom. We need to get a real move on, get him back to the States quickly."

Glenn nodded. "I'll tell the crew you're ready to roll. I guess takeoff will be sometime this afternoon. We'll get you there as soon as we can."

20

It was actually on the day David Ross put an end to the suffering of Mir Gholam that thousands of physical miles, and millions of cultural ones away, a package arrived in the mail at his Washington apartment, addressed simply "Ross."

Not Mr. Ross, or Mrs. Ross; so Elaine opened it and found a slim volume of poetry entitled *Us*. It wasn't anything she'd sent away for, and she doubted David had done so before he'd left for . . . wherever it was he'd gone. She flicked through it and frowned.

"Good lord," she murmured as she scanned some of the verse. "What on earth is this?"

That was when she came across the poem entitled "David," and as she read it, she realized it was about her husband.

She inspected the cover, but the name Julie Klein meant nothing to her. Then on the back flyleaf was a photograph of a beautiful girl: someone Elaine thought she recognized.

She sat on the sofa and read every poem, or tried to, feeling old and sick: made worse when she suddenly remembered where, and under what circumstances, she had met Julie Klein. She was the girl who had been so rude at the party.

Elaine was glad David wasn't there at that moment. She needed time to think and plan.

It took almost a week for the hurt and humiliation to recede sufficiently for her to reason clearly, and when she did, she took another look at the wrapper which she'd carefully kept.

Ross.

There was no doubt David had had an affair and, worse of all, with that particular girl. But when? And was it still going on? Surely it couldn't be, not if the book lacked an inscription and was addressed ambiguously "Ross." It sounded like the revenge of a jealous woman who hoped his wife would see it. And if Julie Klein, this young beauty on the cover, had been dropped by David, then she'd been dropped in favor of Elaine. It could, she supposed, even be looked upon as a victory.

She searched the telephone book for Julie's address and, that afternoon, returned the book to her with a note.

> Dear Miss Klein,
> Thank you so much for sending David and me a copy of your interesting poems. I was sorry to see you hadn't signed it, so I'm returning the book in case you would like to do this, and perhaps—as David is the subject of so much of your work—you might care to add a small inscription?
> With good wishes for your next project,
>
> Sincerely,
> Elaine Ross

She never got the book back. She decided not to mention the matter; and that was even before she knew about Afghanistan, or what had happened to her husband.

*   *   *

The UN talks were still in progress when Yardley's survivors arrived unannounced in Washington, and scientists began work on the samples they'd brought back.

The Russians were moving hastily now, trying to force the pace and get a signature on arms limitation and the banning of neutron weapons. But the White House, tipped off about the latest events, was taking its time while the changed circumstances were considered and the evidence carefully studied.

The first decision was actually taken by Yardley, and that was to keep his agents out of all publicity. The White House had two nuked Afghans in hand and a batch of scientific reports still to come, and that had to be enough.

The first announcement would simply say that Americans had been involved in finding the victims and bringing out the proof, and if people assumed that meant the CIA, Yardley didn't care. Those who mattered in the United States knew who was responsible.

After days of hints and rumors in the press, the news was officially broken a few hours after doctors confirmed Mahmud was dying. His bone marrow function had been lost. His skin was becoming ulcerated and he was susceptible to internal hemorrhage and infection.

Mahmud's Biblical face and the veiled image of Nasreen became internationally known and, at Ross's urging, Mahmud used the last of his strength for press conferences and interviews about the fight against the Russians and what was being done to the Afghan nation.

In one television interview, he was asked straight out for the first time, "Do you know you'll die soon because of this bomb?"

"There is no one in Afghanistan who would not gladly

die to get the Russians out," Mahmud replied. "For us, this war is holy."

Lyle and Ross were admitted to the DIA hospital and subjected to everything from lumbar punctures and sperm tests to whole body scans.

Yardley ordered satellite photographs of Ruka and the Panjshir Valley south of the town, so the men could identify exactly where they had been when the shell detonated. They pointed out the side valley by locating the waterfall, finding almost the precise spot they laid Mir Gholam; and they showed where Mahmud had been helping to herd sheep.

This information was taken away for analysis.

At first, the UN talks were postponed for four days at America's insistence. During that time, scientific proof that this had been a neutron explosion became available and was made public.

The Russians retaliated as best they could, not only denying they had used the weapon, but adding that the world's attention should immediately be focused on banning it internationally. They accused the U.S. of deliberately sabotaging the peace talks.

But as Mahmud's condition worsened, the wave of protest and revulsion grew. The interviews with him became shorter and were sometimes disjointed.

Every night, he came into millions of homes on television and died some more.

Yardley, Dr. Peter Barry, Ross, and Lyle gathered in the Director's office when the results of all the tests were in.

Barry checked through a file of records and computer printouts. "You were both at the same spot at the time of the explosion, and there's no significant variation in our finding on you," he said, "so everything I say affects you equally."

He spread a printout on the glass table. "The assumption from all the data is that the Russians exploded a one-kiloton shell at five hundred feet. The bombardment of fast neutrons decreases the further away you go, and it's also slowed by obstacles.

"Now Mahmud who was in direct line of sight would have taken, at that distance, maybe two or three hundred rads, which is why he's lasted so long. The two of you, in the side valley, would have got a lower dosage, because you had partial protection from the mountain."

He pulled out a satellite photograph and with it an artist's cross-section. "You can see there's a lot of mountain and rock between you and the blast."

"Does that mean we didn't really get zapped?" Lyle asked.

"No, you got hit all right, no doubt about that." He paused and looked seriously at them. "Both your sperm samples show genetic damage."

"Which means?" Ross asked.

"It means neither of you ought to father any children. They would almost certainly be badly deformed."

The agents considered this in silence. It was a sick feeling knowing that something inside you had altered to the point that any kids you had would be monsters.

Eventually Lyle shrugged. "I wasn't planning on a family anyway."

"It wouldn't be safe for Elaine to have children," Ross said.

"But otherwise, Peter?" Lyle asked.

"Sexually, you shouldn't have any problems at all," Barry said. "Physically . . . well, the fact is, we don't know."

"When will you know?" This from the Director.

"Fast neutron radiation produces early effects and late effects," Peter Barry explained, "and the period between these two we gauge to be sixty days."

"So if we're not dying in another month, what then?" Lyle asked.

"Then you could live for years. It would mean your bone marrow function had repaired enough for that. Just how many years depends on how strong a rad dose you took, and that we don't know. Meanwhile, you'll be predisposed toward leukemia, cancer, cataracts, and general infections."

Yardley inspected his fingernails thoughtfully. "But let's say, Peter, that these two remain at their present level of health. How would you rate their operational functioning?"

Ross and Lyle waited anxiously for the reply because their jobs depended on it.

Barry considered the matter. "If they stay as they are," he said, "then they're fine. Their responses and reactions haven't changed. They could do with putting on a bit of weight, I guess. From that point of view, there's not a problem." He paused. "We just have to wait and see how long it keeps that way."

"Sixty days, you said," Yardley remarked, staring at the wall.

"Yes."

"And they're fine right now."

"As I said, they are. At the moment."

"So you wouldn't have any medical objection to them doing a job for me?" Yardley asked.

"I do think, Lyndon," Barry said, "they deserve some time off."

"It won't take long," Yardley assured him. "I just thought they might like another crack at Rabinovich."

He could see he had both men's attention.

"The Russians are pulling out tomorrow," Yardley told

them. "We've won. The talks are finally off. The President'll be announcing tonight there can be no possibility of a neutron ban with Moscow." He glanced from one to the other. "Rabinovich is going to be on that plane, and we all know what that means for him. A labor camp or a death sentence. With the mood the Kremlin's in, I can guess which one it'll be. Hell, Rabinovich is the guy who started this whole thing. They'll be after his blood."

"I'm after his blood," Lyle said. "He's the bastard who helped design that nuke. He's what Scimitar was all about."

"But he did try to defect and tell us about it, Clive," Ross pointed out. "It wasn't his fault he was handed back."

Lyle grunted. "Well, what do we do?"

"We've fixed it so we're going to peel Rabinovich off from the others into a little room, just as they go through Immigration," Yardley said. "The two of you will be there. Explain the position to him frankly. Offer him asylum. If he takes it, fine. If he doesn't, he catches the plane and he's no worse off. But at least we give him the choice, and some of us don't have to have him on our consciences."

Ross grinned at the Director. "I think that's a great idea," he said. "We'll do it."

"No objections, Clive?" Yardley asked.

"No, General."

"What about you, Dr. Barry?"

"Just let them have time off afterward," Peter Barry said. "Uh, and the other thing is, if this sixty-day mark passes and there's no change, I'll want both of them in for a major medical every three months. And I do mean a major medical. I also want their word that if they feel something's going wrong, and they're getting sick, they're not going to try to hide it. Okay?"

It was an easy promise to make. In any case, not much got past Yardley's eagle eyes.

Yuri Andreyevich Zhikin was told in the afternoon that he was to present himself at the First Chief Directorate's conference room precisely at nine the next morning.

He had no doubt what it meant. The UN conference was off. Rabinovich had defected. The Soviet Union was taking a bad public relations beating, and nothing he could do, no campaign he could mount, was having the slightest impact while this bandit commander, Mahmud, died slowly before the eyes of the world: the first known victim of a neutron bomb.

And now he himself was being summoned. Zhikin, when he left his office that evening, stood at his door, looking back mournfully. Tomorrow, someone else would be at his desk. And where would he be?

He went home and got drunk.

In the morning, because he felt so bad, he had a bath and washed his hair. In his closet was a freshly cleaned, pressed uniform that had been there for some time. It would be his last chance to wear it, so he put it on.

Exactly at nine, he entered the conference room and saw it was a full meeting of all the First Chief Directorate heads and their immediate subordinates.

He was going to be made an example of in some style.

He took a deep breath and walked forward, trying to hold himself straight and not show them how ashamed he was, and how scared.

At the end of the table he paused and looked up toward the grim portrait of Feliks Dzerzhinsky under which was General Gorsky's seat.

But Gorsky was not there. Instead, Sanko of Department V was in his place.

"Well, Yuri," Sanko said, "don't just stand there, find a seat."

Zhikin looked around in a trance. There was a spare chair close to the top. He took it and sat quietly, not fidgeting.

Sanko began. "Comrades, the Central Committee has received, and accepted, the resignation of General Igor Vladimirovich Gorsky as head of this Directorate. I have been appointed in his place. Until my successor for Department V has been chosen, I will continue to play an overseeing role there. Are there any questions?"

Zhikin stared, incredulous. He couldn't believe it. It hadn't been him after all who was the scapegoat, but Gorsky!

"And now we must look to the future," Sanko said. He turned to Zhikin. "Yuri, we need proposals for our international image. Is there anything you have in mind?"

Zhikin shook his head numbly. "Until this Afghan is dead, I don't think we should do anything. It would be wasted. But later, when people forget—and, as we know, in the West they forget quickly—then we will have initiatives prepared."

"I will leave that in your hands then," Sanko said.

The meeting turned to other things.

When it broke up two hours later, Sanko called Zhikin aside.

"I like the way you're looking today, Yuri, my friend," he said. "Clean. Smart uniform. Neat hair. We must keep it like that in future." He looked pointedly. "But I think you forgot about your shoes."

Zhikin looked down. "I will have them polished, comrade."

"Excellent."

Feliks Dzerzhinsky stared in frozen contempt, but Zhikin felt his eyes weren't particularly looking his way any more.

*   *   *

Mahmud suffered and wasted before the cameras of the world.

Then for a day he went into a coma, and when he died without regaining consciousness, there were violent demonstrations outside Soviet Embassies in a score of cities around the world.

Mahmud's body was flown back to Pakistan, where *mujahideen* buried him, his face toward Mecca, as they volleyed bursts of defiant rifle fire into the air.

For a while, Mahmud became a symbol not only of the Afghan struggle but of the cruelty and duplicity of the Soviet Union.

Later, when memories faded, as Zhikin predicted they would, those who thought of him at all remembered his face: the fine features, the calm serenity of the green eyes, the Biblical beard, the dignified suffering at the end.

He reminded them of Jesus who, as far as Islam is concerned, is only a minor prophet.

Epilogue

Nasreen passed the sixty-day barrier, which meant her bone marrow function had repaired to some extent. Unhappy in the United States, she returned to Pakistan. There was little media interest in the event.

She married a *mujahed* in Peshawar. Then, either disbelieving or disregarding the advice of doctors in Washington, she gave birth a year later to a son. Few details are known of this child. Only a handful of Afghan women ever saw him, and later refused to speak of it, except to say the evil eye had looked on Nasreen. The boy died after two days.

David Ross and Clive Lyle also passed the sixty-day mark, and as General Yardley said when he confirmed them as staying on active operations, from now on they just had to take each day as it came.

But then, as Ross remarked later to Lyle, what was new about that?

ABOUT THE AUTHOR

Peter Niesewand's most recent novel, *Fallback*, was a main selection of the Literary Guild and a national bestseller. A foreign correspondent, he suffered solitary confinement for seventy-three days in Rhodesia for his reporting of the guerilla war in 1973. He covered the Lebanese civil war and was twice named International Journalist of the Year, in 1973 and 1976. He got the idea for *Scimitar* in Afghanistan while covering the Russian invasion of that country; his work there ultimately cost him his life.